The
Breaking
Strain

Books by John Masters

NIGHTRUNNERS OF BENGAL

THE DECEIVERS

THE LOTUS AND THE WIND

BHOWANI JUNCTION

COROMANDEL!

BUGLES AND A TIGER

FAR, FAR THE MOUNTAIN PEAK

FANDANGO ROCK

THE VENUS OF KONPARA

THE ROAD PAST MANDALAY

TO THE CORAL STRAND

TRIAL AT MONOMOY

The Breaking Strain

BY JOHN MASTERS

DELACORTE PRESS / NEW YORK

For Danielle

The
Breaking
Strain

Chapter 1

V. K. HAWKER SHUFFLED slowly on, his left hand passing along
the Embankment wall, his right hand holding his sister's. Two
hours ago, in the cozy murk above Threadneedle Street, he'd been
able to hear the whoop and growl of tugs on the river. An hour
ago, on Ludgate Hill—or that was where the taxi driver thought
they were—he'd heard, all around, the despairing horns of half-
seen cars and buses, moaning like lost ships. The rumble of engines in low gear had seemed to solidify the air.

Now no sound intruded through the enclosing gloom, as they
inched forward on foot. The Thames flowed close by, at the foot
of the Embankment wall, but no sound came up to tell them
whether the tide raced, straining, past buoys and bridge abut-
ments, or whether the water lay slack and still. No ship moved on
the river. In the roadway no wheeled traffic moved. For a long
time they had met no other pedestrians. The fog lay deep, yellow,
cored with black, over London.

Anne said, "What's that . . . on the right?"

VK peered. "A bus, I think."

A denser bulk ahead glowed a dull red inside the fog. At ten feet distance, he saw three passengers curled up on the seats, asleep or pretending to be, huddled into coats and under newspapers. There was no driver or conductor. A deserted newspaper stand bore a just legible poster announcing RED PROF RAPE CHARGE.

VK shuffled on, his lips tight. The bloody fog hurt his eyes. And you weren't even supposed to call it fog at this time of year. "Temperature inversion" or "metropolitan smog" were the proper names. Whatever the bloody thing was called, it had been getting worse all day. It was full of chemicals, but what made his eyes smart was the effort of straining to see what could not be seen. His eyes hurt worse than that day on Karamala after the wounded lioness—twelve hours, and the sun slashing at his pupils like a hot razor.

"Pardon," a shadow said, cannoning off Anne and disappearing.

She giggled, then sighed. "England, their England! Are you sure we're doing the right thing, coming back here, VK?"

"Damn!" he muttered. "Hold tight."

The wall ended under his left hand. This could be a small gap, where steps ran down to a pier; or it could be a road. He didn't know London well, and today even a Cockney couldn't have been sure just where he was. A road on the left would have to be leading to a bridge, and surely there wasn't one between Waterloo Bridge and Charing Cross. But *was* that Waterloo Bridge they'd passed under a little way back? If he took a couple of strides now, would he be sure of finding the wall again on the other side?

He stepped forward, his left hand out, and soon touched the wall again. He blew out his breath angrily, and muttered, "Jesus." Anne was right. What the hell were they doing in this filthy, foggy drain of a country?

"It's lucky it's so bad that nothing can move," Anne whispered. "Otherwise we'd get run over."

"Shut up," he snapped.

VK went slowly foward. He ought to apologize for snapping at her. He squeezed her hand, and she squeezed back.

"Oh, VK," she said. "Doesn't this make you feel mysterious?

London in a fog! Here we are in 1971, but it might as well be 1871. At any moment, Sherlock Holmes will loom up, hypodermic at the ready. But first we'll hear his fiddle, and smell his vile shag tobacco."

"Shut up," VK said again, but this time with no edge to his voice. She was a nice girl, even though she did spend half her time playing let's pretend. She used to be a good actress as a kid. He remembered the time she had acted out a scene of extreme illness so well that Mother had rushed her 90 miles to Nairobi . . . where the doctor said there was nothing wrong with her; that she was only suffering from jealousy of the attention given to her brother. He had confidently awaited the whacking Dad would give her. But she got off scot-free. There was no justice in the world. But a lot of living.

Was it possibly getting lighter? Had he seen some swirl in the fog substance? Had he heard the rumble of a wheel? Was he hearing it now? A metal-tired wheel?

He was standing under one of the round-globed lamps that crown the Embankment wall. In its murky glow, very close, appeared a Cockney barrow—a fairly large two-wheeled handcart, its load covered by a tarpaulin. Two men were pushing it, a third steadying the load. They must have crossed the road, and now were going to turn along the sidewalk. He waited, ready to step aside.

The men pushing the barrow seemed to have a misunderstanding over which way to go. The barrow lurched violently, catching the third man off balance. In his effort to steady the load, he pulled it off the barrow. The tarpaulin fell away. VK stared into the closed eyes of a lolling woman, who was either unconscious or dead.

One of the men effortlessly picked up the woman and put her back on the barrow. Another jerked the tarpaulin back into place. The vision was gone. Now VK saw only a tarpaulin-covered barrow.

Had there been a woman? . . . Was she not quite young, dark-haired, voluptuous, the skirt unfashionably long, a gold locket glittering at her throat?

The man beyond the barrow looked around, peering into the fog. He was fat, droopy-mustached like a mandarin, very big. He seemed to stare straight into VK's eyes. VK tensed, easing his hand out of Anne's grip. How could the man possibly not see them? But his eyes must have been focused short, for now he gestured strongly, and the other two, without a word, pushed the barrow to the river wall. The big man leaned over the wall and called down, "Serge?"

From below an accented voice answered. "Yes. We are ready."

The small man nearest VK unhooked a rope off the barrow handle and with a couple of quick motions looped it around the girl's body, under the armpits. Then the other two picked her up and lowered her over the wall. The small man payed out the rope.

Anne's gasp and her sucked-in breath at his ear acted like a dash of cold water to clear VK's head. He was not watching a silent film. He was seeing three real men lower a real but helpless woman into the river, or a boat.

The big man heard Anne's gasp and turned, his arms spread as though to screen the others from sight. He looked more like a mandarin than ever, his sleeves flapping. A switchblade suddenly gleamed in his hand. Behind him, one of the other men cried down urgently to the river, "Wait! Come back!" The small man let go of the rope, and VK heard a splash. The small man looked up, consternation clear on his face.

"Take these two out!" Mandarin ordered. They came on together then.

VK tensed. Run, stay, fight? He had less than a second to decide. "Into the river! Get her," he shouted to his sister. Anne took the step to the wall and vaulted over. Then the three men were on him. The amazement blurring his eyes cleared away, even as the numbness of disbelief had left his mind a few moments back. He was fighting for his life. This he understood, and knew how to do, though he had never done it on a city street before.

He made to offer a classical straight left at Mandarin and saw the momentary snarl of satisfaction on the other's face before he ducked, crossed, and kicked him hard on the kneecap. Then he stepped in, grabbing for the knife as he jerked his knee into the man's groin. Mandarin doubled up, and the knife was in VK's hand before the other two reached him. No one had yet made a sound. Even Mandarin, writhing on the pavement, twisted in silence.

VK stepped back quickly. With his back to the river wall, he could jump over if he had to, as long as he didn't let them get a grip on him. He wished someone would come—half a dozen bobbies for preference. He began to shout, "Help! Murder!" That made a man feel a damned fool, yelling "Help!" like someone in a cartoon. His lips were cold and stretched back from his teeth.

Mandarin struggled to his feet, and they came at him all together. VK swayed backward, as though to follow Anne into the Thames, then lunged with the knife at the nearest man on his left, the little man, who looked like Stan Laurel and had the same sad eyes but a wide, crooked mouth. Laurel swayed delicately back. The third man's fist crunched into VK's cheek. Mandarin's boot crashed against his thigh. His knifeblade jarred on bone, he pulled it out, saw it red in front of his face and stabbed again, short-armed, at Mandarin's throat. From nearby he heard the growl of an engine. Mandarin jerked away but the third man turned his head to listen. VK thrust the knife deep in under his chin, then leaped back. The man spun away, gurgling blood.

Mandarin came on, and, Jesus, here was another man, younger, short gray overcoat, gray narrow-brimmed hat, an obvious American . . . VK fell off right-handed, slashing at the newcomer's eyes. The point of the blade streaked red across the man's cheekbone. Following through, VK jerked his elbow into the eyeball. Then something big and hard crashed into the side of his head. Dizzy, stumbling, he thought he'd had it.

Another figure grew out of the fog, this one tall, burly and bareheaded. The engine sound increased to a roar. Graycoat shouted, "*Assassins! Allez-en!*" Not American, but French, VK thought, and not one of the "enemy." Mandarin was holding one elbow. The third man was pouring blood from the throat. Laurel drew a pistol. It was short and fat and equipped with a silencer. "Stay there," he whispered. Then the three turned together and ran away into the fog.

The big, bareheaded man began to go after them, but VK said, "My sister's in the river." The engine sound faded. A bus, VK thought, trying to go somewhere.

The Frenchman muttered, "*Mon Dieu!* She is swimming?" He found his hat and put it on. "My cheek hurts," he said reproachfully. "Also, my eye. What is happening?"

VK told them. Together they looked down over the wall. The water was invisible.

VK said, "Where can we get down? And which way is the tide going?"

The bareheaded man pointed west along the Embankment. He was wearing black loafers and a dark-blue suit, and VK thought he really was an American. Now he opened his mouth but no words came out until, after a time, he said "Gap!" enunciating the G with sudden violence.

A gap in the wall, toward Charing Cross, VK thought. Trust the foreigner to know more about London than the Englishman! They went together, fast, along the wall, found the gap and, leading down from it, steps to the water's edge. Only one step was wet and slimy above the level of the water. The Frenchman put his hand into the water and said, "I think there is very small current. Or none."

Just past high tide, then. Anne would be here or hereabouts, unless the men in the unseen boat had come back. He didn't think they would. They seemed to have been very nervous types, who'd shoved off at the first hint of trouble. From Laurel's despairing call *he* obviously hadn't expected them to come back. He felt no fear for Anne's safety. She could swim like a seal, and it was not cold. In fact, it was the warmth of the day that had caused the temperature inversion and the smog.

He began to take off his jacket. When Anne reached the woman she'd have dragged her toward the bank, trusting the fog to hide them from any enemies who might still be on top. Then she would have moved cautiously along the wall. Which way? Probably with the tide, as it would be easier. "Where are the next steps downriver?" he asked.

The Frenchman said, "By those ships, *Discovery* and the other, I think."

The American waved his arm and shouted "Po-po-po-po-po-po-*police?*"

VK said, "Call the police? Yes. If one of you would do that, I'll . . ." But it would have to be the Frenchman. The American had the most godawful stammer.

Anne's voice spoke from under his feet. "VK?"

He stared down. "Anne? Where are you?"

Her long blond hair caught his eye then. She was coming along the wall, upstream, very close. She was pushing a balk of timber, a body draped over it, the head back and up. The American slipped into the swirling river, reaching her with a single stroke. Then the log floated close, and VK went down the steps till the water reached his knees. "I'll gaff her," he said, and caught hold of the woman and lifted her onto the steps. Her eyes were open, staring into his. The pupils moved. Anne climbed out, breathing hard but steadily. "Phew, the water's dirty," she said. "I'll probably catch leprosy or spotted fever or typhoid or something."

VK patted her shoulder. "You all right?"

She nodded, smiling. "And you? You've got a bruise on your face."

"Several," he said. They climbed over the guard rail onto the flat space at the top of the steps. The fog swirled past, a black and yellow river. The rescued woman lay on her back, her head supported on the Frenchman's hand, the rope still fast under her armpits. She appeared to be in her early thirties, but her skin was creamy, smooth, and white. The gold locket at her neck was in the shape of a pointed-roof chalet, with a cross and two small charms dangling in the high, arched doorway.

Anne asked, "What happened to the three men?"

VK said, "They got away."

The American knelt astride the woman, untied the rope, and began mouth-to-mouth resuscitation. She was quite short, and strong as well as shapely. Good breasts, VK noticed, fine legs, big mouth.

She moved under the American's hunched body, and her hands came up to her throat. The American stood away. His mouth opened, and he said, "Ho-o-o-o-o . . ."

VK said quickly, "I don't know where the nearest hospital is. There are no taxis. But our hotel's close. If we can get her there, the hotel doctor can look at her, and we can call the police too."

"Are you at the Savoy?" the Frenchman asked. "So am I."

The American nodded, and after a time said suddenly, "Coincidence!"

"Not much—considering we're all trying to get home in the fog, and the Embankment's the easiest way," VK said. The man was a sort of black-haired Gary Cooper, but dumber. Literally. Now he was taking off his jacket and offering it silently to Anne.

VK noticed his sister's slight frown. If there was one thing he hated it was the frilly simpering sort of woman, and Anne hated being taken for one. Also, she distrusted this sort of ceremonial politeness. The informal camaraderie of bush camp and safari tent were more her style. Apart from the dank, streaming hair her swim hadn't altered her appearance, because she never wore lipstick or make-up—or girdles or brassieres for that matter.

But her frown faded. She was smiling. Neither of them were great admirers of America or Americans, but this particular Yank was certainly a large portion of man. She was taking his proffered jacket now—and, goddammit, almost simpering. Without the coat, you could see the man's real, solid size. He was six foot three or four, broad-shouldered and narrow-hipped. He must weigh a good sixteen stone, but moved like a big cat. His hands were huge and his nose had been broken a couple of times. His eyes were blue and the black hair thickly curled. He looked a little like the photos of Jack Dempsey in his fighting prime; perhaps he had a touch of Indian blood. His shoes and suit were very expensive. And he smelled of whiskey.

The Frenchman rolled his eyes at VK, gave a small expressive shrug, took off his overcoat and spread it over the woman on the ground. Her eyes moved from him to VK, from VK to the American. They held, staring. The Frenchman stooped over her. "Are you OK? How do you feel?"

"Drugged," she said. "Help me up. I can walk if I can lean on someone." The American was there in a step. She took his arm and leaned heavily on him.

"Now to find the Savoy," VK said. "I was almost lost even before the set-to. Now I really am."

"This way," The Frenchman said. "I visit here quite often . . . and fogs are not uncommon."

Keeping close at his heels they crossed the sidewalk and a wide roadway, another sidewalk, a narrow strip of park. A blur of lights appeared, began to separate out. "The Savoy Hotel," the Frenchman said.

The girl said, "The Savoy Hotel?" She dragged on the American's arm, bringing him to a stop. "Is this the Strand?"

The Frenchman said, "No. That's on the other side. This is the river entrance."

She said, "Where is my handbag? Ah, of course, they would take it . . . I think I can remember. Yes. I was to meet him in Room 415, Savoy Hotel, the Strand. Take me there, please. It is a suite." Her voice was musical, the diction that of English well learned in school.

VK said, "You take her. I'll call the police."

"Because I fell in the river by mistake?" she said. "There is no need."

VK snapped, "We saw three men drop you into the Thames. My sister risked her life to pull you out. The men tried to murder me, and would have succeeded but for these two gentlemen. I'm going to make a full report to the police, whether you like it or not."

The girl stood defiant, a heroine on a statue, wet black hair falling, the locket glowing between her full outthrust breasts, her legs akimbo, green fire in her eyes, the fog swirling like battle smoke about her. VK stared back.

She said, "It is better that you do not mix yourself up in this any more."

VK said, "I quite agree. It's a police job."

The girl turned up her face to the American. "Please, take me to the room, first. It is my father I must meet there."

The American looked at VK. His mouth opened. "If-if-if-if-if-if . . ."

VK said, "If her father's there, then we ought to let her go up, is that what you mean? All right, but we go, too, and if her father doesn't call the police in five minutes, I will."

The girl turned to the Frenchman. "How do I look?"

The Frenchman said, "Damp, *mademoiselle*. . . . So now we enter the chic Savoy Hotel? And we tell the doorman the lady chanced to fall into the river, and your sister and this gentleman chanced to pull her out?"

"Any other story's going to sound worse," VK said. "Come on." He led into the hotel.

The light hurt his eyes after the fog, and it was very warm. The gray-coated hall porter started forward, his mouth open. "Sir . . . Gentlemen . . ."

VK said, "We have rooms here. Where's the lift on this floor?"

"Up those stairs and then right, sir. Has there been an accident? Should I call the doctor?"

"There's no need," VK said.

Waiting at the door of the lift as the others went in, he hesitated. Five floors up from this level. He'd much rather use the stairs, but the bloody little box was brightly lit, at least. They were all waiting, Anne with her hand out to him. He went in. The doors closed, and Anne held his hand. He closed his eyes and imagined spreading yellow deserts. The American had the butt of a gun sticking out under his armpit, and his shoes were made in England. The Frenchman's cheek was bleeding from a knife wound and his suit was made in America. Anne looked funny in the American's jacket, but somehow sexy.

The lift stopped and he opened his eyes, waiting for the door to open. It stayed closed. "Open the door," he said. He heard the grating harshness in his voice.

The operator said smoothly, "Just a moment, sir. We're between floors. I think the power's been cut off for a moment."

VK felt his skin tightening. The walls of the box began to close. It only needed the lights to go out and then . . . Anne's hand was very tight on his. The Frenchman was eyeing him curiously. One more second, just one more second, and he'd . . .

The lift jerked upward again. "Sorry about that," the operator said. "Happens now and then on this lift. I believe they're going to take the motor apart tomorrow. Fourth floor."

Then they were out in the passage, and VK felt the skin of his face reverting from animal to human.

The American, Bill Hammond, stood behind the others outside the door of Room 415. He half expected someone to come out with a gun, and he put his hand to his tie. He carried a gun himself, in a shoulder holster, and had thought, down by the river, that he'd soon be using it. But one didn't pull guns lightly in this country, and by the time he'd decided to, the thugs had run. Now, with his hand at his chest, he suddenly realized that his holster and the gun butt were exposed, because the English girl was wearing his jacket.

The door opened. The man in the doorway was slight, olive-skinned, and sharply dressed. He did have a gun, too, hidden in a shoulder holster. There was something about his eyes that marked him as a retired detective. Bill had observed too many of his own and his father's bodyguards to be mistaken.

The man said politely, "Were you looking for someone, miss?" The accent was New York. The sharp, small eyes strayed to Bill's gun.

The woman they'd rescued from the river said, "I am Miss Tellefsen. I think my father is here."

The man's glance turned to the Englishman. He said, "Then perhaps you gentlemen can identify yourselves?"

The Frenchman looked at the Englishman, eyebrows raised. The Englishman said, "My name's Hawker, if that's what you mean."

A big man in a rumpled blue suit came out of an inner door. He didn't seem to notice them, but turned sharply on the plainclothes man. "Bosco, that was Gorton on the line." His head was round and quite bald, and he had a wide mouth and pink skin, now mottled with anger. "He's lost her! You know what Gregory Parkezian would do to Gorton for this? He'd have him shot."

Bill suddenly saw who this man looked like. It was President Eisenhower of the wartime pictures. This fellow had the same big ears; but his eyes were shrewder and deeper-set than Ike's.

The man addressed as Bosco said, "This lady says she is Miss Tellefsen, Mr. Webber."

Mr. Webber put on a pair of horn-rimmed glasses and stared at the woman. The color came and went in his cheeks. "My God," he said. "It is! I've seen pictures . . . I've just told her father she was missing. In sixty seconds I would have had to tell Washington . . . ." He had a grating, strongly Midwestern voice. He straightened. "Will you come along, Miss Tellefsen?"

The woman said, "These men saved me. I don't know who they are but that one insists I tell the police."

"Who are you?" Webber said, looking at the Englishman. His eyes were cold.

The Englishman was equally cold. "I am V.K.G. Hawker, Esquire, of Nyeri, Kenya. This is my sister, Miss Anne Hawker. This is the Savoy Hotel, London, England. Who are you?"

The man blinked. "Webber," he said, "Joseph Webber, Department of Agriculture, United States Government . . . And these gentlemen?"

The Frenchman said smoothly, "I am Robert de Guise, owner and managing director of the galeries de guise—you spell it without capital letters, that is most important—of Paris."

Now Webber was looking at him, Bill Hammond. Bill opened his mouth, knew at once it was going to be hopeless, and pulled a visiting card from his pocket. Webber read it. His frown changed to a look of surprised recognition. "William M. Hammond, Los Angeles, California. Richard Hammond's son?" he said. "Chairman of the Middendorf Company?"

Bill nodded.

Webber said, "And you all rescued this young lady? You have done a great service to your country. Your countries. Come in, come in . . . You needn't frisk them, Bosco."

"He'd better not try," Hawker said. Then Webber was sweeping them forward, through Room 415 into another room. He stopped in the doorway and said in a loud voice, "Mr. Tellefsen, what I just told you was a misunderstanding. . . . Here is your daughter."

To Bill there seemed to be a lot of people in the room, though when he got to adding up it only came to half a dozen in addition to themselves. As Webber spoke these people ebbed back from an old man sitting alone in the middle of a big sofa, as a wave ebbs to reveal a craggy rock. He was tall, with deep-blue eyes far sunk under heavy brows. He was getting slowly to his feet, pushing away a proffered arm. His hair was thick and gray, and he had a short, thick gray beard and mustache. If he straightened up he would stand about Bill's own height, six foot three; but he stooped, and there was a palish parchment tinge to his skin.

The woman walked forward alone and the old man cried, "Ingrid!" He opened his arms and she went to him. He hugged and crooned over her; tears shone in his eyes, and he murmured words in what Bill thought was Russian. Then he pushed her a little away, holding her at arm's length. Or was he, too, using her to support himself?

He spoke in English. "What happened, Ingrid? This fellow, Mr. Webber, was just saying that you must have been taken away by the HPS. Although his man was guarding you, he said. It seems to me your organization is . . . lousy, Webber."

Mr. Webber's color heightened and he said sharply, "It wasn't entirely my man's fault, sir. I guess Miss Tellefsen's as much to blame as he is."

Mr. Tellefsen said, "What do you mean? How can my daughter be to blame?"

Webber saw how his anger had trapped him. He said, "I withdraw that remark. I apologize."

"What do you mean?" the old man thundered.

His daughter said in a low voice, "The CIA man was nice. . . . I went to his hotel with him. They surprised us there. It was easy for them."

The old man towered higher. His right hand swept up and the slap echoed like a shot in the room. "Strumpet!" he cried.

She said, "He was lonely." She put her hand to her cheek where the skin burned dull red. "You hurt me."

The old man swept her back into his arms. "Ingrid, Ingrid, I am sorry. But you are so bad. . . . Here, sit down. We are together again, and free! When this man, Mr. Webber, said that you had disappeared, I did not know what to do. It was like a bullet to the heart."

Webber said, "These three gentlemen and this young lady rescued her, sir. . . . Permit me to introduce you to Sigurd Tellefsen, the—"

"Infamous rapist!" Mr. Tellefsen said, chuckling, his anger past like a thunderstorm over a mountain. He looked up at the portly, heavy-jowled man standing at the end of the sofa. "Was that your idea?"

The man removed the pipe from his mouth and said, "Not guilty. It was the Prime Minister's, as a matter of fact. . . . I'm Lord Redmond. And you"—he spoke to Anne—"are a very wet young lady. As also is Miss Tellefsen. What have you been doing?"

Anne Hawker smiled and flapped the arms of Bill's jacket. "Swimming," she said. "I don't feel wet or cold, at all. It's so warm in here. Are you the great physicist?"

Bill placed Lord Redmond's name now. Anne had asked the question he would have liked to.

Lord Redmond said, "Great? In the presence of Sven Thorup's chief assistant, who some of us think is greater than the master ever could have been, just an ink-stained hack, young lady. . . . What happened to you, sir?" He indicated the slash in de Guise's face. The Frenchman put his hand to his cheek and looked in surprise at the trace of blood. "Our friends in HPS did it, did they?"

Hawker said, "As a matter of fact, I did, with one of their knives. If HPS are the people on the Embankment."

Robert de Guise thought, This cut is quite messy. He ought to put on a plaster or something; but it would stop bleeding soon, and meanwhile he dared not miss a word. Who would have supposed that he would ever find himself in the same room with Sigurd Tellefsen, Lord Redmond, and Joseph Webber of the CIA? And accepted as a good fellow, from having helped to repel the villains on the Embankment. Certainly, neither Trilby nor the chiefs in Moscow could have asked more of him, and all achieved by chance! No, now he was being unfair to himself. When he arrived on the Embankment, expecting to get a report that Ingrid was in the boat and on her way down to the Russian ship, and found instead a brawl in progress, it was instantly clear that he had two courses open to him. He could join his own men—the blundering idiots—and help them dispose of Hawker and Hammond. Or he could warn them to run, pretend to help the Good Samaritans, and write off that particular attempt as a lost cause. The decision to take the second course had come instantaneously. One was in England—here one did not kill people or leave bodies about indiscriminately; it attracted unfavorable attention; it was untidy. His early instructors had said many times, when a plan goes wrong it is usually best to cut it altogether and start again with a new plan at a new time. How right, in this case!

A gangling man in a charcoal suit was coming down the room, a briefcase in his hand. He was quite young, bald and darkly handsome, and Webber was introducing him to Mr. Tellefsen. Lord Redmond said, "That's Dr. Nathan Berkowitz, who's going to be

Mr. Tellefsen's American assistant at Shiprock, as I will be his British assistant. . . . But of course you wouldn't know about that yet. Nothing is being published until we get Mr. Tellefsen on the other side of the Atlantic. . . . I say, Nat—come over here. How was the crossing?"

"Fantastic. We were delayed an hour at takeoff but then it was two hours twenty minutes from New York to here. Smooth as silk once we got above a hundred thousand feet. The plane was full of conventioneers, though, half of them stewed. . . . Is that Tellefsen's daughter next to him on the sofa?"

"Yes."

"Well, I guess I'll hand over our little welcome present." He opened the briefcase and got out a large locket. De Guise leaned forward with sudden interest. The locket was in an abstract design of turquoise and handworked silver, the chain of strong silver links. This was American art—real American, art of the Indians. This was what the Yankees had suppressed in favor of the jukebox. He would have liked to specialize in work like this, but that would mean frequent visits to the U.S.A.—a soul-destroying prospect.

Berkowitz waited for an opportunity to make his presentation, but Ingrid Tellefsen and her father were absorbed in a conversation, carried on as though no one else were present. De Guise heard Ingrid say, "Then, though I could not move or speak, I heard a man say, 'I'll gaff her.' It was that one, the one with the long sandy hair and the gray eyes."

"Gaff? He said that?" the old man asked. He looked at Hawker. He raised his voice, "Young man . . . come here. Sit down."

Dr. Berkowitz seized the momentary hush and stepped forward. He said, "I'm Nathan Berkowitz, sir, your American assistant. On behalf of all your American staff I've brought this small gift for your daughter, as a token of welcome to the Texas Project." He held out the locket.

"Oh, how beautiful!" Ingrid exclaimed.

Dr. Berkowitz said, "It's Navajo work. The Navajos live in the deserts just west of Shiprock, where your laboratory—the whole plant—is waiting for you, sir."

De Guise thought, Soul-destroying or not—I can't let this opportunity slip. He said, "Is more of this work available? How much is produced? Do they make anything large? Figures? You see, I am in the business."

Dr. Berkowitz said, "I'm afraid I have no idea."

De Guise said, "This could be quite a rage, you know. I could open up a new world to the European collector. Perhaps I could visit these Navajos?"

Dr. Berkowitz said, "Sure. You'll find the country pretty bleak, but . . ."

Ingrid Tellefsen said, "Oh dear, it is a locket. I never wear anything but this one round my neck. It belonged to my mother."

"We can have it made into a brooch," Dr. Berkowitz said. "No problem."

It would look good on the English girl, de Guise thought. She was long-legged and clean-looking, even in Hammond's jacket. Very British, probably, cold on top, sex-mad underneath. Just the opposite to American women. Ugh.

The old man on the sofa said, "You gaffed my daughter out of the Thames, eh?"

Hawker said, "Yes. Used the modern clipper gaff, too, so I didn't have to break the skin." He smiled, and Mr. Tellefsen's eyes, dulled with increasing fatigue, began to sparkle again. He said, "You are a fisherman?"

Hawker said, "Yes. As a matter of fact, my sister and I are going to Scotland tomorrow for a week's salmon fishing on the Tay."

The old man leaned forward. "Salmon? What size do they run there? Do you use fly only? What lure? I like the fly best, usually, but sometimes early in the season, or when the water is strong, you have no chance unless you use a bait. I have used live bait, and artificial. . . . Ah, the salmon is the king of fish! What number leader do you use? Or do you call it cast? I mean, what breaking strain?"

Hawker said, "At this time of year, when there's a lot of water coming down, you have to use No. 3 cast, fifteen-pound breaking strain at least. You'll have your hands full with that and a thirty-pounder on the end of the line, and of course if you hooked into a real big one—the Tay record was sixty-four pounds when I last fished there—you'd probably lose him."

"Sixty-four pounds," the old man said reverently. "This I have to see. When I was a boy, *salmo salar* was all I ate, slept, dreamed, until my mother would drag me back to work or to school. Work seemed very unimportant when the silver salmon were running. It still does, to me. . . . Eighteen point four kilos was my best. That is about forty pounds. On a red and white spinner, with a rusty hook *this* big, and I was standing up on the bank, in full view of the fish. But the ways of the Atlantic salmon are a mystery. That is why he is the king of fish. Of salmon caught in rivers, not one has ever had anything in its stomach. Not even a fly. How do they live, three, four months sometimes, between coming into the river and spawning? If they do not eat, why do they strike at a lure?"

A spasm of pain blurred the craggy features, and for a moment he closed his eyes. He muttered, "For a moment the salmon can make one forget anything. But it comes back, it comes back. . . . In Russia there are no salmon rivers, no salmon. Other good fishing, yes, but salmon . . . Ah, I think I will give up this Texas Project and come fishing for the silver salmon with you!"

Lord Redmond said, "Why don't you? For a week."

The old man's eyebrows shot up. "But, we are supposed to be going to Aldermaston tomorrow, are we not? We have to spend a week with your reactor, right?"

Lord Redmond said, "That was the plan, but it's off, unfortunately. All our manual scientific staff went on strike yesterday. We had to kill the reactor."

Webber had heard. "Not going to Aldermaston?" he said. "Why, then we can go to Washington tomorrow. I'll have the plane sent over right away."

Mr. Tellefsen said, "I think I like Lord Redmond's suggestion better. I think I will go fishing."

There was a hint of anger in his voice that made de Guise look up sharply. Buried under the grandeur of his appearance, the old man was showing the edge of a vast temper, doubtless made more bitter by the frustrations of old age and perhaps some present sickness. Joseph Webber hadn't noticed. Joseph Webber was much smarter than he appeared—Trilby had warned him of that —but he did lack tact. As Trilby said, Webber's Achilles heel was lack of sympathy.

Webber was frowning down at Mr. Tellefsen. He said, "There's work to be done, sir. Very important work. There's a huge plant that cost the U. S. Government ninety-three million dollars to build, waiting for you. I don't think you can go fishing, sir."

And, de Guise thought, *you* probably have the President's written order to get Mr. Tellefsen into that plant at once—tomorrow, today, last week.

Lord Redmond said, "Dash it, Webber, he's not expected for a week, is he?"

The storm burst. Mr. Tellefsen's voice was a heavy thunder, reverberating in the cavernous chest, shaking the windows, making the ornate chandelier tinkle and shiver. "You say I *can't* go fishing? You think I must punch a clock, like a Seventh Avenue cartboy?" He turned to Hawker. "Where can I hire salmon water? It is difficult, I know. . . . Should I go to the fishing-tackle people, like Hardy's, and ask them?"

Hawker said, "It *is* difficult. Practically impossible, at short notice."

The old man said, "My son, will you—can you—take me fishing for salmon with you? Even if only to watch you?"

A thick, careful silence hung in the ornate room. Through a gap in the heavy curtains de Guise smelled a seeping-in of fog from the river far below. So, old Tellefsen was a fishing enthusiast, which wasn't uncommon; and he was furious at Webber, which couldn't be uncommon either.

Lord Redmond said, "You have already done the country a good turn, Hawker, by rescuing Miss Tellefsen. Anything more you can do to make Mr. Tellefsen happy . . . to thank him for the risks he has taken to come over to our side . . . will be very much appreciated by the Government, and by me personally."

Hawker said, "My sister and I are going to fish water belonging to Sir Alan Gobhair. I was at school with him. We are his guests, of course. A white hunter couldn't afford that water in a hundred years."

Mr. Tellefsen said, "White hunter? In Africa?"

Hawker said, "Yes, sir. My father ran a safari business in Kenya until Kikuyu outlaws murdered him in 1958. My mother, too. I was at school in England then, but Anne was there. A servant hid her under his own bed and she got away. I left school and went out to run the business."

The old man exclaimed, "But you are . . . only thirty, now?"

"Twenty-eight. Sir Alan Gobhair's a year older. I visited Gobhair Castle every year I was at school. I had nowhere else to go. . . . We'll be staying in the lodge. There's room for you and Miss Tellefsen, and I'm sure Sir Alan will be pleased to meet you."

Lord Redmond said, "I see Sir Alan now and then in Boodles. I'll give him a call."

Hawker said, "One thing first, though. I still haven't had any explanation of the attempted abduction—or murder—we interrupted on the Embankment. I think we deserve one."

Lord Redmond looked at Webber. Webber shook his head. Lord Redmond took his pipe from his mouth. "I wish we could, but it's not possible, I'm afraid."

VK frowned, and said, "I suggest it will have to be made possible. If I'm going to take Mr. Tellefsen fishing, obviously I must know about any threat to him. For one thing, I need to know whether he is in danger of being assassinated, or only of being kidnaped."

Lord Redmond said, "You know, he's right, Webber. . . . I presume you'll transfer the security arrangements you laid on for Aldermaston to Scotland?"

Webber was looking angry and unhappy. "I guess so," he growled, "though protecting a man fishing on a big river in backwoods country is not the same as inside a top-security atomic plant. . . ." He turned grumpily on Hawker. "As you say, you are going to be close to Mr. Tellefsen, closer than anyone. You'd better know something about the responsibilities you're taking on."

Hawker's thin lips tightened perceptibly. De Guise suppressed a smile and leaned forward to listen. This ought to be interesting, if highly inaccurate.

Webber said, "The Texas Project is a plan to greatly advance the peaceful uses of atomic energy—oh, like desalinization of seawater, producing electric power at several cents a kilowatt less than we can produce it by other means, stuff like that—I'm no scientist, I'm just a . . . a . . . coordinator, you might say. . . . Several plants and laboratories will be engaged in the project, here and in the United States. The current U.S. budget allots three point one billion dollars for this project. The main laboratory and test factory have already been built near Shiprock, New

Mexico, close to the plant where our Bureau of Mines processes most of the uranium mined in the United States. We have been making progress, in cooperation with our British colleagues, but the Russians have been far ahead of us. Because they had the world's top man in the field—Mr. Sigurd Tellefsen. Six months ago our sources reported that Mr. Tellefsen wanted to leave the Soviet Union if he could."

Six months, de Guise noted. HPS had slipped up badly in their surveillance, at the psychological level, if Tellefsen had nursed this intent for six months without them becoming aware of it.

He stole a glance at Hammond. The big face was impassive. Impossible to tell whether he was swallowing this nonsense about cheap kilowatts and seawater. Hawker definitely was not, but would probably pretend to.

Webber went on, "We—ah, my organization—chose this current meeting of the Royal Society in London as the time for his escape. Mr. Tellefsen insisted to his Soviet masters that he must come to London in order to discuss certain scientific problems with Lord Redmond. Once he was here it was easy. The British police were to arrest him, on some trumped-up criminal charge, outside the meeting . . . though I sure don't get why it was necessary to pin a dirty morals charge on him."

The old man said, "They had a strumpet accuse me of rape. It is the British sense of humor." Dr. Berkowitz laughed suddenly and as suddenly suppressed it.

Webber said, "Once he was arrested, he applied for political asylum. That was kept secret from the press, as it usually is until the man's safely hidden. The woman then dropped her charge, said it was mistaken identity, and we were home free. . . . But the HPS only allowed Mr. Tellefsen to leave Russia, even after he'd explained how he had to consult with Lord Redmond, because they were going to hold his daughter in Russia. It was known that Mr. Tellefsen would never desert his daughter."

"Never!" the old man on the sofa said. "She is my past . . . and my future." His head had begun to sag. De Guise thought he would go to sleep soon.

Webber said, "But our organization got Miss Tellefsen out yesterday morning. I can't say how. We brought her to London.

Then . . . then . . . they got her back again. And you know the rest. The HPS men saw the fog building up this morning and took advantage of it. They are very good at improvising. I imagine they planned to get Miss Tellefsen onto a Russian ship in the Pool, and back to Russia. Then Mr. Tellefsen would go back, too. But now . . ."

"We're going to Scotland," Hawker said. "Ten o'clock from Euston, tomorrow morning. If you'll excuse me, I'd like to call Sir Alan Gobhair."

"I'll come with you," Lord Redmind said. "Let's go into the other room."

Webber said, "One moment, Lord Redmond. There'll be two bodyguards, also myself and Meikle—he's my British opposite number."

Mr. Tellefsen lost his drowsiness. His head came up and he looked balefully at Webber. "Two bodyguards? What use will they be, if my daughter is to be there to divert their thoughts from their task? That is four extra people. Is there room for so many in this lodge?"

VK said, "Wait a minute . . . Yes, just."

Mr. Tellefsen clearly had hoped for another answer. He said, "Room, perhaps, but not the need. Or the wish . . . I do not want secret police standing on watch outside the bathroom, asleep on the mat outside the bedroom, tasting the food in the kitchen!" He turned to VK. "My boy, why do we not invite your friends up? These two young men."

"No reason at all," Hawker said. He too had taken a dislike to Webber, de Guise noted. It might be a useful fact to remember, later.

Mr. Tellefsen said triumphantly, "Then there will be no room in the lodge for you and your police, Webber. You can live in the nearest town. And you will not come anywhere near me when I am fishing. Is that understood?"

"Father," Ingrid said, laying a hand on his arm.

Webber said, with remarkable self-control, "Very well, sir. I only want you to realize that you are in danger night and day. And that I am charged by the British and American Governments with looking after you."

The old man said, "It does no good to have a horse in the stable if he refuses to work. . . . You will come?" He looked at Hammond.

Hammond said, "Ye-ye-ye-ye-ye-ye-ye-ye-ye-ye . . ." His head shook up and down and the color poured into his face. Anne Hawker's face was agonized.

"*Oui!*" Hammond shouted suddenly.

Mr. Tellefsen said, "Good!" He turned to de Guise. "And you?"

De Guise cocked his head and stuck out his lower lip in a way they would all say was very Gallic. Of course he must accept the invitation, after perhaps a momentary hesitation. Scotland would be an excellent place for the next attempt. Staying as close as this to the center of the enemy camp, always under the necessity of communicating with his superiors, it could not be long before he was unmasked. But, what would you have? It was a shame to destroy a cover one had spent five years building so carefully; but, as Trilby said, that was the nature of the business. To make an omelette one breaks an egg. Next omelette, next egg. And, if nothing happened in Scotland, there was America ahead. He didn't know how he could stand it.

"*Oui,*" he said. "Thank you very much. *Enchanté.*"

Webber said, "And now, we should leave Mr. Tellefsen to rest. The guards will be within call if you need them, sir. And I'm in Room 416, of course." He took Bill's arm and muttered, "Let's have a drink. Get your jacket. I've got to talk to you. . . . No, downstairs. I want to see something down there."

Then they did not speak until they had gone down in the elevator, walked through the lobby and past the grill room, and entered the American Bar. There Webber chose a table in a corner, leaned forward, and spoke in a low voice. "Did you see that man in the lobby, sitting on the right?"

Bill nodded. The man had a very red face and was holding a pearl-gray trilby hat—the kind gangsters used to wear around 1924—in his lap. Webber said, "That is the head of Section 4 of the Russian Department of Health and Public Sanitation—the HPS. Section 4 is like our CIA. Big joke. What'll you have?"

Bill licked his lips. How many had he had before lunch? Four, was it? He recalled the sympathetic pain in Anne Hawker's face while he had been trying to say "Yes" just now. Goddammit. He said, "Bo-bo-bo . . ."

"Bourbon?"

He nodded and held up two fingers.

"Double? Straight? On the rocks?"

He nodded again and Webber beckoned a waiter. When the drinks came Webber said, "That man outside—we know his real name but always call him Trilby—has some godawful skin disease. The color on his face is rouge. He's a lousy cosmetician."

Bill took out one of the little scratch pads he always carried and wrote, *Why not arrest?*

Webber shook his head. "No can do. Ever. He's owner of a firm that distributes St. Louis Adding Machine Corporation products in Europe. Cable address SLAM. Big joke. Headquarters in Geneva. Wherever we run into trouble, he's around. Always with a legitimate reason. We used to try to pin trouble on him, but we gave up. First, because he'd pin trouble right back on me, or whoever our man on the job was, then the local police would have to pull everybody in, which made them mad. Finally, we came to see we were well off at that, knowing who their head man was, and where he was."

Bill wrote, *Gregory Parkezian?*—the man who would have had Gorton shot.

Webber said, "Head of all the Russian security and secret police. Way above Trilby. Equivalent to . . . well, Hoover and our Director combined, plus the power to order secret unexplained deaths. . . . Those are the people we're up against, and they make it a rough job at any time. And now, Mr. Tellefsen's making this one hell."

Bill signaled to the waiter for another drink. When that was gone, words came more easily, as they always did. He said, "If Mr. Hawker is going to look after Mr. Tellefsen for the next week, d-d-d-don't you think you should check up on him?"

Webber gave him a curious glance. He said, "That's partly what I wanted to see you about. You're going to be the only American in that lodge, Mr. Hammond. And you're a man who has a big stake in our country. I have to keep out of the old man's way until he cools down a bit. . . . I'm asking you to see that Hawker and the others really guard him. I guess you've been under guard

yourself, for fear of kidnaping? And that's why you carry a gun?"
Bill nodded. "Then you understand. This is serious. Cheap electrical power's all-important to the growth of our economy—the President emphasized that only last week."

Bill nodded. Mr. Webber must think he was mentally retarded, to believe that story. It was easy to think so, with this impediment.

Webber said, "As to the checking up—it's being done. The man at the door—Harry Bosco, he's one of my top assistants—called British security as soon as I took you all in to meet Mr. Tellefsen. And the FBI about you. And Paris about de Guise. I may not be the nicest guy in the world, but then I don't often finish last, either."

VK came out of the bathroom in pajamas and robe. He raised his voice. "Anne, damn it, you've left your lipstick on my dressing table again. They'll think we indulge in incest."

"More likely that I'm not your sister," she said, coming through the connecting door from her bedroom. She was wearing a white batiste night dress embroidered with blue flowers, and carrying a long-handled silver hairbrush. She brushed up his hair the wrong way and said, "Your mirror has a better light than mine. What a day! The most exciting of my life."

VK said, "Messy, I'd call it. Violence in a city seems so . . . squalid. Well, we're leaving tomorrow. Just as well."

"Is it very expensive here?"

He nodded. "I'm not complaining. You know we decided to have a real blowout before disappearing into the crowd . . . but the time has come to confine ourselves to dry bread and water."

"After Gobhair," she said. "I'm looking forward terribly to seeing it, after hearing you talk about it for thirteen years. The great castle in the mountains! The purple heather! Beautiful men with kilts! Do you think Sir Alan will fall madly in love with me and ask me to marry him?"

"Over my dead body," VK said grimly.

"Why, VK, I thought you liked him. He's your friend."

VK cut in. "I do like him, very much. He is my friend. The closest I have, probably. But he's a born bachelor. Any woman who married him would go stark raving bonkers within a year."

She brushed her hair with long, even strokes. "And you? Are you a born bachelor, too?"

"No," he said. "I like the girls too much. Someday one will trap me."

"I . . . " she began. He looked up and saw that she was staring at him, her eyes wide, the brush in her hand. She said, "And then, what will I be? I can't imagine not looking after you."

He got up and put his arms around her. "You'll be Anne," he said gently, "the most wonderful girl in the world. And what about you? Suppose it's you who wants to get married. Then what?"

"I don't know," she said slowly, "I just don't know. I can't imagine anyone meaning more to me than you do. But it would happen, wouldn't it, if I really fell in love, sexually I mean?"

"Yes, it would," VK said. "So we'd better pray we don't fall in love." He patted her hand. "There, Anne, we're the babes in the wood, apparently. Run along. Sleep well."

The Secretary said, "The last item on the agenda, Mr. President, is the Texas Project."

"A big name for a big idea," the President said. The narrow face drooped into lines of fatigue. "I've read the presentation and it looks as though we have no choice. If I am not to be outgunned when Lao Chi and I meet in Moscow next year, the Texas Project must be completed by January 1, 1972. Today is—" he glanced over his bifocals at a wall calendar—"May 8, 1971. How long is the job going to take?"

The Director said, "We can achieve ten thousand thorups now. To reach the Project target of a million thorups . . . a minimum of four months after we start the computers . . . maybe five."

"Make it four," the President said coldly. "And that only gives us three months for the unexpected snags every project runs into. There's no time to waste. But nothing starts until Mr. Tellefsen reaches the plant. Is that right?"

"Yes, sir."

"The indispensable man, at last."

The Secretary, who was a favorite, said, "There are plenty of things in this country that don't roll until one particular man gets there."

The President tapped the folder in front of him. "According to this, we were due to get Tellefsen yesterday, in London, and I see there's a note that it came off well. So he's flying over today?"

There was a silence. Everyone looked at the Director. He cleared his throat. "No, Mr. President. You'll see lower down that he was supposed to spend a week with the British nuclear men at Aldermaston."

The President cut in. "That had to be canceled because of a strike. So why isn't he here already? Who's responsible for the delay?"

"Mr. President, he insisted on going fishing."

The President leaned back in his chair and took off his glasses. "He's gone fishing," he said slowly. "Who's in charge?"

"Webber . . . Joseph Webber."

"The fellow who told me back in '66 that I'd given Mr. Johnson bad advice about Vietnam?"

The Secretary said, "He's a very capable man. Tact isn't his strong point. He called last night to say Tellefsen insisted on going fishing. He wanted to know whether he should pretend to go along, but actually take the first opportunity to bring him over by force."

"Webber said that?" the President said. He looked at the Ambassador across the table. "That's just what we need now, isn't it?" He pointed at the Secretary. "Mr. Tellefsen is one of a kind. He must be treated with great care . . . and sympathy. Why does Webber imagine he left Russia? To have us treat him the same as the Russians did? For money? Certainly not. He left Russia because somewhere, somehow, he came to believe we had a better answer. . . . We want him to work for us, of course—I've just been saying how badly we need him—but if Webber turns him against us mentally, spiritually . . . Well, I think we understand each other. What's the cover plan for the Project?" . .

"The peaceful uses of atomic energy, sir, particularly large-scale desalinization of seawater and cheap electricity. Lord Redmond is the world's top man on that, and Dr. Berkowitz on desalinization. They're the two Deputy Chiefs of the Project, under Tellefsen. It ought to work out fine."

"It's your head," the President said. "Are you satisfied, Mr. Ambassador?"

"Quite, Mr. President. I spoke to the Prime Minister an hour ago. Mr. Tellefsen's left for Scotland."

The President adjusted his glasses. "Right," he said. "That's all. But let us all understand the position. This Texas Project is a fantastic step forward in science, as long as we keep pace with the Russians. If we don't . . . if we get left behind, it will be the end of freedom in the world as we understand freedom. But we won't fail, will we?" He stood up.

"Thank you, Mr. President . . ."

"Who's next, George?"

"Monroe Barnett, President of the American Bar—"

"George, even I know who Monroe Barnett is. Tidy the desk. Give me a clean handkerchief. I just said that Sigurd Tellefsen was one of a kind, but Monroe Barnett's rarer than that. He's an honest lawyer."

Chapter 2

IN THE IMMENSE HALL darkness and sheer distance dimmed the farthest trophies. Down there, far away, Anne and Bill Hammond paced the bare stone flags, looking up at the heads and horns and brief inscriptions. Opposite, between walled-in arrow slits and small leaded windows with ogival arches, primitive African masks shared the stone with claymores and banners and round, embossed Highland shields. Some of those masks were excellent, de Guise had noted. Like many another red-faced milord, Sir Alan or his father had better taste than one would expect.

Near the main door a few logs flickered in the cavernous fireplace, their flame and light soon lost in the hall's sheer size. Ingrid Tellefsen, perched on the forward edge of an oak bench, huddled into her overcoat and crouched closer to the fire. De Guise stood in the open door beside VK, Sigurd Tellefsen, and Sir Alan Gobhair, the owner of all this splendor. The northward view swept down to Loch Tummel, then rose past Tulach and the cleft of Glen Garry to the purple haze of the Forest of Atholl.

Sir Alan was wearing the kilt, as he apparently always did in the Highlands. It was easy to see how he and VK had become friends, for they were both strangers to their environment. VK belonged to another place and Sir Alan to another time. He was a gaunt, almost bald young man with wild blue eyes and a big ginger mustache. He and Mr. Tellefsen had taken to each other on sight, to VK's relief, which de Guise could well understand. It was all very well for Lord Redmond to assure him that Sir Alan would be delighted; and it was true that VK and the baronet had been at school together (ah, the British and their school days!); and it was true that the lodge was quite separate from the castle. Nevertheless, to arrive seven strong when only two had been invited! They might have guessed that Sir Alan's reaction would be pure Scottish patriotism—to get Mr. Tellefsen a good salmon.

Salmon, salmon, salmon . . . VK and Sir Alan and the old man had talked of nothing else for an hour now, himself throwing in appropriate exclamations of wonder or surprise, as they paced the unkempt gravel on the north front, or sat on a bench close outside the huge front door.

"The day of the big hook is finished . . ." Sir Alan said didactically.

De Guise sighed and looked out across the immense view. He wondered where Trilby was out there—or would appear; and whether he himself could get any warning before violence exploded around him. He was expendable, as Trilby had taken care to remind him so often. What came next depended much on whether it was still the policy to get Mr. T. back to Russia. If they'd decided not to bother—just to kill him—then anything might happen—a sniper's bullet from the bank when they were in the boat; a bomb planted in the lodge or their rented car; a car swooping down on the old man while he was walking to the river—and there'd be no hesitation, no swerving, if *he* happened to be walking with Mr. T. at the time.

There was no gooey American sentimentality about *his* bosses. It was ironic to think that if he were to be erased during the next attempt, which was bound to come soon, Bill Hammond, the American, was probably the only person who'd give a damn.

Sir Alan looked at his watch and said, "Anderson'll be telling us lunch is ready soon. Time for a drop, I think."

Mr. Tellefsen paused in the arched entrance, looking back across the sweep of the view. "Mountains," he muttered. "A river. The great fish. What else can a man want?"

"Youth," Sir Alan said, smiling.

"And fighting, alas. And love. Especially love . . ." He turned in and strode slowly to Ingrid's side.

Ingrid looked up. "Ah, you were never a man of peace, father."

Mr. Tellefsen said, "The blood still runs hot, Ingrid. But the flesh grows cold."

Ingrid said, "In this place, mine too! And *I* am not old." She pulled the overcoat more tightly about her.

Sir Alan opened a bottle and said, "This is what you need. Pure malt whiskey. None of your milksop blends." Mr. Tellefsen nodded.

De Guise said, "Not for me, thank you. Nothing at all."

"A teetotal Frenchman?" Sir Alan cried, peering at him in the gloom. "Can it be true? Wait, I'll get you some tomato juice."

He strode off down the hall, the kilt swinging, his heavy brogues thudding rhythmically on the stone. Outside the sun shone warm on the weed-cluttered lawn and the gravel sweep of the drive. Inside, Arctic draughts blew round the cold stone. Ingrid rubbed her hands. "This is terrible! No wonder he cannot find a woman to marry him. This is worse than Siberia."

"Central heating's bad for the soul," VK said, grinning. "Also, it causes chilblains."

Ingrid said, "Why did they build it looking toward the north? And hundreds of meters above the lake!"

Anne and Bill Hammond returned from the far end of the hall. When the whiskey was poured Hammond wouldn't be far away, de Guise thought. Ingrid said to Anne, "Ah, now I know why you wear woolen underclothes, and big thick shoes, and have red noses! It is . . . it is barbaric!"

Sir Alan strode back, like a one-man clan, out of the far caverns of Castle Gobhair, carrying a silver beaker of tomato juice. He turned to Anne. "Are you girls comfortable at the lodge?"

Anne said, "Very, thank you," and Ingrid said, "Yes. It has real plumbing, and heating."

Sir Alan said, "Another whiskey! You look a little chilly."

He poured out a generous tot. "There. Interesting locket of yours. That's a Roman arch, isn't it?"

"It's a church, I think," Ingrid said, shrugging. "It belonged to my mother."

Sir Alan looked at Mr. Tellefsen. The old man raised his head slowly. He said, "I cannot speak of her. Except to tell Ingrid that she was good and brave. It is for your own good that I keep silence, Ingrid. That, and the preservation of my life, perhaps. You could never keep a secret."

Ingrid said, "He won't say whether she is alive or dead."

Mr. Tellefsen said, "I do not say because I do not know. . . . But I will tell you this. That is not a chalet or a church, as you have thought. It is a bridge, in the town where you were born."

"But," Ingrid said, "the cross hanging from the arch? And these little things at the side that have been rubbed so much . . ."

"They are alpha and omega," Mr. Tellefsen said. "None of them were there when I saw the bridge, neither the Greek letters nor the cross, but she said they used to be. Perhaps they are again. Enough now, child! I tell you, it is for our lives' sake that I say no more." He picked up his whiskey.

De Guise tried to conceal his interest in what the old man had said. Trilby had briefed him thoroughly on Mr. T., of course, before giving him this assignment; but about his past, before he reached the Soviet Union on July 17, 1939 . . . nothing, because nothing was known, and Mr. T. had never talked—not even this much.

He caught VK's eye on him, and raised the glass of tomato juice. "VK, *mon vieux,* you promised to tell me how I can get in touch with the man who carved the Mau Mau ritual clubs. For you it is just a bit of Empire, but for me . . ." He rubbed forefinger and thumb together. "It is more important. It is money."

An old man in butler's livery approached with measured tread. A few paces distant he stopped and said, "Luncheon is sairrrved, sorr."

Sir Alan put his glass on the great stone mantel. "Thank you, Anderson. . . . Ready, ladies? And after lunch, a little ride around the estate, eh? There's a sick doe somewhere on Beinn Eagagach I'd like to put out of her misery, and there's always the chance of getting some of the hoodie crows and wildcats that have been massacring the young grouse this season."

VK said, "If we can get back by about four, Alan. We'll have to go down then, as I'm taking Mr. Tellefsen on the river. . . . We saw the ponies in the stables just now, but I didn't see Walton."

They passed down the hall, through a doorway with open, iron-studded doors into another hall as large as the first. A mahogany table was set in the center of it. Sir Alan said, "He's gone. Death and taxes. Anderson looks after the ponies, too, in another pair of trousers. Sit here, will you, Miss Tellefsen? You know, VK, I'd like to have a day on the water with you. What about Thursday? I'll get you a salmon—a good one. . . ."

The boat floated slowly stern-first down the Tay, VK in the bow, Sir Alan rowing, and Mr. Tellefsen on the angler's seat—a plank set athwart the gunwales to give extra height. There had been heavy rain in the headwaters and on Rannoch Moor the past three days, and the river ran high and fast at about four knots. Sir Alan rowed at a fraction less, keeping the bows upstream, so that the little boat drifted slowly backward.

Mr. Tellefsen cast methodically into the slight wind. He was using one of Sir Alan's fourteen-foot spliced greenhearts from Grant of Aberdeen, with a twelve-pound breaking strain cast and a Thunder-and-Lightning fly tied with a No. 3 hook. The first day, when he took the rod and practiced a cast or two on the bank with it, he had cried, "This little thing . . . for salmon?" But now, after a week on the water, he said, "It is lucky for me that the seventeen-foot rods we used to use, like tree trunks, have gone. I would be dead by now. . . ."

VK looked at the grassy bank, where the others were practicing archery. Anne was showing Hammond how to use the bow. Hammond's arrow went far past the big target. Now it was de Guise's turn. His arrow quivered near the center. Ingrid lay voluptuously asleep among the daisies.

It was a good place. The ripple of the river and, even more strongly, the faint clean smell brought back days of his boyhood, and long hours watching this same sparkling surface. Even the twang of the long bow and the thunk of the arrows had not changed, for they had always practiced archery here by the boathouse. But it was said that you could never put your hand in the same river twice. . . . Well, he missed the faintly feral smell of old John Craig, the gillie—pensioned off five years back—who used to row the boat in the old days. And he missed the sense of timelessness, of no tomorrow: because there was an awful tomorrow, hanging like a black cloud over him. This was the grand finale to his life in the open air. Today was Thursday. On Monday he was due to start as a trainee in the administrative department of the John Lewis Partnership. He grated his teeth. What the hell had he, V.K.G. Hawker, Esquire, been thinking of, when he accepted that offer from a man his father had shown good sport to?

He wasn't cut out to be an administrator, at John Lewis or anywhere else. What England needed was a landed aristocracy, each lord to have a hundred thousand wild acres and a force of twenty gamekeepers, under a head gamekeeper. That's where he'd come in. It would be nice if the lord had had the family jewels shot off in the war, too. . . . He'd give a lot to have been born in Alan's shoes, heir to Gobhair. It wasn't the streets or the wet slates or the gray faces or the rain that made one quail. It was . . .

Sir Alan said, "Why did you leave Africa, VK? Remember how we used to talk about it? All our plans. I was going to come out and go partners with you . . . marry Anne . . . we'd spend six months of every year in Kenya and six here."

Mr. Tellefsen sent out a long, easy cast, and spoke over his shoulder. "Yes, why?"

VK thought, What's it got to do with them? Then he thought, I'll say I'd had enough of discomfort and heat and fevers. But Alan was his friend, and Mr. Tellefsen was a big man. They would not laugh at him.

He said, "I lost faith . . . purpose. The clients thought they were hiring me to get them a lion or a kudu or whatever, but I didn't see it that way, not inside myself. To me, I was a teacher, an apostle almost. . . . I was showing them visions, not trophies for their rumpus rooms."

"They were deprived," Mr. Tellefsen said, "shut in by their money as much as by the concrete and glass of their cities. I understand."

"Yes," VK said eagerly. "They had no idea of the relationship between themselves, as human animals, and the rest of creation. I tried to show them fear and loneliness, courage and self-mastery, survival . . ."

"Death," Mr. Tellefsen said. "Life. Dignity." The boat drifted down, the water purling under the bow. The oars creaked gently in the rowlocks.

VK said, "God, I knew well enough that only one man in twenty saw anything beyond a head to hang on his wall. For the other nineteen the things that really mattered—the being alone, the being afraid and hungry—were no more than nuisances which they had to put up with in order to get the trophy. For a while I fooled myself that the twentieth man made it all worth while. Perhaps he did."

Oh God. It was true. But out there the sun *did* shine, there was dust and mud underfoot, thorns on the trees, wood crackling under the pot. There was grass and water and rifle oil. . . .

Sir Alan said, "I was going to look after the men and the whiskey, remember? While you took care of the women and the champagne."

"It wasn't enough," VK said. "Not without a purpose."

Sir Alan said, "So you're going into business, where your purpose will be the efficient sale of preshrunk shirts, plastic lampshades, spandex-trimmed panty girdles?"

Mr. Tellefsen said, "There is a very big salmon lying out there, I think."

Sir Alan said, "Do you see him?"

The old man shook his head. "No, but I saw a very big fish come into the tail of the pool . . . just his back and the top of his dorsal fin, but he's a great one, I'm sure. And the water swirls strangely sometimes. I have seen a few trout swimming fast where they should be swimming slowly . . . but I am getting tired. In a few minutes, my boy, you must take the rod."

"All right," VK said.

The black-and-gold fly sailed out to the side—the casts were shortening noticeably, though—hovered over the water and settled gently. The current sent it fast downstream and, as the line straightened, also across, until it was due astern. Then the water pressure dragged it under. After about a minute Mr. Tellefsen began his backswing, drawing the fly out, then easily into the next cast.

VK glanced at the bank. Ingrid was awake, admiring Hammond. She had something to admire, dammit. The man had never held a long bow in his hands before today and there went three arrows into the center of the bull, and they'd stepped back to a hundred and fifty yards now. It was tempting to believe that women like Ingrid steamed with lust over men like Hammond simply because of their money. In civilization it was usually true enough. It took the heat and excitement of an African safari to strip their lusts down to essentials. Then it was to him, the disheveled hunter in the dusty trousers and the faded drill jacket, that they turned, eyes moist and bodies pleading. But with Hammond he wouldn't like to bet. The bastard was a natural athlete, and with a little practice might cut him out even on safari. But there'd never *be* another safari. . . .

Real life next week.

Did "real life" *have* to mean routine, the absence of danger, of physical challenge? Must the skills he had cultivated so carefully now die because no one had need for them in "civilization"? He swore under his breath.

Mr. Tellefsen said, "Eh? Take the rod now, please."

Sir Alan rowed in to the bank and VK changed places with Mr. Tellefsen. The others were putting away the target and archery equipment in the boathouse. De Guise came out and called, "But, sir, where is this salmon we were promised for supper?"

Old Tellefsen shook a huge fist at him. "In the water, for a little more," he said. "VK will get him now. You wait and see."

They pulled the boat up to the head of the pool on a rope, and then started again.

Bill Hammond had felt the sweat breaking out on his body, and the senseless knotting of his muscles, when Anne suggested, at breakfast, that they spend the morning on the riverbank, watching the fishermen. He'd have to talk, and he couldn't. So he went up to his room, took out a fifth of Scotch from his suitcase, poured a stiff jigger, tossed it back, poured another . . . then looked at himself in the mirror. Twenty-eight, still in good shape, but for how long? Besides, it was the erosion of will power that really mattered. He poured the second jigger down the basin.

Thank God for the archery. No need for conversation there. But now it was over and now he did have to talk, and that one jigger wasn't enough. Anne Hawker didn't ask for conversation, and de Guise stuck his nose into a book—but his own screaming need insisted. Talk. Tell her. So it began, and so it continued, the miserable da-da-da-da-da-da and wa-wa-wa-wa-wa-wa and, worst of all, the minutes with mouth open, straining to make a sound but nothing, absolutely nothing, coming out.

De Guise spoke without looking up from his book. *"Mon ami, qu'est-ce que vous voulez dire?"*

Bill unclenched his fists. OK, so he could speak if he put it into French. Come to that, he could get the words out if he sang, or put on a Mexican field hand's accent—anything that was not his real self. These acts were almost as degrading as the stammer. Still, sometimes they had to be faced.

Small talk was out. With this curse on your tongue, you never wasted communication on the weather, or minor aches and pains. He said, *"Je veux savoir pourquoi le frère de mademoiselle a quitté le—le business de safari."*

There, terrible high school French, but it was said. Anne said, *"Mon frère a quitté . . ."*

She looked at him and suddenly doubled up with laughter. "Why am I speaking French?" she cried. Bill's aching face muscles slowly relaxed. He smiled. He laughed. She had wonderful eyes, crinkled at the corners.

Ingrid yawned and stretched like a lazy cat.

Anne said, "We left Africa because VK began to feel that he was a sort of . . . pimp, bringing the game to the clients, to be killed. The clients got more and more on his nerves."

De Guise put down his book. "Once you start thinking like that," he said, "it is all over. Incidents which you once would not have noticed become hugely important. . . ."

"Oh, I know, I *know*," Anne said. "There was a female eland, pregnant . . ." Her voice rippled on.

Bill took a long careful look at VK in the boat. Brother and sister had a distinct resemblance, particularly in the shape of the face. VK was lank, a thin man with long sandy hair. The thin high-bridged nose gave him the look of a pale eagle, especially when he was concentrating, as now, projecting his will behind the cast of the long floating line. He and Anne both had gray eyes, too, wide-set and long-lashed—if anything, VK's were longer than Anne's. They were intense, deep-set eyes, but VK's focused out away on the object he was looking at, like a range finder, while Anne's seemed to bring the object back inside, behind the eyes, and examine it there.

". . . and this German millionaire wounded it! At ten feet, he only broke its leg. VK felt he couldn't go on any more."

"So now he is going to this John Lewis? And you?"

Anne said, "Oh, I'll keep house for him, the same as usual. . . . I'm not trained for anything else. I can cook a bit—shoot, of course—ride. What else could I do here? Besides, I like it."

De Guise's voice had a touch of mockery. "You don't want to be someone's Girl Friday? To have a flat of your own, and wear pretty clothes and be a beautiful, desirable, unattached female in London? Marry?"

Bill watched her wriggle uncomfortably. She said, "I'm quite happy. Of course if Mr. Right, horrible word, came along, I'd love to get married, but . . . What about you? We've spent a week together, and we know you are an art dealer, but that's all. It's not fair." She smiled.

Bill thought, She has class. She was tall, for a woman, and steady-eyed. At first glance you thought she must be wearing white lipstick. Then you saw that she wasn't, and the blond eyelashes were her own; and she'd never had a permanent wave—her hair was swept back and gathered in a loose, thick pony tail at the nape of her neck. She was simple, unspoiled, natural . . . but did she want it that way? Or did her brother insist? VK could be a real mean one. When he was unhappy about anything he padded up and down like a leopard, with an intense, hungry expression. You felt that if you offered him something to eat you'd better pull your fingers back quickly.

De Guise said, "Robert de Guise, born Hanoi, the capital of Tonkin, French Indo-China, July 14, 1943. In spite of such an auspicious birthdate, for a Frenchman, we were still kicked out of Indo-China. My father saw what was coming, and did not believe the assurances from Paris. In 1950 he sold out his business in Hanoi—import and export, and what I think you call factoring. We went to live in Pau. We were well off—not fantastically rich, but very comfortable. I became a modern young French milord. A ski champion. Alpinist. At the University of Toulouse I devoted myself to man's proper study—girls." He shook a Lucky Strike out of its pack. "My parents died. I left Pau for Paris. I took my place in the world."

Anne said, "I'm sure I've seen your photo somewhere. Did you buy or sell some special picture recently?"

De Guise said, "I don't think so. It was probably in a society column that you saw me. I am a member of what is called the Jet Set, I believe. I am seen dancing the Fink in St. Tropez or Sardinia. I am always staring into flashbulbs with the fourth-best-dressed woman in Tangier."

"Ame-me-me-me-me-me-me-me . . ." Bill stammered.

De Guise spread his hands in a deliberately Gallic gesture. "Do I visit America? Once, many years back. . . . Your great country is not for me, Bill. It is a matter of taste."

Bill detected a venomous backlash to the word "taste." De Guise wasn't saying that liking America was a matter of taste, but that America had no taste. Well, plenty of Europeans had said that before him. And plenty of the ones who said it had been wearing Levis and loafers, and smoking Luckies, like Robert. De Guise put on these French gestures now and then, as though to joke at himself, but the man himself was just the opposite of the volatile old-type cartoon Frenchman. De Guise had a lot of cool, an oddly American kind of cool at that, in his emotions. Except for the short hair he acted very like the old movies of Kennedy.

Anne's eyes were shining. "It must be terribly exciting, being in the Jet Set." She caught Bill's surprised expression and finished hurriedly, "Of course, I wouldn't like that sort of life."

De Guise said, "Ah, you think? But you are a woman? In truth, it can be very boring—the parties, the champagne, the gaiety hahaha all the time. . . . But these people have a great deal of money, and they buy many pictures and much sculpture from me. And . . . I will let you into a secret . . . really, I am a hard-working professional. There are few dealers in Paris who are as knowledgeable of abstract art and artists all over the world as I am . . . and in the field of primitive art, none. I go everywhere, but I am always working. From Sir Alan yesterday I hear the location of a fabulous collection of Papuan masks. VK tells me about the old Kikuyu. The barman at that little pub in Pitlochry talks of a crazy artist in Aberfeldy . . . well, I have visited him, and he is crazy like a fox. My parents left me well off, but I have made myself rich. *Pardon*"—he glanced at Bill with a smile—"in the presence of Bill Hammond I will say only that I am not a pauper."

Now Anne was looking at *him*. He ought to tell them something about himself; but this could not be in French, just because it was about himself. He would have to write it down.

De Guise said, "*Mon ami, vous permettez?* Mr. William M. Hammond is the son of the late Richard F. Hammond. The M stands for Middendorf. Bill's mother was Nancy Scoones Middendorf, of Pittsburgh. On her marriage she brought Mr. Hammond Senior a sizable fortune. . . . You don't mind these details, Bill?"

Bill shook his head. He kept his expression neutral. It was funny that de Guise should know so much about him, but not really odd. Privacy didn't exist for people saddled with his particular burden.

De Guise said, "Mr. Richard Hammond formed a private investment company—the Middendorf Company—and by skill and energy increased the company's assets very considerably."

He glanced at Bill and Bill nodded again. One hundred and fifteen million dollars was the current figure, and de Guise probably knew it. Anne was looking at him with an odd expression. He cursed his wealth: Now he was becoming, in her eyes, another hirer of VK, another potential butcher of beautiful animals. Ingrid Tellefsen was looking at him, too, her eyes big and round. She might be a Communist but the presence of great wealth obviously affected her the same way it affected most people.

De Guise said, "Bill's father died last October, so Bill inherited the Middendorf Company. But he is better known as one of America's great amateur athletes."

Bill made a gesture of dissent and de Guise did not pursue that subject. He said instead, "So much was in *Time* magazine last October, Bill. And, you understand, an art dealer who does not know the difference between the rich and the rich-rich of this world will not survive very long."

Anne cried, "You won the one hundred-meter free-style at Mexico!"

Bill said, "Ye-ye-ye-ye-ye-ye-ye-ye-ye-ye-ye-ye-*yes*."

Ingrid slid to her feet. "Come, Beel, take me for a walk. I am so stiff and the grass is damp."

Unwillingly he got up. He looked at Anne, but she did not take the hint and invite herself along too. Perhaps she thought he wanted to be alone with Ingrid. Ingrid had linked her arm in his. She was a sex bomb, but a good loyal woman, too. Old Tellefsen was glaring at her from the boat. A daughter like Ingrid must be nearly as much of a trial as if she were your wife.

He walked at Ingrid's side along the riverbank in silence, thinking of Anne Hawker. . . . He wondered how much de Guise knew about his athletic record. It would sound great in the recital, but a person like Anne would have no idea of the price he had paid—unwillingly—to hang up that record. Time and again he had cursed the physique and natural coordination which enabled him to accomplish the feats his father drove him to. Why hadn't he had the guts to tell his father to go to hell? For the sake of his mother—who was dead. . . . De Guise had told them his father had made a lot of money. Right. But no one could tell them about the remark he himself had overheard in the men's room at Trader Vic's. One Ivy League type to another: *Do you know who I saw upstairs? Richard Hammond . . . Who's he? . . . One of the most unpleasant human beings ever turned out by a malevolent deity.*

Ingrid was warm and feminine against him. It wouldn't be hard to lay her, obviously. Well, it would, for him, because in her own way, and underneath all her mannerisms, she had class, was *decent*. His mother had said you could always tell, and she was right. She had shown him how—by their manner, their dress, their way of responding to compliments, to new situations—and it was amazing how keen her insight had been. At least half a dozen times he had thought he liked some girl very much, in spite of his mother's warnings about her; and in the end she had been proved right, every time. They were his father's sort of women, not his.

Anne Hawker was something different, though. How did you make a girl like her understand what it was like to live with wealth such as his—even if you could speak properly? How did you explain that even now, in this remote Scottish quiet, by this lovely river, you were watching the trees for the hidden kidnaper, the thug, or, almost worse, the crackpot who knew he could cure the ills of the world if he could just get you alone to explain his ideas about . . .

He ought to be on the alert, too, because of Mr. Tellefsen. It was an odd and pleasant sensation to realize that it was someone else he was protecting, not himself. If the HPS really meant to murder the old man, it would not be difficult here. Kidnaping would be harder. Webber and Meikle and Bosco were probably around somewhere, out of sight. The old man was making his guardians' task just as difficult as his own father used to with his . . . especially when he wanted to be alone with a floozy.

Ingrid said, "Shall we sit down here, Beel? I'm tired."

He sat down beside her, where she patted the grass, smiling invitingly. They were in full view of the boat and a road bridge. She could tempt him as much as she liked here, he was in no danger.

She said, "Why were you in London, Beel?"

He said, "*Je fais un voyage autour du monde.*"

"I don't understand French." He made an encircling gesture and she said at once, "Oh, you are going round the world. All Americans do that all the time, don't they? The travel agencies send them, and arrange everything, so they never have to eat anything but hamburgers and ice cream."

He nodded. Why try to explain? Actually it was Monroe Barnett, the Middendorf Company's attorney, and his own, who had sent him off. When he inherited the company he had, of course, also inherited a slew of aides, assistants, comptrollers, and secretaries, all efficient, devoted, and still too frightened of his dead father to be dishonest. They had advised him, in chorus, to invest and reinvest in the U.S. economy, and so make more money . . . and more . . . and more . . . But good God, he was making money at the rate of twenty thousand dollars a day already, without lifting a finger. He wanted something else, and he didn't know what. By mid-March he was almost out of his mind. That was when he went to Monroe Barnett. Barnett, Weiss & Ferguson's offices were on 16th Street NW in Washington. From Monroe's window you looked down 16th Street at the White House. The thought had crossed Bill's mind, staring at the colonnaded portico, that *that* would be a goal worth all his time and money. But the thought, once translated into a shape, made him give a single mirthless yell of laughter.

Monroe understood. He was a man whose appearance commanded respect—a long face, hollow-cheeked, a shock of white hair, deep brown eyes, deep cleft lines from nostrils to mouth. When you came to know him, your respect only deepened, because he had probity, dignity, and a great capacity for sympathy. Bill sometimes thought that Monroe Barnett was the only person in the world, after his mother died, who understood the first damn thing about him.

Monroe had said, "You feel that there must be something better to do with your money than use it to make more. Of course . . . Why don't you go around the world, to see if there's an answer outside this country? Avoid personal aid programs. And one-shot deals, like building and endowing a university, or a hospital. You should look for something continuing. It must challenge you. It must involve *you*, not just your money, all the time."

So here he was. Paris. London. Talks with economists, scientists, politicians, sociologists. A deepening certainty that he would find no answer . . . and now this interlude beside a Highland river. Time wasted?

Ingrid said, "I think VK's hooked a fish."

Sir Alan said, "Let the fly hang longer in the stream at this time of year, VK. Let it come right round behind the boat. The water's roiled and they'll not be seeing it so easily."

VK said, "I'll try a brighter fly."

"Yes," Sir Alan said. "And a heavier cast. When there's such body in the water, you need the twenty pounds if you're not to let fish go. The rush of the water is using half the breaking strain of the cast before the fish itself puts any force against it."

Quite right, VK thought. The ceaseless thrust of the river was like the permanent strain that office work would impose on him.

What would he have left to live with? Every man had a breaking strain, which he could increase by self-discipline, but usually only in one area. He himself could go for days without food or water. But hours in an office? That was a strain he had not been born, or trained, to stand up to.

He reeled in, cut off the Thunder-and-Lightning fly and put it back in the fly box. He considered the choices.

"The Silver Wilkinson," Sir Alan said. "Or the Mar Lodge. I've killed many a salmon with the Mar Lodge in weather like this."

"What size?" VK asked.

"Oh, size? Ah . . ." Sir Alan laughed. "Now that you mention it, pretty small. Twelve to sixteen pounds. But clean run."

VK selected a purple-hackled Silver Wilkinson and began to fasten it carefully onto the new cast. Sir Alan rowed the boat back upstream. VK watched his own fingers tying the knot, but his thoughts were elsewhere. . . . John Lewis, a noble firm, a forward-looking pillar of the mercantile ship of state. The thought depressed him immeasurably.

He finished fastening fly and cast, and began paying out line, gently curling the rod tip to and fro, the fly floating in gradually lengthening parabolic curves over his head. When he had forty feet of line out he flicked his wrist and let the fly shoot.

The fly fell on the water. The line began to swing. The fly disappeared.

Ingrid and Bill had gone for a walk along the bank. Now they were sitting down.

Mr. Tellefsen's voice was low and hoarse. "Right, VK, twenty yards. I saw his back."

VK drew back and cast again. The fly drifted across the place Mr. Tellefsen indicated, the line straightened, the fly disappeared underwater.

Twenty seconds later the rod moved in VK's hand, the butt coming slowly up under his arm and the point down. He held steady against an increasing strain.

Sir Alan said, "You're into a fish, VK! Let him take it now, let him take it."

Mr. Tellefsen sighed. "This is the one."

The line snaked away on the surface of the water, then went down stiff and taut. VK waited, his breath tight as the line. What was the fish doing? Probably trying to ease the sharp, hard thing out of its mouth. Perhaps just biting through the cast.

The salmon took the fly and moved on—slow, unhurried, and very powerful. The reel screamed in a rising crescendo and the line slid across the water, cutting the surface like a cheese wire.

"That is a big fish," Sir Alan said.

"Very big," VK said, suddenly exultant. "This is the biggest fish I've ever hooked into."

"Ah. Yes. Then careful now. Mind the rocks, VK."

Here on the Gobhair Estate water, the Tay ran between low grassy banks, which rose on the south side—the right—to the fields and woods of Grandtully, on the north more steeply to a narrow winding road. Oak and ash trees, now brilliant in early summer foliage, lined both banks. The river ran a hundred and eighty feet wide between banks. The boat was now under the right bank, the salmon closer toward the middle of the river.

"Give him all he wants," Sir Alan cried.

Fine, VK thought, but he's going downstream like a torpedo—all the hand slack's gone, and most of the line, and the reel's ready to smoke. The boat dropped faster downstream and Sir Alan said, "Ease the ratchet a bit, VK. I'll have to row again when he reaches the tail of the pool."

For a full minute the line stretched taut from the empty reel, over the bent rod tip to the salmon underwater. He was already only a few feet from the broken water marking the end of the pool. One short run now, and he'd break the cast. . . . The line slackened and VK reeled in as fast as his wrist could turn the ratchet. Several seconds passed before he felt the strain again. Now the line ran straight across the river, the far end moving upstream.

"Do you want to get onto the bank?" Sir Alan gasped, straining at the oars.

"No," VK said, "I'd rather be in the boat for this one."

"Move over," Mr. Tellefsen cried. "Give me the right oar . . . There." He joined the baronet on the thwart and the two of them bent to the oars, rowing with all their strength to keep up with the salmon as it cruised upriver against the swift current. The salmon stayed near midstream, the boat close to the bank. For a time they kept pace, the line running straight across the stream. Then the line went slack, and a moment later the salmon broke water in a high, powerful leap.

VK shut his eyes.

Old Tellefsen cried, *"Cone-yo!"*

Sir Alan muttered, "My God! . . . And clean run! Did you ever see such a color?"

VK watched the river, praying that the salmon would not make such a leap again, for he could not fail, soon, to throw out the hook. Yet, what a sight! New-sliced lead was the usual description of a salmon's belly color, and that's what he'd seen under the thick ocean-colored back. Forty, fifty pounds? At least . . . but he refused to think about that. This fish could not be presumed upon.

The river curved and still the salmon worked upstream toward the top end of the Lairig Pool, where a narrow road bridge crossed on eight arches, over shallows and rock outcrops. Now, with the heavy volume of water in the river, the rocks were hidden under tossing white foam. VK swung his legs over the bench, to face forward, for the salmon was beginning to gain on them.

With the bridge forty yards off, Sir Alan grunted, "You . . . must . . . tighten on him . . . If he reaches the rocks . . . he's gone . . . He wasn't born yesterday."

Or last year, VK exulted. He touched the reel brake and began to wind in slowly. For a time the salmon allowed himself to be drawn in with the line, then the direction of the line reversed, the reel screamed against the brake and the monster resumed his cruise. VK tried again. A twenty-pound breaking strain, with this salmon, in this water, wasn't enough—but it would have to be. The fish gave the impression of intelligence, of not worrying. Perhaps he meant to swim up under one arch of the bridge, and down under another. That would fix everything in short order. Anne and de Guise and Ingrid and Hammond had run to the bridge. A crowd was gathering there, and as the salmon again broke water in a magnificent leap, all their arms flung up. VK could hear nothing above the roar of the Tay, but there was no need. Those were fishermen, and he and they had just seen the biggest salmon any of them were likely to see.

His arms began to ache. The salmon, as though getting the message, turned without warning and headed downstream at full speed. Again the line sang and the reel screamed. Again the

rowers had to backstroke to keep pace. Again at the foot of the
pool, in water so shallow that the salmon's bull-like shoulders
swirled out of water as he turned, they held him on the empty
reel. He started tirelessly upstream. . . .

The sun came out, went in, came out. The wind blew down the
river and the sweat dried on his body. . . .

"That's two hours now," Mr. Tellefsen said. "Do you want a
drink? This might kill me. I hope so! It is the best way to go!"

"Water, please," VK said. He was very thirsty. The salmon was
working leisurely upstream for the fourth time. The bridge was
lined with people. His arms hurt, his wrists felt thick and bruised,
and his fingers burned from using them to help check the line
against the salmon's remorseless drag.

Once more the fish reached the tail of the Lairig Bridge rapids,
this time heading for sharp rocks below the central abutment. VK
tried to hold him, but it was no good. . . . He was going. Ten
seconds and he'd be among those rocks. The cast couldn't hold
him.

VK said, "I'm going to slack off."

It was breaking every rule of fishing, but when correct methods
failed, you had to try the incorrect. He payed out more line, until
he could barely feel the presence of the fish on the other end. For
twenty seconds nothing happened. Then the salmon, feeling no
pressure in his mouth, turned back downstream.

After counting another twenty, VK began to reel in. With sixty
feet of line out, he took the strain. The line now ran almost dead
astern, with the boat upstream of the fish. VK reeled in more
firmly.

The salmon's reaction was quite different this time. After a short
dragging pause, as though in disbelief, he began a fight of frenzy.
. . . The line sang and the salmon raced downstream, almost on
the surface. If he had gone on, nothing could have saved the line,
but for no reason, controlled now only by panic urges, he turned
on his tail, arched twice into the air and came back upstream as
fast as he had gone down. The line went slack again, this time
because VK couldn't reel in fast enough. But at ten feet the
salmon saw the boat and shied away, leaping once more into the
air.

"I'm keeping above him if I can," Sir Alan said. "That way . . .

he'll have to get by the boat . . . to reach the rocks . . . he'll not like that . . ."

"Three hours," Mr. Tellefsen said, what seemed days later. He and Sir Alan rowed mechanically, heads bent. A wide swirl in the water under the right bank marked the salmon. VK reeled in with a dull, exhausted efficiency. The boat swung slowly across the current.

Sir Alan said, "Can you hold her steady, Mr. T? I'll take the gaff."

The line stayed taut. There he was, huge, slow. Sir Alan leaned over, the jaws of the gaff flashed . . . "Got him!"

A roar sounded in VK's ears. He looked around and saw fifty people clapping and waving their caps on the Lairig Bridge. Then the bow touched the bank, and Sir Alan was out, the boat secure, and *it* lay blue and silver on green grass. Sir Alan held it up, then the people from the bridge came running down and he stood alone, holding it up by a cord through the gills. . . . His arm was cracking under the strain. They were talking all around. . . . *Sixty pounds . . . fifty-five . . . seventy . . . Bigger than Miss Ballantine's, that she killed in '24 . . . Not as big as Miss Ballantine's . . . Do you notice the sea lice on him, he's not twelve hours in the river! . . . Take him to the scales quick, VK . . .*

VK sat down on the grass. He took the fishing knife from his pocket, cut off the bloodstained hook and bright fly that had caught the fish and stuck it into the band of his old tweed hat. Soon he'd feel the excitement and the thrill. Now he saw only the great fish's sad, dead eye. He wanted to close his own eyes and share the salmon's sadness before returning to savor the triumph. Old Tellefsen was there, his cheeks wet, patting his hand. He understood.

Bill Hammond awoke with a throbbing head and saw that it was past ten o'clock in the morning. Boy, had he knocked it down last night! But it was worth it, not only because he'd been able to talk, but because it was Anne he'd been talking to. And she *had* asked him why he was going around the world, and he had told her, right out of the deep-down truth which he could almost never dredge up and give to people.

What a party! He remembered the bottles of malt whiskey

crowding the table, and Sir Alan's ginger mustache permanently buried in whiskey, and Mr. Tellefsen remorselessly upending glass after glass with no apparent change in his craggy features until the very end, when he keeled over slowly, chair and all, and lay beard skyward on the floor, smiling; and Mrs. Turner, the lodge housekeeper, giggly on a thimbleful; de Guise, awash in tomato juice; Anne, transfigured; VK, the hunter-hero . . . but VK hadn't looked so happy. Perhaps VK thought that his interest in Anne was only a crude seducer's. Or could it be that he was jealous? Then there was Ingrid, flushed and loud, letting herself in for another of her father's formidable tempers when she flung her arms around his, Bill's, neck, and kissed him deeply on the mouth. Old Tellefsen had raised his hand and thundered, "Let go of that young man, Ingrid. Have you no shame?" But Ingrid dodged the blow and the old man returned to his good temper, his whiskey, and his rapt contemplation of the great salmon, packed in ice on the center table.

Bill rolled out of bed and doused his head in cold water. Half an hour later, dressed and shaved, he walked into the breakfast room. The lodge faced west along Loch Tummel. Sir Alan's grandfather had built it so that he could fish Gobhair's Tummel water all day, and in the evenings would not have to ride back up the six-mile drive to the castle and its Siberian draughts. It was not so convenient for the Tay water, but even so was much better than the castle.

Mrs. Turner met him at the door of the dining room. "No one else is down yet, sir," she said. "You're the first."

Bill peered under the silver covers. His head was clearing. A good Western breakfast would complete the cure. He wrote, *Steak? Rare?*

Mrs. Turner said, "Certainly, sir. Angus beef." She handed him a newspaper. " 'Tis the *Scotsman* from Edinburgh, sir. The London paper's not in yet."

Bill read desultorily until the steak came, then settled into his food. It was excellent, and so were the fried eggs, bacon, and potatoes. VK and Anne came into the room. VK paused in the door. "Good God, man, where's the rest of the platoon? Besides, you're in the United Kingdom now. Not done to eat cow for breakfast here. Quite unconventional."

Bill grunted. That was a word he didn't often get applied to him.

VK said, "The last time I had cow for breakfast I nearly got sacked from my school." His thin smile widened. "It wasn't a steak, though. I was boring a hole in a cow's neck to drink blood, as the Masai taught me. The farmer saw me. The way the head-master—and later the rest of my so-called friends—treated me, you'd have thought they'd caught a new Dracula. And all I did was take a little drink off a fat Friesian."

De Guise came in and poured coffee.

Anne said, "It's just what you're used to. The Masai drink blood all the time. So do all cattle-keeping tribes, really. Sometimes mixed with mealie. It saves the animal, you get the protein just the same, and . . ."

De Guise lowered himself into a chair. "Please, my friends, re-member I am only a weak-stomached European. . . . *Bonjour, M'sieu-dame,* did you sleep well?"

Mrs. Turner came to the door. "It's the laird on the telephone, Mr. Hawker."

Anne sat down next to Bill. He smiled at her, willing her to hear the good morning he could not say.

Anne smiled back and Bill caught de Guise's quizzical look over the rim of the coffee cup.

Anne said, "Here we are in the Highlands, with moors all around us, and the only excitement is catching a fish. There ought to be Scotch mists, and huge deerhounds bounding out of them, and muffled screams. . . ."

"You are mixing *The Thirty-Nine Steps* with *The Hound of the Baskervilles*," de Guise said.

VK came back. "Sir Alan wants us to have a farewell lunch up at the castle, all except whoever's fishing. That'll be you, Robert, won't it? You haven't had a day yet."

De Guise said, "It seems such a waste, when there are experts. . . . Well, I'll be delighted. Will the old gentleman be going up to the castle?"

"I'm sure. He slept well, after he—er—decided to lie down. No head, either, I'm told. . . . Sir Alan's sending the Daimler down for us, so you can take the Austin."

Bill thought, Suppose I ask Anne to come for a walk along Loch

Tummel, until we go up to the castle? It was a blustery raw day, but pleasant for walking. They'd have an hour, at least.

VK pushed away his plate and turned to his sister. "Daggers in the library, as soon as you're ready."

Anne turned to Bill. "Daggers is a two-handed game of patience we practically invented," she said.

Bill nodded, and managed a smile. He was beginning to dislike V.K.G. Hawker with a special intensity.

VK stood up, his coffee cup in his hand. Mrs. Turner, passing behind his chair, knocked the cup from his hand. The hot coffee splashed his chest and face. He grimaced in pain and Mrs. Turner gasped out a horrified, "Oh, *sir!*"

VK whipped around on her, his hand rising, but even as he turned Bill saw the fury vanish from his face, and the hand only took Mrs. Turner by the shoulder. Then he was smiling. "Don't you like the color of my shirt, Mrs. T.?"

"Oh, sir, I'm *sorry*," she gasped. Her Lowland burr came through her training. "I didna loook whaur I was . . ."

"Forget it," VK said. "You're too pretty to cry." His hand slipped from her shoulder and passed caressingly across her shapely buttocks.

"Why, Mr. Hawker!" she cried. "*Well!*" She hurried from the room, smiling. From the passage they heard her call, "Bring me the shirt and jacket as soon as you've changed, sir, and I'll clean them at once."

Bill picked up the *Scotsman*. Perhaps dislike was the wrong word for his feelings about VK. Interest was better. And as for Anne . . .

VK looked at his watch. A little past three in the afternoon. There had been a shower about midday but it had stopped, though the sun did not come out. Not that it made much difference inside Gobhair Castle. He felt heavy and liverish . . . the party last night, and now a large lunch, more malt whiskey, then Drambuie, Bill Hammond talking like a human being, old Tellefsen drooping, Ingrid giving Anne looks that should have stretched her dead on the floor, Alan half stewed.

Alan leaped to his feet. "What we need is fresh air! A shaking up of the liver! I'll tell you what! Bill and VK and I will ride down the mountain! Anderson can bring you and the girls in the Daimler, Mr. T."

"Good, very good," Mr. Tellefsen mumbled. "I wish I could ride with you, but I get tired . . . so tired."

"G-g-g-good idea!" Hammond exclaimed.

VK thought, Anne would like to ride too, but she was too well trained to suggest it. Besides, she wouldn't want Ingrid to feel left out.

Half an hour later they left the stable yard on Gobhair's three best horses—Bill riding Paddy, a fat gray cob; VK astride Flora, a shaggy old roan mare usually used for the deer stalking and to bring the deer's carcasses back to the castle; and Sir Alan on Captain, a young gelding pony, son of Flora. In leather buckets behind the saddle on the offside two of the ponies carried the usual vermin-shooting weapons.

Sigurd Tellefsen waited at the front door, leaning on Ingrid's shoulder. He put up his immense, frail hand to Sir Alan. "Sir, you have given me nobler moments than I ever expected, or deserved. Thank you."

Sir Alan leaned down from the saddle. "It has been my privilege. Come back. . . . Anderson, give us half an hour or so and then come down. But get into riding clothes. You'll have to bring the ponies back up the hill."

"Aye, sorr."

Then they rode away, across the north front, under the empty windows and the crenellated battlements. Sir Alan said, "We have to start down the drive. There's no road even for ponies until below the gorge. Then we can take the bridle trail straight to the lodge. But I don't have to tell *you* this, do I, VK? Look, Hammond, that's Glen Errochty. From here you can just see Blair Castle."

The road dipped off the ledge on which Castle Gobhair was built. As VK looked back a light breeze ruffled the water of the Lochan Sgaradh Gobhair—then they were in the valley.

Sir Alan cried, "Geddup, you idle beast! These animals have been eating their heads off without exercise. Let's shake 'em up!" He took in his reins, leaned forward and kicked his heels into Captain's flanks. The young pony whinnied and bounded forward. Sir Alan's kilts flew and his bare thighs gleamed. Hammond kicked his horse, but Paddy was cunning as well as fat. The resulting buck-and-saw nearly put Hammond into the road, but he held his seat and the cob broke into a rolling gallop. VK banged his heels into Flora's fat sides and bellowed, "Come on, old girl!" Flora put herself into a trot and then, with patent disgust, into a galumphing canter.

The first mile ran fairly straight and steeply downhill. The horses held back, as though querying their riders—Do you really mean us to go down at this lunatic pace? Then the slope eased and the road wound in sharp curves down the gorge of the Gobhair torrent. Here the beasts let out, Paddy with a triumphant kick and neigh, the others after him as fast as their shorter legs could carry them.

"Scotland forever!" Sir Alan roared.

Bill, in the lead on Paddy, whirled out of sight around a corner. Sir Alan followed on Captain. Then Flora tucked her legs under her and whipped around the corner.

There was something wrong. VK registered the scene with near-instantaneous comprehension. First, Paddy was in full leap, Bill crouched along the neck, his seat firm in the saddle. Second, the reason for the leap: a dead fir tree across the narrow road. Third, thought like a flash fuse: The tree can't have fallen in that place of its own accord—it must have been placed—a road block—but horses can get over it easily—the ambushers didn't expect horses, they expected the car, which would have to stop—then they'd seize or kill Mr. Tellefsen—but he wasn't with them—what would they do? Try to escape. . . . Two shots exploded from the trees lining the bank. The bullets whined well overhead. That was meant to deter pursuit. The bastards had picked the wrong men to try to frighten with a couple of shots fired in the air.

"Go for them!" he yelled at the top of his lungs.

Flora's head jerked around under his savage tug at the reins. She squealed with astonished pain as he fumbled at the straps holding the rifle in its bucket. *Crack-crack* came more shots from the firs.

"Up the bank!" he shouted.

Flora leaped the narrow torrent of the Gobhair stream and galloped at the slope. VK's rifle came free. To his right Sir Alan raced at the bank on Captain. Captain made ten feet up the steep slope on his first run, struggled, kicked, found a rock projection for his hind hoofs and forced himself up the remaining ten feet with a heave of his powerful quarters. Then Flora was dancing up on tiny hoofs, and had reached the top before VK had time to wonder how she was going to do it. He slid to the ground, the rifle in his hand. Sir Alan yelled again, "Scotland forever! What the hell's happening, VK?" But the silly bugger hadn't drawn the shotgun, and right beyond him a man rose from the undergrowth at the top of the bank, a man in nondescript gray flannel trousers and an old tweed coat, a pistol in his hand.

"Behind you!" VK yelled, raising his rifle. Then the prancing horse blocked his shot, but Sir Alan had seen, swung around in the saddle, snatched the *skean dhu* from his stocking top, and stabbed downward. Steel flashed, the man fell, the cairngorm hilt of the dagger glittering in his back. A bullet cracked by, and VK dived flat. He heard Sir Alan's gasp. Two more shots followed. One of the thugs from the Embankment, the man who looked like Stan Laurel, was kneeling in the trees behind Sir Alan. Blue smoke drifted from a big automatic in his hand. He ducked and disappeared before VK could fire. Sir Alan Gobhair slowly slipped sideways from Captain's back. Captain jerked uneasily, and the baronet fell head first into the bracken, the reins tight in his left hand.

Laurel appeared a hundred yards away among the young firs, running hard but with an awkward body motion. His arm must still be strapped up from the stab wound he'd got on the Embankment, VK thought, centering his back in the sights. His hair stirred as a bullet cracked over it, very loud and very very close. He dropped his head, noting that Laurel, too, had dropped from sight. The bastards were cunning, and worked well in combination, one tempting you to make a target for the other, but dropping before you could actually fire.

He crawled to Captain, who stood sniffing the body of his master. To the left of where Laurel had disappeared VK caught a momentary glimpse—not long enough to aim or fire—of the big man from the Embankment, the one he had thought of as Mandarin. Sir Alan Gobhair was dead. Two .45 bullets through the back of his head had blown out half the familiar, bony face, and the ginger mustache was drenched in blood. In the gorge a car started up with a frantic roar.

Hoofs pounded and Bill Hammond slid down off Paddy's back. VK said, "Take Captain—he's got the shotgun. Follow me."

He mounted Flora and set her at a gallop through the pines. At the foot of the gorge he turned onto the bridle path. It was ill-kept and very steep, but passable to hill-trained ponies, and it ran almost straight down to Loch Tummel just west of the lodge. Flora broke her gait from a canter to a run, almost human in its steady rhythmic pacing, her head stretched and intent on the bracken and the twisted heather roots. VK's mind raced. . . . Laurel and Mandarin had realized, once their ambush had failed, that their only hope was to vanish among the woods and moors. Those two would escape. A third lay dead with a fifteenth-century *skean dhu* embedded in his back: an honor for the bastard. A fourth man was escaping in the car. And he must be an indoorsman, because he thought that since cars went faster than horses, he could get away. That sort of man would have no sense of direction. He would not realize that for the first three miles below the gorge the drive swung far to the west, while the final hairpins brought it back to join the main Tummelside road heading east. A horseman going straight down the mountain would be cutting across the one short side of a triangle while the car traversed two long sides.

He sat down firm in the saddle, let the reins go loose and urged Flora on with crooning. She seemed to realize the urgency. Wherever the slope eased, she broke into a gallop, her hoofs squelching in the bog patches. Captain kept up well, his extra size compensating for his lack of experience. Hammond was trying to control him too closely. Captain was young but he knew enough to follow Flora without question, and Flora knew the Meall Fead better than any human, except perhaps old Anderson. VK shouted, "Give him his head."

They entered the birch wood directly above the Mains of Duntonlich, and then VK knew they'd make it. From the top of the wood, just before Flora ducked into it at her fast run, he saw the car, an ancient black Humber, come out of the long Gobhair drive, headed east. The car had a mile to go, he and Bill barely two hundred yards. Another car, coming east along the main road, fell in behind the Humber.

Flora reached the high road, her hoofs beating sharp on the tarmac. VK yelled, "Whoa girl!" and slid down, the rifle in his hand. A moment later Bill joined him with the shotgun. The Humber appeared almost at once, the second car now close behind. It was a red Triumph, a young man and a girl in it, and it was trying to pass. At VK's side Bill Hammond was crying "Yo-yo-yo . . ."

VK had the thug's mouth sitting on the bead of the foresight. His finger stiffened on the trigger—then Hammond pushed VK's rifle up. The thug saw them. As the Triumph drew out right to pass, with a roar of its engine and a blare of its horn, the thug trod on his brakes and swung sharp left. The Triumph buzzed by, the Humber heaved and screamed around on two wheels, heading down an unpaved road to the loch side.

VK began to run after it, but at once broke into a walk. His eyes felt cold and his hands were papery and dry. Bill Hammond had lost him the certain kill. But one thing at a time. The dirt road ended in a jetty. There were no trees, only open grass, and then the loch, half a mile wide. The thug was already out of the Humber and running. He had reached the end of the jetty. Hammond stopped and aimed the shotgun. It roared once, twice. The range was too great, and the man ran on and straight off the end of the jetty into the loch.

Bill rammed fresh cartridges into the shotgun as he ran. A minute later they reached the end of the jetty. The man was well out in the loch, swimming hard and well. Bill put down his gun with an angry shrug.

VK said, "They were after Mr. Tellefsen. Two of them were on the Embankment."

The swimmer's head was close to the far bank now. The range was about six hundred yards. VK put the rifle to his shoulder and peered down the sights. Hammond was looking at him in surprise.

It was not a telescopic sight, just a bead and V. The wind was from the left at about ten miles.

Hammond cried, "I-I-I-I . . ."

The dark head centered. The man must be very nearly in his depth. The zeroing of the rifle would be good. Alan had been a perfectionist in matters like that. The head rested on the bead of the foresight, deep in the base of the backsight. He squeezed the trigger.

There was no splash. The head disappeared.

VK eased the next round into the magazine, holding it down with his thumb while he slid the bolt over it. The Mannlicher was a beautiful weapon, no doubt about it. He pressed the trigger on the empty chamber and applied the safety catch.

He turned to Hammond. "Well, what do you want to say? That you didn't know I had any ammunition? That I'm a shit to have waited so long, and let him think he was going to get away? Alan Gobhair was my friend, Hammond. Why did you knock my rifle up, back there? Because if I'd killed the thug at that moment, the Triumph would have been involved in the accident? I saw that. I'm not blind. But making sure of that man who'd had a hand in killing Alan matters more to me than the fate of two strangers in a sports car. If the thug had turned right around, or forced the Triumph to drive at us, he might have got clear away. Because of you. If you do anything like that again, my friend, I wouldn't be a bit averse to putting a bullet into *you*. . . . We'd better get along to the lodge and call Webber."

The fire burned dull red in the library fireplace. The curtains were drawn and the lights glowing. It was midnight. Mr. Tellefsen sat hunched in a big chair by the fire, staring into the flames. The rest stood.

Bill Hammond looked around at them, a group from all over the world brought together by a chance encounter on the Victoria Embankment. Anne Hawker, a Norse maiden with the firelight under her eyes; Ingrid, brooding behind her father's chair—she really was Norse, but looked Mediterranean; VK, padding, padding up and down in front of the curtains, smoking black Rhodesian cigarettes; Webber, solid, alert, bad-tempered; de Guise, eyes like dark cherries . . . Sir Alan Gobhair lay in his great hall. The two HPS dead had been recovered, one from the moor and one from Loch Tummel. The bodies had been searched, identified, and disposed of under the orders of Meikle, the British secret service officer. There had been no publicity. Once the British decided to play rough, Bill thought, they had at their disposal an immense, well-oiled machine, subject to no constitutional limitations, every part obedient to a single policy.

VK stopped his pacing. He looked at Webber. "What's going

on? That stuff about the peaceful uses of atomic energy is nonsense. We pretended to swallow it because it was none of our
business. Now it is. I want to know the truth."

Webber growled, "OK. You probably deserve to know. But I
can't tell you."

VK said, "Are the men who murdered Alan going to be caught
and punished?"

Webber said, "No. . . . Look, Hawker, this is not a criminal
affair we're in, it's war. We're not trying to get justice, only vic-
tory. If an enemy soldier kills your buddy, you don't make your
plans with the object of killing that particular guy, although he
may happen to run into the barrage or the machine-gun fire. . . .
We aren't going after Mandarin and Laurel now—as you call
them—for lots of reasons. Suppose we catch them. What do we
do? Try them? And have a judge demanding evidence, motive, et
cetera? Bump them off privately? We could do that, and it has
been done, even here in England—"

"Scotland."

"—but as I told Mr. Hammond when we were talking about
Trilby, the big boss, every man we get rid of means a search to
identify his replacement. . . . No. As far as I'm concerned, we
won a battle this afternoon because Mr. Tellefsen's safe. But now
for God's sake let's get him to New Mexico, where we can guard
him properly."

Mr. Tellefsen said, "Twice this young man's eye, his hunter's
eye, his hunter's mind, has saved us."

Webber said, "Sure. But it was his lack of experience that put
you in danger this time. He was supposed to have called me that
you were going up to the castle for lunch, and he didn't."

"I had a hangover," VK said.

Mr. Tellefsen turned his massive head slowly on Webber. He
said, "I want him to come to America with me. You regard me as a
pheasant to be preserved. Let him be gamekeeper. I presume you
will have no objection to that?"

Webber did not speak for some moments; then he said, "Well,
there was supposed to be a British agent in Shiprock. He got flu or
something. Of course, he was a trained operative. But . . . if you
want Mr. Hawker—"

VK said, "Wait a minute, sir. I'm not sure . . ."

Mr. Tellefsen turned to him. "Next week you were going to start work in a haberdashery store. Because you cannot find anything else. You, a hunter! It is ridiculous! Come to America! I have only a daughter." He reached up and took Ingrid's hand. "You know how I love her. But I would like a son, to go to the river with, as we did here. To drink with a little, perhaps, as we did here. To talk with at night, of mountains and great fish . . . Will you come? It will not last long. A few months. What can you lose?"

Bill looked at Anne. Her eyes shone with excitement. VK said, "If I can bring Anne."

Ingrid muttered, "Oh, no."

Her father seemed not to hear. "Of course! Ask for any salary you want, my boy! They are spending so much on me that if you asked for a million dollars a week it would not make much difference. . . ." He stood up slowly, pushing himself upright on the arms of the chair. He took VK by the shoulders. "We will find out what fish there are near this Shiprock, New Mexico, where we are going, eh? I will feed the computers in the morning, and in the afternoon we will go to feed the fishes, with little hooks hidden in the meal, ha!" He swept out his arms. "Robert, come too, for a visit! Bill, you too! You young people have lent me some of your youth. And we have been through such noble, such tragic hours together. . . . There is room on the airplane?"

"On the plane, yes," Webber said slowly, "but inside the security fence at the plant . . . I don't think so. Only for the Hawkers, because he'll be on the staff."

"I understand perfectly," de Guise said quickly. "For my part I do not want to be inside the security fence. For me, it is a chance to visit these Navajos. I think I can make a great deal of money from silver and stone work such as that locket Dr. Berkowitz gave Ingrid. For that I can stand even American food! Bill? Come with us. Then we will all be together for another week, at least."

Ingrid said, "Beel, please!"

Bill shook his head. It was a powerful temptation to spend another week close to Anne Hawker. But where would he get to if he quit his search to trail after every girl he liked? Two girls, as a matter of fact, because Ingrid was nice in her way. As for Anne . . . her sweetness counterbalanced her brother's intense, immoral sense of values, but those were the values you had to have if you wanted to succeed. They had been his father's.

He scribbled a note: *Sorry. Work. Always reach me through Monroe Barnett, 1130–16 St. NW Washington, D.C.* He gave it to Mr. Tellefsen.

The old man shook his head. "I am sorry, too. But I understand. Work is work." He looked suddenly gray and weak.

Bill stepped back. He wished there was a dark, private corner to hide in, where they'd forget him and he could forget them, and not think of them growing closer to each other in the great, barren country of New Mexico, which he knew and loved.

VK said, "One thing bothers me. How did the HPS get to know that Mr. Tellefsen was up here?"

Webber unfolded the newspaper under his arm. Without a word he turned to the back page. It was the London *Daily Mirror* of that morning. The back page was a full spread, taken with a telephoto lens from the Lairig Bridge, of the great salmon leaping, the rod bending. VK and Mr. Tellefsen were easily recognizable. The caption gave VK's name only.

Anne said, "You had to go and catch a record fish!" She laughed, half rueful, half proud.

Webber said, "This edition was on sale about one o'clock this morning in London. The paper substituted another story in later editions, and we didn't happen to pick this up. The HPS could have seen it, though this doesn't prove that they did. They might have trailed us up here from the Savoy, in spite of all that we did to prevent it. They might have been tipped off. . . . However it was that they found out, they chartered a plane and were in Edinburgh before dawn. Harry Bosco saw Trilby at the airport this evening. Just waiting to confer with one of his salesmen, of course. Only . . ."

"Only even he," VK finished, "couldn't foresee that Sir Alan would take a few drops and insist we make a cavalry charge down the mountain."

Webber said, "And now, sir, the President's aircraft will arrive at Leuchars RAF station in two hours, and we'd better go. . . . Are you sure you feel all right? You look a bit pale."

"I'm not ill," Mr. Tellefsen said angrily. "Mind your own business, will you?"

Chapter 3

VK DECIDED that he liked America, after all. Three weeks wasn't a very long acquaintanceship, but it was enough. The country came surprisingly close to expectations. Not so surprising, perhaps, considering the number of flicks one had seen, but one always suspected that Hollywood's America couldn't be the real one. In detail that was true, but for the overall impression—the feel of American streets, of country and city—Hollywood had been true to the reality.

It was hotter than he had expected. This New Mexico desert country was very like Kenya in its high, dry climate. There was a majesty of sheer size. In the vast emptiness mountains could fall, and no one would hear. The colors were magnificent, the gorges tremendous, the rivers huge. Only the towns seemed insignificant and ugly.

He walked slowly down the main street of Shiprock at Mr. Tellefsen's side. He wanted to have his hair trimmed and the old man had come along for the walk.

It was a hot, sunny afternoon. The people in the shirt-sleeved crowd were as various as the cars that lined the curb; average people with average, anonymous faces; shabby people in hard-worked overalls; gloomy, proud people; a few Indians somnolent on corners; burly, red-necked police. And somewhere, out of sight, a pair of CIA men. At least, they'd better be out of sight, VK thought. Today's pair were pretty clumsy. They were in a Valiant sedan, had followed too close and been forced into the next place in the parking area. The old boy gave them a long suspicious look but didn't say anything. He'd seen them before, of course, but perhaps he didn't remember their faces. But they'd better be careful. Mr. T. talked a lot about the perpetual surveillance in Russia and what it felt like to know that never, ever, did you have any privacy.

Mr. Tellefsen sighed. "Look at these people! So . . . so human! Why can't they be left alone? Why do we have to have governments? I trust the common man, like these. That is why I first became an anarchist. . . . So how come I turn to Communism, you are asking me? When to go from anarchism to Communism is like standing on your head. I can't answer, except that you find the Communist next to you in the *trincheras*, the fox holes, shooting at the same enemy you are fighting, so you think he is your ally. But he is not. . . ." He sighed again.

VK had grown very fond of him. He wasn't easy to live with. He had a violent temper and a strong will, but he was big, in every way, and you put up with his lesser faults. He was also sick, but would not let a doctor near him. His temper was running a race with his physical weakness. He was at his worst with the other scientists who shut themselves up every day with him in the huge back rooms where the computers purred and clicked, and the blackboard was shielded by lead-lined curtains and coated with a radioactive paint that would destroy a film image. Every day the old man scribbled up basic formulas to be fed into the computers, and it was VK's job to wipe that board clean every night. Webber and his fishy-eyed colleagues who'd examined him in Washington soon found that he knew nothing about their bloody formulas, and didn't want to.

Mr. Tellefsen really lived for the afternoon excursions into the wild country around Shiprock, but even there his zest was weakening. He still talked a good deal to VK—but he didn't say much. It was as though he could only share some shallow surface pool of experience. Below it, a closed sluice gate prevented the outward surge of the deep waters. Sometimes, after long troubled silences, VK thought that inward pressures were about to burst the gate open, but they never had.

"That's a barber's shop," Mr. Tellefsen said.

The barber's pole was short, thick, made of glass, electrically lit, and it revolved steadily. Inside the shop, on the left, four barber's chairs, marvels of chrome-plated automation, faced the long mirror. A high bench lined the opposite wall, with a lower level for the feet. The place stank of hair oil and stale cigars, but only two of the chairs were occupied. The other two barbers sat on the high bench, reading newspapers. An old Negro, his frizzy white hair making him a caricature of Uncle Tom, sat at the far end of the foot bench, a shoeshine box by his side.

Old Tellefsen said, "That's what *I* need." He climbed carefully up to the bench as VK took a chair. A barber folded his paper and stepped down.

VK hitched his left arm a little forward, to be sure that it hid the bulge of his snub-nosed pistol in its shoulder holster. In Africa he had always carried a heavy .45 Smith and Wesson revolver, as his father had taught him. It was not a weapon you expected to use more than once in a lifetime, in big-game hunting; but that once —you were apt to need it very badly. He'd carried it openly, in a leather holster on his belt. Now he felt that the bulge under his left armpit was very conspicuous, though frequent examinations in the mirror had shown that it was not. Another disadvantage was that it forced him always to wear a jacket of some kind. He'd bought this one off the peg in a Washington shop, on their two-day stopover, and it was light and comfortable enough, but he'd have been happier in shirt sleeves. . . .

The click of the scissors and the buzz of the clipper sent him into a warm torpor. In the mirror he saw that Mr. Tellefsen had taken up the barber's discarded paper, while the old Negro, working with slow, ancient skill, polished and rubbed at his shoes. His eyelids grew heavy. It was hot and perfumed. Through the open door there seeped the odor of cooking toffee.

Mr. Tellefsen's voice awakened him. "How much?"

The Negro said, "Two bits, mister."

In the mirror he saw Mr. Tellefsen take off one glove, pull a wad of notes and coins from his pockets, and select a coin. He gave it to the Negro, and stepped down. "That's a good job," he said. "Thanks."

When it was his own turn to ask the price, the barber merely pointed at the wall. VK read a list of authorized prices: *Haircut $2.75.* Two dollars and seventy-five cents was about . . . nineteen and six. For a haircut! That stuff the man rubbed into his hair must be boiled out of rare orchids! No wonder Mr. Tellefsen always carried a pocketful of fifty- and hundred-dollar notes.

He pulled the change from his pocket and began to find the right coins. This was a ten-cent piece, that was a twenty-five-cent piece. The barber was looking at him with disgust. The man would expect a tip even on top of that monstrous charge. He found three one-dollar notes, handed them over and hurried out. Dollar bills, not notes, he corrected himself.

They walked slowly back up the street to their car. It was a Ford station wagon and at first had felt mushy after the Land Rovers he was used to driving; but it was good for the conditions here. The door was red-hot to the touch and the air inside burning and still. "We will go for a drive," Mr. Tellefsen said. "Anywhere. Just to move the air." He leaned back and closed his eyes.

VK said, "You ought to take a couple of days off soon. I'd like to camp overnight on the Mancos. I think we'd get some good fish."

The old man said, "Perhaps . . . I don't know, boy. The fish are not right here. I am restless. . . . I think, at night sometimes, that I am an old salmon trying to find my river for the last time. . . ."

"To spawn?" VK said.

The big fist punched him gently on the shoulder. "Ah, you young *schlemiel* . . . No, it is only that I am old, and frightened."

VK headed north. The dark spire of the Shiprock, an immensely bigger, steeper Mont St. Michel, gradually sank below the horizon behind. The road ran north, black and ropelike in dwindling perspective, its length stretched tight over the slow heaves of the land. A big truck steamed south to meet them, a plume of black smoke trailing eastward from the short stack behind the cab. VK held the wheel a little more firmly—wham, bam, the truck passed at seventy. The suck and buffet died. The engine of the Ford hummed again in the silence.

Route 666, VK intoned to himself. A hundred miles south of Shiprock it took off from Route 66. *Route Sixty-six!* It used to be just a song from a TV show that some older people used to sing in Nairobi a few years back. Now, for him, it had become a road, lined with petrol pumps and diners and beer cans. This western land was like the moon, bleak and huge with fresh air and high champagne mornings.

To the west a flock of goats and sheep moved across the desert, an Indian woman herding them, stick in hand and dog at heel. The road lifted and bent and dropped again over a fault in the earth. The cathedral rock disappeared from the rear-view mirror.

"Stop now," Mr. Tellefsen ordered. "Wait till the CIA men come up, then flag them down."

VK pulled over, sighing. Trouble, trouble. Mr. Tellefsen patted his arm. "It's not your fault, my son. I know that. But, although I am sick and old, I would not like Webber to think I am also blind."

When the CIA men in the Valiant saw the Ford pulled over and VK waving, they came up fast, braked fast. The two agents tumbled out of opposite doors, guns drawn. One ran to the car, the other asked VK, "What's happened?"

"What has happened is, I am tired of being still in Russia," Mr. Tellefsen said. "Get back into your car. Follow us to the Project."

VK drove back in silence. At the Project the old man went into his office, beckoning VK to follow, and slumped into his chair. He pressed an intercom button on his desk and said, "Come here."

Webber appeared at once. Mr. Tellefsen gestured out of the window. "Those men were following me, in Shiprock and on the road."

Webber looked quickly at the parked Valiant and the two agents standing beside it. The wide mouth tightened. "I apologize," he said. "They won't trouble you again."

Mr. Tellefsen said, "It was made plain that I strongly object to surveillance, was it not?"

Webber said nothing. His pink face gleamed with perspiration. VK detested the man, but could not suppress a twinge of sympathy for him now. It was true that Mr. Tellefsen hated surveillance or close guard. It was also true that Webber was responsible for his safety, and no excuses would avail him if he failed.

Mr. Tellefsen said, "The Project will now close down for one week. I am locking the doors of the laboratories and shutting down the computers. At the end of the week we shall start work again . . . until there is any more of this, this harassment, *which I will not have!* Now go." He pressed another button. "Lord Redmond, will you come to my office, please."

VK followed Webber to the latter's office. Webber sat down carefully, put on his horn-rimmed glasses and looked up at VK. "So—you win, eh?"

VK said, "I don't know what you mean."

Webber said, "I think you know very well. You don't like me, and—"

"That's mutual," VK said.

"Right. And you want to see me in real trouble. Well, you've done a good job. Whether you've done as much for your country is another matter."

VK said, "Look, I agree that Mr. T. has to be guarded all the time. Hasn't it struck you that there's only one person he doesn't mind having close to him at all times?"

"V.K.G. Hawker, Esquire. Yes, I've seen it. But a man with no training or experience in this field, working alone, doesn't stand a chance against Gregory Parkezian, when he's pulling out all the stops, which he'll do in this case. . . . Were my guys very stupid?"

"Yes. Also, Mr. T.'s much sharper than you give him credit for."

"Especially when he sees a chance to stick a knife into me. I should have let someone else tell him about Ingrid going to bed with Gorton. Honesty is never the best policy." He picked up a green telephone on his desk. "I'll be going to Washington tonight. I don't know when I'll be back. Or whether." He dialed a number. VK left the room, closing the door carefully behind him.

VK surveyed the scene: the Great West . . . a big hall out at the back of the Uranium Tavern on the northern outskirts of town; blue jeans and cowboy shirts and belts low on lean hips; long skirts and many flounces—and all contorting to raucous Oriental-sounding rhythms from a violet-glowing jukebox. Still, they were having fun, and the men's faces had the real burned-rock texture, even when they weren't Indians. It was a pity Anne wasn't here; but she didn't feel up to a night out and had promised to read to old Tellefsen instead.

It was an education to watch de Guise. He'd obviously never seen this dance before, but he was learning fast, hands level at his sides, moccasined feet shuffling in the short bound-foot steps, eyes intent on the feet of the girl he was dancing with. Just as well that he concentrated on her feet, VK thought; she had a face like the back end of a bus and chewed gum steadily . . . but she could dance this dance, whatever it was; something that hadn't yet been exported from America.

Ingrid was dancing with an Indian. Judging by his expression and the steam almost visibly coming out of his ears she would shortly be raped, unless, as the old Chinese proverb had it, woman with skirt up could indeed run faster than man with trousers down. But Ingrid was not a woman to run. She'd either stop and enjoy it, or knock the man endways. He'd danced with her himself a couple of times—old-fashioned dances where you held the girl in your arms. Just to do that gave you ideas, and the ability to put them into practice. She was two hundred percent female.

He turned back to the bar and signaled for another whiskey and a beer chaser. They called it a boilermaker here. The music ended and de Guise joined him. He was wearing a sky-blue cowboy shirt with yellow piping and big silver buttons, and a Western tie with a huge silver and turquoise buckle. He perched on a stool beside VK and asked for tomato juice. VK said, "What have you done with that girl? Think you'll make it?"

De Guise said, "If I'm not careful."

"What's the dance? It looks mad."

"It's the Sapporo. A sort of rock. Copied from Japanese dance steps, I believe. Like most things in this country."

"You seem to enjoy it."

De Guise shrugged. "When in Rome . . ." He drank his tomato juice.

"How's business?" VK asked idly.

They'd seen de Guise around, off and on, since they'd been here, but he lived outside the Project in a motel and had hired his own car, in which—so he told them—he had been driving all over the Southwest in his search for Indian arts and crafts.

De Guise said, "It is good. Of course I have not sold anything yet—I am only buying. And I am only now beginning to get below the work the Indians produce for the tourist . . . work that is made not in their own image, but as a reflection of the image the tourist—the white American—has of them . . . has made of them. You understand?"

VK nodded. De Guise was speaking with more enthusiasm than he usually displayed. He was a man whose normal manner was cool, cynical, the *nil admirari* of a Guardee.

De Guise said, "There are real artists here, VK, primitives of enormous sophistication. There is in this art a strong link between the earth where these people live, the sky that holds their religious beliefs, and their art. . . . I could spend a lifetime unraveling this art, tracing its sources, its springs, the streams into which it has split, the—"

"Why don't you?" VK asked. "You like it here."

De Guise puffed out his breath explosively. "Me? What do I use for women? Girls like that secretary I was dancing with? There is chewing gum at both ends, VK. . . . By the way, you know who owns the mining rights in most of the land from here to Durango? The Middendorf Company. . . . Here's Ingrid. Without her brave."

Ingrid said, "Let us go home."

De Guise said, "All right. . . . How's your father?"

She shrugged. "He doesn't talk, even to me. About the same, I suppose. . . . "

"And everyone's still out on . . . I think 'vacation' is the word they are using."

VK said, "People are talking?"

De Guise said, "Naturally. What do they expect in a little place like this? They say the Big Boss is angry and has closed down the plant."

Ingrid said, "Why should they worry? They are getting paid. . . ."

It was a little after midnight. VK dropped de Guise off at the Montezuma Motel and drove on with Ingrid. At the Project fence the guards were as thorough as ever.

He parked the car in the garage and walked at Ingrid's side toward the Tellefsens' house. A young moon was setting and gold points of light sparkled in a deep violet sky. He stopped, turned up Ingrid's face and kissed her. Her lips parted under his, but passively. Oh, oh, he thought, this was not how she would respond if she really wanted a kiss.

When he withdrew his lips she swung her right hand and slapped him gently on the cheek. She said, "When I want you to kiss me, you will know it. . . . Let us walk awhile. It is so beautiful." She linked her arm in his. "No kissing, though. Well, perhaps later. . . . Do you sleep with Anne?"

VK tensed. He didn't like to think about it . . . because he had thought of it. Most women were such artificial bitches: Anne wasn't. That was all. But when you'd lived together, alone, as master and mistress of a house since you were fifteen and she twelve; and perforce seen her naked, looked after her when she was sick, seen her through her first curse—it couldn't be quite the ordinary brother-and-sister relationship.

With anyone else he would have been angry that the question was asked; but Ingrid asked so naturally that there could be no offense.

He answered the question carefully. "No."

"She's in love with you," Ingrid said. "That's all I ever hear from her, when you men have gone out somewhere and left us. 'VK says . . . VK thinks . . . VK likes . . .' Well, it is not love, really, it is obsession. How can she ever marry anyone else when she feels like that about you?"

VK did not speak.

"You must let her go," Ingrid said. "But"—she went on before VK could speak—"*not* to Beel Hammond. He will come back to her, I know."

Her tone of certainty stung VK into replying sarcastically. "Not to Hammond. Naturally not. I quite understand."

"Ah, you think I am only jealous. . . . VK, I watched Beel in

Scotland. I talked a lot with him . . . to him. I *know* him, because I have known other men like him. I am not a virgin, you know. Beel needs a woman who will show him that we women are all one. Now he thinks there are two separate kinds, good ones like his mother, whom you marry and look up to and feel ashamed with . . . and bad, dirty ones, whom you relieve yourself on, like going to the toilet, and just as necessary, just as unpleasant. . . . Which of these do you think he imagines Anne is? And is that what she wants—or needs?"

If Ingrid was right, Hammond was one of those men who was a stallion to the tarts and a blancmange to his wife. It could be so.

He collected himself. "The question's academic," he said. "Bill Hammond is in Oslo or somewhere, and he's not going to ask Anne to marry him. Good night."

Ingrid was eyeing him speculatively. "You are a sort of tiger with an ache always in the belly, I think. And you don't know why. Who do you love? No one but Anne? Is that what is aching? Well, I like tigers. Sometimes. Perhaps. Who knows?"

"Don't madden me beyond control," VK said coldly, and turned away to the little house he shared with Anne.

"Wait," Ingrid said. She took his arm again. "You see more of my father than anyone. How is he with you? I am worried about him."

VK said slowly, "So am I. He sort of switches on and off. . . . Now he's there, talking to you, now he's not, he's talking to himself, no words of course, and you've ceased to exist. Same with his appearance. Sometimes he's almost OK, then he turns pale, can hardly walk. But what can we do? He's over twenty-one. Good night."

Anne awoke when he went into her room and mumbled, "VK? Mr. T. wants you to take him camping tomorrow. He said you'd know where he meant."

Two streams met a hundred yards above the three pines. The car stood in the sun outside the pines. Under them stood the tent and an old folding table set with beer cans and a loaf of bread and a hunk of cheese. The valley curved gently from south to west across this step of the mountains and, four miles below their clump of trees, fell off sharply. Out that way, toward the Grand

Canyon and the Navajo deserts, there was no horizon. The red land, stippled with green pines, rose to a sheer cliff across the river. It was past five; the sun shone directly on them over the edge of the rim rock and a cool wind moved downstream off the snow glittering along the northeastern peaks.

VK watched a rock in midstream. There ought to be a fish behind that rock. He flexed his wrist, the fiber-glass shaft responding like a supple woman in a dance. He let the line shoot, releasing the gathered slack from his left hand. The fly settled thirty feet upstream and well out in the white water. He watched the speck of green—it was a Turnberry Clansman—swirl with the current, make to dip, race over the dark shoulder of water above the rock, then slide fast down the near side.

The water surface broke white around the fly, the green vanished in a blur of darker green and the line jerked taut. Just in time, VK thought. A second earlier and the line would still have carried a little slack. He struck firmly; the rod tip arched gracefully and the reel screamed. The fish went downstream fast. About three pounds, he thought.

"You have another?" Mr. Tellefsen called.

"On the reel's not in the creel," he shouted back.

The trout came upstream, swimming so fast and pulling so hard that he knew the fight could not last long. Rainbows were game fish, but they didn't have the human intelligence, still less the sheer strength and stamina, of salmon.

Five minutes later, after the bright fish had made two last panic flights from the sight of his waders in the water, he eased it to him. Putting his net under it he lifted it out of the water. The spring balance, lying on the bank beside his rifle, gave the weight as two pounds thirteen ounces. He worked the hook from the fish's mouth, looked it over carefully, and dropped it back in the river.

He wrote down the weight in his notebook and lit a cigarette. The old man, fishing upstream, shouted, "You are having a rest? You think you are so far ahead? What was it?"

"Rainbow, two thirteen," he said. "That puts me two pounds two ounces ahead of you, with thirty five minutes to go, and what about our supper?"

"Ah, you wait, you wait, my boy." VK saw the bend of the rod, the silver flight of the spoon, the splash as it hit deep water near the tail of the pool above the pines. He turned away and looked west, and sucked in a deep breath. This was what life ought to be like . . . primitive, clean, companionable. There ought to be women, but the old boy had made a point of going alone, just the two of them. Still, it would have been good to have Anne and Ingrid along. Neither of them were indoor hothouse flowers.

He finished the cigarette and picked up his rod. They'd reached here before noon. After a little desultory casting and a long slow lunch, cooking hot dogs on sticks over an ash fire, the old boy had taken a nap. Then, about four, they had started fishing on a bet. Mr. Tellefsen swore that in this water you'd catch more fish on lures—spoons, twisters, plugs, and the like—than with a fly. Privately VK agreed, but he'd taken the opposite side—for five dollars, even money. So far he'd got five rainbow and Mr. T. three, but all a little bigger.

He changed the fly to a Royal Coachman, picked his target, and cast well across the stream. The old man's triumphant cry floated downwind: *"Cone-yo!* Got him! Four pounds if he's an ounce!"

VK grinned and watched his fly float downstream. Before the tug of the line could pull it under, he turned his wrist, raised the fly in a slow back cast, and let the curved line straighten.

He had a fish on when Mr. Tellefsen shouted, "Six o'clock!" It was a big cutthroat, and would make a good supper. He played it happily, while the old boy came down the bank and stood beside him. "You can't count that one," he said. "Time's up. I win."

"You win," VK said, "by cheating. I saw you putting those salmon eggs on your hook."

"Salmon eggs? Me! Why . . . Ah, you young *schlemiel,* you pull my leg, eh?"

Later, the fire burned high under the pines, and twilight crept out of the east toward them. The sun set in a red sky, making the rock cliffs glow with fire. VK watched the old man shaking the trout in a paper bag with flour and salt. Bacon fat sizzled in the pan, he held a Dixie cup of whiskey in his other hand, and he looked content. Then he put the trout in the pan and the blue smoke billowed and the trout crackled, and the stars came out.

"A great day, VK," Mr. Tellefsen said, when he had scraped his plate into the fire. He leaned back in the little camp chair and stared into the fire. After a time he said, "You know, I have not had a day like this for . . . thirty-three years. How many more such days will there be for me? It is better that one does not know, eh?"

VK puffed his cigarette in silence. The old boy didn't expect an answer when he talked like this. He looked very tired now, but exalted. If there had been light, he'd go back to the water and fish some more. He'd draw on the inner strength the fishing gave him. Or perhaps the running water . . . or the mountains . . . or the sheer space.

"Why are you here?" the old man asked suddenly.

VK considered. Now Mr. T. did expect an answer . . . and what was it? Had he come to look for revenge against the murderers of Sir Alan Gobhair? A little; but, as Webber explained, this business wasn't personal enough for revenge; it was more like signing up in an army. The murderers were in the enemy army, but you weren't likely to meet them in personal combat.

For the sake of Mr. Tellefsen himself? Yes, the old boy was a large part of the answer. As the job had worked out, it was very like the one he had left in Africa. Yet this was a delight . . . because of Sigurd Tellefsen. The man was a giant. You felt good just standing in his shade. You felt very good, almost noble, knowing that he needed you and in a way loved you.

Patriotism entered into it, too. When a man like Lord Redmond said you were doing an important job for your country, you had to feel it mattered. But he hadn't lived in England long, and had not liked it much when he had. He wasn't here waving a St. George's banner. Then . . .

Anti-Communism? Communism, by itself, was not a word that would send him to the barricades. He needed something more personal, and he thought he could define it. There'd been a Russian delegation in Nairobi last year. While talking to them he understood with chilling clarity that they intended to destroy the kind of free-form, gypsy world he loved and needed. Other factors threatened that world just as definitely and rather more closely than Communism—improved education, for instance; increased material wealth; universal leveling of ideas and cultures—but in all these cases elimination of the gypsy was only a by-product, a chance result, even an unwanted one; to Communism it was the end, complete and necessary in itself.

He looked at Mr. Tellefsen. "I'm here for the money," he said.

"You do not trust me," the old man said reproachfully.

"I do," VK said quickly. He tried to summarize in words the thoughts that had been running through his head. At the end he said, "And you, sir? It must have needed a strong pull to bring you out of Russia?"

Mr. Tellefsen said at once, "It was Ingrid. Gregory Parkezian came to visit my laboratory—it was in Khrushchev's time—and at the airport I noticed that Parkezian was secretly watching her. It flashed upon me like a bright, painful light in the eyes, that she had never known freedom—freedom to hear everything, to touch everything, to look at whatever anyone in the world wanted to show her, and then to choose, or not to choose. . . And all her life the secret eyes would be watching her—Parkezian, Parkezian's agents, and after he was purged, the next man's . . . then the next's."

VK said, "Mr. Webber mentioned his name just the other day. Who is he?"

"The head of Soviet security and secret police." Mr. Tellefsen's mouth was unusually tight-drawn as he spoke. His voice came out flat and uncommitted, as though he had spent a lifetime training himself to speak with total neutrality of this man, giving away nothing. He said, "Nor has he been purged, so far. There were three brothers, all fanatic revolutionaries, at the same time cold, ruthless, brilliant men, Armenians from Georgia. Gregory is the youngest, and he's sixty-one. The next elder, Ohan, was killed in Hungary, helping put down the Budapest uprising of 1956. The eldest and most brilliant of all, Martin, was killed in Spain, in 1937 . . . and Gregory has sworn to lay the corpses of a hundred thousand counter-revolutionaries on their graves. . . ." He shook his shoulders violently, as though shaking drops of cold water. He said, "Enough of him. Once, I had the freedom I wanted for Ingrid, and I rejected it for Communism. There were reasons, which seemed good at the time. But in that hour when I saw Parkezian and Ingrid, I knew that Ingrid would die as a half person, a crippled soul, unless I could get her out of Russia. . . . I had, too, a wish to make up to my people—to you, the West, the free ones— for any harm I had done. There was a wish, oh so strong, to be free, and *feel* free. . . . That is why Webber grates on me so much, but you know about that. . . Principally, I am here because of Ingrid."

VK said, "She is hurt that you have never told her anything about her mother."

Old Tellefsen shook his head. "Yes. Some day, soon, perhaps I can tell her. Now, I dare not. Not even to you. I lack the courage."

VK laughed.

"Ah, you think I am brave? Only in some things. You are brave too, my boy, but not in everything. We are human. We are subject to panics that we cannot control because the causes are inside us, not outside. We are like the leader—the cast—of a fishing line. We each have a breaking strain. Sometimes we know what it is. Sometimes we have to find out the painful way—by being broken. Sometimes, in life, we know what ought to be done, but are afraid to do it. . . Give me some more bourbon and branch, my boy."

"Branch?"

"Water, from the river. . . . Soon I will go to bed. We will get up early. I have a thought that if there are any steelheads here they will bite best before the sun strikes the water."

VK said, "Don't leave the pines once you've got into the tent, sir. I'm putting a thread round them all, connected to that alarm Webber gave me."

"Always careful, aren't you?"

"I have to be, if you won't let the professionals look after you. I'm going to sleep in the back of the car. Just call if you want me. I'll hear."

"Good night, my boy."

The mournful howling of coyotes awoke him at three, and for a while he lay awake, listening. Then he slept again, and by half past five they were on the river. This time Mr. Tellefsen used the fly rod and VK the spinning rod.

They fished slowly down the length of a long narrow pool, sheltered to the east by a pine wood clinging to the red slope below the red cliff. Tendrils of morning mist curled along the water, the sun had not risen, and in the flat sheen of the river VK saw a big back. For a moment he thought, Salmon! But that was impossible. He called quietly to Mr. Tellefsen, "There's a steelhead under the far bank, not moving, facing upstream."

The old man looked, nodded, drew his rod slowly back and made a few gentle S curves with the line to dry his fly. Then he cast gently, the tapered line slid out with no whip or curve, the tiny fly shot straight, hovered, and settled on the water a foot in front of the steelhead's nose. The cast hovered invisible in the air; there was nothing on the sliding river surface but the brown, newly settled fly. The steelhead struck with a slow swirl, the brown dot disappeared.

"He's big," VK said."About ten, twelve pounds."

"He doesn't feel it," Mr. Tellefsen said. "Or he's lazy."

The fish was on the bottom of the pool, its tail stirring up a fine red discoloration in the ice-clear water. "He's not fighting," Mr. Tellefsen said. "He deserves to die, then. He shall be our breakfast."

He reeled in carefully, and the big fish came like a dull prisoner, its head turning slowly this way and that. Near the old man it made a couple of slow strokes of the tail, then he had the net under it and it was out on the bank. It was a long, graceful fish, but thinner than VK had expected from its length. The skin was like dull steel. The red spots of its early days as a rainbow trout, before a year at sea had changed it to a steelhead, were just visible beneath the ocean sheen. The old man hefted it on the line. "Hardly eight pounds," he said. "Well, it'll do for breakfast." He banged its head against the heel of his boot and started back for the camp. VK picked up the rifle and followed.

At the camp he began to blow up the fire from their dawn coffee-making while the old man took a knife and cleaned the fish in the river. He was on his knees, blowing life into the ashes under new wood, when the old man called, "Here, VK!"

The voice sounded odd. VK looked around quickly, but no one else was in sight. He picked up the rifle with the gesture that had become automatic in Africa, and went to the river. Mr. Tellefsen was standing, staring down. The steelhead, slit down the middle, lay on the flat stone beside the water, flesh up. The entrails had not been removed.

"See," Mr. Tellefsen said.

VK looked. Then he saw that what he had taken for roe was not—it was the steelhead's liver. The liver, which should have been a small wedge-shaped organ the size of a thumb, up under the shelter of the rib cage, occupied most of the stomach cavity, squeezing the entrails down toward the vent.

"The liver's a strange color, and very swollen," he said. "Anything else?"

The old man said, "No . . . no, that's all . . . " He kicked the fish into the river. "I don't want to eat it." He looked frightened and old, and the rising sun was unable to give light or life to his gray beard.

"We'll have bacon and eggs," VK said, and turned to cook.

After breakfast, Mr. Tellefsen said, "VK, I think there will be fish in there." He pointed at the right fork of the river.

"Not there, where it comes down from behind the cliff," VK said. "The water's too roiled."

"No, I mean higher. I think there may be a lake or pond up there. If there is, the fishing will be excellent in it."

VK looked up. The right fork came down in rapids and small falls from behind the red cliff, pines growing thick along the line of the stream bed. There probably was a lake on the shelf behind the cliff. Probably no one had fished it for years, if ever.

"It's quite a stiff climb," he said.

"I can make it," Mr. Tellefsen said. "But I have no energy to spare for wild-goose chases. Please run up and see if there is a lake—make a cast or two if you like—then come back, or signal from the edge there, to tell me whether it is worth the effort."

VK shook his head. "I can't leave you alone here. A nasty eagle might snatch you away."

"Don't be like Webber," Mr. Tellefsen said irritably. "You can see ten miles that way, and five that way. How can anyone come?"

VK looked at the slope. Mr. Tellefsen would be under his eye all the way, until he reached the top. If he took the rifle, he could pick off anyone who did try to approach the clump of pines.

He said, "All right. You have the whistle? Just blast it if you see anything strange, or anyone." He took rod and rifle, leapt from boulder to boulder across the river, and started up the slope.

Five minutes later, working up the hill beside the stream, he thought he heard a new sound. He stopped and looked around. For a moment, peering down past the edge of the climbing pines, all seemed as it had been the five previous times he had looked around—the pines, the tent, the car, the old man in his camp chair. But now the old man was gone and the car was moving. It was the sound of its engine he had just heard, above the roar of falling water. The old man was at the wheel. The car drove faster along the dirt road to the east.

VK sat down on a rock and gazed blankly after the receding car. What in the name of God was happening? Would the old man turn around and come back? Was he joy-riding? They had come in from the west. That way it was thirty-five miles to the main road, with not a house, shack, or farm en route. Eastward, the way Mr. T. was going, it was about fifty miles to another road. If the old boy didn't come back, he'd have a little thirty-five-mile walk ahead of him, and a friendly interview with Joe Webber at the end of it.

The car disappeared around a bend in the valley. The old man wasn't coming back.

Lord Redmond sat behind the big desk, half hidden in a cloud of tobacco smoke. Berkowitz was on his left, but Webber, on the right, was the one in charge. He wasn't enjoying himself: VK gave him credit for that. What Webber had gone through from Washington could not be exorcised merely by being unpleasant. He *was* being unpleasant—very—but he wasn't getting the pleasure out of it which he was entitled to.

"The agents told Bosco that you sent them back," Webber said. His mouth was stretched and turned down at the corners. He looked just like a large photograph of Ike in a bad temper that VK's father had pasted on the dartboard at the time of the Suez crisis.

"I didn't," VK said. "I signaled them not to follow us up the dirt road. Mr. T. was bound to see them, and you know what happened last time. The best thing they could do was see that no one else followed us up. . . . Do you want the Project closed forever?"

"It is, isn't it? Why did you leave him alone, by this river?"

Lord Redmond said, "Mr. Tellefsen actually sent you away, though, didn't he?"

"That's no excuse," Webber said. "Hawker should have refused to go. . . . I don't think there's any doubt that Tellefsen's on his way back to Russia. Having found out just how much *we* know about . . ."

"The peaceful uses of atomic energy," Dr. Berkowitz cut in.

Lord Redmond's jowls hung down like a saddened bloodhound's. "I don't know . . . I don't think so. Mr. Tellefsen has not been acting quite normally, but he didn't strike me as being a . . . devious man."

"Nor me," VK said.

"They never do," Webber said. "Well, can you two get on without him? With what's been learned so far?"

Dr. Berkowitz said, "We haven't learned very much yet. We . . ."

"That's what I expected."

"We were still feeding the computers."

"With stuff that's no good, I bet. . . . He could have crossed into Mexico before you got the news through last night, Hawker. Of course, we're looking for him, and we'll keep at it. . . . I guess we'll terminate your employment as of now. Vacate your quarters, with Miss Hawker, by noon. Hand in your ID discs and TP numbers and photos to the security officer. Your pay check will reach you within half an hour."

"Right," VK said. "What about Ingrid? She asked me to tell you she doesn't want those new guards around the house. She's worried and frightened and they don't help—just the opposite."

Webber said, "She'll have to learn to live with them. Platonically. She's no longer a free agent."

VK said, "But . . . Oh, I see. You think Mr. Tellefsen will be getting in touch with her, telling her how and where to join him."

Webber said, "It's a possibility . . . that's all. When I said you couldn't be trusted to look after him on your own, seems I was right, eh?"

VK went out. The bastard was entitled to that much. If only he cared one little bit about Mr. Tellefsen for his own sake.

He walked across the central square to the Tellefsens' house. A CIA guard let him in. He called, "Ingrid? Come here a minute, please." She came out of a back room, frowning, and he said, "Let's walk outside. Fewer beetles."

"Bugs," she said. She followed him into the yellow glare. He said, "They've sacked me. You're in protective custody."

She didn't look surprised. VK said, "They—Webber—thinks your father's defected back to the Soviet Union."

"He would not do that without telling me," she said. "I knew from the beginning about the plot for him to leave Russia. I had to. If I had said I did not want to leave, he would have stayed. . . . No, the HPS have got him. My poor, poor father!"

VK said, "I swear we were alone in that valley. And, dammit, I saw him drive away, by himself."

"Someone *must* have been there, hidden. It *must* have been the HPS. They have perhaps killed him already. The best hope is that they want him to go on working for them. Then, sooner or later, they will tell me to join him, because he will not work without me. He would rather die."

"Will you go?"

"I don't know . . . I am breathing a different air here. It is frightening sometimes, drastic, but already I don't think I can go back. Yet, if they threaten to kill him . . . what else can I do? VK, *please* help me find him."

VK laughed without mirth. He said, "I don't have any money. I am as popular as a polecat with the CIA. I don't even know who to go and see, in this country."

"Beel Hammond has money," she said. "Everyone listens to him because of it. You saw how even Webber acted with him. He knows everyone."

VK said, "You are determined to get him back, aren't you?"

"Don't joke now, VK. Telephone him. Please. That lawyer in Washington will tell you where to reach him . . . Anne will be happy, too."

VK walked away from her, his head bent. The old man's disappearance—obstinately, he called it "flight" in his own mind—worried him intensely, but it did not frighten him. Gregory Parkezian and Trilby and the rest of them might be almost supermen—but they weren't quite. Sigurd Tellefsen had driven away of his own accord: He had not *been* driven, at least, not by any external force. From inside, then—by what power? What urge? What fear?

And what was his own concern any more, now that he had been sacked? Why not go back to England, a couple of hundred pounds richer?

Goddammit, he liked and admired this man more than anyone

since his father. If anyone was to understand the causes of Mr. Tellefsen's actions, and so trace him, he could. Webber had the heavy artillery, but it wasn't always possible to catch your salmon with a howitzer: the best tool was usually a supple rod and an understanding eye.

Behind and below the curve of the girl's buttocks as she passed by the open window, the lights of a liner moved up Amsterdam harbor. Red and green and yellow jewels of light were scattered on the water, their reflections like long enameled pendants. The girl took off her bra, and shook out her long fair hair over her bare shoulders. The liner's siren boomed a deep bass applause. Bill Hammond sat forward on the edge of the bed. She smiled at him, wide and welcoming, and half opened her arms, as though to say, *You can touch.* The smile wasn't as forced as some he'd seen. She must have been laid by worse-looking men than himself. He gulped down the bourbon and poured another shot.

She was maybe nineteen, twenty, no more, quite tall, blond, slim above, big below. Her breasts were high, smaller than he liked them, but good, shaking like firm jello when she moved, the nipples big. She put a foot up on the big chair by the window and started to take off a stocking, smiling at him. She had on only the stockings and shoes and garter belt and wide-legged frothy black panties now. She was undressing like a stripper.

Why not? She *was* a stripper.

She was showing him the view up the panties and he had it big and hard for her. Her clothes were clean; she had a run in one stocking and the shoes were cheap and worn at the side. All she had was youth and the appearance of innocence. The reality of it men like himself had taken away. Why? What drove him to this sordid lust, sitting on the edge of the bed in the most expensive room in the hotel, rampant like a farmyard animal, smelling woman on his hands?

She took off the second stocking and waved it gently, the way VK used to make the line curl with the fly rod, snaking S's in the air. Then she took off her panties, curving her hips this way and that, and slowly the bush appeared. A miracle, she was blond all the way! The garter-belt suspenders hung straight down like frames on either side of the golden curled V. Then she took the belt off and came to him, her hands up and out.

He met her halfway and held her tight, bending her head back to kiss. At first she twisted her head away and he remembered that whores don't kiss. Then she remembered that he had promised her a lot of money, and she turned her face up, the lips open. He lifted her and she parted and the slow surge and hammer in his loins began. He took her to the bed, threw her down, and rammed at her. At the violence her eyes opened with fear. She stared at him, so close, wondering. Then understanding came, and she gave a little cry as of pain but she wasn't really hurting. How did girls this age understand, so soon?

He groaned and felt her ribs creaking and her breath wheezing in her chest. His convulsive spasms came up inevitably, shiveringly upon him and for a moment the girl's face was suddenly another's, the purest, and he was committing the worst sin a man could commit, and couldn't stop it, and thereby heard himself screaming in silent ecstasy. He moaned aloud, "No, no, no!"

Slowly, as his strength pulsed from him into her, her face changed back. She was an Amsterdam chippie, with a plain, young face. She was anxious to please and her thighs were heavier than they should be. She lay on her back on the bed, naked, legs spread.

She sat up, closing her legs. She said, "You want me dress now?"

He nodded. He took a deep slug of the whiskey and coughed and choked. Hell, he'd forgotten to put any water in it. He went to the window and looked out, watching the liner's lights move on up the harbor. How long had that taken? Just long enough for the captain down there to walk from one side of the bridge to the other and back. Just long enough to turn from man to animal and back.

She dressed quickly. He found his wallet, pulled out a wad of notes, and gave them to her. She looked at the notes in astonishment. "But . . . this is very much money. Much more than you promised. I am not a cheating."

"I know," he said. "Take it."

"We are going to the night clubs? You said, afterwards, I taking you night clubs."

"No, no," he said. "I'm tired. Take it."

She took the money and put it quickly into her big, cheap hand-bag. She said, "I go. Don't afraid about me. Not sick VD." He was afraid she would try to kiss him, but she didn't. She understood his disgust. Why? How?

The bourbon bottle was empty, and he got another out of the cache in his wardrobe. He washed himself where he'd been in her, and washed his face and hands, and drank some more.

What misery, what shame. Why did the woman turn into *her* every time? Then, if he knew that was going to happen, why did he rush so lustfully to the act?

No luck in his search. Everyone with their hands out, though, from prime ministers to whores. No, not the whores, he'd just seen that. Some did it with more dignity, that was all. Giving money away—no problem. Involving yourself—impossible, apparently. Money was a means of exchange. If you tried to look beyond the money to the inwardness of the thing you were exchanging it for, the goods or services that you were creating or enlarging, you often didn't understand what you saw. Perhaps you had to get a special skill of some kind first, and then use the money. Suppose he took a doctor's training. Then, when he graduated he'd be in a position to found his own hospital, staff it, and *involve* himself in it.

Suppose it had been Anne Hawker undressing here, walking las-civiously back and forth in front of the open window, ten stories above the harbor. It never could have been! But the strange thing was, he felt she might. . . . Was it really so bad for a girl to act horny, the way *she'd* always told him? Anne was a great girl. Like a little kid sometimes, especially the way she imagined things. "Let's pretend there are unicorns in that wood," "Let's pretend we're looking for buried treasure." The analysts who'd spent so many hours trying to cure his stammer would have said she es-caped into her imagination because she wasn't happy in the "real" world.

"Anne is a good, beautiful girl," he said aloud. He said, "No, she is not beautiful. Her nose is too long and she looks too much like VK for that. She is attractive. The lady is not a tramp."

Too much bourbon, that was the trouble.

He picked up the telephone and said, "Get me Miss Anne

Hawker, at the Texas Project, Shiprock, New Mexico. Yes, the United States." He put it down and went back to the window. Two minutes later it rang.

It was her. He said, "Hullo. Bill—Bill Ham-Hammond here. Is that you, Anne?" He was stumbling over the words, but perhaps she was happy he could say them at all.

"Bill! Where are you? In the town?"

"Yes. The town of Amsterdam."

She laughed. Her laugh was loud, like a bell. She said, "You are very clear. Of course, you're on the Satellite Beam, aren't you?"

"I just wanted to find out how you all were. Are you enjoying my country? It's full of Dutchmen here."

"It's marvelous here. It couldn't be more exciting. Only . . . VK wants to speak to you."

Bill held the phone away from his ear in disgust. He didn't want to speak to VK.

VK's light nasal voice came on. "Bill, we need your help. The prize plant we imported has disappeared and I've been sacked— fired. Ingrid wants me to stay and help find it, and I'm willing, but I'll need money and advice. Will you come over right away?"

"At once," Bill said. "Tonight if there's a plane."

Anne was on. "You're coming? Oh, that's wonderful, Bill! We'll all be looking forward so much to seeing you again." She hung up.

He picked up the phone and said, "Get me on the first SS to Washington, with onward reservation to Albuquerque, New Mexico."

He started packing quickly. It was afternoon in Shiprock now. He ought to be with them before they got up tomorrow morning, depending on the flights from New York to Albuquerque. And he felt contented, his guilts and frustrations gone.

Why? Why was he really going? VK needed him, but that was no reason. Far from it. . . . Because Anne would want him to help her brother? Yes, that did enter into it. . . . He respected Mr. Tellefsen, and would do a lot to help him; but if the Russians had kidnaped him back, what could he do? It must be more complicated than that, and VK had not wanted to discuss it on an open satellite circuit.

So, why was he going? Patriotism? Sure. They could laugh their damn heads off, but he loved America, and would do anything for it. To answer a call for help was the right thing to do, especially when the country had given so much to you. His father would have approved. Well, maybe. Dad didn't like working for the government, especially for what he called Democratic pinkos like Roosevelt and Truman. . . . Mother would be proud of him. He winced, seeing the face again, in the climactic moment, and took another drink of bourbon.

The phone rang and the man at the desk said deferentially, "We have you on the SS to New York that's due to leave Schipol at midnight, Mr. Hammond. There's an immediate jet connection to Washington."

Chapter 4

THEY WERE IN VK'S ROOM at the Montezuma Motel, in Shiprock
—Robert de Guise sprawled on the bed, back and shoulders supported by the headboard, legs outstretched, loafers on the floor
beside him, a glass of Coca-Cola in his hand; Bill Hammond leaning against the wall, surreptitiously examining Anne Hawker;
Anne on a hard chair, looking at her brother; VK in the armchair,
looking at the ceiling.

De Guise said, "*Bien.* We are all gathered in the library. Now
tell us who did it."

VK said, "Are you sure this place isn't bugged?"

Anne said, "It was. But Bill found it and took out the transmit-
ter transistors."

"All right. Well, I was in the Uranium Tavern just now, having
a drink. An oldish man, an Indian, signed to me to follow him to
the gents."

De Guise said, "You are so attractive." He wondered whether

he would ever get over the feeling of elation that came when he heard the working-out of his own plan described by the victims of it.

VK said, "I can look after myself. I went to a good public school . . . In the gents, this Indian asked if I was VK, and then he said, 'Mr. T. is in the cabin on the San Juan River. He wants you to go and talk with him. Don't tell Ingrid or Webber.' He said that three times."

"That's strange," Anne said. "I would have thought that he'd want Ingrid to know he's all right."

"I'm telling you what the Indian said," VK said. "Well, I asked him whether he had seen Mr. T. at the cabin, and he said, Yes, he had. He was passing on his way to Tuba City from some place called Aneth. The old man, meaning Mr. T., came out and promised him a hundred dollars if he came here instead and gave me a message. I said, How do I know this message is genuine? He said the old man with the beard told him to give me the weight of my fish. I said, OK, what was it. And he said sixty-five and a half pounds. And that's the right figure, but you'd have to have been in the lodge that night to know it, when we weighed the fish again."

Anne said, "Yes, because we let the first weight of sixty-four and a quarter stand for publication."

VK nodded. "So I gave the Indian sixty dollars, which was all I had, borrowed forty more off Pete the barman, and came back here."

He stopped. De Guise waited, hoping someone else would start the ball rolling again—but who? Bill couldn't; would need many drinks to speak without his stutter. Anne wouldn't, though she was very perceptive: Her remark about Ingrid was telling and dangerous. He'd have to speak himself.

He said, "Do you know this cabin?"

VK nodded. "It's at the end of a long unpaved road, which takes off from the main road to Tuba City about twenty miles west of here. It leads to the San Juan River inside the Ute Indian Reservation. The cabin's actually in Utah, I think. Mr T. and I went there early on to see what the fishing was like in the San Juan."

De Guise winced. VK, a true Englishman, pronounced the word *Jew-an.*

VK said, "It's really at the back of nowhere. I think I told you about it."

Anne said, "I remember. At the Uranium Tavern the first Saturday we were all there. You'd just come back."

VK said, "The question is, what do we do now?"

Precisely, de Guise thought. Five days ago, the day after Hammond returned from Europe, he had been discussing this same problem in a Gallup motel room with two of Trilby's more unpleasant deputies. One was Jim, a tall, urbane Negro. The other was a white with the infuriating American confidence that he was always right, and even if he wasn't, hell, he possessed the power to make his opinions stick. It was ironical, but none the less annoying, to find this attitude so firmly ingrained in a man dedicated to the destruction of this same country. The question the three of them had spent hours over was just this: What will they do then?

VK said, "There are three possibilities, assuming Mr. T.'s at the cabin. First, he's there because the CIA persuaded him to go of his own accord, to avoid some danger here. I don't believe that one. He would have told me, or Ingrid. . . . Secondly, he means to desert back to the Russians, and wants to explain it to me. He would probably get me to pass a message to Ingrid when it's safe . . . and perhaps persuade me and Anne to go to Russia, too."

They had not thought of that, de Guise reflected. What conceit VK had! But justified. Old Tellefsen might easily think just that, given the supposition.

VK said, "I think that's quite likely. Thirdly, he can have gone off for some purpose, or reason, of his own. In which case, he now wants to talk about it. I think I have to go and find out."

Bill Hammond nodded, and pointed to himself.

Anne said, "Could it be a trap?"

VK said, "It's possible, though if the HPS have Mr. Tellefsen, I can't think why they would want to trap me, and if they don't have him, what's the point?"

De Guise nodded in apparent agreement, privately thinking that VK hadn't really worked the thing out very deeply. If he couldn't think what the HPS purpose was, here in the motel room, he would see it readily enough when he had been tested to his breaking strain. "And do you know what this VK guy's weak point is?" the unpleasant American had asked, at the Gallup conference.

"As a matter of fact, I think I do," de Guise had answered; and, leaning forward, he had explained.

VK took up a note Bill had scribbled. He read aloud: *"Go at night, secretly* . . . Yes. That's what I was thinking."

So were we, de Guise thought. How nice.

"We have to get rid of Webber's men. It won't be easy. They're in Room 28, across there, two of them, with one car."

De Guise cut in quickly, for if he missed this lead he might have a hard time, later, controlling his own role. He said, "I was thinking about that. The important thing is that we have three cars— yours, mine, Bill's. I am sure that is the secret. . . . Suppose Bill drives east—that is, in the opposite direction from the cabin— some time after dark. By the way, are we going tonight?"

"Why not? The sooner the better," VK said.

"OK. . . . Webber's men see Bill go, and perhaps they follow, but I do not think so. It is VK whom they suspect of knowing something. So, a little later, VK slips out in the dark and lies on the floor of my car. Webber's men are well trained, and they will see this. Then I get into the car and drive east. They will follow, but not too close—probably only one, leaving the other to keep watching. Suppose I leave exactly twenty minutes after Bill. At that same moment, Bill turns around, wherever he is, and comes back. We will pass ten minutes from here, *n'est-ce pas?* We both stop—"

"Blink lights as a signal," VK said. "It's impossible to recognize a particular car coming towards you at night, unless its headlights are set in a special way."

"Yes. Good . . . VK jumps from my car into Bill's, lies down, we each drive on. Moments later Webber's man will pass Bill, going towards Shiprock, but I don't think he will turn back after him. He will keep following me. And I will lead him a chase all the night."

"Very good," VK said. "That'll do it."

But certainly, de Guise thought. It had taken two hours to work that one out, with alternatives in case the idiots decided to drive to the cabin right away, in broad daylight.

Bill stood up. VK said, "Sit down, man. . . . In case this is a trap, we have to approach the cabin secretly. We mustn't let them hear the engine, so we must walk the last mile or so. And we must do five or six miles before that without lights. We must be there well before dawn so we can be hidden nearby and make sure when the light comes that no one's lying up for us. Now, let's start working backwards. If we have to reach the cabin at, say, four-thirty A.M., then . . ."

Perfect, de Guise thought. One could always trust the British to do the right thing, carefully and with thorough planning. It was the Americans, mongrels with no sense of form, who could not be relied on.

Anne said, "I wish I could think why Mr. T. didn't want Ingrid told."

VK said impatiently, "If we find him, we'll learn soon enough. My guess is that she couldn't hide her emotion. Webber would suspect something. Or she'd insist on coming too, and of course he has enough men on her so she would find it impossible to give them the slip. . . . Look, in case this is a trap, we should have a way of letting Webber know where we've gone, if we don't come back within, say, twenty-four hours."

De Guise thought, Well, we had planned on forty-eight, but twenty-four would do, and he could probably delay it a few hours by timing his own disappearance right; for they had decided at the Gallup meeting that everything possible should be done to preserve his trusted status. That meant that the HPS must appear to make a determined attempt to eradicate him also. Whatever they did, it would be painful, but effective: perhaps too effective. The HPS didn't believe in half measures.

He said, "I will do that. I will be back here early tomorrow morning, after my night ride."

Anne said, "I'll be here, too."

VK said, "Now, let's get back to this timetable. . . ."

Bill looked at the dashboard clock. It was a little before half past one in the morning, three-quarters of an hour after he'd left the Montezuma Motel. VK was lying on the floor of the wagon behind him, and he was heading west out of Shiprock on New Mexico Route 504. De Guise's plan had worked out fine.

Behind the tunneling light, he held the car to a steady sixty. Glancing away from time to time to rest his eyes, he could see the stars, and the close, black spire of the Shiprock. He remembered the Middendorf Company's local agent telling him, years ago, that the Indians believed it was the ship that had brought their tribe here from the place of their creation. When you looked at it in the evening, with the sun setting behind it, it really did look like a tall ship, too big to have been made by men.

He wondered, as he had many times since arriving here and hearing the story, why old Mr. T. had run away. It sounded to him like a sort of amnesia, a temporary derangement perhaps. He must have been under a great strain recently, particularly the last few weeks in Russia, when he knew that the CIA were planning his escape, but also knew all the dangers involved and had a special fear of Gregory Parkezian, the Russian security chief. He hoped Mr. T. was not sick or in danger, though, because he felt very happy, and his conscience would give him a hard time if he felt this happiness at Mr. Tellefsen's expense. Anne's smile when he arrived was like a . . . like a . . . he grinned to himself. Damn it, now he was stammering even in his thoughts. And that, he thought, was the first time his stammer had ever made him smile, in any context.

The dashboard clock showed one-forty-eight. On the right two low buildings came up as a dim blur. No lights in them or in the gas pumps out front. That must be Teec Nos Pos. . . . But brilliant lights bored over the dark horizon to the north and shone in his eyes from the center mirror. From the back VK said, "A big truck coming. I can hear his engine. Down that road from the Four Corners. He's going like hell . . . He's turned onto the main road behind us now."

Bill said, "How-how-how . . ."

"About two miles."

Bill slowed. The turnoff to the cabin must be pretty close now. He'd have to let the truck get ahead. In the mirror he saw VK lie down on top of the 30/30 Winchester pump gun. The truck's headlights shone more brightly. It was a big truck, and the driver would be able to look down and see VK. VK would pretend to be sleeping off a drunk. Robert de Guise had thought of everything.

The truck flashed its headlights and drew out to pass. The rumble of the diesel engine roared louder—the smoke drifted in through the windows—the sound faded.

"Navajo Trucking Company," VK said. "He passed us right at

the corner where we should have turned off. We'd better stay on the main road for a few miles, then come back."

Bill nodded. The chances that the truck driver would notice what they did behind him, or care, were very small; but they existed, especially since he would be a local Indian. Suppose he stopped for coffee twenty miles farther on and asked who in hell would be turning off onto Joe's dirt road at this time of night? Suppose the man in the coffee shop was in CIA pay? That was quite likely, with the Texas Project obviously a cover for something really hush-hush. It was best not to take any avoidable chances.

Five minutes later VK said, "I think we're OK now. No one coming from behind."

Bill switched off the lights, reversed the car in the road, and headed back eastward. It took ten minutes to reach the turning. There a faded half board on a drunken post read *Kaylabito Min,* and underneath *Priva.* The right part of the board had disappeared. A dirt road led north. VK said, "This is it. But we don't go to the mine. Keep right at a fork about ten miles in."

Bill checked the trip-mileage counter. It read 56.3. He heard VK rolling down the rear glass.

The Ford rolled on, without lights, over the rough surface. The exhaust burbled softly under the tailgate. The stars wheeled around Orion in the huge dome of the sky. The silhouette of the Shiprock had long since sunk into the blurred horizon. Wind from the west, very light. The dashboard clock showed two-twenty. The world was still and empty—no people, no animals, no birds, no sound but the engine, no smell but dry rock.

At two-fifty, with the mileage counter reading 67, he dimly saw a bifurcation of the road, and swung right. The moon was rising, the stars fading, and a small cloud haze forming low in the east. Darkness crowded closer on each side. The horizon, once amorphous and distant, swung close and formed a hard line against the stars. Rock outcrops appeared, the Ford's nose tilted up, the engine note rose in pitch as she faced the grade.

VK's voice was suddenly urgent. "I smell thyme, crushed thyme. Out!"

Bill rammed the drive lever into P and pushed open the door, falling out with it. As the door opened the ceiling light went on and for a long two seconds he crouched bathed in light. The expected shock of a bullet did not come. He slammed the door shut and the light went out. As he drew his automatic a voice from somewhere ahead called, "Get behind them!" Gravel crunched and stones clinked, then the voice called, "Hawker! Hammond! We don't want to hurt you! Stay where you are, and—"

VK fired twice, and the voice cut suddenly short.

VK came to Bill's side, crawling on his belly. "Someone's moving to get behind us. Two men," he muttered. "I wish I'd got that man who shouted but I didn't. He ducked." They crouched together among dark rocks, facing outward, silent. Bill eased his automatic forward in his hand. His heart was beating so loudly he thought the assailants must hear it. His left hand brushed by chance against VK's face; it was cold and dry.

One man had shouted; a second moved on the right; and VK said two more were behind—four in all. He heard sounds from all around now, and wondered which were real and which he was imagining. VK listened, like an animal, nose up. Then he lowered his head, tugged Bill's sleeve and began to worm through the scrub, moving away from the road. Bill followed. Now he could smell the "thyme" that had alerted VK to the ambush. He'd call it sage, himself, he thought. . . . These people's car had crushed it as they drove off the road into hiding. That couldn't have been long ago. And where was the car? It must be upwind—west—left.

Behind them the headlights of the Ford came on suddenly, flooding the red road in white brilliance. They shone on a narrow steep-sided cut where the road passed through the crest of the red rock ridge ahead and showed three large boulders blocking it. That was where the ambush had been set for them; that was where the man had shouted from.

Bill turned and fired three times, aiming carefully. The headlights went out, smashed. Four rifle bullets cracked high overhead and VK muttered, "What the—? They're not trying to hit us. . . . Run, while they're still blinded by the lights."

They ran, crouched, along the ridge away from the Ford and the boulders in the cut. A car engine roared into life somewhere below them. It wasn't the Ford—it must be the enemy's. A moment later headlights switched on. The car began to turn in a slow circle, its lights sweeping the ridge. Just before the lights touched them, VK pressed him flat. Slowly the lights passed on. They jumped up and ran forward.

The surface changed underfoot. They were on the road again. But that was impossible; they were two hundred yards from it by now. It must be another road, perhaps the left fork from back there. The surface was pitted, and covered with stones and small boulders.

Below and to their left the headlights moved forward across flat pink desert, going the same direction as they . . . now drawing level . . . now passing. A quarter of a mile ahead the lights began to sweep to the right, up the hill. Bill crouched, touched VK's rifle, pointed at the lights.

VK paused, raised his rifle, and then lowered it. He muttered, "Not worth it. Better not let them pinpoint our position too closely."

The sound of a second car engine grew from behind, coming along the side of the slope. VK said, "They're using our Ford, too. Like beaters, one driving us toward the other . . . We'll go down the hill, between them."

They moved, crouching low among scattered rocks. A thin pole loomed against the moon. They moved now among stone foundation walls, formless pits, rusty iron bars, a wheel.

"The old mine buildings," VK said.

The sky glow from the headlights clearly showed the black square of a mine entrance in the hillside. The headlights crept up and on, white fog across a purple sea, the hum and grind of engines like unseen ships.

Bill thought, *The mine!* We'll be safe there. The jumpy, new experience of being under fire, and its dulling effects on his brain, suddenly vanished. He ran toward the black mine entrance.

VK stopped. "I'm not going in there!"

Bill waved his arm helplessly. The crazy idiot! What else could they do?

From the corner of his eye Bill caught a blur of movement. He ducked and the short club whistled harmlessly over his head. His attacker recovered in a flash and the second blow, following backhanded from the first, took VK on the right temple. VK went down heavily. The man swung like a cat but Bill stepped back, his hand flung out and the gun in it exploded once. The man rolled back and began to scream, his legs thrashing the ground. To right and left car engines revved up. Their lights jerked and swung. They came on fast, for the shots had told them where to go.

Bill stooped, took VK under the shoulders and dragged him into the mine. Instantly, it was black. The mine shaft began to dip. The floor was obstructed by fallen rock and the remains of a narrow-gauge railway. Light grew in the mouth of the mine behind him. He lowered VK to the ground, turned, and dropped. A car's headlights appeared in the mouth of the mine. The car stopped, and Bill fired. A headlight shattered. At once the engine roared and the car backed out. The engine stopped and it became very quiet.

Bill began to crawl backward, pulling VK with him. When he thought he was safe behind a hump in the floor, he stopped. A minute later lights again cast distorted shadows on the rough ceiling. He could no longer see the mouth of the mine, or the source of the light. They had probably put the cars where their lights shone into the mine from the side. That was fine. He'd get anyone who tried to come down the shaft silhouetted by these lights. He refilled the magazine of his automatic from extra cartridges in his pocket. He wondered whether his father would be proud of him now. Probably tell him he was a goddam fool to get mixed up in the government's business. He paid enough taxes, didn't he?

Watching the lights on the roof, he felt for VK's chest. The heart beat steadily. The reflected light showed blood on his own chest, where VK's head had rested when he dragged him. He felt carefully around VK's head . . . a cut, not serious, in the temple, where the club had hit. From the mine mouth he heard no sound but that man's bubbling, ceaseless scream. His shot must have touched the brain.

A voice called, "Mr. Hawker! Mr. Hammond! Can you hear me?" Bill thought it was the man who had shouted from the ridge. He listened carefully. This could be a trick to attract his attention while something else was being done.

The voice said, "I don't know how you-all got wind of our reception when you did, but you sure have made things awkward for all of us. . . ."

It was an American talking: vaguely Southern accent, an educated man.

VK stirred at his side.

"We wanted to talk out there in the open air. We wanted to ask you where Mr. Tellefsen is. We don't want to hurt you. We could have killed you half a dozen times over if we'd meant to. . . . Come on out of that mean black hole and talk to us."

VK groaned. Bill covered his mouth with his hand.

"You just come close to the entrance, and tell us where they hid Mr. Tellefsen. Then we'll go away and leave your car about a mile off. OK?"

VK's voice was low and groggy. "Why's dark?"

The voice outside said, "Is that you, Mr. Hawker? You're in a mine. Don't you want to come out?"

VK screamed suddenly, a mouthing nearly as terrible as the bubbling of the man with the damaged brain outside.

"That's it," the voice said encouragingly. "Come on out, we won't harm you. . . . Come on."

The body beside Bill heaved, the voice burst out cracked and screaming. VK struggled like a drowning man toward the mine entrance. Bill leaned on the heaving body and fought with all his weight to hold it down. Horror and amazement nearly overcame him: VK had become less than an animal, something below reason or instinct. The spine arched, like a fish fighting for breath, the mouth babbled. Suddenly he remembered VK's face in the Savoy elevator that first evening in London, and understood. VK had claustrophobia, and the primal fear that had contorted his face in the elevator now twisted him like a hooked, frantic eel.

"Come on out!" The voice was wheedling, soft.

Bill slid one hand to VK's throat and tightened his grip. VK's hands struck at his face but he did not mind. He knew that VK was attacking not him, but the dark prison. He winced to hear the thud of the flailing fists against the rock. He drew back his other fist to knock VK out . . . but that might be bad, on top of the head wound. He tightened his grip on VK's thin throat. The thrashing grew weaker, and, very suddenly, stopped.

The voice said, "What have you done? Is that you, Hammond? Are you going to bring Hawker out?"

Bill was glad he could not answer. The darkness and the closed space didn't worry him, but he felt the imminence of danger. He didn't see how the men outside could harm them now, but . . .

"Look, we don't want to harm you. We don't *need* to. Come on out and talk."

Bill waited, silent and watchful. He heard muttering from the tunnel mouth. After a time, the lights began to fade. The car was backing away.

A long gleam on the floor of the tunnel caught his eye. Something shone among the broken ties and gap-toothed rails. Wires. They'd been there when he dragged VK in. He remembered noticing them now. Outside, a shot boomed and the monotonous screaming stopped.

Someone laughed. As though the laugh had been a shouted message, Bill understood. He half rose in fear and fury, ran forward, and immediately flung himself down as two bullets hit the tunnel wall beside him simultaneously. They had the wires well covered.

He raised his automatic and aimed, but to cut the wires would be very tricky. He could make better use of the time. He slid back fast, careless of cuts and scrapes—reached VK, lifted his shoulders. VK groaned, making his first sound since Bill had throttled him into unconsciousness. Bill began to drag him farther into the mine. Sweating, aching, he had gone fifty feet down the gradual slope when a thudding blast of air pressed him onto his face. The noise, following immediately, didn't seem so loud. Behind that came clods of earth and splinters of stone. A big rock whizzed by like a shell, low and direct down the shaft in its trajectory; but most of them hit the roof and fell harmlessly.

In total blackness, the air became thicker. VK began to cough. Bill lay down, shielding his mouth with a handkerchief and breathing very slowly.

VK whispered, "Oh. Oh. Ooooh." The mouthing died away. A little later he spoke, the voice dull and exhausted. "All right. I . . . I understand now. Here . . ." Bill felt a stir and wriggle and a flashlight was put into his hands. "Use that."

Bill pushed forward the switch. Through a thick reddish pall the wandering beam showed a pile of rock and earth blocking the tunnel. He could not tell how thick it was. In the other direction the bent rails and shattered ties wound on down into darkness. It would be a long time before they ran out of oxygen, at least.

He turned the light onto his companion's face. VK was green-white in color, and he held his eyes tight shut. Dusty blood covered the right side of his cheek and neck, and blood was still oozing, slow and thick, from the cut. He was trying to hold himself still against powerful rigors.

Bill searched around for a length of rail he could use to attack the earth and rock barrier. They'd probably die of exhaustion or thirst before they'd got far into it, but what was the alternative?

He found a rail and set to work to ease a rock out of the mass. He wondered why he didn't need a stiff drink. Perhaps what he needed to balance his life was not bourbon but the fear of death.

What had happened? In spite of their caution they'd walked into an ambush, that was obvious. Its object was to make them talk about Mr. Tellefsen. Perhaps it had been set here to make use of the mine shaft as a weapon against VK, through his claustrophobia. And they'd saved them trouble by walking into it of their own accord! No, that had spoiled the plan because it was one thing to threaten VK with confinement—it was quite another to make him talk sense when confinement had already driven him out of his reason.

In any case, the mine was already wired, ready to be their tomb whether they talked or not. And the HPS knew nothing about Mr. Tellefsen. That was the really interesting fact about the ambush, if he could survive to tell anyone. Perhaps Webber would have the intuition—or the logic—to see it when Robert de Guise went to him in twenty-four hours time.

De Guise would tell Webber that they had gone to the cabin on the San Juan River. No one would think to come and look at the mine unless the shooting and the explosion had been heard. Here, scores of miles from anywhere, not a chance . . .

They might be here a long, long time. Unless mine gases got them. Even then. He'd better find out how far the tunnel went in the opposite direction. There might be better tools lying about, abandoned. There might even be another exit, or an air shaft. . . . No, that was impossible: no air current, even before the blast.

VK's hand gripped his elbow. "Don't leave me."

"I want to explore the shaft," he said.

"Take me with you."

"OK. Hold onto my belt."

Chapter 5

MONROE BARNETT carefully placed a long cigar in his mouth, lit a match, lit a wooden toothpick from the match flame, and lit the cigar from the toothpick. He puffed gently, savoring the Director's hypnotized expression and the mingled aromas of cigar smoke and black coffee. At last, releasing a stream of blue smoke toward the frescoed ceiling, he said, "To answer your question— no, I don't think that it's only the presence of this English girl that has brought young Hammond back. . . . I *must* stop calling him 'young Hammond,' now that his father's been dead eight months, but it was the father who hired me as his personal attorney and attorney to the Middendorf Company twenty-five years ago and I'm still apt to think of Bill as the little boy he was then. Did you know his father? A very difficult personality—but he had good in him."

The Director said, "Monroe, you're the only man in the world who'd say that of Richard Hammond."

Monroe shook his head slightly. These compliments embarrassed him, for he knew that everyone had something shameful to hide, himself definitely included. He went on. "My guess is that Hammond has found in this situation some things he badly needs. . . . First, he's helping the U.S. He's intensely and simply patriotic, and he also feels that he has to make up for his father, who never scrupled to work against United States interests if it would make him more money . . . Then, he has been looking for someone, something that needs *him*, not just the Middendorf Company. Of course, they're inextricably interwoven, but he's too young to be able to accept that yet. And it was him, not a Middendorf representative, that this Hawker fellow asked for. . . . The element of risk is important, I think. Some years ago there was a lot of sneering about the millionaire playboy-athlete, comparing his life to that of a GI in Vietnam."

"Why wasn't he drafted?" the Director said. "I seem to recall there was quite a stink about that."

"Father," Monroe said. "He pulled strings."

"And the boy didn't rebel? Go out and enlist in the Marine Corps, for instance? That seems to be the accepted way for the young of the very rich to spit in the eye of protective parents."

Monroe said, "No. He didn't. He wasn't strong enough, then . . . which is another point. In this matter his decisions are being made by him alone, without the advice of long-established vice presidents and comptrollers."

The Director said, "He sounds like a good guy. I'd like to meet him some time." He picked up his coffee cup.

Monroe puffed carefully, enjoying the busy Italian nymphs romping across the ceiling. The acoustics were excellent in Coccioletti's. The famous ruched crimson silk walls damped the clatter of china and the tinkle of glass, and also absorbed the diners' talk before it had left their booths. Just as well, he thought, in his own case, not to mention that of the Assistant Secretary and the twenty-year-old girl just beyond the cold table. The man was a fool to think he could get away with bringing her to Coccioletti's.

He bit his lip. The man was *only* a fool, he should have said; he himself was a knave as well, and, perhaps you could say, a coward, because he didn't have the guts to bare his heart at Coccioletti's. It was all very well to tell yourself, there's a difference . . .

between an anonymous typist and the best-known woman in Washington; between a few stolen nights in motel rooms and a long, passionate agony of frustration. He'd nearly burst out with the whole story five or six weeks ago when the President had treated him with an extraordinary and generous courtesy. He needed to tell someone, and the Chief Executive's respect had actually hurt, knowing his own unworthiness.

He turned to the Director. "You asked me earlier what Hawker and Hammond can do that you people are not already doing. Nothing. But they can do something different. When Bill passed through here he gave me the story from his point of view. In writing, of course. You know he has a terrible speech impediment? He thought that one big trouble lay in Webber's personality."

"And Mr. T.'s," the Director said. "It takes two to make a conflict like theirs. Webber's a very capable man. Plenty of people like his manner. It gives them confidence. With Mr. T. the result was just the opposite, but no one could have foreseen that. With a little luck Webber might have got onto this special personal basis that Hawker seems to be on."

"I doubt it," Monroe said. "There's a strong father-son element in that. Which is my point. A loved son can do more with a father than any stranger can . . . and he's more likely to find him when he disappears."

"If he's findable," the Director said.

Monroe said, "Bill Hammond told me to make sure that you understand his position. He's not trying to act behind your back, or Webber's. He's not saying that Hawker's right and you're wrong. He just thinks, from what he saw in London and Scotland, that personal action might help find Mr. T., especially if Hawker can be involved. . . . I presume you have had Hawker checked?"

The Director said drily, "Certainly. And his sister. And Hammond. And the French art dealer who's been involved from the beginning—the one who's had a car crash and is in the hospital with a concussion."

"I didn't know about that."

"It was early yesterday morning, or in the night, near Brazos, New Mexico. . . . They've all been investigated, and all found clean. Which means that they're good boys and girls. Or that this is their first assignment, so we have no previous record. However I can tell you that Webber is suspicious of all of them. Why did Hawker allow Mr. T. to disappear? Is public service—or even love—really the only thing that brought Bill Hammond all the way from Amsterdam? Is this de Guise man really so interested in Navajo jewelry? Webber hasn't been able to act so far out of fear of offending the old man . . . who seems to love them all because Webber doesn't . . . but he has a little plan on the stove right now, and . . ."

The maître d' hovered near. He stooped to the Director's ear and muttered, "A call, sir, from your office. Shall I transfer it to my room?"

The Director glanced at Monroe. "Thanks, Attilio, I'll take it here."

The maître d' plugged the phone into the jack beside the table. Monroe thought, now the Director's paying a compliment to my reputation. Usually, he'd take a call in Attilio's private room, which was bugged—by Attilio Petronzi, CIA.

The Director spoke softly into the mouthpiece. "I see . . . When? . . . I see . . . Right." He put the phone down and remarked conversationally, "Young Hammond has disappeared. With Hawker." The cherubic face showed no perturbation.

Monroe Barnett ran a hand through his dense white mane. "Napoleon swore you could kick Talleyrand in the seat of the pants and the man he was talking to would not know it," he said. "Any details?"

"They left Shiprock the night before last to find Mr. T., who was supposed to be in a cabin on the San Juan River. They never came back. Anne Hawker told Webber an hour ago."

"What's he doing about it?"

"Going to the cabin. If it exists."

Monroe began to dial a number. He looked up. "I'm going to Shiprock. . . . Miss Wright, I have to get to Shiprock, New Mexico, at once."

There was no hesitation before the answer. "The quickest is via Albuquerque, sir. TWA flight 169 from Friendship at six P.M. It reaches Albuquerque at nine-eighteen P.M., Mountain Standard Time. Frontier Airlines' first flight to Farmington—that's the nearest commercial airport to Shiprock—leaves Albuquerque at seven-fourteen the following morning, reaching Farmington at eight-eighteen."

"Too late," Monroe said. "Find Mr. Jefferson of Colorado Western Mining, please, and ask if he can put their Lear Jet at my disposal, at Dulles, immediately, for a couple of days."

Miss Wright said, "I'll call back if I can't arrange it, sir."

Monroe said, "Thank you . . . I'll be leaving for Dulles in five minutes. Get a Miss Anne Hawker and put her through to me in the car. I think she's at the Montezuma Motel in Shiprock. If not, try the Texas Project, care of Mr. Webber." He returned the phone to its cradle. "Are you coming down?"

"Tomorrow, early," the Director said. "There are a few other small matters on my agenda, you understand—Vietnam, India, Geneva, Ulan Bator, Cuba, Chile, Djarkarta, the Congo . . ."

Monroe Barnett sat up, rubbing his eyes. The leading edge of the jet wing inched across the tangle of savage gorge and snow-splashed crest below. The cabin attendant, a well-upholstered blonde, intoned in mellifluous airlinese, "Sir, we shall be landing at Farmington Airport in twenty minutes."

Colorado Western Mining did themselves well: champagne and caviar by the bucketful, and the girl had been a beauty queen. The skirt of her powder-blue costume was stretched like skin across her buttocks. The pilot and copilot were straight-nosed junior-executive types. No wild-blue-yonder nonsense here.

The girl intoned, "It is now five-thirty-seven P.M., Mountain Standard Time."

Monroe yawned. He was too old for these sudden flights on top of a good lunch. What had he been thinking about when he dozed off? The story Anne Hawker told him on the car telephone, while he was being driven out to Dulles. A mysterious old Indian with a message. Hmm. The correct weight of the salmon as the identification clincher. Not the published weight, which had been given, mistakenly, as somewhat less. How many people would have known? He'd have to check into that. Complicated maneuvers to shake off Webber's men, ending in disappearance of Hawker and Hammond and crash of de Guise. He'd have to check into all that, too.

He looked down. To south and west the desert stretched away and away. North, the mountains turned harsh profiles to the low sun. All was inhuman, empty, hostile. Incredible to think that people actually lived there. Yet there were people who found such desolation beautiful. For himself, he liked humanity; or at the least, some form of life—trees, grass, flowers . . .

The copilot left his seat, came back into the main cabin and poured himself an orange juice from the bar section. Monroe asked him, "What's that straight line down there?"

The young man leaned over him to look down. "That's a range fence, sir. It's not the fence that you see, actually, but the trail made by the range riders' horses' hoofs as they check the fence for breaks. Now, see that double line?"

Monroe clearly saw two parallel lines across the desert.

"That's not a road, that's the wheel marks of a car, probably a prospector's jeep. The tracks are visible because the sun's low, and it's throwing long shadows from humps and ruts."

Up front the pilot turned his head. "You can see the Shiprock, now, on the left, sir. We'll be landing in five minutes."

An idea crossed Monroe's mind. He said, "Do you mind if we fly on to the San Juan?"

"Plenty of fuel," the pilot said. "We filled her right up in Denver. Could you show me where you want to go?" He unfolded a flight map.

"We want to fly to . . . here . . . by this route." Monroe pointed out the route taken by Bill and Hawker, as Anne Hawker had described it.

The pilot said, "What are you looking for?"

"A blue Ford '69 station wagon . . . other car tracks . . . a cabin by the river . . . anything out of place, suspicious."

"We'd better fly at about two thousand feet, then, and I'll go as slow as I can."

Losing altitude fast, they passed over Farmington and the Texas Project. The Shiprock glided by, black, silent and alone, its shadow reaching toward the town and the uranium plant. Monroe at once located the main road to the west. And there was the road coming in from Four Corners. He saw a store and a gas pump. He found the place on the spread map: that must be Teec Nos Pos. The little jet swung north.

A far, dark gash, red-rimmed, split the western land. "The Grand Canyon," the copilot said. "Straight ahead, a little left now . . . those are the Goosenecks of the San Juan."

The dirt road running northward across the desert showed up more clearly than Monroe had expected. A car was parked at the point where the trail left the main road: The red globe on top showed that it was a police car. From this low altitude tire tracks showed as paler streaks on the dark-red surface. After a few miles the trail forked, one branch soon ending at a tangle of faint, squared lines. "The Kaylabito Mine"—the copilot's finger pointed to the map. "Used to belong to a predecessor company of ours. Copper. It was closed way back. Those are the remains of storehouse and dormitory foundations."

The other branch of the trail ran north across an empty, undulating plain. They came up fast on the San Juan River. Monroe saw a single cabin high above the south bank. There were a lot of blurred wheel marks around it, but the cabin itself showed no sign of occupation.

"Finished?" the copilot asked.

Monroe nodded and the jet's right wing dipped in a long, slow turn.

Monroe settled back and fastened his seat belt. He'd seen a lot, but the light was getting poor and he wasn't trained. There should be proper air photographs taken and interpretation by experts. He'd speak to Webber about arranging it as soon as he landed.

They landed in pink twilight and taxied up to the airport building just as the passengers were going out to board a Frontier Airlines Convair drawn up on the ramp. The air blast, as the Lear Jet swung round, whirled the ladies' summery dresses up around their waists, and blew one man's pearl-gray trilby flying off his head, to roll fifty feet along the tarmac before a mechanic caught it.

Monroe Barnett sat in the open door of a police car, munching a gritty sandwich. Two o'clock in the afternoon, the sun was hot, the view forever. Out here the wind never seemed to let up. It blew from the west now, sending whorls and drifts of red dust east across the desert. Wherever he looked Monroe saw grave, worried faces. With reason. It was Webber who had pointed out that Mr. Tellefsen might be in the mine, if Hawker and Hammond had been able to get him away from the cabin. And the experts at the Bureau had warned that, where there was no exit to the open air, copper mines were apt to accumulate sulfur dioxide gas, which was lethal.

The desert air shivered in the heat and shook to the continual clank and roar of a squat tracked vehicle working in the mouth of the mine. Webber and Lord Redmond conferred in the shade of a big gray truck. The Director talked with the President of the Navajo Tribal Council inside the chief's Lincoln Continental. Miss Tellefsen walked by herself, apart. Anne Hawker paced up and down near the mine entrance. She was wearing low-heeled shoes, a lightweight tweed skirt and a pale-blue blouse. She walked with long, flowing strides. Monroe had noticed last night, when he first met her, that her eyes were brilliantly clear and her skin golden-tanned, though it seemed pale from the absence of make-up. Her years in Kenya—a climate very like this, she said—had etched wrinkles at the corners of her eyes and given her hard, strong hands. She was nothing like Bill Hammond's mother—a hypochondriac, octopus mom of the worst type—yet he saw at once why Bill had apparently fallen for her.

He poured hot coffee from a Dixie cup and sipped it. Time was running out, and who knew how much time there had been to begin with?

A thrashing sound grew in the air. A Utah State Police chopper settled heavily on the sagebrush. A police lieutenant jumped down. Monroe Barnett got up and went to meet him. Webber was there already.

"We found the car," he said. "It's in the San Juan, about two miles below the cabin. It's hung up on a rock in midstream. Blue Ford wagon."

"How is it?"

"Pretty battered. We went way low to look. It's on its side, windows smashed, doors hung open and one gone . . . Anything here?"

Webber said, "Not yet. But the engineers confirm that the block in the shaft is recent, and they're sure it was blown in, it didn't just fall."

The lieutenant said, "That car sure looks like it had been driven over the cliff, sir, and then washed downstream. If these guys were in it, their bodies will turn up farther down still."

"I know," Webber said. "We have to make sure they're not in the mine, first."

They *must* be in the mine, Monroe thought with irritation. He'd been sure of it as soon as he saw the stereo pairs of air photographs, which showed car tracks wandering around the desert, off the road, to the west of that little cut in the ridge. The car tracks went right to the mouth of the mine and then backed off. The Air Force interpreters said that one set actually showed the mark of two men crawling side by side, down the gentle slope toward the mine. The photographs had been enough to focus the search on the mine, rather than on the cabin.

Then more clues began to turn up: cartridge cases of the sort used by Bill Hammond, found in the sage; a wisp of wool which Anne said was from VK's jacket; then a Navajo policeman noticed that a big boulder near the cut in the ridge was not lying the way it had lain for millions of years—some dried earth which should have been underneath was facing upward . . . No, they were here all right. The question was—alive or dead? And was Mr. Tellefsen with them?

Now, let's see, who knew the salmon's correct weight? According to Anne Hawker it was—Bill Hammond, both Hawkers, Ingrid Tellefsen, the lodge housekeeper, de Guise, Sir Alan Gobhair, who was dead. Seven in all. Plus Mr. T. himself, damn it, and he might have told anyone, whether by chance or under duress. Surely one could strike Hawker and Hammond off the list of suspects, after what had happened to them. That applied to de Guise, too . . . Well, Webber had better spring his trap soon.

He stared grimly at the faded lettering on the board at his feet. *Kaylabito Mining Co. Inc.* There was a dark splash on a stone beside it. It rubbed off on his wettened finger. Blood.

Another chopper landed, and took off. Webber conferred with the engineer of the borer. The Director joined them, then Redmond walked over. Finally they all came toward Monroe.

Webber said, "The roof's fallen in some more, Mr. Barnett." He tapped the paper in his hand. "Colorado Western had a blueprint of the mine and flew it in to us from their Denver office just now.

Look, it's nearly two miles long. God knows how much of it collapsed when they blew this front section in."

"What are you going to do?" Monroe asked. "Keep boring, and shore it up as you go along?"

Webber shook his bald head. His lower lip stuck out. "Too slow. This gas is collecting all the time."

"Well, what *are* you going to do?" Monroe asked. Webber and Lord Redmond seemed preoccupied, as though their attention was not really on this problem.

Webber said, "We've decided to use a new borer which the Bureau of Mines has been developing. It's top secret at the moment, because it has military applications. It bores fantastically fast. We've decided to bore down close to the mine shaft about a mile and a half back from the entrance. Then we'll let off a big charge. The crater will be deep enough to uncover the shaft. This blueprint shows the shaft to be eighty-six feet below the surface at the place we've selected."

"It'll be a very powerful explosion, won't it? Rather dangerous?"

Webber said grimly, "You bet it will be. We can't afford slow, sure methods. It'll work out OK, Mr. Barnett. We radioed for the borer to come out a while back. Here it is now." A black-painted semitrailer, with two windows in the trailer portion, came grinding up the ridge to the east, followed by what looked like an ordinary well digger.

Monroe walked thoughtfully to his car. They were taking a big risk, making an explosion like that, even if the trapped men were a mile away, near the entrance. And supposing they'd gone back in a mile for some reason? If they were alive . . . Webber was right: with sulfur dioxide gathering in the mine, they had no choice.

"Move your car back, please," an Indian policeman told his driver. Most of the other vehicles had already started to move, leaving only Webber's car and the new borer at the mine entrance. Monroe's police driver drove off in the wake of the other vehicles.

They didn't stop for over three miles. Monroe's apprehension increased. It must be an enormous blast they were proposing to let off if the spectators had to get back this far and behind another ridge for safety. He resented his feelings of ignorance, of being completely in others' hands.

Anne Hawker sat in a police car, her head in her hands. The Director and the Navajo chief were here. Webber and Lord Redmond had stayed forward. Monroe waited, biting his lip and thinking of young Hammond's short, plush, twisted life. Twenty minutes passed.

The ground heaved, the car doors and windows rattled, and everyone's head jerked up, looking toward the north. Seconds later the roar of an explosion reached them. Seconds later again, a cloud of red earth and crimson dust rose and hung in the desert air beyond the ridge.

"Can we go back now?" he called to the Director.

The Director raised a hand. "Wait. Webber will come and tell us when it's safe."

They waited ten minutes. Then Webber's car drove fast over the ridge, trailing a dust plume. Webber swung the car around by the Director, leaned out and shouted, "We've exposed the shaft. Lord Redmond and three of my men have gone in. You can come forward now."

Monroe's driver swung onto the road and headed back in the procession of cars. The air was still full of dust beyond the Kaylabito Mine ridge, and from the crest Monroe saw why. A huge crater gaped raw and red-black in the empty desert a mile beyond. Big boulders were scattered everywhere, and the rim of the new crater rose twenty feet above the desert floor. Monroe whistled under his breath. No wonder they wanted to keep their new borer secret, if it could bore a hole a hundred feet deep and make a chamber at the bottom big enough to hold tons of explosive in that short space of time.

The car stopped below the rim of the crater. Monroe climbed slowly up the loose rock and looked down. There was the mine shaft, like a worm hole in sand sliced by a spade. A couple of men stood by the entrance, looking in.

Another man came running out, a gas mask swinging in his hand. He looked up at the crater rim, cupping his hands. "They're OK. Weak but breathing."

Webber called down, "Who's there?"

"Just two. Hawker and Hammond."

Monroe pulled out his case and began the ritual of lighting a cigar. With the first puff hanging blue in the air he paused, frozen. Where was Ingrid Tellefsen? She'd been put in his care by Webber for the day. She'd driven out with him. He'd seen her on the ridge by the mine entrance. Then she'd walked off, by herself, along the ridge. Then . . . Good God! He'd driven back without her!

She came walking around the crater from the western end of the ridge. His panic subsided as he hurried toward her, his hands out. "Miss Tellefsen! Where were you? Are you all right? How can I forgive myself?"

She shook some red dust out of her hair. "A big stone fell out of the sky and nearly killed me, but it did not. . . . I was sitting against a rock out there, thinking of my father and Beel. Where did you all go? I did not hear anyone tell me to go back. I did not notice anything here on the ridge. Lord Redmond and Mr. Webber just walked out here with a box and a big sheet of blue paper."

Monroe said, "The ditch digger didn't come out? Nor the big black trailer?" Anne Hawker had joined them and was listening intently.

Ingrid Tellefsen said, "No. Just Mr. Webber and Lord Redmond. They walked up and down, then they put the box down—here—where the crater is, and came back . . ."

Webber had joined them and was listening.

". . . then there were two explosions. A small one, and five minutes later, the big one."

Anne Hawker said, "The black trailer was still back on the ridge? And the well digger?"

Miss Tellefsen nodded.

Monroe said, "But this is . . . most extraordinary."

Webber said, "You were out on the ridge, Miss Tellefsen? We were in such a goddam hurry we didn't account for everyone properly . . . They're carrying Hawker out now. OK, miss, you can go down and help them if you want to."

Monroe said, "There is another extraordinary thing here. I detect no smell of explosives . . ."

Webber muttered, "Not here, Mr. Barnett, please. I'll explain at the Project. Probably tomorrow, after I've reported to Washington."

Forty-eight hours had passed since the rescue at the Kaylabito Mine, and Monroe Barnett was impatient to get back to Washington, his work and the secret *her*. But Hawker had taken longer to recover than was expected, and the doctors had only just allowed de Guise out of the hospital. They were all here now, gathered in the main conference room of the Texas Project—the three young men looking pale, a plaster on Hawker's forehead, Hammond's finger tips heavily scarred, de Guise's head bandaged; the two women; himself; and, the other side of the table, Webber, Redmond, Berkowitz, and, inconspicuous as always, Harry Bosco, Webber's assistant.

Webber said, "Ready? You feel all right, de Guise? I haven't had time to find out what happened to you."

De Guise said, "My head aches, that's all. I suppose it is like what you call a hangover . . . In our little plan to shake off your men at the Montezuma Motel, I was to drive east, drawing one of your men to follow me. I did so, but near Brazos the car came up very fast behind me and it suddenly came to me that this was not Mr. Webber's man. This was someone else. Too late. I tried to escape, but he forced me off the road. I remember the car going over the edge, but that's all."

"You were lucky," Webber said. "Your car was a total loss. And you were lucky someone came along as soon as they did, otherwise you might have lain in that gully a long time. Did you see the driver of the car that pushed you off the road?"

De Guise said, "Just for a moment. He had a long, thin red face and was wearing a light-gray hat. That's all."

"Trilby," Webber said grimly. "Yes. He'll be around. . . . Well, I have here written permission from the Director to give you all TP One status—that is, the highest security classification in the Texas Project. It's not the best way, usually, but events and personalities have played hell with sound procedures in this case. . . . Because there was a chance that Mr. Tellefsen was in the Kaylabito Mine, and time was vital, we used the product which is the Texas Project's real, top-secret, purpose: EAD. Lord Redmond, will you take it from there, please?"

"Right you are. . . . You have heard of EAD?"

"Energy at a distance?" Monroe Barnett said. "The thing that can burn paper inside a box, or diseased human tissue inside a man's skull, without burning the box or damaging the skull? It's measured in thorups."

"Any idea why?"

"I suppose some Scandinavian genius called Thorup invented it?"

Bill Hammond pushed forward a note. Lord Redmond glanced at it: "'Laser, maser beams?' Yes, they are examples of EAD, in a fairly mechanical form. Let me go back a bit. . . . In 1948 a Russian scientist called Sven Thorup published a series of mathematical problems, with speculative solutions to them, which postulated the capacity to transfer energy from one place to another without the use of wires or carrying waves. The papers—appearing in the journal of the Soviet Academy of Arts and Sciences—created quite a furore. Then Thorup died suddenly, no more articles were published and interest died down, or appeared to. You see, EAD was only *postulated*. It was as though Einstein had suggested the existence of relativity without any mathematics to back up the suggestion."

Ingrid said, "This Mr. Thorup . . . was he a Dane, like my father? I think I know the name."

Lord Redmond said, "One moment, my dear. . . . Nothing more was heard about EAD from Russian sources, though I myself continued with the calculations for a time and was the first to use the term 'thorup' to denote a unit of this theoretical EAD—the same way 'watt' is a unit of electricity."

Webber leaned forward and took up the narrative. "Late in 1969 we learned, from various sources, that the Russians were working all out on EAD. Their headquarters was a plant near Samarkand. The chief of the project was a Mr. Sigurd Tellefsen, another Dane who had fled to Russia about the same time as Mr. Thorup, and had been his assistant."

Ingrid said, "I was in Samarkand with my father then. He was not working on this EAD—I never heard of it—but on building a powerhouse, worked by atoms."

Webber said, "That was the cover plan, just like ours. . . . Well, we learned that the Russians had started work on EAD in 1948, secretly, while we fooled around with less sophisticated ideas like lasers and masers. Twenty-one years' start they had, not to mention the only scientist who even knew where to begin! Of course, there are plenty of showy uses for EAD, like moon landings, orbital stations, trips to Mars, and so on—but the guts of the matter is in defense. How do you defend yourself against an enemy who has the capability of creating energy—and *releasing* energy—at a distance, with no material means of transmission? In the present state of the art, there *is* no defense."

Hawker said, "Except by having the same capability yourself."

"Precisely," Dr. Berkowitz said, nodding his head like a schoolmaster in approval of a bright pupil. "It took the Russians many years to get out of the theoretical stage of EAD. The problems—which *we* are only just beginning even to comprehend the nature of—are horrendous. But about a year ago they started on a development program aimed at a one-million-thorup capability. Mr. Tellefsen told us that the target date for completion was January 1, 1972. Do you realize what a million thorups means? It means one megaton at a thousand miles. Do you know what our present EAD capability is? Ten thousand thorups. One-hundredth of the Russian target figure! We just can't afford it. The Pentagon Rednecks, as we call them, the hit-'em-first school, had a good case for unloading onto the Russians before this impossible gap opened. Someone Up There must really like us, though, because when we were getting really scared, we got the word that Tellefsen wanted out. We couldn't believe it. But it was true. . . . The Texas Project exists solely to make use of Mr. Tellefsen's researches. The Project's target is the same as the Russians'—a one-million-thorup capability by January 1, 1972."

"We were just beginning to see the way ahead when Mr. T. disappeared," Lord Redmond said sadly. "You see, Mr. Tellefsen holds the secrets of twenty years of stage-by-stage advance. For twenty years he guided the Russian research through a labyrinth of theory, before they could even begin to think of hardware. Some of the formulae he brought us are in the computers, and will be for days yet. But there is so much that only he knows. Twenty years! And there is a complicated adaptation to be made with our own infant system, which has certain advantages that we don't want to lose."

They sat silent. After a time Webber said, "OK. So now you know. Don't talk, hint, or mention EAD in connection with the Texas Project. . . . We have to find Mr. Tellefsen if our country, or yours, Hawker, is to survive. Because, rather than let them have this EAD power, we'll start a preemptive war."

"You . . . you know that?" Anne Hawker asked quietly.

Webber's wide mouth turned down at the corners. He said, "I don't *know* it, miss. And I'm not in the Pentagon, but I'm what Dr. Berkowitz calls a Redneck. Others call us Hawks. There are plenty of us, civilians and military men, too, who don't aim to see the U.S.A. go under without a fight. . . . So, if we want a future, we'd better put all our brains and experience and money, everything we have, into finding Mr. Tellefsen. Whose real name is Sven Thorup." He shot the next question at Ingrid: "Isn't it, miss?"

Ingrid seemed to consider a time. Then she said, "It must be. I think I would have forgotten already, but I was told very often, when I was seven or eight, that my father's name was Tellefsen, and so was mine, and I was to forget the other. But I couldn't . . . quite."

Webber said, "Back in '48 some high-up in the Party learned about the EAD theory and told Stalin. Stalin had Thorup 'die,' and the Academy articles stop . . . the dust settled. Then Thorup's assistant Tellefsen took over, thousands of miles away. Of course, some Russian scientists recognized Thorup in Tellefsen, but in Stalin's Russia, with Gregory Parkezian looking over your shoulder, you didn't talk. Remember that Mr. Thorup was unknown until he published those articles. He went to Russia in 1939—no one knows where from—to help in what he thought of as a struggle against Fascism everywhere. Of course, the first thing the Russians did was help the Nazis carve up Poland. Then they attacked Finland. But by then it was too late."

Lord Redmond stood up. "I feel better, now that I don't have to lie to you, VK."

VK said, "How did you get us out of the mine? There was a small explosion first, I think. I was practically unconscious." Bill Hammond nodded.

Lord Redmond said, "Yes. We set off a small EAD blast to frighten you to the other end of the mine, in case you were near. Then the big one—it was one thousand thorups—just below the line of the shaft."

They were all silent for a minute. Then Dr. Berkowitz said, "I wish we could put ourselves into Mr. T.'s shoes—into his mind. Do you think he was in a frame of mind to go back to Russia, Ingrid?"

A light at Webber's elbow flashed, and he picked up the telephone. Ingrid shook her head decisively. VK said, "I agree with Ingrid. He was frightened. Generally scared. Especially frightened of Parkezian, I think, and what he'd do to him. Other things he didn't—couldn't—talk about."

"That is right," Ingrid said.

Webber put down the telephone and said, "Mr. Tellefsen . . ."

"Mr. Thorup," Ingrid interrupted. "We will never find my father if we don't know which man we are looking for."

Webber said, ". . . has been located."

Ingrid jumped up, her arms out. "Yes?"

"He's on an Aeronaves de Mexico non-SS flight from Mexico City to Rome. It's due to land in Rome four hours from now."

Chapter 6

ROBERT DE GUISE stood up with the rest. His head ached and throbbed behind the bandage. . . . Why was Mr. Tellefsen flying from Mexico City to Rome? He must remember to think of him as Mr. Thorup. How typical of his employers—on the one hand to risk killing him in order that a part of his story might have more verisimilitude; on the other, to keep from him a vital piece of information about the principal object of the whole mission! For Ingrid was right; if you didn't know the inner reality of a person, you could not follow his movements, still less forecast them. But perhaps even Trilby did not know that Tellefsen and Thorup were the same person.

Webber was ushering them out of his office, and the obvious question now was—is this story a trap? It fitted the requirements of a trap perfectly—that is, he did not have time to check its truth; and the news was so important that he had to pass it on. The HPS action in ambushing Hawker and Hammond, and trying so desperately to get them to talk, had shown Webber that the HPS had no idea where Mr. Tellefsen was . . . and that they were desperate to find out.

He heard his own animated talk as he walked beside the Hawkers toward their parked cars. He was uttering Gallic exclamations, such as *Formidable!* and *Mon Dieu!* Unhappily, these phrases came to him automatically when he had to think of two things at once.

Very well, then. The expected moment of exposure had come. He must not loose his cool, but he must act. If it were a trap, set in just this way, and announced at this moment, Webber had set it in order to find out which of the group was an enemy agent. All five of them would be closely watched and their telephones bugged. The one who sent out a message, no matter to whom, would be regarded as the traitor. But in that case, Webber could not have warned the Hawkers, or Hammond, or Ingrid. So none of them would be on their guard.

They reached the cars. A dozen other cars were parked in the lot. A couple of men were stooped under the raised hood of one, a man was reading a paper in another. All these were of the CIA, obviously. More probably were watching from behind windows across the way.

He started the engine of his car. Anne was riding with Bill. Ingrid was riding with VK, and talking and gesticulating like a woman drunk with joy. She would scratch Webber's eyes out when she learned that the story was not true. If it was not . . .

He paused for security inspection at the gate, then drove out behind the others. He wondered whether he could still preserve his secrecy. A moment's thought, as the car rolled quietly along the black road in the noontime glare, showed him it couldn't be done. Webber had got him. He *must* send the message out. He *must* do it now. Very well—in that case he should try to protect himself against the more violent consequences.

At the motel VK called, "Let's meet in the Uranium Tavern in a quarter of an hour and celebrate a bit, eh?"

He called, "Fine." He went into his room and straight through to the back door, and checked that the bathroom curtains were drawn and the back door locked and bolted. In the front he pulled the Venetian blinds closed and drew the curtains. The air conditioner hummed quietly. He checked the small automatic in his trouser pocket and went along the patio to Anne's room. She came out at once at his knock, her face scrubbed and eyes sparkling. "Oh, Robert," she said, "I thought . . ."

He bowed. "I apologize that I am not a tall, handsome, blue-eyed, dark-haired . . . Anne, I have a little problem, about a present I want to give Ingrid. Please come and advise me."

Anne said, "I'm sure I don't know any better than you, Robert."

"Ah yes, because you are a woman," he said. He guided her along the patio, talking. "It is a matter of choice, between two pieces of turquoise. . . ." He held open the door of his room. A CIA man was certainly watching from that room across the courtyard. Too late now. He closed the door, put on the chain, and pressed the lock button. He drew the automatic.

He said, "Do not shout, Anne, and I will not hurt you. Sit down there. On that bed, where I can see you." The look on her face was surprised, but not very. Certainly there was no trace of panic. He'd have to watch this woman. He picked up the phone and said, "Get me Area Code 303, 445-8997." He waited, the gun in his lap pointed negligently at Anne.

A voice at the other end inquired, "Is this Mr. Carey?"

That was Trilby. He said, "He's on a flight from Mexico due to land in Rome in three and a half hours. It's a feed, and they'll be listening." He put down the receiver.

Well, now Trilby knew. And he knew that the information came from the CIA and therefore might be a plant. And he knew that the CIA had permitted the call to be made, which strengthened the likelihood of a trap. And he knew that Robert de Guise was no longer a secret agent—he was just an agent.

He said to Anne, "What's Webber's number?"

"4422."

Webber came on at once. He said, "Mr. Webber, I have Anne Hawker here with me." He heard the smothered exclamation at the other end. "Sorry," he said, "but it was necessary. I want free passage out of the country."

"Like hell," Webber said. "And don't touch Miss Hawker or I'll see that you're charged with murder and go to the chair for it. There's good precedent for that in this business."

"I don't want to harm Anne but I certainly will if you force me to. Call me when you are ready to discuss ways and means that will ensure no possibility of cheating. Meantime, remember, if anyone tries to break in, I shall shoot Anne." He put down the phone and looked at Anne, who was standing in the door of his bathroom. "You can't get out that way," he said.

"I wasn't going to," she said. "I suppose we've all been wondering whether there was a traitor among us, and—"

"Traitor!" he said, his anger rising. "Do you think *I* owe anything to America? I, whose eye they spat in? Better *you* should call yourself a traitor for betraying Europe to this . . . this barbarism, this paradise of bad taste."

"But you like America," Anne said. "Look at your clothes. The way you speak, when you forget to be French. The—"

"Quiet!" he cried. With an effort he moderated his voice to the amused timbre that he wanted people to notice about him. He said, "I am only surprised that it took so long to unmask me. Webber would have done it much sooner if there had not occurred this most fortunate clash of personalities between himself and Mr. Thorup. It is an exciting game, this espionage, is it not?"

"Sir Alan was killed by your people," Anne said. "You're a murderer, Robert, not a spy. . . . Did you drive your car off the road just so that Mr. Webber wouldn't suspect you?"

De Guise shook his head, then winced. The reality had been bad enough, there in the darkness beside the road. He remembered the car behind flicking its lights twice, so he stopped. He remembered Trilby pulling alongside, and saying, "The CIA man turned back half an hour ago. You must be more alert, de Guise. All right, get out." He remembered standing beside the car, and seeing Trilby's eyes gleam, and his arm draw back, the rubber truncheon bending in obscene silhouette. But that was all, until he awoke, cut, bleeding, stunned, in the wreck of his car. The nerve of these people! How did they know what he would or would not say while concussed?

Someone knocked firmly on the door. He heard VK's voice: "Let her out, Robert."

He motioned with the gun for Anne to come up to the front of the room where he could keep an eye on her. He did not go near the door but spoke loudly enough for them to hear outside. "I will only talk on the telephone, VK. I don't want to see anyone outside the windows or doors, front or back, or I shall take steps. Go back to your room and call me."

He heard their footsteps receding and almost at once the telephone rang. There'd be a tape recorder plugged in to the switchboard, but at this stage what did it matter?

It was VK again. He said, "What do you want?"

De Guise said, "Safe conduct into Mexico."

VK said, "Have you harmed Anne? Let her speak."

De Guise looked at her and held out the phone. She said, "No, I'm all right."

"Well, let her out. If she's OK, then you can go free."

"I think I prefer to take her to the border. I think you drive me, alone, and I sit in the back seat with Anne. When we get to the border, wherever it is—it is a long way, I know—Anne and I will get out and go to the border control together. Then she will turn back and I will go on."

VK said, "All right."

De Guise said, "I have a better idea. Let me speak to Bill. . . . Is that you, Bill? Say something in French. I understand the language."

"De Guise, ne dommagez pas à Anne!"

"Ouch, *ma pauvre langue!* No, I won't *dommager* Anne, unless any of you try to *dommager* me. . . . Bill, VK is a very unreliable fellow in some ways. I would not rely on his promise any more than a man-eating leopard's. It is you who must drive Anne and me to the border. And I want to hear you swear, yourself, that no harm will come to me, that I can cross into Mexico with my belongings, and that the Mexicans will not arrest me once I am over."

"B-b-b-b-b-bon."

"That is a promise, from Bill Hammond?"

There was a long pause then. Someone had put a hand over the mike, of course. Webber was in there, and they were all telling Hammond he couldn't give the promise—or, if he did, they'd break it, OK? And Hammond was saying—how was he saying it? Just by looking obstinate?—that if he gave his word, everyone must keep it.

The voice came on, sudden and loud: *"Oui, je promets."*

"All right," de Guise said, sighing with relief. "Bring the car to

the front of this room when you're ready. Just you. I'll come ou.
with Anne, and, please, Bill, see that Webber or VK or the agents
don't try anything."

He looked around the room, at the Zuñi mask, and the Hopi
dolls, the silver and beads and turquoise, the carpets and tools
and ornaments. Dear Lord, it was indeed a wonderful art the
Americans—the real Americans—had brought to fruition in these
Southwestern deserts. How much of it could he take? Could he
ever come back?

Anne said, "I'll send the rest to Paris, Robert. We have your
address."

He looked around sharply. Ah, it was a trap. It must be. But she
was calm. *Le flegme britannique.* Was it possible that she meant
it? One could only wait and see. The cursed woman made him
feel sentimental, lonely, afraid. He selected a few of the best ornaments, and then Anne said, "Bill's car's outside."

He said, "Very well. Let us go. Walk slowly. Close to me. Open
the door."

Bill watched from the driver's seat. He longed to get out, but at
this point he didn't want to make any move which might provoke
de Guise. It was nine o'clock, the night hot and gusty, thousands
of moths fluttering in the torrents of light over the border posts
and customs sheds. He saw de Guise walk out on the Mexican
side, carrying his briefcase and a suitcase. He got into a taxi and
waved jauntily as the taxi drove away. Bill didn't respond.

Anne came toward him, walking slowly, with no spring in her
long thighs. The overhead lights accentuated the dark circles
under her eyes. He thought, She's had a gun in her side for more
than eight hours. She reached the car and suddenly her eyes, the
gray, wide eyes, filled with tears. He hurried out and gingerly
tried to take her in his arms. "It's OK," he said. "Don't worry. It's
all over."

She stood awhile, half leaning against the car, her head turned
into his work shirt. He kept his right arm around her shoulders,
his fingers working gently to knead the flesh, firm and shallow
there over the bone. His left hand hung down his side, and her
body was pressed against it, one breast swelling into his ribs.

She stood away, twisting her head so that her blond hair shook out in the hot wind. "What a silly thing to do! I'm a real crybaby, sometimes."

Oh, damn, oh Christ! She was dabbing at her eyes, and he couldn't take her in his arms again. It was too late. The moment was over.

A police officer came out of the border immigration post and walked to them. He said, "Mr. Hammond? Mr. Webber's on the line from Shiprock."

Bill nodded, wondering vaguely how the cop knew. But of course Webber had telephoned ahead, long since. De Guise had probably been under three or four guns all the time he was in the control post with Anne. They could easily have picked him off, too, and he'd never have known what hit him. Well, another time. A promise was a promise, and Anne was safe, and that was what really mattered.

In the little back room Anne took up the telephone, throwing him a little smile as she did. She said, "Hullo . . . Yes, quite all right. A bit tired. Not to worry. So's Bill." Then there was a long time when she said nothing, listening. Then she said, "All right, Mr. Webber. I'll tell him. We'll call back later."

She turned to Bill. "Mr. T.'s car has been found abandoned in a back street on the outskirts of Mexico City. Mr. Webber knew that before the conference this morning, but he couldn't say anything then because he and Mr. Barnett had laid this trap to catch whichever of us was a traitor. They said that Mr. T. was on a plane from Mexico City, rather than some other place, in case the traitor had already heard from his side about the car being found there. . . . Robert got awfully cross when I called him that—traitor. But, you know, I think it's because he really wants to be American, almost." Her stomach rumbled loudly and she giggled, clinging to Bill's elbow. "Stanmore train! Can we get dinner at this hour?"

An hour and a half later, replete with steak and beer, he spread his hands and looked questioningly at her.

"Well!" she said. "I've never eaten so much in my life."

It figures, he thought, smiling. She had eaten the way small girls often do, putting away a large bowl of soup, a pound of New York cut steak, salad, mountains of French fries, and two helpings of lemon meringue pie with whipped cream.

He signaled for the check. It was late and the waitress was hovering nearby. Now, in a moment, they'd have to discuss what to do next. There wasn't much choice, at that. They'd have to take a couple of rooms in a motel, and drive back tomorrow. Anne could call VK and tell him.

Anne said, "Wait a minute, Bill . . . I didn't say much during dinner because I was thinking . . ."

It's nice of you to say that, he thought. The truth is that you didn't say much because I can't reply. Besides, your mouth was full most of the time.

She said. "Why are you smiling? I was thinking about poor Mr. Webber. You know, he apologized on the phone just now because he didn't protect me from Robert. I had to laugh because what he really wanted to say was that none of us mattered a ha'penny in comparison with finding who the traitor was—and he'd found out —and he was happy as a sandboy."

Bill nodded. She could go on talking forever as far as he was concerned.

She said, "And I have an idea about Mr. T. I think he may be very ill. Or believes he is. . . . Did VK tell you about the fishing trip? When Mr. T. caught a big fish that had something wrong with its stomach? VK just mentioned it, but I think it may have been important. Suppose Mr. T. thought *he* had something terribly wrong with *his* stomach? You're thinking, why wouldn't he have just gone to a doctor? That's what Mr. Webber thinks, too. But people aren't always brave, and they don't always act sensibly, Bill, particularly if they think they have cancer. . . . Yes, cancer."

Bill wrote on his pad *Webber had hospitals checked.*

"I know," she said eagerly. "But in the States! Bill, I think we should drive to Mexico City tomorrow."

He wrote, *1,000 miles.*

"Oh dear," she said, "I can never get it into my head how big everything is here, even after today's ride. Well, we could fly down, couldn't we? I think we should have an advertisement put in the Mexican papers at once, asking any doctor who saw or treated a man like Mr. T.—with or without his beard—to come forward."

Bill began to speak in French, but his French was only good enough for the simplest ideas. He wrote, remembering grimly what his father had often shouted at him: "For Christ's sake, write clearly, Bill! You can't make up for stuttering by scrawling!"

After a few moments he handed the paper over. Anne read. She said, "I suppose you're right. We ought to tell Mr. Webber, so as not to cross his wires . . . if he has any. Who is McCaffery, who you say can act less conspicuously in Mexico City than any of Webber's men?"

He wrote, *Private detective agency. Branches everywhere. Worked for my father, also our company.*

She said, "Good . . . Now, let's get to a motel, and call Shiprock, because—" she yawned, half hiding the gape with the back of her hand—"I shall be asleep before it's done . . . and I shall dream of the back of your head and the way your ears stick out. I've been staring at them all day. They kept floating on ahead of me, hour after hour across the deserts and through the mountains and I kept repeating, It's a bird, it's a plane, it's Superman! Thank heaven it wasn't, in the end, though. It was you."

The waitress was there, impatient, with the check. Bill's heart waltzed and dipped. Hurriedly he found his money. This was a girl for him.

Webber finished talking and sat back. Four of them were gathered in Webber's living room—Ingrid, Mr. Barnett, VK, and Webber himself. It was late and the air conditioner had developed asthma. VK grabbed up his beer and took a deep draught. Webber's eyes were fixed on him. The bastard was laughing behind that wide monkey face.

Ingrid said, "Are they in separate rooms at the motel?"

Webber said, "I didn't ask. You could make a surprise call at three A.M. if you want to find out."

Mr. Barnett said, "That's not a very seemly remark, Joe. . . . What do you think of Miss Hawker's idea?"

VK controlled his bad temper. Old Barnett had a manner that forced you to dignity and calm in his presence.

Webber said, "Right now, her guess is as good as anyone's. And better that McCaffery should check it out than us. With Mc-

Caffery on the job people will think it's some old guy that ran off with his nurse that they're after, because the wife wants him caught before he can change his will."

VK thought about Anne's theory. She was probably right, and he wished she had spoken earlier of her suspicions. But one saw things at random, not in formed sequence, and it took time for the mind to collect them and arrange them into coherent expression.

He thought about Mr. Thorup: a genius; a simple man; a strangely informed man. A memory struck him. He said, "What's a bit?"

"A bit?" Monroe Barnett said, smiling. "*You* ought to know. Isn't it British slang for a girl?"

"No, in American money. The shoeshine man in Shiprock asked Mr. T. for two bits."

Mr. Barnett stopped smiling and said swiftly, "And he didn't ask what that was?"

"I don't think so. No, he just gave him some money."

Mr. Barnett said, "That is interesting, indeed. It's the sort of thing that isn't taught in English courses. To know that two bits is a quarter, I would guess that he must have lived here."

"My father was never in America before in his life," Ingrid said.

Mr. Barnett said, "It would have been many years ago. I haven't heard anyone say 'two bits' or 'six bits' in a long while. My father frequently did."

VK said, "Mr. T. often used words and phrases that sounded very slangy to me. Of course he could have picked them up from the pictures—I mean, Hollywood."

"He never went to the pictures," Ingrid said.

"Or reading American gangster thrillers."

"He only read books about science—or fishing," Ingrid said.

VK said, "He did use odd phrases, though. . . . He said several times 'All right already.' And he called people *schlemiels*. And he said *cone-yo?* And he wished he could buy bagels in Shiprock. What's *cone-yo?* What are bagels?"

Mr. Barnett said, "Salted doughnut-shaped rolls . . . very tasty. Everything you've quoted, except *cone-yo*, is New York Jewish jargon. My partner Bernie Weiss gives very amusing recitations in it sometimes. He was practically raised in the garment district. I don't know what *cone-yo* is."

VK said, "Now that we are thinking about it, I remember other things. He wrote dates the American way—six-slash-twelve for June 12, not twelve-slash-six. He used the right words to telephone operators, like 'connected' instead of 'through.' "

"Why do you keep hinting he has been here before?" Ingrid demanded. "I tell you, he has not! He said so!"

"He might have been hiding something from you," Mr. Barnett said gently.

VK said, "I think he was here. And, by God, I believe he went to prison here!"

"In prison?" Ingrid said. "VK, my father may be very ill, and I love him. Please don't . . ."

VK said, "I'm not joking, Ingrid. You must agree that your father was—is—capable of violence. I've seen him lose his temper half a dozen times."

"Why do you think he's been in prison?" Webber asked.

VK said, "He was damned odd about his fingerprints. He wore those thin gloves all the time."

"Yes."

"I thought he must have a skin disease, but he did take the gloves off sometimes and then I saw that there was nothing wrong with his hands."

Mr. Barnett said, "We could check on whether he's been to jail easily enough . . . . if we had his fingerprints. And we don't, for the reason you gave."

VK said, "I think we might have them. On a casting reel he gave me one day when we went shopping in Farmington. It's in its box still. But he took it out to show me, and he wasn't wearing gloves. I haven't touched it since—or before."

Dr. Alvarez was small, gray and sloe-eyed, with a small gray toothbrush mustache. He had been in a business suit when they first saw him, but he had excused himself, darted out, and returned wearing a white coat. Now he placed the tips of his fingers together and cleared his throat. Bill thought that he would do well on TV commercials, except that he'd left his stethoscope lying carelessly on the table, instead of hanging it around his neck. Bill balanced his notebook on the edge of the table. Anne sat beside him, her hands folded in her lap.

The doctor picked up a sheet of paper. He spoke in fluent English. "When I had confirmed that it would be proper for me to discuss the medical aspects of this case with you . . . the Hippocratic Oath, you understand . . . I made some brief notes, to clear my own mind. . . . Mr. Amieva—that was the name he gave—came first to me at about four P.M. on Thursday, June seventeenth. He had no proper appointment, but he had telephoned a few minutes earlier, saying he had heard I was a specialist in internal medicine, and he urgently needed an appointment. As I had a half hour to spare—an unusual event, I assure you—and he sounded genuinely sick and worried—I spoke to him myself—I told him to come up. I noted on his entry that he was very tired, very dusty, very dirty, as though he had driven a long way. He told me he had cancer of the stomach. I told him that was for me to find out, and started with my examination. I will not waste your time with all that I did *not* discover. But I did detect an enlargement of the cervical glands and the spleen. I took a peripheral smear and examined it microscopically at once. Blood platelets were markedly down, and there was an abnormally large number of immature white cells. I next administered a local anesthetic into the sternum, and with the blunt-needle technique took a sample of bone marrow. I could do no more then. It was essential that the bone marrow should be examined by a specialist in pathology. I asked Mr. Amieva to return the following day at the same time, and arranged for the marrow sample to be sent to my colleague Dr. Echeverria."

Poor Mr. T., Bill thought—alone, in a strange country, half out of his mind with worry.

Anne interjected, "Did he have stomach cancer?"

Dr. Alvarez said briskly, "No. Dr. Echeverria's report was unambiguous. Mr. Amieva is suffering from acute leukemia."

After a silence Anne said slowly, "Is there any hope?"

The doctor said, "None. . . . My problem was what to tell him. Sometimes one should tell the truth, sometimes not. I did not know Mr. Amieva well enough to be sure. The matter was taken out of my hands by an unfortunate chance. . . . Mr. Amieva came. I had his file on the desk. Just as he entered the room, my nurse told me that a certain lady had just arrived and must speak to me for a moment. She is a valued patient and friend, so I went

out . . . leaving the file. I was not gone more than three minutes
—five at the outside. As I came back here, Mr. Amieva walked
past me. He didn't seem to see me. I saw at once that the file was
open. . . . It is the sort of careless mistake that we all make sometimes, Mr. Hammond. Only, if you are a doctor, the results can be
very dangerous. I think of that poor old gentleman . . ."

"Don't blame yourself," Anne said.

The doctor spread his hands. "He brushed past . . . not seeing
. . . I hurried after him, tried to hold him in the waiting room.
There were two patients there. He looked at me—he looked
through me—and said something I couldn't understand. It
sounded like *ow vith like yamott.* I took hold of his arm—you
understand, *señor,* it is hard to know how to behave in front of
other patients, who are in a nervous state themselves, ten floors
above the solid earth—Mr. Amieva flung off my arm with great
strength and left. He threw a handful of American paper money
at me as he went. I have been most unhappy. Should I have told
the police that this poor man had left in such a condition? Should
I have accompanied him? How, when he threw me off so violently? That is why I was overjoyed to see the advertisement in
yesterday's newspaper. . . . Mr. Amieva knows, at least, what is
wrong with him, and can get the best treatment available."

"What's that?" Anne asked.

Dr. Alvarez said, "It is called the VAMP treatment, from the ini-
tial letters of the drugs used. Perhaps most important is that he
should start taking 6-Mercapto-Purine. It comes in pill form, and
can give complete remission within weeks. That is, all the blood-
forming elements revert to normal, the hemoglobin count rises,
pallor goes . . . Did you notice a pallor, by the way?"

"Yes, though he got a suntan in New Mexico that hid it."

"Ah . . . Pallor goes, full vigor is restored. For a time. Relapse
recurs within three, four, six months, with the same symptoms as
before. This time there is no response to 6-M.P. Another drug,
Prednisone, will give an excellent response within ten days, but
only for a few weeks. . . ."

"Someone looking for Mr. Amieva should carry 6-Mercapto-
Purine with him?"

"Every moment would help, I suppose. He may be using the
drug already. I made a note about it, on Dr. Echeverria's report—

look here—and he will have seen that. It's not easy to get without a doctor's prescription, even in Mexico, but it can be done. Mr. Amieva seemed to have plenty of money."

Bill wrote, *Ask if Mr. A. had a beard.*

Anne asked the question, and Dr. Alvarez said, "No, he was clean-shaven." He glanced from one to the other.

Anne stood up. Bill followed suit. The doctor closed the file and handed it across the table. "Here," he said, "keep this. It will help the next physician to deal with the patient. I am sorry I could do no more for the gentleman."

Bill handed over a card given to him by McCaffery's chief agent in Mexico. It read, in Spanish and English, *If you receive any further inquiries on this subject, please refer them to the undersigned*—then the agent's name and address. The doctor read it with a little *moue* of surprise, then said, "I understand." He bowed them to the door.

In the street again, Bill went to the curb to hail a cab, but Anne said, "Let's walk. . . . Isn't it awful? He was, is, such a kind old man really."

Bill nodded. He too liked Mr. Thorup; and his own mother had died of cancer. But right now all he could think of was the easy swing of Anne's stride down the wide sidewalk, and the way the sun put lights in her thick hair and the wind blew the stray ends of it around her face. Anne pushed a strand back into place and said ruefully, "The wind and the dry heat are going to make my hair worse than ever. . . . What's the time, Bill?"

He showed her his wrist watch, the hands pointing to noon. She said, "We just have time for a sandwich. Unless you think it would be better to eat at the airport."

Bill said, "*Oui.*" They'd been in Mexico City nearly twenty-four hours now. Last night, when they called to tell VK where they were staying, VK insisted they should return to Shiprock as soon as possible. Why? Was he jealous? The hell with VK. Anne was looking at him with raised eyebrows. *Oui* was no answer to her question.

He braced himself. He knew what he wanted to say, and now prayed that he could say it without the curse on his tongue turning it into something suggestive or sordid. The inability to speak was liable, at any time, to make him blush like a damn schoolgirl.

Not now, not now! He gathered his strength, feeling the sweat lining his forehead and damp on his upper lip. How did it go in French? To hell with French. This was too important.

He said, "Anne . . . I'd like to . . . take you dancing tonight . . . here in Mexico City . . . Will you stay?"

She looked up and over the tops of the skyscrapers for a moment. Her heels clacked firmly in the lilt of her stride. He was thinking that she could not have heard him, when she said, "That would be lovely, Bill. We must see McCaffery's man first, and give him the message about Mr. T. so he can pass it to Mr. Webber. And we should call VK, so they don't expect us. After that, we're free, aren't we? Oh, my hair!"

Bill thought, Might as well be hanged for a sheep as a lamb. He said, "Coiffeur?"

"Oh," she cried. "Have a perm? Those awful tight curls? They look so artificial."

Tight curls weren't necessary, he thought. There were younger, more modern styles. Sort of piled up, or loose chopped hay stuff. He pointed suddenly at a brunette in a red Cadillac.

"Like her?" Anne said.

"Oui," he said, "mais vous seriez plus jolie qu'elle." She glanced at him, laughing uncertainly. When she saw his earnest face the laugh left her lips and her eyes became large and soft. Then she laughed again, and turned away and thrust her hand recklessly through her hair.

"No one can do anything with this! Anyway, VK likes women to look natural."

Bill began to speak, but cut himself short. It might be none of VK's business how his sister dressed and wore her hair, but she thought it was. Actions spoke louder than words. He took her by the elbow and guided her firmly toward a shining glass expanse labeled Peluqueria. The window was full of dummy female heads with cool hair-dos.

He said, "Nous faisons un appointment pour l'apres-midi. Et ce soir . . . we dance!"

"No Fink or Sapporo!" she cried. "I can do the Frug, and that's all."

He crossed his heart, and held the door of the peluqueria open for her.

Ten minutes later, back at their hotel, Webber called. Anne took the phone.

She was smiling when she turned to Bill. "He said don't leave Mexico yet as he may have some important news for us soon. . . . See, they *want* us to stay! Now run along, Bill. I have to powder my nose. I'll meet you downstairs in ten minutes."

The FBI man flew in from Albuquerque at one in the morning, and reached the Project at two. Webber, VK and Ingrid were waiting for him in Webber's office. Monroe Barnett had returned to Washington, to VK's regret. VK thought him a good and wise man. It was at his urgent pressure that Webber had allowed VK back into the inner councils of the search for Mr. Thorup. As Mr. Barnett pointed out, the fly had been found in the ointment, and removed: the news from Mexico proved that Mr. T's flight had been of his own volition and therefore could not have been prevented; and, that when it came to finding him again, VK knew him best—in some ways better even than Ingrid.

The FBI man cleared his throat. VK leaned back in his chair, balancing it on two legs, his hands in his pockets. Ingrid recrossed her legs, giving a momentary clear view. The FBI man's eyes flickered. VK hid a grin. Ingrid couldn't help giving any man that much of a reminder that he was in the presence of a woman. Sometimes she didn't even know she was doing it. Sometimes.

The FBI man's eyes returned to the papers spread on the desk. He said in a monotone, "This report will be handed to you in its entirety, Mr. Webber, per instruction of our Director. Presently I am only summarizing its findings. . . . On processing the fishing reel, Case HZ 493278, dash 14, three different fingerprints were identifiable. By closed-circuit processing, and the cooperation of the personnel concerned, we were enabled to determine that two of these belonged to the owner of the Farmington Sports Goods Store, and a Mr. Durward Kellogg, who had also handled the reel. The telecom print of the third was returned with this annotation; and I quote: *Sigurd Thorsson. 150 West 65th Street, NYC. Booked 10th Precinct, Manhattan, August 13, 1936. Drunk. Public disturbance. Striking officer. Sentenced 10 days by Judge Blauvelt, Manhattan Night Court.*"

"My father used to fight when he was very angry," Ingrid said with some pride, nodding her heavy black hair. Her eyes opened and flashed green. "But that is not my father! That is Mr. Thorsson."

The FBI man continued in his nasal monotone. "As stated on this report, miss, we have no means of equating the print on HZ 493278 dash 14 with the person known as Tellefsen stroke Thorup. We have no proven specimen. But we can state with certainty that the print on HZ 493278 dash 14 was made by the same individual who gave the name of Sigurd Thorsson in New York City on August 13, 1936."

Webber said, "What about that address?"

The FBI man said, "It no longer exists. The edifice was demolished in 1961 to make way for the Lincoln Center."

"The arresting officer? The policeman he hit? What was it all about? Just drunk?"

"The arresting officer, we have ascertained by reference to the New York Police Commissioner's office, was a Patrolman Edward McCready. He had less than fifty-two weeks departmental seniority, and resigned soon after. As he was not eligible for pension and he did not maintain contact with any police benevolent or social organizations, he has not been traced."

VK said, "So no one knows, now, where Mr. T. was doing his drinking and fighting. What is August thirteenth? Any special day? Danish New Year?"

A gleam of respect came into the FBI man's prominent eyes. "We instituted inquiries into that," he said. "The answer is in the negative."

"My father would not need a special occasion to fight, when he was well," Ingrid said. "But it is not my father!"

The FBI man pushed a sheet of paper across the table. A photograph was stapled to it. Ingrid took it. She stared for a long time, then passed the photo to VK. It showed a man with thick blond hair, a black eye burgeoning on the left side, holding a police number board in front of his chest. The hint of a grin lit his craggy face.

"That is my father," Ingrid said with sudden determination. "I was doubting—but I remember, a picture came into my head, of being a very little girl, I was stamping my foot, I was so angry with him about something, and he looked at me just like that. . . . But why did he call himself Thorsson when his name was Thorup?"

The FBI man said, "We have negative information on that, miss. I have totalized all we know. We are unable to locate any transcript of the case. Judge Blauvelt has deceased."

"Can you trace the owners of the building where this Mr. Thorsson lived, and get a list of tenants from them?" Webber said. "Perhaps some of them could tell us something. Put a tracer on that name in all departments—relief recipients, hospitals, births, marriages, deaths, etc.—between, say, 1920 and 1939."

"We are taking all possibilities into consideration, Mr. Webber. We might achieve quicker results by using publicity, but I understand that is prohibited."

Webber said, "For the time being, yes. Later, we might want to. Thanks." The FBI agent left the room.

Webber said, "We'd better break it up. . . . I'm going to Washington tomorrow—today—and then probably on to Europe."

"Europe?" VK asked.

Webber nodded. "We're getting the cards out on every cancer specialist and institute in Europe, including Russia. I think that's where we'll find him."

"He won't go back to Russia of his own accord," VK said. "I'm positive. . . . But he might well go to some other country in Europe for treatment, since he wouldn't want to risk coming back into the States."

"What risk is there?" Webber said crossly. "Am I going to arrest him? Is the President going to have him flogged?"

"He is not acting rationally," Ingrid said, "otherwise I would have heard from him."

"You're right," Webber growled. "Well, I'm closing down my office here, until we get Mr. T. back, of course. Meantime I'm going to work out of my office in New York. That's more central now."

VK said, "We'd better go there too."

Webber said, "I'd prefer that. I'll make reservations for all of you at the . . . I think the report said that the Plaza was Bill Hammond's favorite. Will you call your sister, VK? Tell them to come back here as soon as possible. Then close up here and move to New York. Harry Bosco will help you."

I bet he will, VK thought sourly as he left the building. And keep an eye on us. Ingrid linked her arm in his. "Make the call from my house."

VK nodded absently. The FBI man had given them another fact about the old man. It threw a brief light on a far-off time, like a flash of distant lightning, and then vanished. It showed no path to follow, and indicated neither a past nor a future for the event it so eerily illuminated. Where had Thorsson-Thorup-Tellefsen come from, to get into a public brawl on August 13, 1936? Where did he go, after he had served his ten days in jail? How did he earn his living? There might be a report of the brawl in a New York newspaper of the time, but it was unlikely. And, as they were searching for the famous Mr. Thorup in 1971, how could it help to know more about a 1936 brawl engaged in by the unknown Mr. Thorsson? The answer was that any and every bit of knowledge helped. If you were hunting a lion you had to know about lions in general, but it was especially important to know the habits and character of that particular lion. Then perhaps you'd know in what sort of places to look for him.

Ingrid pressed a button beside the front door and after a moment, during which VK knew the resident agent was scrutinizing them on the tecvision, the buzzer sounded and Ingrid opened the door. Now she would not be able to open that door—or any other door or window—without a similar check.

Ingrid waved at the telephone. "Call them. I will get out of this awful thing." She tugged impatiently at her girdle.

She went down the passage. VK stared at the telephone. Half past two in the morning. Even later in Mexico, wasn't it? Suppose they didn't answer? Or suppose he got Anne's room and Hammond answered? Jesus, it made you feel the cold of the cave, the way the short hairs crept around the back of the neck. That big, muscle-bound Boy Scout, pawing Anne. She wasn't used to big cities. Perhaps he was making her drunk. He could take a lot more booze than she could, God knew.

He picked up the phone and asked for Miss Anne Hawker at the Mexico City hotel, person to person. Ingrid came back, her flowered nylon and lace nightgown floating behind her and her hair loose, her feet bare. She waited beside him, her eyebrows raised. After a time VK heard the hotel operator say, "She doesn't answer." He hung up quickly.

Ingrid said, "They are still out? Do not glare at the telephone, VK. Come and sit down. Have a drink. Give me one. There."

He poured two shots of vodka and sank back in the armchair. One of Ingrid's full breasts curved half out of the gown, but she didn't give the feel of wanting sex, particularly. Perhaps he could make her. He ought to concentrate on her, instead of imagining Anne in Hammond's arms.

Ingrid said, "Stop grinding your teeth. . . . Tell me, I do not think your sister has had many lovers, no? But when she has a man she is good at making love with him. Yes?"

VK managed a somber grin. A great woman, Ingrid. She wanted to know something: She asked. Well, what was the answer? To the first question, probably "One." There was that smooth Italian millionaire playboy who'd taken Anne in. He'd been slow to see what was going on, but once he had . . . Ordinarily he didn't like to fight with his fists; he wasn't strong or big enough for that sort of nonsense; but he would never forget the pleasure of feeling the Italian's nose crunch under his fist, of seeing the blood spurt out all over the expensive safari suit.

As for Ingrid's second question . . . even though the answer to the first question might be "Only one," the answer to this was probably "Yes, she's very good." It was difficult to tell about your own sister, but he thought that Anne would be a passionate, total lover.

Ingrid said, "You are sure she has not made love with Beel since he came back from Europe?"

VK's mouth tightened. The bloody woman wasn't interested in him at all, only in Bill Hammond. He said abruptly, "No. They haven't had an opportunity. Until now."

Ingrid's eyes widened, her creamy forehead furrowed. "Then what has changed Beel so much toward her? I have tried everything to make him see me, but he sees only her. Is he truly in love with her?"

VK said, "I don't suppose he knows himself. Anyway, I'd be the last person he'd talk about it with."

The big eyes focused suddenly on him. "Ah," she said. "You don't like him?"

"I didn't say that."

"You don't want him to marry your sister? To make love with her even?"

"I didn't say that, either."

Her gown slipped a little wider open. She said, "But you like me, though?"

"Sometimes," he said. He finished the vodka and stood up. "But if you think I can steer Bill Hammond's attention away from Anne toward you—or that I want to—you're mistaken."

Her gown parted. Her eyes softened. Her skin was firm, ivory and cream, the breasts big and round with big, strong upstanding nipples, the hips firm, the bush big, sharply defined, dense black. "You look like a statue," he said. "Fertility. Woman. Sorry . . . When we make love, Ingrid, it's going to be in my time, not yours. Good night."

De Guise said, "Thank you. No, nothing more now."

He scribbled his signature on the bill, picked up the slip of paper under it, and dropped a quarter on the tray. The waiter said, "Thank you, sir. Good night, sir."

De Guise checked that the door was locked and sat down under the light. Vancouver lay spread like a glittering carpet below. He read the note carefully: "You have not been traced beyond Mexico City, so continue using Duchamps name and papers t.f.n. Reported from usual source that among fingerprints asked for by CIA in the past week one request originated from Webber. This was of Sigurd Thorsson, booked for drunkenness, New York City, August 13, 1936. We are tracing. Move Montreal at once, keep closest touch here as we must move fast on first information. They will be working on same information and we have to get ahead of them somewhere. For information: Hammond and Anne Hawker went to Mexico City not after you but because Case Subject's car was found there. They visited a Dr. Alvarez specialist internal medicine but we have so far been unable learn object of visit. Later they danced all night in night clubs, then flew back to El Paso, picked up car, and drove to Shiprock."

De Guise burned the paper carefully in his ash tray and lit a Lucky. So Bill was making time with Anne at last. He was a slow starter, but perhaps a strong finisher.

He looked wistfully at the Zuñi mask he had arranged on the mantel. Now he'd have to pack it again, and start the endless business of calling airlines, finding space, checking that his papers were in order. How much more exciting it would be, really, to codify and classify all this wonderful, living world of Southwestern art and artists.

But it was impossible. The ridiculous, ludicrous Americans. He switched on the TV and turned the dial to Channel 2, KBSL, Seattle.

Chapter 7

HARRY BOSCO brought the note up to their Plaza suite himself, then hung around looking as though he would like someone to invite him to have a drink. No one did, so he left. Bill and Anne stood in the window, looking out over Central Park shimmering under the high sun.

VK read the note aloud: *"FBI report: Sigurd Thorsson, bachelor, was married to Yetta Rapkin, spinster, on February 13, 1933, by Rabbi Morris Landau. Mr. T.* gave the address the FBI have, the one that doesn't exist any more. Miss Rapkin gave 403 Second Avenue, New York. They're checking who lives at that address now, and they've told Webber. He's in Vienna. . . . That explains the Jewish slang Mr. Barnett was talking about."

Ingrid turned the pages of a telephone directory. She said, "There is a Yetta Rapkin in New York now. 388 Riverside Drive. The telephone is 662-3557."

VK picked up the phone and called Bosco's office. He wasn't

back, but VK told the secretary, "Are you tracing the Yetta Rapkin in the telephone book? 388 Riverside Drive. I think we should, urgently." He hung up.

Anne said, "If this is the woman Mr. T. married, she'd be Yetta Thorsson, wouldn't she? Oh, I suppose she might go back to her maiden name, particularly if there'd been a divorce, or if she's in business."

Ingrid jumped up. "What good does all this do? We are trying to find my father, not this person he once married."

"She may be your mother," Anne said.

Ingrid's expression changed from frustrated anger to outrage to wonder. "My mother!" she whispered. "I never thought . . . Of course she could be. We don't know when they parted. We must find her, at once."

"We're doing our best," VK said. "But as you said twenty seconds ago, the person we're really looking for is your father. We've been rushing along behind Webber, as though we were tied to him and the CIA and the FBI and all their whirring, bloody computers. But we came into this affair in the first place, and Mr. T. asked us to stay in, on a personal relationship. That's what we have, a personal sympathy, and Goddamnit, we're not using it!"

Anne said, "Yes? Go on."

He strode up and down the room. "Mr. T. runs away from me. He learns he's dying. He may have suspected it before, but in Mexico he *knows* it. What does he do next?"

Ingrid says, "Webber thinks he goes to look for the best doctors he can find, outside the United States."

"That's the logical answer. But if he was being logical, he would never have run away. He would never have gone outside the U.S.A. . . . or even his house in the Project. He'd have picked up the phone and asked Webber to get him a good doctor. Damnit, the President's personal physician would have been on his way in an Air Force SS inside ten minutes! Mr. T. knew that . . . but he wasn't thinking logically. A man given a sentence of death doesn't act the way a man does when he's cut his finger. He thinks . . . he feels . . . the time has come to do what has to be done. There will never be another chance. This poor, sick, lonely old man . . . what would he do?"

"Go fishing," Ingrid said promptly.

"This is no time to joke," VK snapped.

Then they all fell silent, and VK thought, Good God, I wonder. After a minute Ingrid said, "I thought I was joking, too. It is not funny, my father's illness, but I am overwrought. . . . Now I do not think it was a joke. It was what I truly felt. Whenever he had trouble—with his work, with me, with the commissars—he would go to the river and walk for miles along the bank. He would take his fishing rod if it was the season. Once I heard him shout, 'If only there were salmon in the river here, I'd never come back to this accursed laboratory.'"

Anne said, "Did anyone tell you what he said to Dr. Alvarez? *Ow vith like yamott.* Does it mean anything in Russian?"

Ingrid shook her head.

Bill wrote a note and VK read, *I think Ingrid's right. Mr. T. probably gone fish. For salmon. But where?* He passed the note to Ingrid. She shrugged. "The world is full of rivers, full of salmon."

"Not good ones," VK said. "There aren't many. . . ."

The telephone rang. Harry Bosco came on. "Yetta Rapkin is a display manager for Goldman and Bloom, ladies' wear, 477 Seventh Avenue. She's in Chicago now, but she's leaving for New York tonight. Goldman says he believes she was married to some kind of a Swede, way back."

"Have you talked to her?"

"No. She's not at her hotel, or the store where she'd been fixing a display. She's coming back to New York on the high-speed train —the New Twentieth Century Limited. It seems she won't fly. . . . We'll talk to her when she gets in tomorrow morning."

"Who's this? What's he saying?" Ingrid interrupted. VK told her. "I will go to Chicago!" she said. "When does this train leave? What time is it? Twelve. We have time!"

Bosco said, "I heard. I bet they heard her in Central Park. . . . The New Century leaves La Salle Street station at seven-thirty —into New York at two-thirty—about two hundred miles per hour . . ."

VK said, "It's mad to fly out there, it must be a thousand miles, and then turn right round and come back."

"Not to meet your mother, for the first time," Ingrid said. "I am going. That is definite."

Bosco said, "If she goes, one of you must go with her."

VK thought, And there'll be an agent hanging around in the background, too, in case Ingrid thinks she's free of the CIA and skips off to join her father. Well, who should go to Chicago with her? If he went himself, he would be leaving Anne alone with Bill Hammond again. So Bill should go.

He said, "Bill, you'd better go. Bosco, will you get air reservations and rooms or whatever for them, on the train back? And keep calling Chicago until you do get Miss Rapkin, and warn her to look out for Bill and Ingrid."

Bosco said, "OK. I'll call in five minutes with the flight number to Chicago. They'd better be ready to go then."

VK hung up. Ingrid was already gone, throwing the single word, "Packing," over her shoulder. Anne was going too, saying, "I'll pack for you, Bill."

VK was alone with Hammond. For the first time since they came back from Mexico City, by God! He said, "That haircut you made her have is bloody awful. She looks like a whore! What the hell business is it of yours how she does her hair?"

Bill Hammond opened his mouth and his big hands tightened into fists. VK waited, poised lightly. He wished the bloody man could speak, then he'd certainly say something which would start a fight. He'd be beaten to a pulp, but he'd show Mr. Hammond enough to keep him off Anne, perhaps.

Hammond's jaw closed, his fists relaxed. He turned his back on VK and followed Anne out of the room.

Bill leaned back on the padded couch at the rear of the lounge car, an open newspaper on his lap. Ingrid leaned eagerly forward beside him. The stream of passengers had died to a trickle. The clock showed seven-twenty-five. . . .

This might be her: a woman of average height, not young, sallow complexion with spots of high color on her cheekbones; plain black dress, one large piece of costume jewelry, one dangling watch charm; her hair strikingly piled. She was looking up at the car. She waved a white-gloved hand. That meant Bosco had got through to her. She passed forward and out of sight.

The board by the platform entrance read 7:30 P.M.—*New Twentieth Century Limited—South Bend—Cleveland—Buffalo— Albany—New York*. It was an odd feeling being in one of the new trains. He hadn't traveled by train since he was a kid, and then only two or three times right after the war.

A sepulchral voice intoned the traditional chant of, *"All abooooarrd!"* The steel pillars supporting the station roof began to glide past. The hum of generators sank under the low rumble of wheels. The New Century rolled out of La Salle Street, picking up speed instantly. Ingrid could not sit still and got up, looking over Bill's shoulder, waiting impatiently.

Then the other woman came. She stood over him, an inquiring look on her lined face. Bill struggled to his feet. Ingrid said, "Miss Rapkin? This is Bill Hammond." Bill shook hands.

"Mrs. Rapkin," she said. "So the shnook walked out on me, but I *was* married. They can't take that away from me. But not Mrs. Thorsson even if I wanted it. Vee not yot many Svedes in the yarment business." She pulled off her glove and showed the plain gold band on her left hand. She sat down, sighing. "My, my, have I become popular all of a sudden. Old Sam Goldman's telling me he's getting inquiries about me like I'm a new Barbra Streisand they just discovered. . . . Could I do with a drink!"

Ingrid said, "I am Ingrid . . . Tellefsen. Mr. Hammond's secretary." She was staring intently at the older woman, as though trying to trace any resemblance to herself in the other's skin, or hair, or nose, or mouth, or eyes.

Yetta Rapkin, aware of the scrutiny, said acidly, "Nice work if you can get it, dear. . . . What's the hurry to see me? What's so important you have to fly out just to travel back with me?"

Ingrid said, "Mr. Hammond has some questions to ask, and they might be urgent."

Mrs. Rapkin said, "Well, why don't you ask them? Does this young lady have to interpret for you, or something?"

Bill said, "I—I—I . . ."

She touched his hand. "Forget it. I'm sorry. I'm such a damn fool I work for Goldman and Bloom, and you know what *that* means. Well, of course you don't!"

Ingrid said, "We would like to talk privately, please. Mr. Hammond has a private room. We could be comfortable in there."

"OK, dear . . . Do you want to order a large dry martini for me?"

Bill led the way down the swaying corridor as the train rocketed past Comiskey Park and through the ravaged wastes of South Chicago.

He opened the door of his room and Yetta Rapkin exclaimed, "You didn't lock it? Why, I've got one too, next door! Oh, you men, you're so lucky, especially when you're *big*. Every time I leave a room I come back expecting to find some gorilla under the bed, ready to jump out stark naked and rape, rob, and murder me. I've been robbed three times in the past eighteen months on Riverside, and once I was gagged. The next time I find a man in my room I swear I'll . . ."

The high spots on her cheeks glowed; she subsided into the arm chair. "Well, it'll depend whether I invited him, I guess. . . ."

The drinks came. She talked on with rapid animation. Her hair was dyed very black, her lips were a wide dark plum gash. Her eyes were large, beautiful, and unfathomably sad, whatever the expression on her face.

She put down her empty glass with a bang. "So, what gives? Don't tell me that Siggie's come back and wants me."

Ingrid said, "Sigurd Thorsson? No. He has disappeared again. He is my father. I said the other name just now because I wanted to look at you. I am really Ingrid Thorsson. . . . Are you my mother?"

Mrs. Rapkin stared a long time at Ingrid. Her eyes became moist and she fumbled for a little handkerchief in the big bag. "No. I couldn't . . . have any children. Perhaps if I had, Siggie wouldn't have left. It's bad not to be able to give your husband a child . . . especially a Jewish child, a son."

Ingrid said, "We don't know where he is. He is a very important person now. Your government is trying to find him, and so are we. . . . He's very ill. When he learned that, a few days ago, he disappeared. Has he been back to see you?"

"No. I haven't seen him for thirty-five years, and only heard of him once, three years later I guess it was. The last time I saw him was 1936 . . . August twenty-third, as a matter of fact. It was the day he . . . well, I remember it. Never mind why."

Ingrid said, "It was the day he came out of jail?"

She looked surprised. "Yes. He came back to the apartment, and said he was sorry, he had to go. Just like it could have been to the little boys' room. But he meant, go—period. He wasn't the right man for me, he said. That was true, but any man's better than no man. Then he said he had more important work to do and walked out. Bingo."

"What was he arrested for?"

"He never told me. When he was sentenced he called me—I was working, too—and said not to visit him, he needed to think. I didn't want to visit him. I was young, I was respectable. Our family never got into *any* kind of trouble, and as for jail! I nearly died of shame. But I wasn't surprised, either. It was some political thing, I know. I told him a hundred times, after we were married, that he'd get into trouble with his politics, and he did. I was mad. And ashamed . . . Where's he been all these years?"

"Russia. You have not divorced him?"

Mrs. Rapkin shook her head. She patted Ingrid's hand. "Sorry if it upsets you, dear, but the answer's no. Unless he got himself a Russian quickie, he's still my husband. . . . At first, I hoped he'd come back. Then after the war I suddenly saw I was thirty-five, and scraggy like a chicken, and I could get a divorce any time I wanted it—if someone else came along. But no one ever did. No proposals. Just propositions. Plenty of them, I'll say that for myself."

"What did my father do for a living here?" Ingrid asked.

"All the time I knew him he was working at a little electric plant over in Jersey City. It disappeared way back, merged with GE or Westinghouse or someone, but in those days they made radio tubes and things. Siggie went to night school at NYU and read books all the time. Scientific books about electricity and radiation and physics . . ." She laughed reminiscently. "He gave himself a hard time, because his English wasn't so good. He'd have a Danish-English dictionary beside him all the time, but he didn't understand some Danish words, then he'd have to go to a Danish-Icelandic dictionary. You didn't know he was from Iceland? Boy, has he been keeping his cards close to his vest! I suppose your mother never knew about me. He wouldn't have told her *that*. . . . But you don't know who your mother is, do you? That's bad. Siggie shouldn't have done that."

Bill wrote on his pad, *Can you tell us anything about his background?*

She said, "Siggie came here from Iceland with his parents about

1920, I guess. Somewhere around there. He was about twenty. His dad was a farmer back in the old country, Iceland, but his farm fell into the sea or the cows got measles or something and a friend wrote them the streets were paved with gold here so old Mr. Thorsson brought his family and worked in a big flour mill in Duluth. He learned about the U.S.A. quick. He went out on strike a few years later. It was winter and he caught pneumonia on a picket line and died. Siggie was twenty-four, I know, because he kept telling me he had to support his mother from the age of twenty-four, as if that were something new. You see, he didn't like her. . . . Well, he came East and worked for a few years in the garment center, pushing carts and starving and studying. I guess his mother did some cleaning, but jobs weren't easy to come by in those days. . . . Then he goes to work for this firm in Jersey City, and meets me, at a bus stop, and we fall in love . . . and get married . . . and the marriage starts to fall apart almost before the rabbi's said *Eloachim Eloi*. . . . I could use another martini. His mother was alive in 1962."

Bill started with excitement. She nodded. "Sure. She went back home to Iceland as soon as Siggie and I were married. That was in 1933. She never spoke a word of English. She hated it here. As soon as someone else was looking after him, she went. Siggie never wrote to her, but I did. That was why I said I heard of him once, later. She wrote telling me he'd been to Iceland in June 1939, with a baby—some byblow he was trying to find a home for, I guess. . . ."

Ingrid said, "It must have been me."

Mrs. Rapkin clapped her forehead. "Oh, my God! You're right. Forgive me, please . . . I remember that it was a little girl. Anyway, his mother wrote that he only stayed a week, looking around, and then left with the baby. No, there was no woman with him, honey. . . . Well, we kept on writing, now and then, me in English and her in Icelandic and I'd have to have her letters translated by a professor at Columbia, until 1962. I wrote then because I wanted to know whether she'd seen or heard of Siggie again. There was a guy practicing the *Wedding March* under my window at that time, and I was just checking up, in case. Wedding-schmedding, I'd met this guy on a cruise, I should have pushed him off the boat deck. . . . Old Fru Thorsson answered *she* hadn't seen or heard from Siggie since his visit in 1939. . . . And he was in Russia all the time! He always was pinko."

Ingrid said, "Where does the lady live, my grandmother?"

"It's not a long address. The place is just a couple of barns and three shacks and a big river, Siggie told me. Likeya Mott, Iceland."

Like Yamott, Bill thought. Those were the words Mr. Thorsson had shouted when he left Dr. Alvarez's office.

Mrs. Rapkin said, "It's spelled *Laekjamott,* but pronounced Likeya Mott. You think I speak Icelandic? Hell, no, but I loved your father, honey, and I tried to find out all about him, where he'd come from. Well, he came from Laekjamott, and he dreamed of that place and the salmon swimming up the river to mate . . . though the way he described what they do, any man *I* know would rather have a bowl of Wheaties."

Ingrid said, "Do you know what *Ow vith* means?"

The other woman shook her head. "No, dear. I told you, I never learned Icelandic."

The drinks came. The waiter left, closing the door carefully. Ingrid said, "Do you love him still?"

The flow of words stopped, the jangling watch charm was still. Her voice was composed and low. "My dear child, yes. He was my husband. . . . But thirty-five years is a long time. The edges get blunted. They have to, or a woman would go crazy." She took a long drink.

The wheels rolled with a cushioned, steady hum. Poles, houses, roads made a close, blurred image. The New Century headed into open country.

"What else can I tell you?" Mrs. Rapkin asked. "Not much, because I'm getting fried and all I want to do is cry."

Bill wrote, *Do you have any other memories? Names of people he saw, friends he brought to the apartment?"*

She said, "We didn't have any friends. He worked and I tried to stop him so he'd pay some attention to me. He was too serious for me. He was a very serious man underneath, and I . . . what I thought was serious was sex and babies and the apartment. He didn't care a damn for any of that. Except sex. That we had. It wasn't enough."

"No relics, clothes, books, letters?"

"Nothing. I threw them all out, oh about 1950, one night when I was feeling blue and blamed it on him." She stood up and Bill jumped to his feet. "You know my address . . . I'm going to my roomette and rest for the next two hours. These trips are murder. The men in the business love them. All the little models make a big play for them, if they know the score. But for a woman—an old dame near sixty, it's hell." She took a step, turned back, one hand on the lapel of Bill's jacket. "One thing . . . My, what muscles! Sure you don't want *another* secretary? . . . One thing, I don't want Siggie back. Just in case you had any idea, or he has. Don't tell him I exist. OK?"

When she had gone Ingrid said slowly, "I think my father might have been happy with her, if she had been older in her head then, like she is now. . . . And still I do not know who is my mother. Oh damn, now I want to cry too."

She tipped her glass, shot the vodka down her throat, and began to cry. After a few minutes, while Bill patted her shoulder, she said, "All right. What have we learned? That the words my father said to the doctor in Mexico refer to the place where he was born. I think he might have gone back to the river at Laekjamott, to die there. He told me that his father used to carry him to a river on his shoulders when he was a little boy, and pull him in under his big coat when it rained or snowed and they were at the river. He worshiped his father and told many stories about him. I thought all these stories and the river were in Denmark, but it must have been Iceland."

Bill wrote, *His mother might be alive. Phone VK. Tell him have McCaffery find out about her. Also what* ow *vith means.*

Ingrid signaled for the attendant and asked for a radio phone. When the man connected it, she made the call to VK, who agreed. "Now," she said. "Let us talk about something else. Wasn't that funny yesterday when Anne cried? Just because her brother said rude things about her hair! I would like to see any man try that with *me!*"

Bill bit his lip gloomily. Anne had told him in Mexico that VK would be furious at her for "tarting herself up," and she was right. But she'd done it anyway and it was right for her. The hairdo VK hated was great on her. It completely changed that sense of personality which emanates from anyone as a combination of their physique, manner, toilet, and clothes. It was a new Anne he had taken dancing—a sophisticated woman who laughed and joked and teased. Even though he had spoken little, and that in halting French, she had made him feel witty and wise. And how she danced . . .

Ingrid said, "She loves VK. That's why she cries."

Bill shook his head and muttered, "D-d . . ."

She leaned back, scowling. "It is true. . . . Now I will say something else that is true? I love you. I want you." She caressed the back of his neck.

"*Non*," he said. "*Nyet!*"

"Oh, Beel . . . what is the matter with you?"

He wished he could tell her. And it wasn't only the blockage of words; he really didn't know what was the matter with him. Tentatively he put out his arms, and she came to him. There was a momentary surprise in her green eyes, then the lids dropped and her lips were warm on his. Surely she was not too nice for him, although he knew she was a decent, loyal woman—at least to her father. He had no need to imagine her curves, or her female secret parts, because they were here. The stocking shimmered under his hand, then the velvet of her thigh above the stocking top. She held her legs apart, sprawling back, her head and lips moving rhythmically under his. The texture changed again to roughness, then wet silk, and she moaned suddenly, and thrust up her pelvis.

And, oh Jesus, nothing for her.

"I don't mind! Don't worry!" she whispered. "We have time."

But it wasn't there. How could you tell her that all women sooner or later looked like his mother? If they were basically decent girls he saw the resemblance in time and didn't, couldn't have sex with them. If they were bad girls—the resemblance came too late, in the actual throes, and then he wanted to kill himself.

She opened her eyes and slid to her knees in front of him. She put her hands on his loins and looked up at him. She spoke softly. "Beel, I have had many, many lovers. But I am not a bad woman. We must spend a night together. Please. Because you need a woman like me to show you that women do not divide up like eggs, bad, good, bad, good . . . but like the weather, like the sea—sometimes good, sometimes bad, sometimes calm, sometimes rough, sometimes pure and clean, sometimes . . . the opposite."

He shook his head wordlessly. He knew she was right, but she was not the woman who could teach him. She stooped forward, kissed his loins, and went out, closing the door gently behind her.

The Century flashed on to the East. The seconds slid back, with factory and field and city blurring together, dusk coming. . . .

Had Anne known physical love? Entry into her body? He didn't like to think about it, but he couldn't stop himself. There was something in her eye, in the way she responded to him in the dance, that made him think she had. How could she give him that sense of awareness unless she had known it all herself—the desire, the act, the completion? With whom? What man? Or men?

Ingrid had said flatly that she was in love with her brother. He shut his eyes tight but the pictures would not go. Was it really possible? He closed his eyes. . . .

He became conscious of an extraordinary drowsiness, and his head felt like a football full of cold wool. Someone was sitting at the foot of the couch, a stubby pistol in his hand. The pistol was fitted with a silencer.

The man spoke softly. "Mr. Hammond? Are you feeling all right? No desire to vomit? Nod your head if you feel well . . . reasonably well." Then Bill realized he was loosely but efficiently gagged. His hands were not tied.

He nodded. The man had a mid-European accent, very slight, and now Bill recognized him. It was Trilby.

"We want some information. We did intend to get it from Mrs. Rapkin, but we found that Bosco has taken the precaution of putting a guard on Mrs. Rapkin . . . and on Miss Tellefsen. We cannot afford to wait, so we'll have to ask you. Tell me, for a start, what Mrs. Rapkin told you."

Bill relaxed, his head on the pillow. They wouldn't get him to talk, not in a thousand years.

Trilby sighed. "I can see by the sparkle in your eyes that you are bracing yourself to withstand boiling oil, rats released on your private parts, water dripping on your forehead all the way from here to New York . . . but I can also see that such methods won't work. Now, what will? Tell me."

Bill stared at the man, trying to imprint the features on his brain so they would never leave him. Big brown eyes, soft, rather prominent . . . thin, high-arched brows giving him a permanent slightly surprised or slightly pained look, like a man affronted by an inferior wine. Bald almost pointed dome. Thin hair at the sides, over the ears. Most prominent of all, the red cheeks. He tried to look through the rouge to see what was wrong with the skin itself . . . was it of a rough texture almost like nubbly linen?

Trilby's voice had an edge. "You need not memorize me like a poem, Mr. Hammond. Webber possesses a good two dozen portraits of me, some in Technicolor. . . . Let us get back to you. We know all about your mother, your father, the ladies who comforted him, for a price . . . your feats on football field, golf course, swimming pool, and race track . . . your friends, your girls . . . all either very superior or very inferior, it seems? Your mother has much to answer for. But you are not a pederast? Fundamentally you are a good person, very genuine, very real. 'Square' used to be the word. It was characteristic of you to feel bad that Hawker waited so long to kill our agent on Loch Tummel. You never talked, did you—that was even more characteristic —but Mr. Hawker had no such scruples. De Guise heard, noted, and told us. . . . The most important thing in this business is to know when and how people break, and to know that, you have to know *everything* about them. *Revenons à nos moutons,* as you would perhaps say in my position. . . . I want to know, at once, what you know about Mr. Tellefsen-Thorup. Here." He pushed forward a pencil and note pad. "Write it down."

Bill let the pad and pencil lie on the sheet and kept his eyes fixed on the other.

Trilby said, "We do have a method, you know. I think it will work, and I must use it, because I must have this information. I work for a very unforgiving organization and a very unforgiving man. You've heard of Gregory Parkezian? Though loyal to his family, good to his father, devoted to the memory of his brothers, he is . . . a murderous bastard. Well?"

Bill said nothing.

Trilby took a box the size of a small transistor radio from his pocket, pressed a button and spoke into it. "Go ahead."

His red face moved into darkness as he got up and stood near the door. Bill waited, at first tense, then growing uneasy in spite of himself. What was he up to? Was he releasing more gas, or whatever he must have done before, when he got in? But he hadn't put on a mask or covered his own nose with a handkerchief. He wasn't close enough to use a needle. . . .

The door opened and the attendant staggered in. A second man was behind, helping him, almost holding him upright. Bill sat up sharply, then Trilby's soft voice reminded him of the gun. "Careful."

They closed the door, and the new man helped the attendant into the chair at the foot of the couch. His head rolled sideways, jerked up, lolled again. He was small and old, with a little friz of white hair and short-sighted eyes. His coat was off and his face wrinkled from sleep. The man behind him was big and young, a light-skinned Negro. This man pulled a handkerchief from his pocket and first gagged the attendant, then slipped a pair of handcuffs on him.

Trilby said softly, "He'll come around in a moment. It was only a nick, wasn't it, Jim?"

Jim nodded. "No trouble. He was curled up on his jump seat. I just gave him the needle and set him on his feet right away."

Bill's head stared at the man addressed as Jim. Trilby said, "Our friend thinks he recognizes you, I believe. . . ."

Jim said, "My voice. Sure. I was outside that mine. . . . My voice is more Southern white than Negro, right?"

Trilby said, "All right. Go ahead." The attendant's eyes were rolling in full consciousness now as he understood what was happening to him—or, at least, that he was gagged and handcuffed, and in the presence of a man with a gun.

Jim leaned forward and a knife shone suddenly in his hand. With his left hand he took the attendant's left thumb and slowly began to force off the nail.

It was a long, loving business, expertly done to produce the maximum of pain. Bill felt cold and very sick, and sweat burst out all over him. He would vomit inside the gag. . . . The nail came off finally. Jim took the forefinger of the same hand, and looked at Bill. He was grinning. The attendant's low moans could hardly be heard through the gag.

Trilby said, "It isn't *fair*, is it? That's what you are thinking

Well, no, it isn't. But as I am sure Webber has told you, this business we are all engaged in is not a sport. It is not even crime, which is also personal, and in which one receives rewards and punishments broadly based on one's performance, skill, et cetera. This is war. If this man were to receive frightful injuries in a bombing raid, it would be no different. The raid wasn't aimed at him . . . nor is this. Go ahead, Jim."

The attendant's second nail finally came out. Blood dripped thickly onto the carpet. The attendant's terrified eyes fastened on Bill. Bill's brain raced and stalled, jerked and raced. He couldn't allow this to go on. He must. What did it matter? Why didn't the son of a bitch do it to him? The pain was agonizing, even on another's flesh.

Trilby said, "Now an ear, Jim."

The bloodstained knife crept toward the old man's left ear. His eyes were full of tears.

What the hell principle was he fighting for?—was he allowing the old man to suffer for, he meant. But there were other principles: Helping people. Not hurting them or letting them suffer. And, God, he could lie to Trilby—conceal the truth. Why hadn't he thought of that before?

He seized the paper and pencil and wrote, *Mr. T. visited Mrs. Rapkin three days ago, told her he wanted a divorce, and was going to England.*

Trilby nodded encouragingly. "Very good. What was his real name?"

Bill wrote, *Thorup,* without hesitation.

Trilby nodded again, glancing at Jim. The big Negro took the attendant by the back of the neck and pushed the point of the knife firmly into his left ear. Blood oozed thinly out and the old man wriggled like a fish on the hook. Then his head suddenly flopped.

Trilby said, "We'll bring him around in a minute. Meantime, Mr. Hammond, don't lie. The name Thorup was born with is Thorsson, isn't it? Now tell me where he was born."

It took Bill a minute to control his hand. Then he wrote, *Laekjamott, Iceland.*

"Good. Did Mrs. Rapkin tell you anything else useful?"

He worked electrical firm Jersey City. Left U.S.A. 1936. Visited Iceland June 1939 with Ingrid as baby. Mrs. R. doesn't know where he is now.

"Hmm. And he arrived in the Soviet Union on July 17, 1939, as we all know. Now, what did you learn in Mexico City?"

Bill fidgeted with the pencil. The attendant groaned. Jim took him by the neck again, and held the knife ready. Bill looked at Trilby's soft, implacable eyes. There'd be a rematch. Sometime. Someplace. To the last drop.

He wrote, *Mr. T. saw doctor in Mexico, learned he has acute leukemia.*

Trilby said, "I see. So, of course, it's Dr. Stegmaier whom Webber's gone to Vienna to see, not the nuclear physicists, as we thought. Very interesting . . . Any more?"

Bill wrote, *No. I swear.*

Trilby said, "I believe you, because you have principles, Mr. Hammond. Like me. Unlike de Guise and Hawker . . ." He looked at his watch. "We'll be in Albany in four minutes. Better put them out, Jim."

Jim put away his knife, found a small metal case in his inside pocket, pulled out a syringe, and slipped it into the back of the porter's neck. The attendant's head dropped as though he had been shot.

Trilby said warningly, "It's not fatal, my friend. Not that you could do anything about it if it was. They'll have a hard time waking you, though."

Jim crossed the room in a stride. The needle plunged into Bill's neck just below the ear. The sudden jerk into oblivion came as a welcome release.

Chapter 8

VK CHANGED down from third to second and then, with a counter-movement of finger and thumb, shifted into low ratio and four-wheel drive. The jeep ground on up the steep muddy slope, lurching between boulders and loose stones. Ingrid swayed easily beside him, her face hidden in a parka. Anne, Bill and the interpreter were jammed in the back. Bill, at least, probably loved it, VK thought sourly. The jeep had no top and a wind from the North Pole cut them with cold blades.

Summer in Iceland: bitter wind, stark tundra, far snow peaks. But the quest for Sigurd Thorsson had developed a sense of movement. He felt that they were at least advancing toward the goal. He could not imagine what help old Fru Thorsson could give them thirty years after she had last seen her son, but he was certain they had to talk with her. For himself, he had to see the place where the old man had been born and brought up. This austere earth had shaped Mr. Thorsson's first senses, just as the dry gold of East Africa had shaped his own. . . .

He felt good, too, that they were physically moving across the face of the earth; better, that every day they moved with more difficulty and discomfort as they worked nearer to the bones of nature. And surely he would come closer to the elemental personality of Sigurd Thorsson in such a place.

The baffled searching ended, and the forward movement began, at the marble museum they called Grand Central Station, though you couldn't smell or see a train. There, two nights ago, he and Anne had been waiting on a red carpet in the bright bowels of the earth. Just before the train was due three policemen and an ambulance crew arrived with a stretcher on an electric trolley. Then Harry Bosco came, in a hurry, and muttered in his ear, "I'll take Mrs. Rapkin. You get your friends." He didn't explain, and then the train glided in.

Bill came down the red carpet, Ingrid hanging on his arm in triumph. He felt Anne stiffen beside him.

Then they were close, and he saw that it was not triumph on Ingrid's face. And she wasn't holding onto Bill, he was holding onto her. . . .

They heard the story at the hotel in the morning. Bill had recovered from the aftereffects of the drug. The big idiot, VK thought, had certainly given Trilby all he needed, on a plate . . . yet he'd tried to get out of it. He'd held his tongue as long as he could. He'd lied—and been caught out at once. He wasn't used to lying, that was the trouble. And he hated to see innocent men suffer. Men like Bill Hammond weren't cut out for this line of work. He felt shame that he had betrayed their secret, yet . . . What else *could* I do, he asked, without words. Anne and Ingrid comforted him, telling him over and over he couldn't have done anything else.

Then the action, accelerating . . . News from Bosco: Trilby and the man called Jim had left the train at Albany. No trace yet.

Rapid unanimous decision: We must go to Iceland, at once. Anne called a travel agency: No jets to Iceland today, but a Loftleidir flight would leave Kennedy Airport at ten P.M., due in Reykjavik at ten A.M. the next day, Iceland time.

Then the Icelandic Consulate General: Where's Laekjamott?

The man had never heard of it, but after a time he found someone who had. It was up the river . . . Wait a minute, spell it . . . Laxa-i-Thingeyjarsyslu, seventy miles from Akureyri. Icelandair has daily service to Akureyri . . . And what did *ow vith* mean? . . . It means "the river at." So *ow vith Laekjamott* means the river at Laekjamott? . . . Yes. And *lax* means salmon. It is a salmon river . . . Does Fru Thorsson still live at Laekjamott? We must know immediately, and we'll pay all expenses . . . In that case a telephone call to the local police can be made. We should get a reply within two hours . . . Thank you. Please go ahead.

Anne looked at Bill, worried and tender. Ingrid wandered around the connected suites, polishing her nails, staring out of windows, frowning.

A conference: Trilby would probably send some HPS men on the Loftleidir flight. At Reykjavik it made a connection with an internal flight due at Akureyri at 11:30 A.M.

They must get to Fru Thorsson before the HPS could. OK, how? Bill scribbled a note and VK called the Lear Jet Company in Wichita, Kansas. *This is the private secretary to Mr. Hammond of the Middendorf Company. Mr. Hammond wants a Lear Jet in New York, as soon as possible, ready for overseas flight, with pilot. Mr. Hammond will copilot. Mr. Hammond will buy the plane if he likes it, meanwhile rental rates* . . . A Lear Jet Model 23 will be ready at La Guardia in two hours. It's been used for demonstrations in the New York area. No problem—for Mr. Hammond of the Middendorf Company.

Then, a reply from the Consul General's office . . . Yes, a Fru Thorsson does live at Laekjamott.

Next, transportation from Akureyri to Laekjamott—and an interpreter. Don't forget that the old lady speaks no English. Direct call to Icelandair office in Akureyri . . . a slow, halting conversation. All fixed.

Passports, vaccination certificates . . .

They flew out of La Guardia Airport at three in the afternoon. The Lear Jet climbed away like a baby rocket, burst out through ten-tenths cloud into brilliant sunlight, and swung north. It was north all the way . . . refueling at Goose Bay . . . the stars climbing, the cloud floor turning gray below, scattering, vanishing . . . Denmark Strait brilliant in moonlight . . . now with Bill

Hammond in the pilot's seat, Anne at his side and the pilot back in the cabin, yawning—"Mr. Hammond has the tickets. Besides, he can *fly!*"

Reykjavik's winking tower lights, customs and immigration at midnight, Iceland time. No night operations at Akureyri Airport, so they had to wait till five o'clock, though the light was strong again long before then. Akureyi: two hours delay before they found the man who'd promised to have a jeep and an interpreter ready. The poor bastard—it was only a few hours since he'd been speaking to them in New York, and he hadn't believed that they could *really* be here when they said they would. But finally he'd produced the jeep and the long-nosed interpreter—a schoolmaster —and off they went again.

On the blacktop, Bill drove. After an hour they turned onto an unsurfaced side road. After another hour a battered sign directed them onto a vast moorland, where green lichen clung to black volcanic rock and only wheel ruts marked the "road." They crawled forward between bogs and cliffs and rushing streams. Here VK said, "Let me drive." This was primitive country, and he had a feel for such places. He needed it, for all trace of road soon vanished. They were in fact driving across country—very severe country. Still, they'd made it—so far.

So far . . . the engine coughed and VK swore. He topped a ridge and then it was downward on a steep bare hillside. He slipped her into high ratio and let her coast. The odometer showed that they'd covered sixty-five miles since leaving Akureyri. It shouldn't be far now.

It had better not be . . . the engine spluttered again and nearly stalled.

Five minutes later, as they crawled around the point of a rocky ridge, Ingrid cried, "Laekjamott!"

Three houses and as many barns nestled in the valley a few hundred yards ahead. Three larch trees caught the eye—there had been no trees since Akureyri. A thin rye crop made a green background for the weathered gray wood of the barns. A river lay like a steel blade along the floor of the valley beyond.

The engine coughed again, and again VK looked at his fuel gauge. Over half full—it wasn't that. Perhaps there was dirt in the fuel line. Or it could be the plugs or the timing. Bill knew about engines. He could have a look at it later. He himself was a driver, not a mechanic. At Nyeri there was always old N'dalau, who had worked for twenty years in a Dar-es-Salaam garage before Dad found him and put him in charge of the safari cars. There was something wrong with this bloody machine, all right. Their arrival would not be spectacular.

A hundred yards from the hamlet, the engine died. VK climbed out, stretching and yawning. It felt good to have rock underfoot again. Down there some children and a woman stood by the farthest house, watching. He saw men weeding in the fields beyond the last barn.

VK walked forward, the interpreter at his side. An old woman came slowly out of the first house, leaning on a stick. "That's her," he said to the interpreter. She had Mr. T.'s eyes, the same big frame, above all the same mouth, but hers was turned down and tight where the old boy's was turned up and relaxed. This was a hard woman. They must have been too much alike on the surface, too different deep down, ever to have got on together.

The interpreter spoke. She answered. He said, "She is Fru Thorsson."

VK said, "Tell her we have come to talk—"

But Ingrid interrupted, her hands spread. "Tell her I am her son's daughter! Her granddaughter."

The old woman looked questioningly at the interpreter. She had no sympathy, VK thought. If she were capable of feeling she would know that Ingrid had claimed some special love.

Ingrid's hands dropped slowly to her sides. The interpreter said, "She asks, are you the daughter of the woman he married in America?"

Ingrid said, "No . . . My father will not tell me who my mother is. He says it would be dangerous."

The old woman said, "You are the baby he brought here before the war. That locket on your breast was pinned to your dress. He would say nothing to me, either, of your mother. I knew better than to ask twice. . . . Come."

She went slowly to the house, her stick clacking on the wooden sill. VK turned to Bill. "Will you have a look at the jeep, Bill? If it's going to take time to fix, we'll have to stay the night here. Anne, you stay out too. If another car comes, call at once." Then he and Ingrid followed the old woman.

In the little room there were only two hard, straight-backed chairs. The old lady sat in one, VK in the other, his notebook on his knees. Ingrid and the interpreter stood beside him. They faced the old lady across a bare, scrubbed floor. VK said, "Tell her we are her son's friends. . . ."

Then, through the interpreter, he told her of Sigurd's fame; of his time in the Soviet Union; his flight to the United States; his illness; the possibility that he had come to Laekjamott, or might try to do so. The old woman listened, her hands folded in her lap. Once another, younger, woman peered inquiringly through the open window, but Fru Thorsson silently waved her away. Twice VK caught the hooded old eyes staring at Ingrid as she leaned against the doorjamb, bosom outthrust, like a primitive sculpture of the Earth Mother. Then the eyes came back, the gargoyle face settled again in its wrinkles.

VK said finally, "Has he been here? If not, where does she think he might go? Anywhere else in Iceland?"

Sentence by sentence the interpreter had translated. Now, sentence by sentence, he gave them the old woman's answer. She spoke in short, tired bursts, and while he put them into English, she stared out of the window at the hills.

The interpreter was speaking. "She says Sigurd has not come here. He will not come here while she lives. But, she asks, does Sigurd know that she still lives? She is very old. He will not come because she was always the weight around his neck. When he was small his father would take him to the river. But she went and dragged him back to read his books and fetch peat for the fire. His father stayed at the river, but she made *him* go to school. He hated her. But he looked after her when his father died, though he hated her. And she looked after him, washing and mending his clothes and working also to clean office buildings. Blood is thicker than water. When he married the Jewess her work was done and she came home. Here. Carl, in the next house, uses her land, and gives her food and clothes in return. She needs no more clothes now."

The interpreter's drone ended. The old woman looked impassively out of the window.

VK said, "Does she know why Mr. Thorsson—Sigurd—would have cried out, 'The Laekjamott River'?"

"She says, I was only the wife of Sigurd's father. His mistress, that he loved, was the river. He brought me here as a bride seventy-four years ago. The river became jealous. We had a daughter. She died of pneumonia from river mist, a week old. Then a son . . . When he was three months old I was walking on the bank of the river in flood time, after the melting of the snows, the baby in my arms. I slipped, and he fell into the river. He disappeared at once. Not even his swaddling clothes were found. Who, what, ate his body? Is it strange that I hate the salmon my husband loved so much? Then I had Sigurd. I swore I would not let him go to the river. It was no use. When Sigurd was five his father took him and showed him the salmon in the pools. He said that showing the salmon to Sigurd had been such pleasure to him that he would show the river to others. We could make a living from it, he said. There was an English lord who paid 800 kronur a year for the right to take fish in the Svalbardtsö, and all the fish he caught belonged to Kristen, the farmer, except what the lord wanted to eat himself. Why not us the same, Sigurd's father asked? I told him he was mad. At that time, he was. Now, that English lord's son pays sixty thousand kronur for that same Svalbardtsö. . . . Sigurd's father said we will make enough money to live on, from the English gentlemen, and in addition we will have the privilege of showing them the ways of God's most wonderful and beautiful creation, the salmon of the Atlantic Ocean. . . .

"But war came in Europe. The English could not come. Instead, a rye blight came, and the crops failed, two, three years, one after the other. We knew we would have to leave Laekjamott. I thought Sigurd's father would die. We left. . . . He never spoke of this river again. Of others, but never the Laxa-i-Thingeyjarsyslu. There are other rivers, he said, where the salmon swim up, and perhaps I shall see them, and catch the noble fish, but this one I shall never see again. He could not bear it. . . . The river is the other side of the house. I never look at it."

The heavy humming of bees filled the air and the sun had come out. Summer here was short and violent in the intensity of all the living, and preparation for surviving, that had to happen inside six or seven weeks. VK frowned at his notebook. He ought to check up on the Thorssons' life in America—where exactly they had lived, whom they had known, details of his job with the electrical plant—but the old woman looked tired, and he had a feeling it would be a waste of time. She could not help them find her son, because she herself, and the sense of responsibility she represented, were what Mr. T. was escaping from.

The interpreter said, "She says, please to excuse her. The Myrdals will look after you."

VK walked slowly out of the house, head bent, his thoughts far away. He sat down on the shaft of a farm cart, staring at the purple and green land as though the heather hid an answer. The ground rose steadily southward to a severe distant mountain, where large plaques of snow patched the northward-facing slope. Sigurd Thorsson's native land was a mystical country, of runes and gnomes, and they had passed steam hissing up through snow banks beside black rivers.

Anne came to him. "We're not going to be able to get away today, VK. Bill says he must take the whole carburetion system down, clean everything and put it together again."

"Where do we sleep?" VK asked.

"Mrs. Myrdal there speaks English. She says two of us can sleep in her house and two in the old lady's. They have tiny single rooms that I suppose were used for farm laborers. The Myrdals also have a sort of cupboard room the interpreter can use."

"All right. Are we going to get something to eat?"

"In an hour or so."

"I'm going down to the river. Don't forget to keep a good lookout."

He walked off. Listening to the interpreter and Fru Thorsson had been like prayers and responses in the school chapel: The old woman whispered low and weak, but full of character, the man answered strong but mechanical. And what had it all been about, finally? A commination against the Laxa-i-Thingeyjarsyslu . . . the river's name was an echo of lonely music a long way off. And *lax* meant "salmon."

He passed among rocks green with lichen. A marmot ran away

from before his feet and vanished down a hole, a moment later reappearing to scold him, chattering, for his intrusion. An eagle swung in slow circles against the sun—a fisheagle, he saw, its tail feathers spread and white against the wind. Light cirrus clouds streaked the big, pale sky.

He came to the river. It was about fifty yards across, a good fly cast from either bank to the center. There were no trees to catch the back swing, but plenty of rocks. The faint path reached the river just below a fall, perhaps four feet in height, where it dropped over a fault in the black lava. Above the fall the water swirled quietly, whorled and curled here and there by hidden rocks. Below, after the froth and bubbles from the fall had died out in the tail of white water, it was the same. He walked downstream, and after two hundred paces came to the lip of another exactly similar fall.

A gleam of dull blue caught his eye. He paused, kneeling slowly until a boulder hid him from the water. There it was again. This time he saw the fish clearly . . . three feet long if he was an inch, holding himself steady against the swift water at the foot of the fall . . . now moving across the water, hidden under the surface reflections, now sliding back into sight. The powerful tail suddenly thrust, the fish surged forward, and an instant later broke surface in a clean twisting leap. The sun limned the long silver belly, the thick blue back, the gleaming eye and shining teeth. The fish plunged into the upper pool, its leap successful. Clean run, VK exulted, about twenty-five pounds. A beauty!

"Not so big as your monster in Scotland, but oh, so beautiful!" a woman's voice whispered in his ear. Ingrid settled at his side behind the rock. "Is he going up to find a mate?"

VK said, "Not yet. They don't spawn until October. . . . Have you come for me? Do they want me?"

She shook her head. "No. They have dragged the jeep into the village. Bill is lying under it, covered with oil. He is very happy. I do not understand why men like to get oil on them. Anne is lying under the car with him. She is very happy, too, but that I understand. . . . Why did you come here?"

VK said, "I don't quite know. My feet brought me. To look at what your father loved. But can't come back to."

Ingrid said, "When I was young, I tried to be a son as well as a daughter to my father. But he did not like it. I was very jealous of any little boy he seemed to show attention to. . . . I expected to be jealous of you, but I am not. I wish you could have been my brother, from the beginning."

"Well, I'm not," VK said quietly.

They walked on down the river, past two more falls, two more long pools. Another salmon, smaller this time, broke surface without warning in midstream, and sailed up and over another fall in a long arching curve.

Ingrid sighed, "So much need, so much strength." VK stopped and looked at her. Her eyes were on the river, her lips parted. As he stared, her eyes turned slowly to his, became luminous, went slowly out of focus. He leaned toward her, and her lips were wide, soft, and cool. She sank down, turning her body a little, easing herself. The golden bridge hung in the valley of her breasts. One arm crept around his neck, the hand tentative at first on the back of his head, then strong, affirmative. After a time she said, "Wait." The wind soughed among the rocks, and their bed was the grass beside the river. When she was ready he found her, and entered her. Her eyes were open, fastened on his, she did not smile. Her other arm kneaded his back, and pulled him more firmly into the cradle of her thighs.

She was like the river—the surface apparently calm, secret depths powerfully whorled and sucking—then a fall, sudden vertigo, breathless turbulence, exultation—stillness again.

They lay for a long time. When he wanted to move his weight from her, she said, "No," and held him.

At last she sighed, and he slipped away from her. He tried to say "Thank you," and found himself more moved than he had expected. His voice was hoarse, and he had to clear his throat before he could get the simple words out.

She said, "It is very good. But it is not love. It is need, like them." She jerked her chin at the river, and the unseen salmon. "Poor Beel," she said after a time.

VK said, "What makes you feel sorry for *him?* Didn't you succeed in getting him to seduce you on the train?"

She said, "You have heard of Oedipus?"

"Too bloody much," he said.

"You are very ignorant, sometimes," she said. "I love Beel because he needs me."

"Possibly. But I *want* you. Tonight."

She looked at him with a sort of open calculation. Finally, "All right," she said. "We must be in the same house."

"I'll fix it," he said. "That ought to make Beel feel jealous, if he's going to. Frankly, I don't think he will."

She said, "Nor do I. You do not need me, but you are a good . . . male animal. You know?"

"Thank you, most humbly," he said.

He wondered whether she would have made love with any man, at this place and this moment, beside her father's river. Or was she working off frustration caused by seeing Bill and Anne side by side under the jeep? Or had nothing happened on the train? She was an athletic woman, an outdoors woman, yet she dressed with flamboyant chic. She used fashionable lipstick and excessive eye make-up, which he hated. She had her hair done in bird's nests, which he despised. But he liked her. She was honest. And she wasn't his sister.

Ingrid said, "Something flashed, up there. On the road."

VK looked quickly and this time saw the flash. It was a long way off, but could only be caused by the windshield of a car, about two miles up the road.

He said, "Run back to the others. Keep under the slope—there. Tell Bill to come out, but from behind the hill. I'm going to stop them somewhere on the road here. It must be the HPS."

He saw no more flashes. The car had vanished in a fold of the earth. Ingrid hurried away toward Laekjamott. VK ran the quarter mile up to the road and searched quickly for a place to hide. The giant boulders, flung over all the landscape by prehistoric eruptions, offered plenty of concealment. It took a little longer to find one sufficiently close to the road, and at a place where the car would be going slowly.

He drew his pistol from its shoulder holster, crouched, and waited.

The car came around the shoulder of the hill. It was a Land Rover. When the sound of the engine was almost upon him, he stepped out, the gun thrust forward.

For a moment the engine raced, then de Guise's face came into focus above the barrel of the pistol and the car jerked to a stop. Two other men were with him. One was the sad-eyed little man with the resemblance to Stan Laurel. The other he had not seen before. VK said, "Out. Hands on head. Eyes front."

He stepped behind them. Three determined men, acting in concert, could overcome almost any lone man if they could see what he was doing. He said, "Walk round the front of the car. All of you—sit down on the side of the road, facing the river."

He sat ten feet behind them, the pistol ready. De Guise said in a conversational tone, "You moved amazingly fast . . . and secretly. Our information is that you are still in New York. Congratulations."

VK said, "We're learning, slowly. Now shut up." He looked thoughtfully at the backs of their heads. The HPS had got important information out of Bill Hammond by a show of ruthlessness. It might be a good idea to show them that his side was equally determined. The landscape was large and empty. The gusty north wind rustled the moor grass and chased the clouds down a steel sky. From here he could see that there was only one more fall below the place where he had made love to Ingrid. Below that, the river plunged into a deep gorge cut into the lava. Suppose he took these three to that point, the beginning of the gorge. They'd never be found again, and certainly never recognized. It might be a good idea to take off their clothes and bury them elsewhere. Belts and buckles would last longer than the bodies.

Behind him he heard the crunch of shoes on stone. To the men he said, "Don't look round."

Bill Hammond stood at his side, automatic in hand. He'd come alone, presumably with some idea of keeping the women out of danger. Chivalrous ass . . . in a job like this you needed all the eyes and hands you could muster.

He said, "De Guise and Laurel, from the Embankment. I don't know the third man. Probably a local, from his clothes . . . I bet no one outside the HPS knows they're here. They think we're still in New York, and they wouldn't want to leave a trail for us to follow. They couldn't have arranged it better for us."

Bill said, "*Je ne comprends pas.*"

VK said, "We can get rid of them for good. Knock them on the head and push them into the gorge there. They'd vanish—just as they were planning for us to, at Kaylabito."

VK didn't take his eyes off the men below him. He was aware that Bill was fidgeting uncomfortably at his side. He said impatiently, "For Christ's sake, they've been trying to *kill* us."

Bill felt uncomfortable but determined. He could not allow the killing of these men here and now. For one thing it might bring trouble on Mrs. Thorsson and the Myrdals. And they themselves wouldn't escape. There weren't enough cars around Akureyri so that a Land Rover could go unnoticed. It wouldn't help the quest to spend the rest of their lives in jail in Iceland. There was another point, which Webber had frequently emphasized: de Guise was an HPS man whom they really knew about; they recognized him, they had lived with him, they knew his habits. It would be foolish to get rid of him—unless to save their own lives, or for some other vital cause. He would only be replaced by another man, whom they did not know.

VK could glare like a leopard deprived of its prey—but Bill could not allow the men to be killed in cold blood.

"*Non,*" he said firmly.

VK raised his pistol, as though to shoot the three then and there. He lowered it. "All right, Sir Bloody Galahad. If it's one of us, or Anne, they kill next time, just remember this moment. . . . Disarm them. Take all papers, money, and keys off them."

Bill worked quickly. They were all armed. He put the guns in his pocket. They had no papers, not even car registration or driving licenses.

VK said, "Now, de Guise—walk. Not along the road. That way, over the mountains. If I see you anywhere on the road I shoot at sight."

"What dreadful-looking country," de Guise said. "And it must be forty miles to anywhere, over those mountains. You are so vindictive, VK." He started to walk. A few yards up the hill he turned and waved. "*Au revoir, messieurs.* Give my regards to the ladies." Then he trudged steadily up the long slope, followed by his two companions.

VK put away his pistol. He said, "I always thought the British public-school type was the most squeamishly sentimental ass in the world. Now I know better. First you risk the future of your own country and mine, and the fate of everyone in them, because you're too lily-livered to watch a total stranger having his ear damaged. Now you throw away a unique chance to even the odds against us, and make the high-ups on the other side treat us with considerably more care. Why don't you take up crochet? Well, it's done now. I want you to come down to the river for a moment. We have to talk about what we do next. We can leave the car here. I've got the keys."

Bill nodded. In one sense VK's abuse was justified. But VK must understand that there was a place, a need, for both of them. If everyone acted like VK, what would be left but a vicious jungle? And without VK, they would achieve an *Animal Farm*—and the farmers would be the HPS. VK was looking at him now with a peculiar expression. No, not at him—past him, up at the sky. His head was cocked, listening.

"Jesus Christ," VK muttered, "a helicopter." Bill looked around but they were in open land near the river now. "Lie down," VK said. "Keep your head down."

The chopping roar was still faint but quite clear. A helicopter, Bill thought, fighting down an unreasoning panic. Where could they have got that from? How did they know, so soon, what had happened to de Guise? The sound increased and VK said, "Draw your gun."

Bill watched, his chin pressed into the turf, as the helicopter swept closer over the undulating terrain. Suddenly, above the Land Rover, it stopped and hovered, slowly swinging around.

VK shouted, "They're ours!" and jumped to his feet.

It was a big U. S. Navy UH-46 Sea Knight, and he could see white Navy caps behind the pilots. Someone in the helicopter saw them then, and it swung toward them with a lurch and swoop. It landed close by, the door opened and Joe Webber stepped down, his horn rims gleaming. When he was clear of the rotor blast he put his deformed gray Homburg onto his bald head, where his ears seemed to be supporting it, and said, "Drs. Hammond and Hawker, I presume?" A faintly triumphant grin twisted his wide mouth. "Didn't expect to see me here, did you? Too slow. Too stupid."

He indicated the chopper behind him. The rotors were circling to a stop. A dozen sailors in dress blues, rifles carried, got out, lit cigarettes, yawned and stretched. Webber said, "We're on our way from *U.S.S. Enterprise* to put on a little show for the friendly people of Reykjavik. You forgotten what day it is?"

"July the fourth," VK said. Bill muttered an exclamation. He had forgotten, although he had remembered, when he boarded the Century in Chicago, that it was then July second.

Webber said, "As soon as I heard about what happened on the Century, I left Vienna for this place. . . . Well, what's going on? Is that your car on the road?"

VK explained as they paced up and down the riverbank. Webber said, "So de Guise and his friends are just up there somewhere? Well, let 'em walk. I'll have a good watch on the air and seaports by the time they arrive anywhere— What in the name of God's that?"

"Salmon leaping," VK said. "Bill and I were just about to discuss what to do next. We've learned nothing here."

Webber said, "Except that the HPS are as much in the dark as we are. They proved that first in New Mexico. They just updated and underlined it by sending de Guise here. Well, I tell you what *I'm* going to do now. I'm going to go on doing what I'm trained to do. What I have the equipment and the men to do. I'm following every lead. I'm feeding names, facts, information, into computers and following every variant explanation the machine gives out. I have close to a thousand men on this right now, and when I want more help from any part of the U.S. establishment, anywhere, I get it. You can see that. . . . No trace of Mr. T. in Vienna but I got the names of nearly three thousand cancer specialists, clinics, and hospitals . . ."

Bill noticed some flattened grass beside the river, and saw VK also staring at it with a momentary withdrawn look, his nostrils pinched.

Then VK said, "Look, Webber, you and ourselves are not supposed to be in a competition. We are supposed to be complementing each other. . . . I've been thinking, ever since we got here and talked to Fru Thorsson, his mother. She's over ninety, by the way, and in her mind still as hard as steel." He pointed at the river. "This is the river of Laekjamott. This is the river Mr. T. left with his father, and his father told him they could never come back to. They could catch salmon in other rivers, but not here. . . . Ingrid has told us that whenever he was troubled, he'd go to the river. He'd fish. He complained only that there were no salmon in those rivers. He said the same thing to me in New Mexico. Salmon, salmon fishing, salmon rivers . . . or all three . . . obsessed him. They filled his mind, just below the surface layer. When the news of his illness broke that surface layer, the salmon thing came to the top—like that."

He jerked his chin at the blue and steel shape that arched out of the water, writhed in air, and plunged back in.

Webber said, "You suggesting that Mr. T. thinks he is a salmon?"

"Not that he thinks he *is* a salmon, but that he thinks *like* a salmon. If you want to get a good buffalo you have to think, *I am a bull buffalo, it is such-and-such time of year, the sun is there, I have fed, I shall rest under the big mimosa in the ravine.* . . . Mr. T. is like a fish, driven in a certain direction by an instinct it doesn't understand. And that direction, I think, is fulfillment of what life was for him as a boy. Salmon."

Webber said, "OK. So where's he gone?"

VK said, "Salmon don't go up just any river. They go to particular ones. Mr. T. said in Scotland that even salmon were nothing to him without love. I think he mentioned fighting, but I'm not sure. Also mountains. A place in mountains where he loved and caught salmon? We must keep digging at his past for clues. In the meantime, I think we have no alternative but to look for him wherever *salmo salar* runs."

Webber said, "There are thousands of rivers."

"There are thousands of rivers," VK said, "but not many where big Atlantic salmon are caught. The old boy wasn't a fish scientist, he was a fisherman. He liked big fish, records. We talked a lot about flies and spoons in Scotland and Shiprock. . . . Salmon fishing is a closed sport. It's usually very expensive. Salmon rivers are becoming fewer and fewer as industrial pollution spreads. You have to book years ahead to get a stretch of good water at a good time of year. In most places—certainly in Scotland—everyone in the district knows who's on what water when."

Bill broke in. *"Peut-être il est revenu à Scotland?"*

"He might have. We should ask the British secret service to

check. . . . The CIA are working on the assumption that Mr. T. is trying to find someone who will cure him of leukemia. I think it's all the more important that we—Bill and I—should follow a different track. We should assume that he's trying to get back to freedom, happiness—being young again, whatever you like to call it. And I'm quite sure that means salmon, though there are other factors we may not yet know about. So we should start systematically checking the principal centers for sport salmon fishing. We ought to use McCaffery again to do the spadework for us. Get a list of the places and the rivers. Find out who's taken out licenses in all those places since June seventeenth. Check which of those people never had a license before."

Webber said, "And you?"

VK shrugged. "Bill and I have to discuss it with Ingrid. . . . We might go to Norway. I believe they have the world's largest Atlantic salmon there."

Webber said, "Canada might be good. I know a lot of American tycoons fish the Miramichi and the Restigouche, and do they pay for it! Well, I think you're on the wrong trail, but go ahead. Only, I must be able to get hold of you in a hurry if I have to."

"And vice versa," VK said grimly.

"Right. Why don't you use Monroe Barnett as a clearing office? Keep him informed. He can always get a message to me through my Director. . . . You fellows want a ride anywhere?"

Bill shook his head, and Webber said, "Of course, you have the ladies with you, don't you. . . . Well, I have to be on my way. To Zurich tomorrow."

A few moments later they watched the helicopter rise, bank, and sweep away.

At the Land Rover VK said, abruptly, "Is the jeep fixed?"

Bill shook his head. It was going to take another couple of hours' work to clean the fuel lines properly. If there was any hurry, they could always use the Land Rover.

VK got behind the wheel and started the engine, but did not put the car in gear. He sat awhile, staring forward, and then, without turning his head, said abruptly, "So we'll have to spend the night here. If Ingrid and I take the rooms in the Myrdals' house, can I trust you not to fool around with Anne?"

The car jerked forward. Bill slowly fought down a desire to

punch his companion in the teeth. He scrawled in his notebook and as they reached the houses thrust the piece of paper under VK's nose: *Mind your own damn business.*

VK left the house after the early dinner and walked alone by the bank of the river. It was broad daylight. Ingrid would be waiting for him as soon as he was ready to go back. Waiting, and wishing he was Bill Hammond.

He saw Anne coming down from the houses, but pretended not to. She came up behind him and linked arms without a word. She knew he'd heard her feet in the grass. After a time she said, "Bill told me what you said."

"How?" he asked. "Chanting in Choctaw?"

"In English. He can sometimes get a few words out, when we're alone. . . . You mustn't dislike him so much, VK. He's a gentleman. He can't help it."

VK laughed sourly.

"Remember talking our last night in the Savoy?" she said. "Well, I think I'm falling in love with Bill, and it terrifies me, because I still don't see any answer."

He did not speak and after a time she left him with a quick kiss on the cheek. He walked on, alone again.

Chapter 9

BILL PASSED the newspaper to VK. Ingrid leaned over VK's shoulder to read it. She looked up. "Is this what you mean? About the British observatory seeing an explosion on the moon?"

Monroe Barnett nodded. VK asked, "Well, what does it mean?"

Anne said, "I suppose it means that the Russians have sent a rocket with a nuclear warhead to the moon."

Barnett said, "It wasn't powerful enough for that. Jodrell Bank recorded it as equivalent to only a hundred tons of TNT. But satellite radars detected no rocket."

VK said, "God! EAD?" He dragged nervously at his cigarette. Sitting around in New York, doing nothing, staring at Bill Hammond, wondering whether he'd seduced Anne at Laekjamott—it was all getting to be too much for him.

Barnett ran a hand through his shock of white hair. "NASA is afraid so. Palomar picked it up, too, but didn't publish, on an urgent request from the National Security Board. They hoped that no one else would notice. But the British did. Now our people are hinting that we did detect a rocket, to turn speculation away from EAD."

VK said, "How much was this—how many thorups, or whatever?"

Barnett said, "The Director explained it to me. . . . The formula's the same as for gravity, that is, the force varies inversely with the square of the distance."

Anne said, "The moon's 238,000 miles away."

VK thought, Suppose it's five thousand miles from the nearest point in Russia to any vital target in the U.S.A. The moon was nearly forty times that distance. So, if they could deliver one hundred equivalent tons on the moon, they could deliver one hundred multiplied by forty squared, tons, on the U.S.A. One hundred and sixty thousand equivalent tons of TNT. One hundred and sixty kilotons. Without material means of transmission. He said, "Why haven't they destroyed us already?"

Ingrid said crossly, "The Russians are not all barbarians. . . . Besides, this may be the only machine they have—my father would know—and before they can fire it again the Americans could send over many rockets."

"Yes. It can't just keep creating energy at that rate."

"But at a lesser rate, perhaps," Barnett said. "The Director thinks that this is how they are going to power their Jupiter probe and the manned Mars shot. He also thinks they haven't yet learned how to change the direction of the transmission. I mean, it has to be a line-of-sight thing. Otherwise, why make this obvious bang on the surface of the moon, where instruments can detect it, instead of bouncing it off a satellite and back to some empty part of Siberia, say?"

VK got up and lit a cigarette. Mr. Thorsson was looking for salmon somewhere, somewhere wild and far away, while they gossiped in this bloody satin-lined hothouse. The acrid smoke from his cigarette filled the room.

Barnett said, "Have you decided where you're going first?"

Anne said, "Norway, as soon as McCaffery's man calls us from Oslo. We have to wait for that. . . . Bill wanted to ask you about the salmon rivers of Canada. He thought he might go there, while

VK and I go to Norway. . . . Do you know the Miramichi?"

Monroe Barnett's hand shot out, knocking his martini glass to the floor.

Anne jumped up. "Don't worry . . . I'll ring for another."

Barnett muttered, "I am sorry. That was very careless of me. . . . What was it you were saying when I interrupted you?"

"Bill said that Mr. Webber mentioned two salmon rivers in Canada. He thought the names were Restigouche and Miramichi."

Barnett said, "Ah, I see. . . . Yes, they are well known. They are both in the Canadian province of New Brunswick. The Restigouche is nearly all owned by private syndicates or clubs of very rich men, mostly from this side of the border."

"Could Mr. Thorsson get to fish on it?"

Barnett shook his head. "Not unless he's a friend of someone belonging to one of the clubs. And we know he isn't." He looked at his watch.

Bill wrote, *The Miramichi?*

Barnett rose to his feet. "He might get a rod in there, but . . ." He shrugged. "You have McCaffery checking into the licenses that have been issued, don't you? That's the best you can do. Personally, I feel in my bones, quite illogically of course, that Mr. Thorsson would go back to Europe for his salmon, or his cure." He started for the door. "Webber's in Brussels, by the way. He reminded me to make sure you kept in touch. So do tell Miss Wright how she can get hold of you. She'll take charge while I'm away. Now, please excuse me. I'm supposed to be dining in Washington with a *very* persnicketty old lady, and the plane may be late. And I haven't packed for tomorrow yet."

VK said, "One thing, sir . . . Are the FBI trying to trace that policeman who arrested Mr. Thorsson in 1936? Good . . . And I think we need expert advice about salmon rivers. We need a list of them all, according to quality, availability of water, et cetera. McCaffery could waste a lot of time inquiring in places where no one in his right mind would look for a big salmon."

"My father is not really well in his mind," Ingrid said.

"About salmon, I think he will be," VK said.

"I'll make inquiries," Barnett said. "*Fish and Wildlife* will know. Miss Wright will call you."

The door closed behind him. VK said, "The Lord Chief's in a hell of a hurry this evening, isn't he?"

Ingrid flared. "He's going to Paris tomorrow, remember? And why do you have to be nasty about everyone? Mr. Barnett's a very proper man."

"That doesn't mean we have to pretend he's perfect. I think he's a little pompous."

"He can't help it," Anne said.

"I didn't say he could, did I?" His temper was getting worse than ever. He *must* get out into the country.

Ingrid said, "Please put out that awful thing, VK, or smoke it in the passage."

VK puffed at his cigarette. He said, "Wait till we hear from McCaffery! Wait till we have heard from a salmon expert!" He fumed in silence. *No one* seemed to know what to do. Not even the HPS. According to Bosco, the last CIA report on Robert de Guise, since he'd reached Montreal from Iceland, had him just sitting in his hotel room, doing nothing. Well, they can afford to wait. They have EAD. We don't.

He snarled, "Wait and see! A lot of bloody twentieth-century Gladstones, that's what we are. I'm going out for a walk. I'm going to walk from one end of this island to the other."

"Shall I come with you?" Anne said.

"No."

He would only take his bad temper out on her, and that wouldn't help. Tomorrow, unless something urgent cropped up, she was going sailing with Bill. He and Ingrid would stay in the hotel. Ingrid would sulk, because Bill hadn't invited her sailing. The hell with all of them. He went out.

Bill took in the sheet and brought the Sprite slowly up into the breeze. Here on Long Island Sound the wind was light from the northwest, and a heat haze almost hid the Connecticut shore. As he worked the Sprite westward, where ruffled water showed stronger air currents around Lloyd's Neck, he kept his eye on a big Shields Class sloop flying the pennant of the Seawanhaka Yacht Club. It was edging up on the port tack. If her skipper held his course she would foul him soon.

Anne was crouched beside him. Her legs looked good in Jamaica shorts. She asked, "Who has the right of way now?"

Bill pointed at himself, then at the sail.

"We do. Oh yes, because we're on the starboard tack? We're getting awfully close. Perhaps he doesn't know the rules."

Bill pushed the tiller hard over to starboard, loosed the sheet, and fell away. The Seawanhaka boat glided ahead, its skipper glancing back with a small, hard grin.

Bill moved over and gave Anne the tiller. He should have held his course and forced the Seawanhaka man to go under his stern. And, if there was a brush, report him. Well, he hadn't done it, because he didn't have the phony competitive fire in his belly, and now that his father was dead he no longer needed to pretend he did. People used to think he had it, in his football days, but all he'd had was terror of his father. Technically, for instance, he was a good enough sailor to crew on an America's Cup twelve-meter, and at one time he'd thought of taking up big-time yachting.

Anne said, "I like sailing. The climate's so wonderful here, compared to England. Of course, I don't really know much about England."

He was amused to see her cast her eye up to the leech of the mainsail, then to the foresail, the compass, the horizon, and astern, just as he had taught her. She said, "Africa's my home. And yet it isn't. No one will let it be."

"VK won't. Is that what you meeee-?" Damn. Just for a moment it had flowed like oil from his tongue.

She said, "The clients just seemed to get worse and worse. . . ."

"*Et vous . . . tu?*"

He stopped. He had been trying to define the question more closely. Do you like *your* job? What *is* your job? How much longer are you going to stay as a satellite to VK? But the words stopped there, and he thought, That's right, they say it all—*And you?* "You" in the special, intimate second person singular.

She said, "I have been very happy, Bill. I can't really imagine any life without . . . him."

After a time, he said, "*Tu dois aller au coiffeur, encore.*" The Iceland winds had blown her hairdo to bits.

She said, "Perhaps." He looked away from her towards the land.

It was hard for her to be disloyal to VK, even in this ridiculous thing of how she did her hair. It was infuriating . . . yet, if she were different, he wouldn't feel the way he did about her.

He said, "And, this eeeevening, we'll g-g-go to the the theater." She said, "Oh yes, I'd love to . . . With VK and Ingrid?" He said, "No."

It was Anne's turn to avoid his eye.

They said no more. Bill realized it was four hours since he'd thought of a drink. The cat's paws of air died away, and the sail slatted feebly in a near calm. Gradually a small breeze grew from dead astern. The little boat glided over silver water past Lloyd's Neck, past Sagamore Hill and into the yacht club basin at Cold Spring Harbor. The attendant said, "Mr. Hammond? A lady asked you to call as soon as you got in. There's the phone."

Bill followed Anne into the little telephone booth, and they stood pressed together while Anne listened, holding the earpiece a little away from her ear so that both could hear. It was Ingrid. "Mr. Bosco called. They lost track of de Guise for two hours this morning, then found that he had flown to a place called Fredericton, in New Brunswick, Canada. Still under the name Duchamp. With two other men. Trilby saw them off. I can't get VK. He is walking around New York again, but I think he will be in soon. What shall I do?"

Bill thought quickly: De Guise had gone to New Brunswick, the province with the famous salmon rivers. Trilby saw him off. He *must* be on Mr. Thorsson's track. Monroe Barnett's hunch, about Mr. T. going to Europe, must have been wrong.

Anne said, "Are Mr. Bosco's men going to pick up Robert's trail in Fredericton?"

Ingrid's tinny voice said, "McCaffery will do that."

Bill scribbled on his pad, *Ready Lear Jet. VK and I will go.*

Anne said, "Bill says he and VK will fly up there in the Lear Jet. Will you call La Guardia to get it ready? We'll be back in an hour."

"Wait . . . Miss Wright, Mr. Barnett's secretary, called to say that she has spoken with the biggest expert on salmon fishing in the country, and he says that the best places for Atlantic salmon are Norway, Scotland, Iceland, England, Spain, Newfoundland,

New Brunswick. She gave me a long list of the best rivers in each of those places. Shall I read them to you now?"

"When we come back, please, Ingrid," Anne said.

"And McCaffery has found McCready, the policeman who arrested my father in 1936. He—"

"Tell us when we come back, Ingrid," Anne said. "We must hurry." She hung up.

She turned toward Bill. She was smiling and excited. The parted lips drew him down and he kissed her. Her mouth was warm and wet and salt-sharp. It opened gently, giving, and her body stirred against his. He thought of his sleepless hours in Laekjamott, knowing she was there through the wooden wall, wondering whether she was awake, imagining her nakedness. The memories stiffened his loins rigidly against her. She pulled gently away, her eyes large.

They were still in the Lear Jet, the compressors whining to a stop, when the battered station wagon drove up to the hangars. It was the last of the summer daylight and the electric lamps shone bright on their towers. A man got out and came toward them. Bill locked the brakes and slid out of the pilot's seat, flexing and unflexing his fingers.

"That's McCaffery's agent, I bet," VK said. "You can tell a retired flattie a mile away."

The burly man in blue jeans, checked shirt and moccasins was waiting as the professional pilot opened the door. Bill went down first, while VK stayed in the doorway, his hand in his pocket. They exchanged recognition codes. This was a McCaffery man.

VK turned to the pilot. "I've no idea how long we'll be." He jumped down behind Bill.

The pilot waved. "Don't worry. I'll stay by the phone."

As soon as they were in the station wagon with their light baggage, the agent drove off. He swung out onto the main road. "I'm Doug Sheppard. . . . Your three men arrived at three o'clock this afternoon. I recognized de Guise from the description the head office gave me. The second man looks like a fat Chinese—big guy with thin black hair and drooping mustaches . . ."

"Mandarin, from the Embankment," VK interjected.

"The third fellow's tall and thin, with a broken nose. Another guy—never saw him before—was waiting for them in a green International Harvester Traveler, license New Brunswick 48490. They drove through Fredericton and north on Route 2—the Trans-Canada—to Hartland. That's a little town about eighty miles up the St. John River. They got there a little after five, and took two motel rooms. The man I had tailing them phoned me an hour ago—at seven."

"Is their car four-wheeled drive?" VK asked.

"Yes. It looks like a camp car only it doesn't have any camp name on it. It's four or five years old and pretty beat-up."

"Inconspicuous," VK said.

Bill saw that VK was looking out of the window, his head up like a pointer, but his mouth relaxed. The dark forest on one side; the great river on the other, scattered lights reflected in its unseen surface; the night air blowing through the car—all were acting to make him a fairly reasonable human being instead of the bad-tempered s.o.b. he'd been in New York.

Bill said, *"Hartland, est-il fameux pour la pêche de saumon?"*

The agent said, "Say, you French Canadian? Oh . . . Well, Hartland's the center for a number of hunting and fishing camps in Carleton County, in the headwaters of the Main South West Miramichi. They get real good fishing up there."

VK said, "So the Lord Chief *was* wrong. . . . Have your people found out anything from checking the licenses?"

The agent said, "It's damn difficult. Practically anyone can issue an angling license in this province—stores, sporting goods retailers, camp operators, the lot. Of course they have to send the names and details to St. John, but they're in no hurry."

"Is it possible to fish without a license?" VK asked.

The agent laughed. "Hell, no! You wouldn't stand a chance, not even if you parachuted into the middle of the forest at night. . . . The law is that to fish from a boat you must have one guide per man. It's one guide per three men to fish from the bank. The guides are responsible for seeing that the dudes have licenses, don't break creel or size limits, and all that. Believe you me, they *do!* Their living depends on it—the same way it depends on no one being able to fish without hiring them."

The car began a jerky stop-and-go passage through Fredericton. They sat silent until they were out of the town and accelerating away through lumber mills sharp with the smells of cut wood and burned sawdust.

Bill's thoughts returned to the brief report which McCaffery's New York office had filed on McCready, the policeman. McCready remembered arresting Mr. T. quite well, because he'd only made six arrests during his time on the force. It was in a bar on Eighth Avenue near 14th Street. He was on his way to another assignment after special duty at some kind of political demonstration. A bartender ran into the street and asked him to stop a disturbance. Inside the bar he found a free-for-all going on. He yelled for everyone to stop fighting, but no one paid any attention, except this man who grabbed his coat and hit him over the head with a bottle. McCready couldn't remember what the demonstration was about, but the files of the *New York Times* were being examined.

The car settled down to a steady sixty and Bill dozed off.

VK knew something had gone wrong as soon as he saw the face of the McCaffery man in Hartland. He came to their motel room as soon as they had checked in. The time was a few minutes past eleven.

Sheppard let him in and, without waiting for introductions, he blurted out in a low whisper, "They left town just before eight, Mr. Sheppard. I tried to call you, but I guess you were at the airport. Three of them went—de Guise, the Chinese-looking fellow, and the tall guy with the broken nose. The other, the driver, stayed back. He's in his room in the motel there across the road . . . unless he slipped out the back way. One guy can't keep tabs on more than—"

"OK, OK," Sheppard snapped. "Where did they go?"

"East on 107. You know it? It goes through the fishing country to Juniper Station and Napadogan, then back to Fredericton. . . . As soon as they turned onto 107 I telephoned a pal in Napadogan to watch out for them in case they were just going right back to Fredericton. Then I followed on again. I didn't see their car at all. . . . There are no side roads, but when I got to Napadogan my pal said they hadn't been through there, so I turned around and drove back. Still didn't see 'em. They must have pulled off into the woods somewhere. There's a full moon, but I couldn't see their car, or anything. I had to drive like hell to get back here in time to meet you."

"Well, for Christ's sake," Sheppard said, "did you have time to call some of the camps before de Guise drove off?"

The local man said eagerly, "Sure thing . . . Sweet Brothers have one new dude, but he's from Montreal and the cook says he knows the guy's family. Tweedie and Maurice Biggar don't have any. Miramichi Camps have twin brothers who say they're from Utah and they're about five feet tall, so they're out. Weddie has dudes just arrived, but he knows them from before. Burnthill's closed, except for one regular couple. Least, that's what the gravel pit guard at Deersdale says and that's the best information you can get."

"Why?" VK asked.

The man said, "Burnthill's way back in. Dennis Parchment, the boss, won't have a telephone, electricity, road, nothing. Just privacy and the best food and liquor and fishing you can get. You have to reserve like two years ahead, and own a piece of Fort Knox. The only way in is by canoe from Deersdale—that's where the Miramichi turns away from the road. This guard has the key to a little hut there, where stores for Burnthill are dumped. I spoke to him on my way back from Napadogan just now. He said Burnthill's closed, except for this old couple, Mr. and Mrs. Andrew Jackson, he calls them, because that's who the man looks like. They come most years, and hire the whole camp. . . ."

VK jumped off the bed and paced up and down the narrow space between the feet of the beds and the TV set bulging out from the opposite wall. He spoke as though to himself. "De Guise couldn't have gone into one of the fishing camps along that road or you'd have seen him. . . ."

"And the owners would have called me," the man said. "They promised to."

"Except that he could have gone to Burnthill? By canoe?"

"No canoes are out from the camps, or the Deersdale dump. I asked."

"By road, then."

"There's no road, like I just told you. Well, there's a kinda logging road goes in four, five miles from near Juniper Station. Not all the way."

"And after that they'd have to walk through the forest? There's a full moon. Bright as day out there."

"Jesus, mister," the local agent cried. "You ever seen that Miramichi country? It's godawful going—fallen timber, swampland, cliffs, underbrush thick enough to skin a rabbit, black flies as big as Boeings and thirstier'n vampires."

"How much farther is it, from where they'd have to get out of the car? It's a four-wheel-drive job, remember."

"To Burnthill? I don't know. Never been in there. No one has. . . . About twenty miles, maybe."

"Anyone know anything about this Mr. and Mrs. Andrew Jackson?" The agents shook their heads.

VK paced in silence. It was possible that de Guise was not going to Burnthill but to some other place that no one had ever heard of. But on the available evidence he was heading for Burnthill camp. Why? There was no clue. He was not going the direct way, which presumably would have been to report to the gravel-pit guard at Deersdale and be taken downriver in one of the camp canoes. He was going on foot then, with two other men. Moonlight or not, they would not get far at night in country such as the agent described.

He swung around. "Can we get a canoe? At dawn?"

The agent said, "I guess so. Sure. From Deersdale. The guard there will go down with you."

"We must go by ourselves."

The agent said, "No soap, mister. Those are real birchbark canoes. They're a dream, *if* you know how to handle them. If you don't—" He shrugged.

VK turned to Bill. "I bet you know how to manage a birchbark canoe."

Bill nodded.

VK said, "I knew it. . . . Look, I think Bill and I must get to Burnthill ahead of de Guise. If we go down the river while they're hacking through the forest, we stand a good chance, even though they do have a start. But we must be in the canoe at first light. . . . One of you ought to keep an eye on the man across the road. The other will have to drive us out to Deersdale. After dropping us, he ought to take the logging road as far as possible, then follow up behind de Guise's party on foot. . . ."

He looked at his watch. Near midnight. They ought to be on the river at four. There was food and drink to get, at least some chocolate, chewing gum . . .

Bill knelt in the back of the birchbark canoe, his folded jacket under his knee. How many years was it since Dad had sent him to Camp Wawenakee in the upper peninsula of Michigan, with orders to come back an expert in canoeing, archery, riflery, and volleyball? Long enough, but fortunately you never forgot the knack of balancing a canoe and handling the paddle.

VK sat in the center of the canoe, looking forward. The river curved down green and broken white under the avenue of the larches. The light grew steadily in a cloud-scattered sky, the water gurgled under the bow.

A long reach opened up, the current slackened, and Bill settled down to the slow voyageurs' stroke they had taught him so long ago. . . .

VK raised his hand and Bill, peering past him, saw the white water at the head of a rapid. VK made the washout sign and Bill turned the canoe toward the bank. They lifted it out of the water, upturned it on their heads, and began the portage. The black flies descended on them, sniffed the heavy coating of protective oil, and hovered maddeningly, buzzing loud in their ears.

The rapids ended a hundred yards downstream. The portage trail came out of the woods and they relaunched the canoe. VK said, "Those bloody flies have become addicted to this mosquito oil. They're injecting the stuff back into me." He slapped angrily at his neck, and with a handkerchief wiped away the blood. They slid on down the river.

"Two hours," VK threw over his shoulder.

Bill said nothing. How far had they come? Nine, ten miles perhaps. In clear water the canoe did a good ten knots, but then there were the portages, and slow careful work in rocky sections . . .

Later VK said, "Look there. On the left."

The forested hills swept down to the river on both sides. A couple of hundred yards forward on the left a strip of the hill, low down, seemed to be bare.

"Tree stumps," VK said. "A clearing . . ." The canoe slid closer. "No, it's not. It's a road . . . the logging road! They must have cut it farther in since the agent last knew it. Turn into the bank! Here!" His voice was suddenly low and urgent. Bill looked up and saw he had a finger to his lips. He bent his back to the paddle and the canoe surged toward the bank. In the shallows VK stepped out, held the canoe steady, and whispered in Bill's ear, "They may have dropped a man off there. . . . Don't go round that corner until I'm at those rocks there. Here, bundle the coats to look like me sleeping, something . . ."

Bill watched him wade ashore, the pistol drawn in his hand. Then he crept along the edge of the river, ducking under over-hanging boughs, once or twice cutting inland and momentarily out of sight. At the big rocks, where the river took a sharp bend, he stopped and waved his arm. Bill began to paddle.

So—he was being used as the bait, in case some HPS thug was lurking around the corner. He felt chilly between the shoulder blades, but it was not the HPS that he was afraid of. This was Anne's jealous brother, up there behind the rock. His life was in the hands of V. K. G. Hawker, who sometimes acted like a man, sometimes like a beast of prey.

He turned the corner and a long stretch of river opened up. He paddled steadily, wondering for how long the bundled coats in the bow would deceive the enemy—if there were one. . . .

Two shots boomed under the trees, the sound dulled by the roar of the river. He saw a man sliding and rolling down the steep earth bank below the cut of the road. The body rolled into the water with a splash, and disappeared. Bill began to paddle toward the place when he heard VK's call. "He's dead."

He swung the canoe with difficulty against the current and inched back upriver. VK was reloading his pistol. He stepped in and said, "Go back to where the man rolled down. It was Manda-rin—the Chinese fellow the agent described. He had a bead on you. Think we'll be able to pick up his body?"

Bill shook his head. He knew the ways of rivers such as this. The man was wearing a red shirt, which would show well if the body came near the surface. But the water was deep and it might stay down there forever, caught on a snag. Or it might strand on a sandbar in five minutes, and stay till the spring floods.

Bill put the bow to the bank and VK stepped out and scrambled up the bank. Bill saw him kneel, stare up and down the road, then walk off. Five minutes later he came back. "Their car's hidden in the woods just up there," he said. "Engine still warm . . . only been stopped an hour or so. The road ends there. Well, if they're only an hour ahead, on foot, we ought to beat them easily now."

The canoe swung easily and fast into the stream. In five minutes the trace of the road disappeared as the river cut away into virgin forest. They rode on among trees and rocks and swooping kingfishers. Bill saw no trace of the dead man, and after a time gave up looking. He settled down to his paddling. He felt that his strength would never give out. He could go on forever, night and day . . . hour after hour . . . after hour. . . .

The sharp point of the submerged bough came down the center of the canoe like a scalpel—hardly a shudder, only the water springing through, the black point of the bough ripping past his knee, and suddenly the canoe losing its youth, growing old and heavy under his hand.

Bill made two desperate strokes, turning the bow toward the nearer bank, then they were in the river. He grabbed his coat and VK did the same. The water was waist-deep and the strength of the current nearly swept them off their feet, but their reaching hands met and together they waded to the bank.

They turned and looked at the river. The canoe was gone, the paddles vanishing in the distance. "*Cone-yo!*" VK said. "Now we've got to walk, too. Or swim. How far do you think we have to go now?"

Bill held up two fingers, then three.

"Two or three miles? God!"

They slipped back into the river and for half a mile floated down on their backs. Then rapids came and they floundered to the shore. A portage trail curved down on the south side, and they hurried down it, their shoes squelching.

At the far end Bill sat down on a rock. "*Fatigué,*" he said. In truth he felt suddenly exhausted. Perhaps it was the sudden disappointment of losing the canoe when everything had been going so well.

VK said, "Sorry. I forgot you've been paddling. . . ."

Bill arched and stretched his back, slowly spread and stretched his fingers, and relaxed. A thought made him chuckle. VK said shortly, "What's the joke?"

Bill said, "*Où avez vous appris le mot coño?*"

"*Cone-yo?* It's a Russian swear word. Or Yiddish. At least, I suppose so. Mr. T. shouted it the first time he saw our record salmon jump on the Tay. It sounded wonderful, better than mere obscenity. I've been using it quite a bit."

Bill hesitated. How did you explain that if you grew up in California, among Mexican field hands and servants, you couldn't help learning that *coño* was the Spanish for snatch? He said, "*C'est le mot espagnol pour la chose des dames.*" He pointed to his crotch.

VK said, "Well, I'm damned. So I've been shouting 'cunt' all over the place! And so did old Mr. T. He must have been in Mexico before. Perhaps that explains why he went back there when he felt that he was ill. Well, I'll mind my language in future."

A thought niggled in the back of Bill's mind and then, like a faulty connection, sparked out. He tried to bring it back but it would not come.

VK said, "If you're ready . . ." Slipping and sliding, swimming and wading, falling and crawling, they plunged on down the river.

Nearly two hours later Bill saw log cabins ahead on the right bank. Here, the Miramichi made a big loop, first turning left and then curving back right. The land on the inside of the curve was almost flat and partly cleared of timber. There, under the slope of the southern ridge, half a dozen log cabins clustered around a larger ranch house. The Canadian flag flew from a tall white-painted pole. A man in a blue baseball cap was waving a fishing rod on the riverback; two others were peeling potatoes outside the ranch house; wisps of smoke curled up from the ranch house chimney.

The man in the baseball cap saw them coming. A moment later he turned and looked across the river. Bill saw two men come down to the far bank, directly across from the camp, and start wading over.

"De Guise and the tall man," VK said. "A dead heat."

Bill and VK walked across the neck of land. De Guise and the tall man climbed out of the water. Their clothes were torn and their faces marked by scratches and insect bites. That's just how we must look, Bill thought—like a pair of murderous tramps.

They all met in front of the man in the baseball cap. He was a big man with a hard jaw hiding under creases of fat. The rod weaved gently back and forth in his right hand. "Well, well," he said. "Visitors." There was no welcome in his tone.

For a moment they stood, locked in a situation that none had foreseen. Bill thought grimly, Now everyone's tongue-tied.

De Guise recovered first. He said, "Forgive us for arriving like this. We have come to talk to a friend. It is rather important. A business crisis, you understand. Your man at Deersdale wasn't there so we had to come by car and on foot. . . . You are Mr. Parchment?"

The man in the baseball cap said, "What's your friend's name?"

De Guise said, "Mr. Tellefsen . . . but he's so well known in his field that he does occasionally use other names to conceal his identity from the press. Thorsson. Thorup."

"He's not here," Parchment said.

"I think he must be," de Guise said suavely. "He might be using any name."

Bill, watching de Guise, thought that he had probably expected to use force at this point. The arrival of VK and himself had prevented that, and de Guise was making up a plan as he went along.

Parchment turned to Bill. "What's *your* story?"

VK said, "These men are Communist agents. We are working for the CIA and the British Secret Service. We have reason to think a famous scientist may have come here to fish for salmon, probably yesterday or the day before, but he might have arrived any day since June 18. These men want to abduct or kill him. We want to protect him from them."

"A perfect explanation," de Guise murmured. "Except that it is topsy-turvy."

VK went on. "Our man is big, gray-haired, looks ill, seventy-one years old, Scandinavian origin, mad on salmon fishing. If he's here, don't let these men get near him. Tell him VK's here. And call the police."

Mr. Parchment carefully rested the butt of his rod on the ground. His jaw stuck out. "I don't know which of you's telling the truth. Fortunately, I don't have to know. There's no one here like you describe. . . . Now, beat it." He put two fingers to his mouth and whistled. Two tall young men came out of the ranch house. The resemblance showed them at once to be his sons. He said, "See these four guys?" The young men nodded. "Get your rifles. If you see any of them around here after five minutes, drill 'em."

"Sure thing," the biggest young man said amiably.

Parchment said, "Now, like I said, beat it. The way you came. All of you."

As the two young men came back out of the ranch house, loading their rifles, de Guise and his companion set out to recross the river, and Bill led VK back across the flat land, into the river, and slowly, painfully, up it.

As soon as the curve of the hill hid them from the camp VK said, "Out here. We'll get onto that slope behind the camp."

Bill said, *"Vous pensez que Mr. T. est ici?"*

VK said, "I don't know. There's something strange. Parchment was worried as hell. And he couldn't keep his eyes from wandering up the hill, as though he expected someone to come down from there. . . . Go very carefully, because those men have rifles and we only have pistols. And look out for de Guise. He isn't going to take no for an answer, either."

They worked up a densely forested rocky slope, on a line that would lead them around in a half-circle to the rear of the camp. After nearly an hour the slope eased, leveled, and fell away. They were above and behind Burnthill Camp. Trees obscured part of the scene but they could see Parchment, at the river, rod in hand, but now a gun belt and holster conspicuous at his waist. One of the sons dozed outside the ranch house, rifle cradled.

Up here, the crest of the hill was like a woman's breasts. A well-defined path ran through between the two swelling rises, and on down into the camp. They were on the left-hand hillock, looking toward the camp.

VK whispered, "We'll stay here and watch till dark, then go down into the camp."

Bill nodded and hitched himself into a more comfortable position. The black flies settled and bit, and he gritted his teeth and swore he would not move. What was the connection that had suddenly lit, back there when he was explaining about *coño*, and gone out again? Not the word itself, but . . . The stiffening of VK's elbow brought him to full alertness. VK's pistol was out, pushed forward, its nose just clear of a rock. Voices drifted through the forest from the south. Someone was coming from the forest toward the camp. Two people. A light laugh, unmistakably a woman. A man, the timbre vaguely familiar. It must be Mr. and Mrs. Andrew Jackson. The midday sun threw careless light and shadow in the shallow pass between the breasts of the hill.

The couple came. Bill saw a man's white hair, strong and thick; dark auburn hair, a woman's. They were holding hands like children—Mr. and Mrs. Andrew Jackson. He saw them clearly. Of course, he might have guessed as soon as he heard that name. He had seen enough pictures of the seventh President and the resemblance was striking. The lovers on the path were Monroe Barnett and . . . he recognized her at once, and had a hard time holding back his whistle of astonishment. No wonder Monroe had to hire the whole of Burnthill to ensure absolute privacy!

The two passed on and down into the camp.

Minutes later, a low voice said, *"Alors, ce n'est pas le guerre, c'est l'amour."*

That was de Guise. Bill looked around anxiously. VK said, "He's across the valley, on the other hillock. They arrived ten minutes after we did, but I couldn't shoot because Parchment would hear. I've been covering him ever since."

De Guise said, "And my friend here has been doing as much for you." He stood up. Bill and VK followed suit. De Guise said, "So we have been leading each other a wild-goose chase. But what is one to think when Mr. Hammond's own lawyer leaves the Plaza Hotel, after a conference with you gentlemen, goes to La Guardia airport, dives into the men's room, disguises himself in quite an expert way, comes out and takes a plane to Fredericton, in Canada. Our man in New York is baffled . . . but we in Montreal assume that Mr. Barnett must be on some urgent and secret business, eh? What else but to meet Mr. T., who is in hiding? So we too go to Fredericton and follow him. And you follow us. So perhaps you do not know, after all, where the eminent scientist is, *hein?* Ah well, one develops a certain cynicism. This affair of Mr. Barnett's must be the best-kept secret in Washington. The only one! And, *mon Dieu,* she is still beautiful! VK, you were the one who suspected that even the Lord Chief, as you called him, had feet of clay."

VK said, "I think better of him than I did. He seemed too inhuman."

De Guise said, "And now we must part. . . . Did you meet a friend of ours en route?"

VK said, "No."

De Guise said, "Really? That is strange. He must have gone to sleep. *Alors, au revoir . . .*"

Bill watched the tall man rise from the undergrowth and follow de Guise down the slope of the hill to the east, diagonally away from the camp. Soon the trees hid them.

VK said, "Back to square one. No one knows where Mr. T. is. *Coño!*"

Bill frowned. The loose connection had sparked again. This time he must not let it go. Spanish was the word. Spanish was the idea.

He burst out, *"Espagnol! On parle espagnol en Espagne aussi!"*

VK stared at him. "They speak Spanish in Spain, too? Of course they do." His gray eyes widened. A long scratch on his jaw slowly dripped blood onto his shirt. "My God!" he said slowly. "Spain was in that list of countries with good salmon fishing."

Bill said, *"La Guerre Civile d'Espagne? Quand?"*

"When was the Spanish Civil War? Before we were born, I know that. . . . Wait a minute, it was the year my parents were married, because they had planned a honeymoon in Seville and couldn't go. 1936. The year Mr. T. vanished. After a political demonstration in New York, which led to a fight. . . . We've got to get back to civilization, in a hurry. And this time we *must* shake off de Guise and his men."

A rhythmic chopping sound grew in the southwest. Bill and VK moved quickly under a tree. The helicopter passed low overhead, circled once, then sank fast to the clear space by the river. It was marked RCMP. Parchment put down his rod and went to it. Two large police dogs bounded down, followed by two Mounties in khaki shirts and blue trousers. The Mounties turned back and lifted something red and gray out of the helicopter. "Damn," VK muttered. "That's the body of Mandarin. It must have beached on a rock."

"*Comment sont-ils arrivés?*" Bill asked.

VK said, "Parchment must have radioed. See the aerial on top of the flagpole? These millionaire clients he gets may talk about how wonderful it is to be out of reach of the telephone, but wait till one of them gets a bellyache and see how quickly they want the doctor then! I know. I was in that business myself for thirteen years. We've got to get moving before those damned dogs pick up our trail. We'll cross the river as a first step."

Bill hesitated. He said, "*Pourquoi n'allons pas au police? Ils sont nos amis.*"

VK said, "I know the police are on our side . . . once all the explanations have been made and checked out. Meantime they have a corpse with two bullet holes in it that match this pistol. Even our explanations may not help. We have committed murder on Canadian soil and they may not be able to let us get away with it, for political reasons. But mainly it's a matter of time. We're just about positive now where Mr. T. is. Let's go!"

VK led, almost at a run, down the left forward slope of the hill as de Guise had gone down the right slope. "Downwind of the camp," he said, and a few minutes later the baying of the police dogs showed that the beasts had picked up a scent, presumably of de Guise and his companion. "Let *them* do some explaining," VK said.

They reached the river a mile above the camp, crossed, swimming and wading, and plunged into the northern forest.

The baying of the dogs faded. VK glanced at the sun and headed uphill, keeping the sun behind their left shoulders. He set a fast pace for the next six hours, turning gradually toward the westering sun. For fifteen minutes, early on, they had to crouch under an overhang of rock while the helicopter cruised in slow circles low over the forest. Then it went away, and they did not see it again that day.

The sun set. The split and broken land began to merge into the fading sky. It became dark.

VK said, "Stop here till dawn. We'll only break a leg or our necks if we try to go on, even with the moon. Besides, I'm bloody tired."

Bill sat down on a fallen tree. Boy, could he do with a drink. Or two or three. The tree creaked as VK sat down beside him. VK said, "Christ, I'd like a smoke. No dry matches . . . As far as I can remember from the map, the American border's about five miles the other side of the St. John River. And that's about thirty miles from here. Two days walk and then a nice midnight swim. We're going to be *bloody* hungry."

Bill heard him breaking boughs off pine trees. Soon they were both lying on the browse, looking up at the stars in a clearing sky. VK said, "Poor old Barnett . . . Parchment will tell him about our visit, and he will get out as quickly as possible. Probably tomorrow. Then he and she will separate. . . . They ought to be all right. Unless de Guise catches them somewhere, somehow. He may figure, Well, we didn't find Mr. T. but we did catch Monroe Barnett in a compromising situation, so let's try to make something of it, for future use perhaps. . . . Well, nothing we can do about it. I'm going to sleep."

Bill curled up, patted the jacket under his head and tried to go to sleep. He dreamed of Anne; of his mother dressing him; of Mexican whores; and awoke bleary-eyed and weary.

That day they marched from just after four in the morning until half past eight at night. Twice they saw a RCMP helicopter, but both times it passed a thousand feet up and a good distance to the east. They slept, torn and exhausted, a mile into tall timber past the deserted railroad metals, the empty shack, and the fading nameboard which were all that marked Lampedo, on the Canadian National. The next day the country became even more broken up, and it was already dark when they came suddenly to the top of a steep slope and saw below them a stream of moving lights, then a dark gap, then more moving lights.

"The St. John River," VK muttered. "There's a road along each bank. Feel strong enough to swim it now?"

Bill nodded. What he must not do was lie down. Once he fell asleep, he didn't think he'd ever wake up again.

The stream of cars was not very thick and they did not have to wait long before slipping across the blacktop and down the bank to the edge of the river. They sat, took off their shoes and secured them by the laces around their necks. VK muttered, "Thank God it's summer. Hell no, in winter we'd be able to walk across! Wait!"

A light played on the water, wandered past them and back to the river. A car had pulled off the road and stopped on top of the bank, half a mile downstream. From it a powerful spotlight scarched the water's edge and the wide surface. After two long minutes the spotlight went out. A little later a police car passed, southbound, its red lights out.

VK said, "OK."

They stepped together into the water and struck out. Bill swam steadily and powerfully. VK fell steadily behind. He was splashing a lot. Bill said, "*Aidez?*"

"No."

They swam on. VK's hands flailed the water but he made almost no progress. He breathed in loud, harsh gasps. Suddenly he went under. Bill moved across with two strokes and took him under the armpits as he went under again.

VK's voice was weak but furious. "Leave me alone . . . bastard."

Bill took no notice but turned on his back and with steady thrusts of his legs drove on toward the west bank, holding VK in his arms. VK began to move, either trying to struggle free or to swim—Bill couldn't tell which. He held tighter.

When his muscles had turned to aching putty, and he was ready to sink, rock grated against his shoulders. He crawled ashore and lay retching on cold rock.

Stumbling, falling, they crawled up the bank, across a dirt road and onto a rising, forested hill. Finally they sank to their knees and fell face forward. And then it was heavenly, blessed dark.

The board over the post office read *Fort Fairfield, Maine,* and the flag was an arrangement of fifty stars and thirteen stripes. VK stood inside the drugstore phone booth, the receiver to his ear and one eye on Bill keeping watch by the door. He didn't look too bad. The heavy rain now falling had messed up everyone's clothes and made theirs relatively inconspicuous in spite of the stains and mud splashes. The three days' growth of beard, more obvious in

Bill's case than with his own sandy hair, was what really made them look a pair of tough customers.

The voice came on the line. "This is Miss Wright, Mr. Barnett's secretary."

The operator cut in. "Will you accept a collect call from Mr. Bill Hammond, from Fort Fairfield, Maine? Go ahead, please."

VK said, "Miss Wright, can you get an urgent message through to Mr. Barnett?"

Miss Wright's voice was neutral. "I can't promise when it will reach him, sir. He travels in rented cars, without a schedule, when he's in France, you know."

VK said, "We know where he is. We've just seen him. Tell him that. And tell him that de Guise and his people also saw him. And the lady. Do you understand? He must move at once to protect himself, in case de Guise tries to make something of it."

After a long pause Miss Wright said, "Yes, sir." VK thought, she's probably the only human in the world to whom Barnett entrusted his secret. He said, "Now, put a call through to Dr. Alvarez, at 943 Avenida de la Republica, in Mexico City. Ask him what language Mr. T. spoke during their interview. . . . You can do that on another line? . . . Good. Be as quick as you can."

He waited, looking at Bill. Five minutes passed before Miss Wright came on. She said, "He spoke Spanish, sir. Dr. Alvarez never thought to mention it because of course most of his conferences are in Spanish. He said Mr. Tellefsen spoke very good Castilian, of Spain, not of Mexico. He said he used the *theta*."

VK said, "That's what I wanted to know. We should have asked at the time."

Miss Wright said, "I have a message for you, sir. Are you secure?"

"I suppose so. We've just walked into a booth in a drugstore."

"Yes, sir . . . This is from McCaffery. Quote. The New York *Times*, August 14, 1936, has a nine-line story about American Anarchist Party rally in support of Spanish Republic against military uprising. Rally held 14th Street and Eighth Avenue six P.M. August 13. Attendance estimated two thousand. During rally several fist fights broke out with Catholic group pickets. Unquote."

VK grinned with excitement. When Mr. Thorsson disappeared in 1936 he had gone to Spain to fight. And now he had gone back to Spain . . . where there were salmon. He looked up and saw a familiar figure leaning behind Bill Hammond at the door. Joseph P. Webber, his jacket sodden with rain. To Miss Wright he said, "Tell Mr. Barnett that we're sure Mr. T. has gone to Spain. That's all for now. Webber's here. Thanks."

He stepped out of the booth and an impatient old lady went in. Webber led them at a trot across the rainy street and into his parked car. He said, "You fellows are giving me an ulcer! I'm just settling down to a plate of Roman spaghetti when a man comes running from the Embassy to tell me that a couple of guys who claim to be ours are being chased all over New Brunswick by the Mounties. For murder. I say to myself, that'll be the Boy Scouts. A talk with Bosco and a look at the map tell me where you'll head for. The Mounties worked it out, too, you know. The Maine state troopers have just had a request to pick you up if they see you. I warned them off. What in hell have you been up to?"

VK said, "Mr. Thorsson's gone to Spain."

Webber's small eyes flickered and he started to light a cigar. "Maybe the Boy Scout system works too . . . because we just learned, by sweat and inquiry and the old computers, that Mr. T. left Mexico on a tramp steamer out of Vera Cruz the day after he saw Dr. Alvarez. The ship landed cargo at Cádiz, Spain, June 28, and Mr. T. vanished . . . though he'd paid his passage to Port Said."

"Two weeks ago," VK interjected.

"Right. And the computer also turned up another interesting thing. You feed it everything every doctor says about other doctors, and about leukemia, and then you ask it the question—whom do you go to if you have acute leukemia and you're told there's no hope. The answer always comes out Dr. Julio Medellin, of the Madrid Research Clinic. I was going to see him today. Now it will have to be tomorrow."

VK looked at Bill, "We'll go to Spain too, as soon as we can get Ingrid and Anne, right?" Bill nodded. VK said, "You go to Madrid. We'll go to the salmon rivers."

Webber said, "OK . . . Wait a minute, who were you phoning just now?"

"Miss Wright, Monroe Barnett's secretary in Washington."

"That ought to be secure. She's a careful woman. . . . Let's get going. I've got a 707 waiting at Limestone. We can talk on the way to New York."

Miss Wright lived in the same poverty-gripped part of Washington's Negro ghetto where she had lived since she came to the capital forty years ago. Every working evening she took a fifteen-minute bus ride from 16th Street, and then walked two blocks to her apartment. She'd been mugged twice, by junkies, and raped once, when she was a good deal younger; but she had not reported these things to the police, or to Mr. Barnett. They had been done by other Negroes, and she abided by the code of silence.

This was the first time, though, that she had ever found an intruder in the apartment. The big hands came over her mouth and throat as soon as she let herself in, and the soft Southern voice said, "Careful now. Take it easy."

She was certain it was a Negro. He gently replaced her spectacles and led her to her own easy chair. "Sit down," he said and switched on the light, just as she would have done. The curtains were drawn, though it was a close, thundery night. She saw that the man was tall, big, young, and pale-skinned. He had a knife in his hand.

He sat on the edge of the coffee table, one arm resting on her knee. He said, "How come you live in this dump? Working for the man and pulling down eleven thousand? You could live in Georgetown."

"I live with my people, where they must live," she said. "When they can move, I can move." The young man had violence and death behind the smoldering eyes and the controlled voice. She said, "What do you want?"

He said, "My name is Jim, ma'am. . . . Two white men called you from Maine today. My boss thinks they said something important. He wants to know. It's worth a hundred thousand."

Miss Wright shook her head.

Jim said, "OK. That's what he said you'd say. . . . See this film? It comes from a camera that was fitted with a long lens. One of our men took these pictures up in Canada. Of Mr. Barnett and a lady. You can have them. Or the newspapers can have them."

Miss Wright gripped the arms of the chair and stared at the

young man. He understood the anger and sorrow in her eyes and said, "I'm sorry, really. But I don't have any choice. And I don't see that you have, either, even if Mr. Barnett were here."

That's it, Miss Wright thought. What would Mr. Barnett do? Play for time? The young man wouldn't allow that. . . . Lie? Perhaps, but she had never lied, and could not start now. . . . To protect the woman he loved, Mr. Barnett might do what they asked. Or would he?

What guarantee would he have that they would keep their word? Suppose they had more pictures? It didn't matter. The problem was *these* pictures. It would be no use worrying about some future breach of faith, when *this* film here could ruin both of them, and half a dozen innocent bystanders into the bargain. No, Mr. Barnett would do what they asked. Then he would kill himself. *The wages of sin is death.*

But first, he would make sure that the photographs were genuine. Then he'd look at them to see if they were actually dangerous.

She said, "Who took these photographs? When? Where? How?"

Jim spoke almost apologetically, but he would have liked to use the knife, all the same. "They didn't tell me everything, ma'am, but I understand two of our men saw Mr. Barnett and the woman in a hunting camp in Canada. Our men got the hell out, quick as they could, stealing one of the camp canoes to do it, so they were waiting with the camera when Mr. Barnett and the woman came out of the woods the next day. They had to come down the river, too, I guess. That was yesterday and this film reached us today, with orders what to do."

Miss Wright said, "Let me see the pictures."

"Here's one print," he said. "Then you got to talk, Miss Wright."

"Let me have it," she said.

She looked carefully at the picture, and nodded her head sadly. It was a good picture, and they were holding hands in goodbye, and the woman was crying. Mr. Barnett would have to speak. *The wages of sin is death,* but it didn't say whose.

When he saw his name on the pageboy's board in the breakfast room of the Crillon, Monroe Barnett felt that a bullet had hit him between the shoulder blades. He raised his hand and the boy came to him with three cables. The first one he opened read: VISIT EMBASSY SPEAK GLAISHER URGENTEST WEBBER.

The second read: MUCH REGRET I TOLD THEM WHERE MISTER HAMMOND IS GOING NEXT PHOTOGRAPHS DESTROYED. RESPECTFULLY BERTHA WRIGHT.

The third read: MISS WRIGHT IN CRITICAL CONDITION OVERDOSE OF SLEEPING TABLETS MISS PARLBY TAKING OVER HER DUTIES I WILL VISIT MISS WRIGHT AS SOON AS VISITORS ALLOWED REGARDS BERNIE WEISS.

Monroe Barnett stared straight ahead, the three slips of paper in his hand. . . . What photographs? They must be of himself with *her*. But who had taken them? Where? Surely no one at Burnthill . . . and they had parted at Napadogan, at the end of the canoe trip. It must have been there.

So they had found Miss Wright's breaking strain. The better and nobler a person's character, the easier it was to break. Because such people cared about more things, more people than just themselves. He bowed his head in his hands, and sat in silence. The waiters left him alone.

Chapter 10

BILL WATCHED the curtains fluttering uneasily in the breeze. The rain—which had followed the rented Beechcraft from Paris to Bilbao, and the car westward from Bilbao along the north coast of Spain—had now lifted. Stars were coming out in a ragged sky. It was near midnight, cool and pleasant.

He wished he could get to sleep, but his mind would neither start nor stop at command. In his thoughts, businesslike reviews of their situation and plans alternated with turbulent thoughts of Anne. . . .

We are in a small town called Cangas de Onis. This is as far as we could get in the day from Bilbao. We are on our way to check two famous salmon rivers farther west. But on arrival here we learned that Cangas itself is on a salmon river, called the Sella.

Anne the long-legged, and virginal? Anne whose cool mouth could become a hot pit. Anne, the first woman he had ever both respected and wanted. Anne, sister of V. K. G. Hawker, s.o.b. Seeing Anne again, after the days without her in Canada, was like turning a sudden corner, from shadow to light, from doubt to certainty. . . .

So Miguel, who is McCaffery's Bilbao man and their interpreter, has found a local guide, and this guide has undertaken to check the Sella waters to learn whether any elderly foreigner is or has been fishing them. A foreigner who speaks good Spanish, using the theta; and coño. The guide's name is Carlos. Carlos is square and quiet and weatherbeaten.

Anne was VK's sister, his housekeeper, his companion. Surely, it was Anne, not he, who must break the strange, almost unnatural ties binding her to her brother? Or VK himself should do it. Any decent man would. But VK wasn't a decent man.

Tomorrow, early, we drive on westward. Carlos will report by telephone or telegram if he learns anything while we are away. In any case we will see him on our way back to Bilbao. It is frustrating to be in the hands of an interpreter, even Miguel, who's good. Miguel is also old, short, and short-sighted, and he has flat feet and bad breath. My heart sank when he met us at Bilbao Airport. But he had all the right papers, enough passports so we can change our identities every day if we want to, a car well stocked with different registration plates, and a rifle. The car's a SEAT sedan and it's rather small for all of us with our fishing rods and sporting gear. But Miguel says a large American car would only make us more conspicuous, and—he pulls down one lower eyelid with his forefinger when he says this—more expensive.

Anne's movements were long and graceful. Her breathing was always even and deep, through her nose, her mouth lightly closed. She was sleeping in the next room, through that door. She had not bolted it. He had not unbolted it. Was it, then, locked or unlocked? If he tried the door, would he solve everything, or spoil everything?

He heard her bed creak, shuffling, a drawer opening. A few moments later, as he lay rigid, hardly breathing, her door into the passage opened and gently closed. Footsteps passed to the head of the old wooden stairs, and steadily, creakingly, down.

Bill slipped out of bed and went to the window. The regularly spaced lights shone on a broad street and wide sidewalks, all empty. The leaves of the trees whispered in the breeze. Anne came out of the front of the hotel, turned right and walked down the street. Her head was up, and she walked with long free-flowing strides . . . but that proved nothing: she could not walk any other way. Her shoulders were hunched; she was unhappy.

She couldn't go walking around past midnight in a strange Spanish town, unable to speak a word of the language. Anything might happen to her. Hesitating, he watched her. At a corner she too hesitated, then turned down a side street. He could not see her any more. He flung on his clothes and hurried down the stairs and into the street.

He came up to her on the outskirts of the town, beyond the last street lamp, where the side street had become a lane and the lane narrowed to a footpath beside the river. She had heard him coming ᵤnd turned, suddenly startled. He cursed himself that he had not thought to call, saying, *It's me, Bill;* how could she know who was following her into the dark beyond the town? She recognized him at once; her hand fell to her side, the tautness in her attitude relaxed, and she waited.

When he reached her he said, "Anne . . . are you all right?"

"Yes, Bill," she said.

"I saw you go out. I was worried for you."

Her face grew clearer as his eyes became accustomed to the darkness. She said, "I couldn't sleep."

He said, "Nnnnn . . ." Oh damn, it had been all right just now. He had started to say, "Nor could I," but managed to blurt out only, *"Ni moi."*

She said, "Shall we walk along the river? It's very beautiful, even in the dark." She laughed quietly.

Her hand fell into his. The skin was cool and fresh, and the hand tightened and relaxed under his grip. She smiled at him. They walked together, slowly, on the path beside the river. Surely daylight was growing again, the sun rising, as it had in that moment returning from Canada when he stepped down from the huge bomber at McGuire Air Force Base and saw her with the wind in her hair. She was looking at him, the look of a woman in a Dutch painting, quiet and domestic, welcoming, saying, *Don't be afraid, you will not fail again.* If he made love to her she would not become anyone else in his arms. She would always be Anne. He took her hand to his lips and kissed it. She stopped and faced him, her lips parting and her eyes very deep. It was under a wide bridge at the edge of black star-touched water.

VK stood at the window of his room. watching the empty street. Nothing was happening, nothing moving: a small, dead town. What the hell was the matter with him that he couldn't sleep?

His telephone rang. After a minute of buzzes, clicks and sleepy Spanish, an American voice came on loud and clear. "Thanks for sending in your address. You're learning."

It was Webber. He said, "Is that all you rang for?"

"No. Our friend visited the specialist I named, the day after landing. He was told they could do nothing more for him. He went away. He didn't say where to."

VK said, "What are you doing now, then?"

"The usual . . . asking questions. Good night."

VK hung up and returned to the window. Mr. Thorsson had visited Dr. Medellin, the leukemia expert, on June twenty-ninth. And been given no hope. And then disappeared again.

He leaned out, suddenly peering. That was Anne leaving the hotel. He watched her as she disappeared into a side street. Poor girl, for a long time now she'd been alternating between worry and happiness. It was Hammond, of course. She thought Bill Hammond was marvelous. And Hammond responded because she was probably the first person he'd ever met who really wasn't after his money; the first person who really had no idea what his kind of money meant. But Hammond could never make her happy. At the moment he had an obvious respect for her, but as soon as she went to bed with him, he'd lose that. And if he actually married her—which he wouldn't: why should he?—she'd just become his worshiped Mom, while he buried his nose in his bloody investments.

He ought to go after her and find out what was the matter. He ought to send her back to England at once. Better still, he should abandon this manhunt, go with her, take the job at John Lewis and settle down. . . . Christ, not that!

He stiffened as the burly shape of Bill Hammond left the hotel and followed Anne down the side street. An assignation? What was the point of that, when they could go to each other's rooms without any trouble? Perhaps Bill, too, had been looking out of his window, unable to go to sleep. The strings of everyone's nerves were tightening. No one could sleep. The finish line was close . . . and then what?

He realized that his breath was coming short, and his hands were trembling. He jerked his jacket off the back of the chair, put it on and headed for the door. Three steps toward the stairs and a low voice called, "VK!"

He turned. Ingrid was in the door of her room, beckoning him. "Come back. Here."

He went to her slowly. She pulled him into her room and closed the door. "I saw, too," she said. She was red-eyed, but composed.

"What's it really mean?" he asked.

"It means I have finally lost," she said. "Well, no one can have everything he wants in this world. That's true, eh?"

"Yes," he said. He started for the door. "Hammond's not going to have Anne, for one thing."

She grabbed his arm. "VK, don't!" she said. "They are in love. Can't you see? Ah, you can, but you won't accept it. . . . You must. Look at me." She stretched out her arms and the robe fell open, to display her fine creamy white body for him. The golden locket glowed in the valley of her breasts. "We'll never be in love, but we do have gifts we can give each other." She put her arms around his neck. "Forget them, VK." She pressed her pelvis against him, and pulled his head down to her. "Help *me* to forget, at least."

He pulled free without a word. She ran to get between him and the door. She was breathing hard. She held out her hand. "The pistol, VK. Or I'll start screaming."

He hesitated. In truth he had forgotten that he had it, in its shoulder holster. Now that she had reminded him, he wasn't sure that he wanted to give it up. Hammond was a big man to tackle without some kind of equalizer. But Ingrid meant what she said. She always did. He took out the pistol and slapped it into her hand. She stepped aside. He passed her and went down the stairs.

The new market and the tiny cathedral stood in a stone waste. The strong shadows cast by the street lights gave all the buildings the quality of models in an exhibition. Bill had followed Anne down that side street on the left. He hesitated. Must he really follow, too? He stood in front of the cathedral, paralyzed by doubt. The inscription on the façade was in Latin, and at each side a Greek letter was carved in the stone, alpha to the left, omega to the right. Some recollections stirred, recent and ancient. But what the hell was he doing here? Was he too scared of Hammond to do anything about it when the bastard was seducing his sister? He plunged down the side street.

When he came to the river he went on downstream for a while, but the path died away. A plank bridge crossed the river at a narrow, deep place and the path went back up the other side toward the town.

He found them under a wide road bridge, locked together under the arch, Anne leaning back against the stone, Bill holding her, kissing. They did not hear him or see him until he spoke. He said, "Hammond, I told you to leave Anne alone."

They came apart with no guilt. Hammond looked big and calm. Anne said, "VK, don't be angry . . ."

He said, "Go back to the hotel."

Bill said, "Yes, Anne, go back. Don't worry."

The bastard was speaking quite plainly: no hesitation or impediment at all. Anne went away. The darkened backs of houses rose above them. Street lights on the bridge parapet shone down on a patch of green grass.

Bill said, "VK, I love her. I want to marry her."

VK leaned back and landed a blow with his left fist, square on Bill's jaw. The big head snapped back, but VK knew he hadn't hurt him. He'd never be able to hurt him with his fists. This was a trained boxer, the neck thick with muscle, the jaw firm and square.

Bill's face seemed to settle into a kind of content, as though he were saying, "So be it! I didn't start it!"

His first blow was a light left jab to VK's nose, followed, as VK parried, with a right feint and a stinging straight left and a right to the eye, all in a single series. Then again, and again, with no break in the pattern, and only infinitesimal changes in the timing so that VK's defense was each time wrong, either too soon or too late. A second series began with the same punches delivered in reverse, from right jabs to left crosses. VK felt his senses going and dropped to one knee. Bill stepped half a pace back. VK grabbed him by the arms and jumped up with all his strength, butting him under the chin. The counterblow landed with stunning force on the side of his head, sending him flying across the grass to his knees. Bill was groggy too, he saw as he looked up— blood pouring from his nose and a trickle of blood from the corner of his mouth. VK advanced on him, fists up, until he was within striking distance, then feinted forward with his left but did not finish the punch. Instead he stumbled back, picked up a round stone from the bank. Then Bill hit him in a low flying tackle. His head smashed to the ground, and pain pierced his shoulder. He sank his teeth into Bill's wrist. Bill's other hand worked free, and a short punch, delivered from no more than two inches, hit him above the ear. His head whipped over, and it went dark.

He awoke to a movement of air on his cold face. Water dripped down his chin, his head ached, and his shoulder hurt. He opened his eyes. Bill was standing by the river, looking at him, his hands dripping water.

VK's eyes slowly came into focus. Beyond Bill surely something was wrong with the pattern of shadows under another bridge a little farther upstream? Gradually he made out the unmistakable silhouettes of two tricorn hats and the tip of a rifle barrel. Starlight gleamed on black leather and oiled steel. Two Civil Guards were watching, immobile, their long blanket cloaks hanging straight from their shoulders. His humiliation had taken place before an audience. He laughed, trying to keep it silent, but a strangled groan came out.

Bill was at his side. "Aaaa . . ."

Good, the bastard had lost his new-found speech again. He rose to his feet, shaking his head. He didn't feel too bad, and he'd marked Mr. Hammond. What had been proved was something else again; but he felt better.

A truck crossed the road bridge overhead with a hollow rumble. The dark, murmuring river beside them here must be the Sella. A salmon river. He dipped his hands in, splashed his face, and straightened up. The Civil Guards had gone. The bridge they had been standing under was an ancient, tall arch, steeply sloped approaches meeting over the center. From the middle of the arch hung an enameled metal cross, brilliantly clear in the lamp light, and from each side a single large Greek letter, alpha to the left, omega to the right.

The recollections of the town square, just now, returned, with earlier ones . . . the swell of Ingrid's breasts and the gold locket between . . . Sir Alan Gobhair: "That's a Roman arch, isn't it?" Sigurd Thorsson: "It is a bridge, in the town where you were born."

This was the place.

Chapter 11

IT WAS TWO O'CLOCK in the morning, and they were crowded into Bill's room, waiting. Ingrid had taken off her locket and held it in her hand, gazing at it as though it was not an ornament of gold and enamel but a living portrait of her mother. Bill stared out of the window, wondering how long he could last before holding Anne in his arms again. VK had a bloody nose and one bruised eye; the other glittered angrily.

Miguel came in with Carlos, the guide. "He was asleep," Miguel said apologetically. "It took him time to dress."

The two Spaniards sat down awkwardly on the forward edges of two stiff chairs.

VK said, "Well, what's he say?"

Miguel said, "We have not had time to speak much yet, but he has said certainly he knows of a foreigner who has been in this district since June thirtieth. He did not speak of him earlier because it is an affair of scandal, not of salmon fishing. Further, the man is not a stranger. Some know him. Also, this affair began so long ago that it could have no connection with the matters we spoke of. But now that he has looked more closely at the *señorita* —" he bowed slightly toward Ingrid—"he thinks this may be the man."

Ingrid said, "To think I was born of love between my father and a woman of Spain. Did I not tell you that it was not for salmon but for love that my father would be searching?" She turned eagerly to Miguel. "Is my mother here? Is she still alive?"

"One moment, *señorita*," Miguel said. "Carlos says there was heavy fighting here in the war. The Reds held all this part, and unfortunately many of the people supported them."

"Why does he say 'unfortunately'?" Ingrid cried. "The others were Fascist animals."

"Possibly," the interpreter said gloomily. "But as Carlos fought on that side he is not likely to agree. . . . He says that early in the war some foreign volunteers came here to fight beside the Asturian miners. They fought well and one of them, a big tall powerful man with blond hair, became famous. To some, infamous. His only name was El Rubio, which means 'The Blond,' though perhaps someone in Spain knows his real name. . . . He was head of a court-martial which tried and executed three land-owners and a police captain for treason and spying. A few months later the Nationalists broke in from Castile, through the Sella gorge, and there was no more fighting here. Only many executions. But they couldn't find El Rubio, whom they wanted to execute more than anyone else. He had gone, together with the other foreigners, to fight somewhere else in our poor martyred country. . . . So they put up a commemorative pillar to the martyred heroes instead, at that place, Prescendi."

Ingrid said impatiently, "This El Rubio, was he, is he, my father?"

Miguel said reprovingly, "I have not had time to find out everything yet, *señorita*." He turned to Carlos and spoke briefly. Carlos answered at length. Ingrid listened, biting her fingernails.

Miguel said, "In Prescendi, the village where El Rubio executed the Nationalists, there lived a respectable peasant couple called Coballes. They had a daughter, Alegria. Some time in 1937, I forget when but it was a little before the Nationalists broke through, she had a baby, here in the house of a friend in Cangas—"

"It was September ninth," Ingrid said. "It was me!"

"—to the great disgrace of her parents, for she was unmarried. Worse, she would not name the man responsible for her condition, and so great had been the lovers' caution that no one else knew, though a few guessed—"

"El Rubio!" Ingrid cried. "The man who fought the Fascists! My father!" She clapped her hands with delight.

"—and the guessers were sure they were right when the baby disappeared at the same time that the foreigners went. Alegria could not feed it. Everyone in Spain was starving then, you understand."

Anne said anxiously, "But surely with Franco still in power, Mr. Thorsson is in great danger here."

Miguel said, "Carlos says, it is true. El Rubio's name is still on the list of those for whom there can be no forgiveness. If he is found in Spain, he will be shot before the sun sets."

VK asked, "How has he survived this long? Two weeks."

"Carlos says many people here are still loyalists in their hearts. Those who recognize him have said nothing—yet. Besides, they are frightened of him. Besides the executions at Prescendi, which were after all a legal thing in their way, all done in the proper form, he killed one of his own comrades for interfering with his girl, this Alegria de Coballes."

"But Carlos himself hasn't talked? You said he fought for Franco."

"He did. But he says he is an Asturian, a guide, and a fisherman, not a police . . . what do you say? . . . a police rat. But, he says, people are talking who do not recognize El Rubio, who were too young to know the war. They are talking because it is a scandal that this man lives with the woman—"

"Then she is alive!" Ingrid said.

"—who is married to another man. You see, after the war Alegria de Coballes married a simple fellow called Pedro Rodriguez. Pedro was wounded in both knees fighting near Madrid."

"On which side?" Bill asked.

"One does not ask," Miguel said reprovingly. "One must live. But as he receives no pension, no allowance, one can guess. . . .

He married Alegria in spite of her shame. Because he must walk with crutches the work of the land is hard for him without help. They have been married these many years but were not blessed with children of their own and—"

"Where do they live?" Ingrid cried.

Anne cut in. "Amieva! Isn't that the name?"

Miguel looked surprised. "The cottage is in Prescendi, thirteen kilometers up the Sella from here," he said. "Where the river comes out of the gorge. But Amieva is where they have a hut on the mountain for the summer grazing and the cheese making. How did you know that, *señorita?*"

"I didn't," Anne said, "I guessed. Amieva was the name Mr. Thorsson gave to the doctor in Mexico City."

Miguel said, "You have great sensitivity, *señorita*. . . . Carlos says that Alegria might be at the Prescendi cottage now, with El Rubio. If not, she will be with her husband at the hut in the high pastures."

"Does El Rubio ever fish for salmon?" VK asked.

"Yes. Or he stands and stares at the water with no rod in his hand. Carlos saw him fishing a week ago."

"But he has no license."

"That is free water."

VK turned to Bill. "There can't be any doubt. . . . Ask Carlos if anyone else has been making inquiries about El Rubio."

"He says no."

VK said, "Well, don't let's waste time. We'll go as soon as it's light. Anne, make sure you bring Mr. Thorsson's medicines. . . ."

The cottage had a tiled roof and geraniums on an upper balcony. At the back a tiny grain store of coarse plank construction, perched on four legs, faced the Sella. The cottage door was unlocked but no one was in. Miguel walked to the next cottage and VK went down to the river. The water was cold and clear. Upstream another of the pointed Roman bridges crossed the river.

Miguel returned. "The woman in that house says Alegria went up to her husband yesterday. El Rubio is fishing. Somewhere above the bridge."

VK said, "I'll go," and Ingrid said, "And I too."

They walked up the road, the river on their right. Serpents of gray mist writhed along the surface of the water. The stones beside the river were green and white, the living white of limestone. For five hundred feet above the mist the air was clear; then a flat ceiling of white cloud lay like a lid on the valley. The steep walls, dense with oak and beech, rose up into it and disappeared. Cold air moved down the valley from the unseen gorge and the passes to Castile beyond. The light was absolutely flat, without shadow or brightness. The measure of a scene, of height and distance and shape, came only from perspective.

VK and Ingrid walked slowly, not talking. He was hungry and it was early—not as early as that hour before dawn when one went out to hunt, but like the hour when one returned from the first sweep and night had withdrawn the last shreds of its protection, and one came back to the silent camp and the smoke was beginning to curl up from the cooking fire and one of the men was awake, blowing quietly on it, and dew pearled on the grass. So here the night was past and the day not yet come.

They reached the place where the Roman bridge sprang across the river, while the modern road went on up the bank. In the angle of the low wall there was a concrete pillar. Its deeply incised lettering, partly overgrown with lichen and blurred by rain and sun, recorded the assassination of four men at the Massacre of Prescendi on February 20, 1937, and declared eternal vengeance against the "Red murderers." A recently painted sign, propped against the pillar, hid the names of the dead. The sign read *Coto No. 4,* and an arrow pointed downstream.

"There he is," Ingrid said softly. "My father. El Rubio."

The old man came out from behind some big rocks fifty yards upriver and picked up his rod, which they had not noticed. VK stared, then relaxed. He had no beard, and looked much younger. The rod was a heavy coarse pole at least fifteen feet long, and he could hardly wield it. The great tip moved stiffly as he prepared to cast—there was no spring in the wood, nor in his arms—the line went out heavily and landed with a splash. It was not tapered line but a strong twine. Whatever he was using as a lure had no shine or color.

Ingrid and VK walked on along the road, and then down a worn path among the rocks until they were near the old man. He made another cast, and VK saw that the lure was a pale-gray river shrimp, tattered and broken after many casts. The hook caught in a twig on the backswing. Sigurd Thorsson turned wearily, his jaw set.

"*Coño!*" VK said. "I'll say it for you."

Recognition came to the old man before awareness. His mental processes seemed to be reversed, for he first let the rod fall and embraced VK, then he stepped back, saying, "Why . . . it's VK, isn't it? You have been fighting?"

Ingrid went to him. "And me, Father."

"Maria Carmen!" he said. "Maria Carmen, my baby . . . But what was it I had to call you?" His brow furrowed. "Ah! Ingrid." Then tears came to his eyes and VK picked up the rod and unfastened the hook from the bough while father and daughter embraced.

Ingrid said, "Can we go now, Father? I want to see my mother."

The old man looked worried. "They need food. . . . They are in the cheese hut, above Amieva." He pointed vaguely up the mountainside. "There is a salmon here. I saw him. Yesterday I had a bite from him but struck too soon. I must try to catch him."

VK said, "With this hook? He'll die of blood poisoning before you land him. Here, try this." He took off his hat and began to work the Silver Wilkinson out of the band.

Mr. Thorsson said, "Ah! The fly that killed our salmon on the Tay! It is called a . . . wait a minute . . . Wilkinson, Silver Wilkinson! . . . I shall never be able to drop a fly with this rod and this line. Look at it!"

"Try," VK said. He gave Mr. Thorsson the fly.

The temperature of the valley was the same as on many Tay mornings. The light was exactly the same as when clouds rested on the shoulder of the moors, mist lay on the river, and all was gray and opal between. Three times, he remembered, a Silver Wilkinson had taken big salmon on such days.

The old man's arms had lost their strength but his fingers kept their skill. He worked the shrimp off his own hook and put it carefully in a puddle on top of a rock. He cut the hook off short to the cast—it was a huge hook, dulled with rust. "This is a poor country," he muttered. "Great, but poor. Or is it that only the poor can be great. What did Christ say? When have riches ever strengthened a character? Your friend's, perhaps. Bill Hammond. It is coming very clear now."

His big fingers fastened the little fly hook onto the cast. Tentatively he swung the heavy rod, and then made his first cast. The line landed like a whiplash and he swore and began to draw it in. But he stood a little straighter, and his head was a little higher. VK, glancing around, saw Anne and Bill watching from the Roman bridge, his arm around her shoulders. Mr. Thorsson saw them too, and called absentmindedly, "Anne . . . Bill . . ." Then his attention returned to the river. Ingrid sat on a rock and watched her father, her chin in her hand.

He was fishing above a line of broken water where the river, barely forty feet wide here, left a long pool and plunged down among scattered rock and boulders, some as large as houses, toward the Roman bridge. The gusty wind made it difficult to control the fly, and after five minutes VK saw that the old man was tiring fast. Once or twice he had put the fly where he wanted it, but it had settled heavily enough to scare any fish close by. And, as he was casting slightly upstream, the fly floated down dry to the edge of the rapids. VK had seldom seen a salmon take a dry fly. They liked it to be drowning, just below the surface.

Sigurd Thorsson spoke almost to himself. "I was fishing here— just there, by the bridge—when I first saw Alegria. It was out of season, but in the war we didn't care about that." He cast again. The fly landed well, drifted and sank. There was no bite.

Thorsson went on, "Maria Carmen, Ingrid, was born on September ninth, and the Fascists broke through a month later. I had to take her with me. Oh, the foster mothers and wet nurses that child had. . . ."

VK said, "Why don't you try a little downstream? See, that pool there." He pointed to a small pool, somewhat like an elongated bathtub, where the water was pale green above the pebbles at the side, shading off to a dark emerald as it grew deeper. Above and below the pool the rapids churned the water into a white, weightless foam.

Mr. Thorsson muttered, "Near the bridge? I don't know if I can put the fly into that, VK. It's a small pool."

He walked slowly down the bank, and, facing the bridge, cast downstream, the wind behind him. The purple hackle overshot, landing on a rock. . . . He drew back, and cast again, with an audible groan. This time the fly hung in the air, then glided over the edge of the limestone to settle on the water near the top of the pool. The fly floated downstream for a moment, then the line tautened as Mr. Thorsson eased back the point of his rod. The fly went underwater. Ten seconds later the rod tip bowed sharply and the reel began to scream.

Mr. Thorsson steadily pulled the rod back. "He's hooked," he said. "He's not big. . . ." The line glided aimlessly across the pool. The point of the rod went down. Marks of strain scored Mr. Thorsson's face. "But too big for me," he muttered. "Here, take the rod, VK."

VK said, "You can land him . . . but let him go down out of that little pool into the big one below the bridge."

"If he will," Mr. Thorsson said.

They were directly under the Roman bridge now. Anne was leaning over. "I see him! Twenty pounds . . . twenty-five!"

Mr. Thorsson eased some line off the reel, enough to take the strain from the salmon's mouth while keeping control of him. The salmon, as VK had hoped, swam around a sharp ledge and into the lower pool. It went fast down the pool, the reel whining, and for a few moments VK thought they were going to have a repetition of the great fight on the Tay, which would mean the loss of the fish, for Mr. Thorsson had no stamina left. But this salmon came back and a battle of wills and strength developed between the strong young fish, not very intelligent or experienced, and the dying old man. . . . VK stood back, biting his lip, as Mr. Thorsson hurried up and down the bank to help the ancient reel deal with the salmon's sudden flurries of activity. He was tired, very tired. The point of the rod hung down every time he failed to concentrate, and those times were becoming more frequent.

VK watched, tensed as though it were his own fish. His hands were damp and stiff, and he found himself praying that the salmon would come to the gaff, and the old man drop dead in that moment. . . .

The salmon came in at last, beaten, and Mr. Thorsson took the old-fashioned gaff from his belt. By a last effort he raised the rod with his left hand, and with his right plunged the steel point into the salmon's flank. Then, slowly, he began to collapse. VK reached him in a stride, caught him and lowered him gently to the stones. "You got him!" he said. He seized the gaff and lifted the salmon to the bank. It flipped its tail twice and then lay still, its dark blood congealing on the white limestone beside the pale-green river.

Ingrid knelt, cradling her father's head. Mr. Thorsson mumbled, "Is it sick . . . like the steel head?"

VK said, "No. It is healthy and strong."

"Good. Pedro and Alegria will be pleased. They need it."

VK said, "As we need you, sir."

Mr. Thorsson said, "Yes . . . I have been waiting for you. Not deliberately, not as a plan. You know what I mean?"

VK said, "Yes. But you are lucky that someone else did not find you first—the HPS or Franco's police."

"I suppose so. I cannot care, though until a few weeks ago I cared about little else. . . . You see that place where the salmon's blood marks the stones? A man's blood marked the stones only a few feet away, once."

"That was a court-martial," VK said. "You were fair in your judgment, I'm sure."

"I was not thinking of that. . . . This man I killed in hot blood, with this gaff, because he had tried to rape Alegria. It was soon after we had met and become lovers, and this man thought that because she gave herself to me, he could take her too. . . . He was trying to pull her under the bridge one evening when I came upon them."

"The guide told us about it," Ingrid said. "You did right. You must not worry."

The old man said, "I do not worry now. At first I did not. Then I did, terribly, for many years. I could not sleep, sometimes, for worrying. I could not tell you, Ingrid, the truth of your birth. I could not let it even be guessed that I had served in Spain. . . . Did the guide tell you the name of the man I killed?"

VK shook his head.

"Martin Parkezian. The beloved elder brother of the head of all Soviet secret security police."

Ingrid exclaimed, "Oh, my God! My God! . . . But he was killed in battle!"

"No, he wasn't. He died a lecher's death, where that salmon lies. They made up the battle story in Russia afterwards. Gregory Par-

kezian is one of the few people who know the truth. He has spent
years sending agents to find out. He knows that a tall foreigner
called El Rubio killed his brother. He does not know, yet, who El
Rubio is. Several times, in Russia, I caught him looking speculatively at me. I became paralyzed, like a rabbit before a snake. No
more . . . It is done. I returned to the Sella, and battle, and love.
And I took a salmon. With my daughter . . . and my son."

VK began to cut out the fly. The salmon had taken it well, and
the hook was firmly embedded into the gristle of the right lower
jaw. He cleaned the fly in the river and put it back in his hat. He
stood up. "We'd better go."

Ingrid said, "I *must* see my mother!"

The old man said, "I must take this salmon to Alegria . . . and
say goodbye to her. Then we will go. I should never have come.
But I could not help myself."

"I know," VK said.

"What terrible dangers I have put upon my friends here! And
they have said nothing! Ah, they are Asturians!"

"*Coño!*" VK said, putting one arm around the old man's shoulder. "Come on. Anne's got some medicine you must start on at
once. Now."

They all squeezed into the SEAT. Bill was happy to be jammed
into a corner of the back seat because Anne was pressed against
him. VK's hostility seemed to have been temporarily suspended,
though not abandoned. Perhaps because of the fight? Well, he
didn't care. He wanted Anne for the rest of her life. He supposed
VK would always be a part of that life—and so of his own, too.
They had to reach some sort of understanding. VK must realize
that for him and Anne it was simply love. If they started from
there, everything would have to work out. In the meantime he felt
that Anne had somehow withdrawn a little, as though to give VK
a better chance to measure what was happening.

A few hundred yards beyond the Roman bridge at Prescendi a
side road climbed away up the eastern wall of the valley. It
wound steeply up and up without guard rail or protective wall,
the terrain grew more fierce, crags jutted out against a clearing
sky, trees hung on the edge of cliffs, a tributary stream growled
down in a steep chasm toward the Sella. The backward view

deepened but did not become longer, for on the other side of the valley the mountains rose as steep and as high as on this. Nowhere, except straight up, could the eye escape.

They passed through the six houses of Amieva, one old woman watching them silently from her door. The blacktop had ended far back. The bare earth road zigzagged across steep pastureland, then into woods and at last again onto open meadows.

"Stop here," Mr. Thorsson said. "By Lothario, that tethered donkey. He is ours."

VK drove the car onto the grass and got out to open the trunk. A moment later he appeared carrying a rifle and said, "Got your gun?" Bill nodded, tapping his shoulder holster. VK said, "I've got mine too."

Ingrid helped her father to mount the donkey. "Don't try to lead him," he said. "He knows his way up this mountain blindfolded. Neither Pedro nor I can get up without him."

McCaffery's man, Miguel, said, "Is it necessary for me to go up?" He looked apprehensively at the slope. "Mr. Thorsson can interpret for you."

VK said, "No. You wait by the car. Here, give me that salmon."

They began to climb the steep grass. The silver salmon gleamed on VK's back. A stone cabin, its roof thatched, broke the smooth skyline of the mountain. A few cattle grazed the lower ridge among scattered chestnut trees. A small black dog jumped up onto a rock and began barking down at them. A man swung into view on two crutches and stood, hung in the crutches, beside the dog. He turned his head, and though they did not hear him he must have called, for a woman came to his side. The dog stopped barking.

Ingrid cried, "My mother . . ." and began to run. The others stopped. The woman waited, puzzled, to receive the fast-climbing girl. She was another Ingrid—a little shorter, thinned by age and deprivation, the thick hair densely streaked with white.

Just before Ingrid reached her, Sigurd Thorsson called out, "*Tu hija!*" Your daughter. The woman above slowly unfolded her arms. The two women embraced, heads meeting, and sank slowly to their knees together.

It was VK who started to go forward again, then the rest followed. When they reached the top Ingrid and her mother were seated together on a rock, hands tight held, gazing at each other.

Mr. Thorsson said, "Come into the cabin. The sun is hot sometimes, even in Asturias. We have milk, a little bread and of course home-made cheese." He spoke a few words to the cripple and said to VK, "Give him the salmon. He wants to clean it at once. Here, tether Lothario. He is a great lover, this one. . . . There."

He led into the cabin, stooping low under the stone slab of the lintel. Inside, one small window at the back grudgingly let in a little light, showing a wooden bunk, straw-filled; twigs and ash on a flat stone platform which was the cooking place; two metal pots hanging from the smoke-blackened roof beams; an earthenware water pot on the floor; and several cheeses, in various stages of ripening, on a rough wooden shelf.

Sigurd Thorsson pulled out a milking stool from under the bunk, offered it to Anne, then carefully sat down on it. He stretched out his arms. "How did you find me?" The cattle down the mountain grazed with a steady tinkling from the bells hung around their necks.

VK put on the safety catch of the rifle with an audible click and said, "We thought you'd go fishing."

Mr. Thorsson looked at his hands. The flesh had fallen from them so that they were mere skeletal webs covered with thin brownish parchment. He was a dying man, Bill thought, and he looks it. But this man was not the same as the one who had fled from Shiprock. This man was at peace.

Mr. Thorsson said, "You know, I had hooked a salmon in that same pool down there at Prescendi, above the Roman bridge, when I first saw Alegria. She came to watch. I caught the salmon. Afterwards, Alegria and I made love. . . . I have never been as happy as I was here. Young. Fighting for an ideal. Fishing for salmon. In great mountains. Among a strong, brave people. In love with a strong, brave woman . . . She served a machine gun on this hill until a week before Ingrid was born. . . . The thing—human, animal, fish, I don't know which—that I became in the doctor's office knew the look of the place it wanted to go to, but had forgotten what it was called or where it was. There was running water in it, and mountains, and violent death, and a language that it had learned, and a mate. I followed my nose, my fears, my desires, not knowing why. . . . Once I reached this place, once I saw Prescendi, I remembered everything. Alegria was standing beside the *horreo* at the edge of the river. . . ."

Bill looked out of the low door, his eyes smarting. Now that the long chase was over, the quarry safe in their hands, he wanted to say, Don't come with us. Stay here. Die here where life took meaning for you. How could he ask Sigurd Thorsson to come away from this place where peace lay like a blanket over a landscape charged with memories of war? Where, far below, white sun-bright clouds hid the lower earth and all smoke and dirt, so that you existed in clean air and blue sky, among austere crags and cattle, untouched with sin? Perhaps he and Anne could stay too, the world forgotten.

The wail of a bagpipe rose above the tinkle of the cowbells. Through the open door Bill saw the cripple on the rock, a single-drone bagpipe under his arms, the mouthpiece in his mouth. The crutches and the dog and the gutted salmon lay beside him. The wild, thin wail of the pipes blew away over the mountains.

Sigurd Thorsson said, "That is a lament. I have heard them play it over men killed in battle here. He is lamenting for Alegria. Now that he has seen Ingrid and you and your clothes and money he thinks Alegria will leave with me." He spread his skeletal, trembling hands. "Damn him . . . It is I who must leave."

He went out. Bill watched him go to the women, take Ingrid by one hand and her mother by the other and walk to a rocky outcrop a little distance down the ridge. The cripple played on, his back to them all, his face to the black snow-ribbed towers of the Peña Santa de Asturias—the Holy Peak of Asturias—three thousand feet above.

VK said, "It had to finish like this if we ever found him alive. We've got to get this news through to Washington right away. And start back, because the HPS—"

The keening of the bagpipe broke off abruptly. Pedro cried something, while the pipe bag still expelled air in a sad moan. Mr. Thorsson called, "A car's coming!" They hurried out and stared down the hill. Mr. Thorsson joined them.

Bill saw it at once, a shiny sedan just entering Amieva village, far down, a mile and a half away.

VK said, "As I was about to say, the HPS won't be far behind. They'll reach our car in five or six minutes."

Ingrid and her mother came, Ingrid running, her mother keeping pace with long mountain strides. "Franco's police," Ingrid cried.

VK said, "I think the HPS. Anyway, they've cut off our way back by road. Can we get you out that way, sir—over the mountains?"

Mr. Thorsson said, "Yes. I know the paths, but—"

VK said, "We'll take the donkey for you to ride on. Both of us will have to come with you—Bill and me. . . . Anne, we've got to get messages through to Washington, and Webber in Madrid. And get our clothes and papers out of the hotel in Cangas. Rendezvous at the same hotel in Bilbao . . ."

Mr. Thorsson pointed down the hill and spoke in rapid Spanish to Alegria. She nodded and seized her daughter's hand, tugging at her to go with her down the hill.

Ingrid pulled free and threw both her arms around Bill Hammond's neck. She kissed him on the lips, pressing her body against him. "There," she said, pulling back. "You will remember that, at least."

She turned to her mother.

Anne started down with them but Ingrid shouted, "I'll do everything. Stay with Bill and my father. You have the medicines."

Alegria looked at Sigurd Thorsson. "*Siempre te quiero*," she said. "*Adios!*"

Pedro was swinging around on his crutches with amazing agility, breaking off hunks of cheese, stuffing sausage and bread into a calfskin pack, pouring wine from a jar into a leather bottle. The dog stood on the edge of the slope, his head cocked, watching the two women run down, their skirts flying.

Sigurd Thorsson said, "I love you always. *Adios*. That's what she said. Nothing more . . . It's better. I hope the last goodbye will be as sudden. Alegria said she can lead Ingrid down to the road by a shepherds' path. Look!"

The two women reached the SEAT on the grass. Miguel had seen them coming and was waiting. He joined them without pause and all three ran on and disappeared into the hanging woods below the road. Less than a minute later a cream-colored sedan swung around the last hairpin bend and reached the grassy alp. At once it stopped. It was a Facel Vega, Bill saw. Five men tumbled out.

"They've seen the SEAT," VK said. Bill edged back from the skyline and dropped to one knee. VK crouched beside a rock, aimed the rifle, and fired.

"Damn!" VK muttered. "That chap must have a sixth sense. Tall man in a pearl-gray hat . . . he stepped behind their car just as I squeezed the trigger. Now they've all scattered. De Guise is there, I think. Three others . . . It'll make them come on more cautiously. Everything ready?"

Anne was helping Sigurd Thorsson onto the donkey's back. He sat far toward the tail, saying, "As you see, I've done this before." He smiled faintly.

Pedro hung in his crutches by his armpits and pointed up the ridge to the edge of the beech forest. He spoke rapidly. Thorsson nodded and, when Pedro stopped speaking, reached out his hand. The other took it in both of his, bowing over it like a man receiving a gift. The donkey started moving.

Mr. Thorsson said, "Go—where he pointed. It's the quickest way for us to get out of sight."

The donkey began to trot. Glancing back, Bill saw the cripple ease himself onto the rock, put down his crutches and pick up his bagpipe. The music pierced through the high air. "*Sirihuelo,*" Thorsson said. "A song of joy."

VK said, "Canter if you can. Until we get into the woods. Anne, beat that donkey."

Bill ran alongside Mr. Thorsson on the downhill side, in case the donkey stumbled.

After fifteen minutes they reached the woods. The beech mast lay thick among the tortured tree roots and a thin gold sunlight showered down through the bright leaves. The donkey broke into a walk, and Mr. Thorsson said, "Let me rest a minute. It's the bumping. . . . Pedro said we would do best to cross the Dobra River near here, go upstream on the other side, then cross the pass at the head of the valley and down to Posada de Valdeon."

VK said, "All right. He knows best." He walked to the edge of the wood and stared back the way they had come, the rifle hanging negligently in his right hand.

Anne said, "Mr. Thorsson, you should take some pills now."

"Must I?" he grumbled. "Very well. Pass me the *bota* to get them down with."

VK returned. "They've got to be slowed somehow. Put off the scent altogether if possible. This is the place to do it. They have to cross the open hillside to get here from the cabin, as we had to. I'm going to stay here and break them up a bit."

Bill said, "I-I—*je resterai avec vous.*"

VK snapped, "No, you won't stay with me. It's Mr. Thorsson we're trying to save, not me. . . . Can you start again now, sir? If you push now perhaps we can rest later."

"Very well," Mr. Thorsson said. "Look after yourself."

"I will," VK said. "Don't you worry. If I can I'll rejoin you in four or five hours. You'll probably hear firing inside ten minutes. Don't stop."

Bill hesitated, tried to speak, then thrust out his hand. VK looked at the hand, then at him, and said, "Get moving."

Bill called out, "Anne, Anne!" as he ran beside the donkey through the beech woods. She turned and he saw that she was crying. "*Te quiero,*" he said gently.

"Good," Mr. Thorsson said. "Don't cry, Anne. VK is a great hunter. And Bill here is telling you he loves you."

Bill kissed Anne quickly, then motioned for her to follow behind the donkey while he led the way. He drew his pistol and ran forward till he was fifty yards ahead, then kept that distance. After a time—it might have been twenty minutes, it might have been half an hour—he heard the crack of a rifle shot far up the hill behind. At that moment the donkey was picking its way across the Dobra torrent while he held Sigurd Thorsson's right arm and Anne held his left, for the current was strong and the rocks slippery.

As they rested on the far bank he heard two more shots, then one with a different sound. That last one, he thought, was from a revolver. Twenty minutes later there were two more rifle shots and two more revolver shots. Finally, silence. Sigurd Thorsson said, apparently out of sleep, "It is no good worrying, dear Anne. VK will survive if anyone can."

Four hours later, resting among rocks in a stony waste under the north slope of a high peak, Bill sat at Anne's side, her hand resting in his. Her face was heavy with misery and Bill thought,

VK *must* come back and I *must* make him accept this love of ours. Mr. Thorsson slept on the ground. Lothario stood motionless, heavy head and long ears hanging.

A stone moved behind him and Bill turned to find himself looking down the muzzle of VK's rifle at three paces. VK said, "What sharp ears you have. And you, Anne! What's the matter with you?" He sat down. His shirt was black with sweat and his arms scratched and bleeding, his face drawn with fatigue. The eye from last night's fight was a greeny-purple color. He spoke jerkily. "I ambushed them there—edge of the beech wood—got the lead man, killed him—de Guise was there, he's a good hunter—good eye for country, never gave me a shot—they worked round behind me—hell of a time getting out, had to double back past them—cross the Dobra lower down—I put a bullet close to de Guise—but it was long range—didn't see Trilby."

Bill thought, No, Trilby would not have joined in the chase. He'd be back on the main road by now, figuring what to do next. Trilby liked to be a step or two ahead of the game, not actually in it.

"Lie down and sleep a bit, VK," Anne said. "You look done in."

VK stood up. "Not a chance. We must get off these mountains before dark."

When they tried to start, Lothario refused, braying loudly. Bill looked anxiously around, but VK said, "De Guise's crowd gave up hours back. They'll be trying to get round in front of us, but I think I persuaded them we were headed north, not south. . . . Keep moving."

Hours later, coming down a steep hillside, they saw a rocky cart track clinging to the slope below. After a cautious, slow descent the donkey stumbled onto it and Mr. Thorsson said, "Turn right." An hour later again, as twilight dimmed the mountain walls on each side of the valley, lights appeared ahead. Bill tramped on almost in a trance, one foot after the other, until a voice rasped in his ear, "Wake up, man. See what it says on that sign?"

Bill peered up at the rusted, discolored lettering: *Posada de Valdeon.* Mr. Thorsson muttered, "The motor road begins here."

VK said, "Wait here, off the track. Behind the rocks, out of sight. I'm going into the village to see what I can find. Taxi, car, Vespa, anything . . . Steal it, if necessary." His knees suddenly buckled and he leaned against the sign post, his eyes closing. Bill pushed him down, and said, "*J'irai.*"

VK spoke without opening his eyes. "All ri' . . . go ahead. . . . Be French. Hope God you don't meet any real Frenchmen." He stretched out flat and was unconscious, Bill saw, before Anne could push her folded cardigan under his head.

Bill stepped out along the dusky track. Bats swooped around a church belltower near the first houses. Down a narrow street to the right a few cars were parked outside an inn. More cars and two buses crowded the churchyard. From behind the inn he heard the rattle of a drum and the distinctive wail of the Asturian bagpipe.

An English male voice made him prick up his ears. "Well, enough's as good as a feast, is what I say."

"One fiesta's much the same as another, really, except for the bagpipes. I never expected that!" That was a woman. She went on. "Did you understand what that man was saying about a murder in the mountains?"

Bill drew back, pressed against the wall.

The unseen Englishman said, "Not all of it, but I think a Civil Guard's been murdered by some bandit called El Rubio, not far from here."

The woman said, "Well, that explains the roadblock outside the village, and all those Civil Guards in the inn."

The man said, "Good thing we brought our passports . . ."

Bill listened no more but hurried back, walking fast through the dusk. He reached the rocks and the gaunt signpost. Someone stepped out of the shadows, and he said, "P-p . . . Is that you, Anne? The p-place is full of p-police. They s-say El Rubio murdered a Ci-civil Guard near here."

VK appeared, yawning, reeling. "I heard," he mumbled. "That'll be Trilby's work. Cunning bastard. He found out Mr. T. is El Rubio—then shot a Civil Guard—said we did it. Now we have the whole Spanish government after us. Now we can't turn to the police or authorities for help, whatever trouble we're in."

Chapter 12

THEY WORKED CAUTIOUSLY around the village through fields of ripe wheat; then moved southeast, always uphill, at a slow pace till midnight; rested an hour among oak trees; and went on again. They saw no one. The big, steep land seemed deserted. There were no lights ahead, only a few gleaming far off and scattered in the bowl of the valley behind. VK went a few steps ahead of Anne, Mr. T., and the dead-weary donkey; Bill a few steps behind. For the moment they had no plan beyond getting away from this area where the police were out in force looking for them. Then perhaps they could hold up a car, or steal a truck. Perhaps, Bill thought, they should separate, Anne and Mr. T. holing up in a cave somewhere while he and VK made separate tries for Bilbao or Madrid . . . or a telephone booth: He had never thought he would want to talk to Webber, but he did now.

Bill walked with his gun in its holster, for he needed both hands to protect his face from bushes and branches. Every now and then he stopped, turned, and listened. The land sloped ever upward. The night chill of high altitude tingled in his cheeks. On the donkey's back old Thorsson rocked left, right, left, right, in a coma of fatigue. It began to rain.

He walked into the donkey and realized that they had all stopped. VK said, "We've got to rest." Bill nodded. The rain was mild and felt warmer than the earlier wind on his skin. They helped Mr. Thorsson down, and Bill tied the donkey loosely to a small tree. He took off his coat and gave it to Anne, who spread it over Mr. Thorsson. The old man sat down with his back to a beech tree and his legs stretched out in front of him. Whether his eyes were open or closed Bill could not see, but he did not move again. VK curled up beyond Mr. Thorsson. Bill took Anne's hand and they sank to the grass, lying curled together, he behind her, one arm under her head, the other around her body. He found her breast and she stirred comfortably to let his hand cup it, then her head was suddenly heavy on his arm and her breathing slow and even. He stared across a mountainside illumined only by a faint glow from behind the clouds. The rain pattered on the beech leaves, then he was asleep.

He awoke, suddenly warm and alive. He knew he had not slept long—there was no change in the light, or the rain, or his position, and his shirt was no wetter than when he lay down—but now he was not tired. This was Anne curved inside the curve of his body: Anne, moving languorously, thighs stirring, a hand pressing his hand to her breast. She too had awoken. Perhaps it was these slow sensuous movements that had aroused him. She was awake, so she knew the urgency of his desire for her, because his sex had risen and pressed against her buttocks. She turned over suddenly, her arms came around his neck and her mouth opened below his. Her tongue pressed rigid into his mouth, drew back, slid in again, caressed his tongue, retreated.

Mr. Thorsson sighed and Bill tensed, listening. After a minute he rose, pulling Anne with him. It had to be now. But not here. A few yards away would do. They stumbled together away from the tree. At ten yards, the rain dripping on his head, he took her in his arms, but she whispered, "There, Bill, what's that?"

A few paces away, he saw a straight edge black against the dark. Going cautiously to it he found a low stone hut, its entrance sheltered from the rain. There was no door or window and inside he could see nothing, but there was a smell of woodsmoke and old ash. Anne followed him inside and in total blackness he turned and found her. In a moment she lay under him, spread, holding, drawing him, her lips salt and wet. He mounted with power and entered tenderly, to whisper "Darling . . . oh my darling." She was deeper and firmer than any woman he'd known, and the first who was not a whore. Her pelvis heaved and thrust under him, she was a slippery trench, becoming hotter every second. She engulfed him in velvet ridges, her legs gripped him tight, and suddenly he had to hold himself onto the earth as the spasms began to thrust him into her, pinning her with his weight, she struggling and crying under him. The pulsing jets came white-hot now—then red, glowing, warm. He lay gasping on her, her mouth was full of tears and salt. She did not move and her inner flesh relaxed in slow spasms. A deep muscle thickened and caressed him. He had lost nothing of his size in the depths of her, and her rhythmic contractions brought him slowly to press and release, hold and thrust, until she moaned and sucked his tongue from his mouth, and moaned again, and remote lights began to glitter behind his eyes and the aching of his loins released.

When he rolled his body off her she held him so tight with arms and legs wrapped around him that he remained in her. She took his hand and passed it down to her slippery swollen flesh. He touched himself, and her, and knew that they filled each other. Her lips were at his ear, whispering, "Bill, I love you. . . ."

His sex was a long, rubbery projection of himself that she had created for the two of them. She was astride him, her body arching and bending, her wet cold hair slapping his face, the lips of her sex massaging his loins. "*Coño,*" he whispered. "*Coño!*" His spasms began in sheer pain, turning to helpless ecstasy as she writhed, an unseen she-cat, twisting on him, then suddenly stopped, flopped, the lips flaccid.

A face grew in his mind. A woman's face, lost in animal passion. He froze with terror as the features took shape. Then he recognized her. It was Anne, only her, no one else. No other woman who had ever lived.

Again, he knew it would. He'd seen a bull elk in rutting season, rampant, hypnotized in a sexual drive that shook his whole huge body, and thrust him to a climax every few minutes for hours, days on end, whether with his cows or alone did not matter, he could not help himself. Bill knew the same urge now, his maleness no longer triumphant—that had been the first time—but helpless. He would go on now until he dropped. He could make love. And because of it, he could speak. Nothing could stop him now, for he had found *her*, the mother and whore—Anne.

But she slid away from him, and kneeling over him whispered, "Darling . . . soon it'll be forever. I'll bring the others now, though. We must get them into shelter."

She was gone. He zipped himself and lay back against a wall of the hut. Soon a match flared and he saw VK's face framed in the door. The yellow glow died but he had seen VK's eyes, and in them, that VK knew. Perhaps he had seen them go. Perhaps he had heard them as they cried and moaned together. At this moment, if they had been completely alone, VK would have tried to kill him. On these Spanish mountains, in this hut, as the light of a second match showed a pile of wood, gray ash, goat droppings, the bare earth where he had covered his woman—it was customary, and fitting, that a man should avenge what he felt was his sister's shame. And if VK were to overcome him, then it was good and fair that he should die in this entrancement, caring only about the permanent enlargement of his heart and body, the aching throb . . . if only she would open the cradle of her thighs toward him.

"Go to sleep," VK muttered. "I'm going to light a fire."

And now Anne was with him again, curled again in his arms, her back to him, and he went out on a sudden river, toward the night, on a fading knowledge that he was pressed against her and would never go soft again. VK's eyes shone in the red glow of a burning twig, and Anne's breast swelled in his hand. . . .

He awoke to a sense of danger, and saw the silhouettes of a man and a dog in the door. They were about the same size. He fumbled for his pistol, Anne groaned, and the dog—was it a bear? —growled cavernously. It wore an immense steel-spiked collar around its great neck. The little man said a curt word, addressing it as Baturro, and the beast fell silent. They all awoke and sat up. A small fire burned dimly in the middle of the floor.

Sigurd Thorsson and the stranger spoke in Spanish. Bill looked at his watch. It was seven o'clock in the morning, and the night's rain had turned into a heavy upland mist. Visibility was less than fifty feet. The little man came into the hut and crouched just inside the doorway, and Bill saw that he was not a man but a boy, twelve or thirteen years old, wearing ragged black trousers, a torn blue shirt, and for protection against the weather, an old sack, one seam cut open. His bare feet slopped about inside large ancient shoes. His skin was brown-weathered and his eyes were a strong gentian blue. He carried a staff in one hand, and under the sack, which he now shed, he had a goatskin pack. From this he took out a loaf of bread and a hunk of darkish cheese. He held them out.

Mr. Thorsson said, "He's offering us his food. That's all he has for a week. . . ." His voice was stronger than VK remembered it since the early days in Scotland. He went on. "His name is Marcos and he's a shepherd—from a village below the pass."

"What pass?" VK asked.

"The San Glorio. It's ahead of us, less than a mile away. A motor road goes over it from Riaño, on our right, to Potes, on our left. He says there are some *Guardia Civil* on the pass. Four of them." Bill stared at Anne. She smiled openly at him, with no trace of languor or sexuality—a fresh, clear smile.

"What are we going to do with him?" VK was looking coldly at the boy. "Now that he's seen us, he's a danger, especially with Civil Guards so close."

Old Thorsson spoke, almost dreamily. "A score of times, on patrol, our lives depended on shepherds like this boy. Perhaps his father, his grandfather . . ."

The boy spoke, through a mouthful of bread. Thorsson said, "He asks whether we are bandits." He laughed. "Shepherds aren't afraid. Any Spanish bandit knows *they* have nothing worth stealing. . . . I told him the police are after us for something we didn't do. I'm going to ask him to help us."

VK looked at Bill and shrugged. Bill said, "With n-no m-map and n-no idea where w-we are or w-where to go, w-we need help from someone."

Thorsson began to talk. The boy answered, every now and then jerking his chin toward the swirling mist. Bill gazed at Anne. He knew VK was watching him.

Thorsson said, "He says he can guide us across the road between the Civil Guard posts. Beyond, there are more mountains. He can lead us through them as far as the next road. After that he doesn't know the country and will have to come back to his flocks. I've told him we can do nothing for him now, but later we can give him a proper reward. . . . He says the mist will lift soon. We should go at once."

For a time Bill thought they would not be able to start because Lothario would not get up; but after the great dog had growled at him, the donkey allowed himself to be dragged upright.

The shepherd boy said, "*Venga Baturro*," and led off. In the mist the great dog at his heels looked like a cross between a grizzly bear and the Hound of the Baskervilles. Bill thought their direction was south, though with the sun hidden he could not be sure. The donkey paced wearily, head down, VK tugging at the rope. From time to time Baturro growled with a cavernous subterranean rumbling. The hair stiffened along his back and he peered into the mist, his head turning sharply from side to side. The boy spoke a few words and Sigurd Thorsson said, "He smells wolves. There are many on these moors. That's why he wears the spiked collar."

After a time the dog padded on in silence and the hair lay flat again along his spine. The way led at first uphill, but slightly; then over a gradual crest and for the next twenty minutes steadily and sometimes steeply downward over rock and bare grass. A sudden break in the mist would be bad here, Bill thought. Without its protection, on this slope, they would be in full view.

The boy stopped and pointed. Bill saw the black of a tarred road ahead. The boy pointed to the left and whispered, "*Guardia Civil.*" His hands made the gesture of the three-cornered hat. Then he led on and they all crossed the road. A small wind kept the mist moving slowly from right to left.

Dogs began to bark, close, and Bill saw VK push forward the safety catch of the rifle. Black and brown shapes ran out of the mist—two police dogs, Alsatians, barking. VK aimed but did not fire. Bill swore silently. A shot, fired now, would give everything away. Then the police dogs were on him, leaping forward in a snarling pair. The shepherd boy spoke a single sharp word: "*Matalos!*"

Baturro moved out silently from behind the donkey and caught the nearest police dog in mid-air. The dog thumped to the ground, half stunned, with Baturro astride, the huge jaws clamped into its throat. The police dog writhed in frenzy. Its companion leaped at Baturro's back, and fastened its teeth into the heavy brown and white fur at the back of Baturro's neck, behind the spiked collar. Baturro shook and rolled and Bill stepped back. "Go on!" he muttered to VK, pointing forward.

A man shouted in the mist, not far off. The shepherd boy answered in a plaintive whine. VK and the donkey and Anne and Sigurd Thorsson began to disappear up the slope beyond the road.

For three, four endless minutes the three dogs fought in the mist-enclosed arena on the pass. Bill saw then that the under dog was dead, his head bleeding into a yellow gorse bush. Baturro held on a moment longer, then suddenly rolled over, using his great weight to throw the second dog off balance. In a second it was all over. Baturro didn't go for the throat, but took the back of the police dog's head, bit deep, and with a savage jerk whiplashed the animal's body, breaking its neck. The corpse fell six feet off, onto the road. Baturro bayed once. The boy beckoned to Bill and they ran together up the hill. The voices were calling more peremptorily, and from closer.

They caught up with the others after a few moments. Mr. Thorsson said, "Baturro killed them? Marcos shouted to the *Guardia Civil* that their dogs were fighting his. They believed it at first and did nothing, but just now they were telling him to stay where he is while they came to investigate."

To Bill, VK said, "Stay at the back with me now. Anne, keep the donkey close behind the boy." His voice was noncommittal but there were dark rings under his eyes.

They had gone about three hundred feet up the hill and a quarter of a mile beyond the road. The mist thinned, as the boy Marcos had predicted. VK unslung the rifle and dropped a few paces behind Bill. The mist condensed on Bill's eyebrows and dropped cold onto his cheek. His hair was wet and cold. He was wearing strong shoes but not the mountain boots needed for the travels of the past twenty-four hours, and his feet were wet and his socks soaked. He could barely see Anne, twenty yards ahead.

The current of air blew stronger against his right cheek and he looked anxiously upward. The gray murk began to lighten. Ahead and to the right front the mist was pearled and haloed. The sun was on the point of breaking through.

He opened his mouth to cry *Hurry!*, but there was no need. Marcos had increased the pace. Anne strained at the donkey's rope, Mr. Thorsson slapped its rump. They hurried on and up through thinning, swirling tendrils of mist. Gorse and broom glowed into yellow flame as the diffuse sunlight strengthened.

A strong westerly gust ripped the fog curtain from them. They stopped, motionless, on a bare hillside. Six hundred feet below and half a mile back Bill saw the road, and a big signboard and a tent. To the east the earth swooped endlessly down to a distant trough. Beyond the pass a frieze of snow peaks glittered in the sunlight.

Four green-uniformed Civil Guards were gathered around the bodies of the two dogs. Bill saw rifles. One of the men was using binoculars, as the mist blew away, to search the hillside. Marcos, squatting at VK's side, muttered a word. Mr. Thorsson said, "They have seen us." The Guards spread out and started up the hill. VK was examining the way ahead, his back to the Civil Guards. He said, "The ground's very broken. We won't always be in sight of them, and for the moment the range is too great for them to fire, even when we are. But at the rate this bloody donkey climbs, it won't be long before they'll be able to . . ."

Bill thought, Suppose VK and I try to hold them here while Mr. Thorsson and Anne escape. It would be very hard to manage any real delay without killing some of the Guards, and they were not members of the HPS.

Marcos spoke rapidly. Mr. Thorsson translated. "He says . . . let him ride the donkey . . . on up the mountain . . . while we go there . . . around the left side of the Peña Prieta . . . that mountain ahead . . . It is very steep, but . . . we can perhaps do it."

Down the mountain the Civil Guards had disappeared into a fold of the ground. They wouldn't come out for five minutes or more, and they had made the mistake of leaving no one behind on the pass to watch the whole hillside.

VK said, "OK. Tell him not to fight when they catch him. Tell him to say we hid here and recrossed the pass when they went on after him . . . that we forced him with us at gunpoint."

The donkey moved to the right across the hill, the boy riding, Baturro at heel. VK led the others along the slope to the left, in the direction the boy had pointed out. If the ruse was to work, they must all be out of sight around the spur of the mountain before the Civil Guards reached this spot, where they had parted.

Five minutes later they reached the spur and passed around it. Bill and VK crouched among the bushes, looking back. The green-cloth hat covers came over the ridge below. The four Civil Guards stopped, looked up, then seemed to hold a consultation. One of them pointed to the right. They moved away and, soon, out of sight. Bill and VK hurried forward.

Half an hour later Bill, now in the lead, stopped with a shiver of vertigo. This must be the steep place the boy had warned them of. To the right the mountain rose very steeply in rock and heather to a rounded crest. Plaques of snow lay in the gullies and under the cliffs on this northern face of the mountain. To the left the steep grass slope ended, replaced by a nearly vertical rock chute which dropped two thousand feet to a black tarn, ice-rimmed. Below the tarn the land swooped on down three thousand feet more to a toy village amid miniature fields. Black rocks and small layered cliffs linked the precipices above and the chute below. Across them was the only way.

Bill's stomach felt empty and queasy. He had a fair head for heights, but vertigo and dizziness had sometimes assailed him, and they were upon him now. And how was Anne to cross? And Mr. Thorsson?

VK came back from a close inspection of the rocks. He looked at Bill as though to speak. He's going to ask me to help him, Bill thought. And now he's seen that I can't, that I will need help myself.

VK said, "I'll guide everyone across, one by one. You first, sir . . . while I'm fresh. The rest of us are expendable." His lips twisted in a small, hard grin as he said it, and the bloodshot black-ened eye looked at Bill. Bill knew suddenly that he meant to have his vengeance here.

Mr. Thorsson said, "I do not get dizzy, VK. It is only that I have little strength."

"Don't worry," VK said.

They started off. Watching, Bill could see that there was only one really bad place. For the rest, it was a matter of VK going slowly ahead, guiding Mr. Thorsson's foot, holding his hand. At the bad place, though, VK stood astraddle across some unseen drop, facing the mountain, while Mr. Thorsson slowly passed around outside him, holding to his arms as though to scaffolding.

Anne said, "I love you." He started. The dizzying heights had turned his thoughts away from her. The deep-gray eyes were looking into his.

"Aren't you afraid?" he said, pointing.

She shook her head, smiling. "I can't think about it . . . only of when we shall always be together."

VK came back, long-striding across the heather. "Anne," he said. "You next."

Bill watched them make the same careful passage across the rocks, although this time it went faster. Anne hardly needed any help except at the bad place and even there passed over with no more than three careful sideways steps, hands gliding along a rock shelf, instead of Mr. Thorsson's painful progression.

Then VK was standing over him, his eyes glinting. "Your turn, Hammond."

He stood up and went forward. VK threw single words and curt instructions over his shoulder. "Follow my footsteps here. . . . Right foot here . . . Left foot first, then right . . . change hands . . ."

A turning haze slowly sucked his attention into its vortex, and he was looking down. He swam, floating on a surface of air, and gazed on delectable, misty pools far below. His arms moved in long slow circles, circling wider, more swoopingly around the far, deep, central pool. And in the middle of that, the center of the whirlpool, VK's eyes, sharp flints, no light in them, the thin lips tight, the long jaw set. Below, a hand was stretched out to him, but unmoving. He could reach the hand easily, but first he had to control himself, to arrest the long circling dive on which he had launched himself. Slowly, working as hard as to make his tongue form words, pushing through a swaying curtain, the blue haze now above, now below . . . his hand moved out and clasped the other.

At once he was jerked forward. The swooping circle ended abruptly and he stood on a rock ledge, three inches wide, pouring sweat, his forehead ice cold. He was shaking, looking a million miles down the chute. A stone dislodged by his foot leaped out and down, bounding farther, longer, steeper until it sprang out of the chute and down the last thousand feet in a single dive, landing in the middle of the tarn. The sound of the splash never came to them.

VK said, "Nearly fell then, didn't you? A little touch of vertigo? There's worse ahead. Much worse. There. Look down there." They were in the middle of the bad place. VK's lank blond hair shone with sweat and he was rubbing his hands dry on his trousers. "Think you'll make the next bit?" he said. He was grinning like a wolf.

Bill looked him in the eye. "If I live, VK, I am going to marry Anne. No one's going to stop me. No one and nothing. Now blindfold me, because that's the only way I'll make it across there."

He pulled his dirty handkerchief out of his pocket and began to tie it around his eyes. Before he had finished VK said, "All right. I'll tie it. . . . Here. Hold this hand. Left foot first. There. Hold . . . Slide right foot past. Wait till you feel my hand, then step along the ledge sideways . . . Now a long step straight down, about three feet, stop dead against a rock. Hold it . . ."

Hours later he heard Anne's triumphant cry, "There!" In her voice he heard her double triumph—*See what a man my brother is! See what a man my lover is!* Then her hands were behind his head, unfastening the handkerchief. He looked back the way he had come. At VK's sardonic grin, he turned away and vomited his guts out, while Anne held his head.

He got up. "Come on," he said. "Let's get going."

Four hours later, from the edge of a high hayfield, they saw a village and a tree-lined stream below. The wheat stood gold in the slanted fields. Thorsson said, "That must be Cardaño de Arriba, and that's the road Marcos told us about."

They sprawled down, resting. VK said, "What now? I think we should hold up a car and drive into France."

"We'd never get across the border," the old man muttered.

"Ingrid's waiting for us in Bilbao," Anne said.

"That doesn't matter," VK said impatiently. "We have to get

where we're safe at least from the Spanish police. I wish church altars were still sanctuaries."

"We ought to g-get to Bilbao if w-we can," Bill said. "Then use the B-b-beechcraft. They can't put roadblocks in the . . . air!"

Anne said, "A man's coming . . . an old man. He was resting under the wall."

Thorsson turned his head. *"Buenas tardes!"*

The old man squatted companionably with a polite word. Bill looked around as they talked. To the left was moorland. Ahead, the valley ran south to a big lake, probably artificial. There was a village in the valley close below and another by the lake. A huge white limestone mountain dominated the right side of the valley. If Marcos had led the Civil Guards behind that it would take them all day to get back and pick up the proper trail again.

Mr. Thorsson said, "He says that Civil Guards on bicycles came to the village this morning early, and went on. They are not here now. He knows, because signals are made from that lower village when they come. If we wait here he will bring us food, and after dark he will guide us past the end of the lake. Some of the way he can take us in his oxcart. There is a railway over those next hills that you can see beyond the lake. A mining railway, but it has some passenger trains."

"Where does it go from and to?"

"León in one direction, Bilbao in the other."

VK looked up, startled. "Bilbao! . . . I suppose we'll have to trust him."

Thorsson said gently, "We have come to no harm through trusting Marcos, have we? But, my boy, if we are to travel all night, I must rest now."

Bill hitched his back more comfortably against the thin ash tree and glanced at VK and old Thorsson. VK slept sprawled as though dead, but his right hand lay on the rifle; and at any alarm —as had already happened once when a child screaming in the houses across the field had aroused him—he would come instantly awake and sit up, the rifle pointed and his finger on the trigger. Old Thorsson dozed, like himself, with his back to a tree. The morning sun, pouring down almost unobstructed through the leaves, showed a touch of color in his parchment skin, and he breathed well and evenly. Meter-gauge rail tracks gleamed in a cutting below. It was ten o'clock of a mid-July morning.

A cluster of houses lined a low ridge a quarter of a mile to the north. Behind the houses the land climbed away to the high country they had been crossing all last night and the day before. Dogs barked fitfully, and he could hear a faint whirring from a coal-mine elevator a mile to the west. Once a horsecart and twice rackety old trucks had passed on the road behind the wood. But that was all.

His gaze returned to Anne. She lay on her side, his coat rolled under her head. Her skirt was rucked up and he looked wonder-ingly at her thighs. Since their passion in the shepherd's hut he had not had a chance to exchange more than a word or two in private with her; and when those moments came the most impor-tant thing to say always seemed to be, *I love you.* Looking at her now, he wanted to ask whether she had enjoyed his love-making; but that would be an insulting question. Obviously she had. Then he wanted to ask her what caused her to respond, and lead, with a more animal directness, a sheerly greater skill, than any whore—Mexican, French, Cuban, or Egyptian. Physically she had not been a virgin, but that was almost beside the point. What she knew—what she did—could not come from a few fumbled seduc-tions. It had to be instinctive, natural; or it had to come from an intensive experience in very imaginative brothels. He did not need to ask which. So the question answered itself: She was a natural maker of love. That was why, for the first time, he had felt no shame. Why he knew he was not debasing a woman but fulfilling her, and she him. Anne was . . .

A faint, far rumble crept into his reverie and he sat up straight. The unmistakable boom of a diesel horn sounded in the east, and he stretched out his hand to awaken VK. But VK was already awake, the rifle cradled. The diesel horn boomed again. The ap-proaching train was headed for León—the wrong way; but they had better examine it closely, to see how they could get onto one going the right way. Mr. Thorsson's eyes opened, and he said, "I'm ready. Just give me a hand."

VK said, "Not this time. We just want to look at it. Keep down, sir."

The horn boomed again, close now. Bill crept to the edge of the

wood and looked up the mile-long straight to the east. A bright-
blue diesel locomotive came fast around the distant bend, followed by one, two, three . . . nine tiny freight cars and two passenger cars. The horn blared loud and imperious, straight down
the track, and Bill crept back into the wood. This train was going
fast, downhill. So a train headed for Bilbao would be going slow,
uphill.

The diesel passed with a rumble and a stink of oil smoke. The
quick rattle of the car wheels began. Bill watched, his face thrust
between the roots of a small bush at the edge of the cut. The cars
were open and shallow. Some were empty, some full of coal.
Some had a hutchlike sentry box mounted on one end-frame.
These boxes must be open on the far side, because the near side
was walled with wood. . . . The two passenger cars held few
riders. A conductor sat at a seat writing something. On the back
platform of the rear car there were two men in green, black belts
and hats shining, rifles gleaming.

The clack of the wheels echoed into silence. The last cars
curved around a sharp bend to the west and vanished. The diesel
horn blared away in a dying fall. Creeping back into the wood
Bill saw that Anne had not awoken. VK knelt beside her, a sad
look on his face. Then he pressed one thumb gently below her ear
and her eyes opened. She did not move. VK said softly, "How can
you sleep, you lazy cow, with that horn blasting in your ear?
Didn't you sleep properly last night?" Her arms came up and
pulled his head down and she kissed him on the forehead. Bill
looked away.

VK recalled him. "Here. What did you make of our chances
with a train?"

They discussed what they had seen. The southward-facing sentry boxes must be for brakemen, but how many men had actually
been in them it had not been possible to see from this side. Then,
were the cars turned bodily around at the far end, so that the
boxes would all face north on trains going the other way? It
seemed unlikely. And did every train carry a pair of Civil Guards,
or only passenger trains?

VK said, "Did you see a way to get up on the wagons?"

Bill nodded. It wouldn't be hard, as the cars were so small.
Onto a low step, then onto the platform, then up and over. A full

or half-full car would be better than an empty one. Then they could hide under the coal, at least so that a casual glance wouldn't show them. He said, "We'd better jump the f-first eastbound f-freight. I'll give the signal."

It came very soon, heralded by the shrill call of a steam-engine whistle. That was better. A steam engine would really be laboring to climb the grade here. They waited, crouched at the edge of the wood. The locomotive's asthmatic whistle came closer. The black boiler rolled around the curve, wreathed in steam from leaking pipes. Behind it followed open coal cars, and Bill saw at once that the brakeman's hutches still faced the opposite way, south. He could not see which, if any, were occupied. There were no passenger cars, just a boxlike van for the conductor.

The locomotive passed—No. 93—a polished brass nameplate—JULIAN—a glimpse of the engineer leaning out the far side—the fireman shoveling coal—the glare from the open firebox dimmed by the sun. Bill waved his hand and jumped to his feet.

They ran out beside the laboring, lumbering train. The wheels screeched slowly against the curve of the rail, the iron coupling links rattled, woodwork groaned, stones crunched. Bill shouted, "This one!" Anne swung up first, VK on her heels. VK dropped his rifle over into the car and reached back down. Bill, slowly running with Mr. Thorsson on the cinders, bodily lifted the old man onto the steel step, while VK took his hand. Bill thrust, VK pulled, and Mr. Thorsson stood on the platform. Bill followed with an easy step and a long stride.

One after the other they climbed over the side of the wagon. Inside, the coal was almost to the top of the wooden framework. They lay down and began to move the small anthracite nuggets with their bare hands, to make hollows to lie in.

Bill noticed VK pause in his scrabbling, raise his head, and look up and down the train. He lowered it again, and reached for the rifle. He said grimly, "The brakeman in the next wagon has seen us. He must have seen us get on. . . . I can shoot him where he is. No one will hear. Then push him off on the outside of a curve. No one will see."

Mr. Thorsson said, "VK, you are a very violent man. Sometimes you are like one of those beasts that kill for pleasure. . . . You have a much better weapon than your rifle."

Bill understood at once, but VK frowned. "I don't have a big knife, or that would be best. If he would let me get close enough to use it."

Anne said, "Money!"

Mr. Thorsson said, "Yes. In your pocket, my son. The other one, I think." VK pulled out his wallet. "Now, take out a note. Hold it up. Wave it. Has he seen? Let go of it."

VK grinned suddenly and Bill lifted his head to watch. It was a Spanish hundred-peseta note, worth about a dollar and a half, that VK let fly. The brown paper rose in the air, swooped, and fluttered past the brake hutch like a leaf in the wind. The brakeman's head turned to watch it. Suddenly he leaned far out, and VK released another note. This time the brakeman tried to grab it as it passed, but he missed and almost fell off the train.

In all the world no one else seemed to be aware of the little comedy being acted out between two clattering coal cars. Ahead, the high black back of the locomotive's coal bunker blocked the engine crew's view. To the rear, the conductor did not look out of his van. Up and down the train the other brakemen slept in their hutches. To the right wheat fields, thick with poppies, stretched empty and gold and red to a pale horizon. To the left the mountain wall kept slow pace with the train.

Mr. Thorsson said, "Beckon him to come to us. We must talk with him."

VK picked out a five-hundred-peseta note and waved it in one hand, beckoning to the brakeman with the other. The brakeman made a downward gesture that clearly said, *Wait*.

They returned to their task, laboriously digging forms in the coal. The train rattled on eastward along the foot of the mountains. Sparks showered on them, gradually riddling their clothes with tiny burned-out holes. Then, as the train rushed down through dense woods of beech and oak, the brakes began to squeal and the wind became sharp with the smell of hot steel. Grinding and bumping, the train stopped at a station.

From forward came the clang of steel and the gurgle of water. Feet crunched on clinker beside the tracks. After a few minutes, a voice spoke nearby, softly, in Spanish. Mr. Thorsson answered. Bill raised his head and saw that the brakeman was standing on the forward buffer beam of their wagon, looking at them over the rim of the wagon's side. A cigarette dangled from his mouth and he was pretending to examine the brake wheel. After question and answer, Mr. Thorsson said, "Give him the five hundred pesetas now, VK." The coal heaved and VK's black hand came out with the money.

The brakeman murmured, *"Gracias,"* and Bill heard him jump down to the roadbed. Soon after, the train started with a fearful series of jerks and clangs.

Mr. Thorsson said, "You only have to be against the government to have friends in this country. Any government! I've promised him more money, and he's promised to hand us over to his relief in Mataporquera. He told us to get farther under the coal. He said we could be seen very clearly from above—signal boxes, bridges, and so on."

As the train rocked and clanked on, Bill wriggled free and looked around. Anne knelt laughing on the coal. "I don't think I've *ever* been so dirty. VK? VK! Come out and do some work."

VK was bursting free of his pit in the coal. One look at his grim blackened face and Bill's smile vanished. VK said, "Did you see the man up the bank? He saw you. The three of you. It was the man we call Laurel. You all had your backs to him. I don't think he saw me. So he doesn't know that we've seen him."

Bill looked over the side. The train was climbing steadily on an open hillside, the engine exhaust thundering straight up. A town lay in the valley to the left. A road ran down from the hollow of the hill behind them, where the station was, to the town. From the town another road ran along the valley floor, parallel to the railway, but lower. A small blue car was racing toward the town from the railway station.

VK said, "That's a Fiat 1100 . . . SEAT, I mean. Probably Laurel's. What do you think he'll do? Telephone his bosses from the town, or . . ."

"Not on Spanish telephones," Mr. Thorsson said. "He would never get through in time."

Bill said, "I d-don't think he'll telephone. He'll d-drive like hell, get ahead of this train, and have the C-civil G-guards w-waiting for us somewhere ahead."

VK pointed at an overbridge up ahead. He said, "He can't trust the Civil Guards to kill Mr. T. on sight, any more than we can trust them not to. . . . I think he'll wait on a bridge and put a bullet into Mr. Thorsson as we go under."

The old steam engine up front leaned into the collar as the grade stiffened. The bellow of the exhaust vanished in the large silence. The pace slowed to a crawl.

"Christ, we're practically going backwards," VK exclaimed. "If he does go to a bridge, I don't know whether he'll wait on the near or far side. . . . I'll guess the far—then the engine driver and fireman won't see him. So if I'm to get him when he leans over the parapet to shoot down into this wagon, I have to be farther forward. I have to be looking backwards, and I have to be hidden at the moment that I pass under him."

Mr. Thorsson said, "The next brakeman's hutch forward is empty. Our man said so."

"Good. Mr. T., you get into my hole. Bill, make another hump at the other side, which might be Mr. T. If Laurel has to hesitate, just a fraction of a second, wondering where to shoot, it may make all the difference. . . . I'm going forward."

Bill held his arm, pointing. "Isn't that Laurel's car? Wait, or he might see you."

The train ran more freely now between an avenue of poplars. Straight back the pale limestone pyramid of Espiguëte, which had been their companion all last night and the day before, pierced the scurrying clouds. In the valley to the left a small blue car raced along the dusty road, rapidly overtaking the train.

As soon as the car disappeared in a fold of the ground VK took the rifle and swung across to the next wagon forward. Bill watched him until he slipped into the sentry box two wagons ahead. He sighed with relief. Laurel had signed his own death warrant. At fifty feet, with that rifle, VK would not miss, however badly the train jolted and swayed.

The gradient eased and the beat of the locomotive's exhaust lightened. The wheels clacked faster over the rail joints, making a merry sound in the flashing poplars. Bill took off his coat, bundled it, and heaped coal on it at one side of the little wagon. Mr. Thorsson buried himself in VK's deep trough. Anne kneeled at Bill's side to help him.

His hands stopped working. He looked at them, side by side with hers, all four black and shiny. She was turning to him—her face black-streaked, hair disheveled.

He said, "You look like the girl in the old Dodge commercials!"

She laughed, her black hand drawing a wide smear on her face as she tried to push a floating strand of hair back into place. "What girl? We didn't have TV in Kenya, you know."

He said, "She was a very nice blonde who kept blowing herself up. When she came down, she looked just like you do now."

Anne said, "VK has accepted you. Because you trusted him." Her eyes began to fill and their grimed hands joined. The engine shrieked out a sudden whistle, the wagon banked hard to the left for a curve and plunged into a tunnel.

A cloud of black and yellow coal smoke enveloped them. Then it was dark. He pulled Anne's head toward him and kissed her on the lips. They clung together as the train gathered speed in the tunnel.

His eyes began to smart, and when he had to draw back his mouth to breathe the acrid smoke made him choke and cough. It was dark, black dark, like the inside of a tube, or a mine. It was like the Kaylabito Mine shaft, and the noise and dense smoke somehow only accentuated the resemblance.

The Kaylabito Mine shaft, where VK had lost his self-control.

The wagon jerked hard right, and light burst down the tunnel, coming on fast. He thrust Anne away with a heave and a yell, but she clung, not understanding, as he reached for the gun in his armpit holster. The wagon burst into the open.

Fresh air wreathed around him in the smoke, but he saw Laurel plain, crouched beside a thorn bush close above the tunnel mouth, a sawed-off shotgun to his shoulder. Time froze. Anne saw Laurel, too. Laurel's eyes searched for Mr. Thorsson—detected the false hump—saw the real man. The scene exploded. Anne dived forward to hide Sigurd Thorsson, her arms outspread. The train noise buried the quick one-two blast of the shotgun. Bill dropped to Anne's side. She was dead, the back of her head shattered.

Bill looked at the blood on his hand. There was an automatic pistol there, too, covered with blood. A hundred and fifty feet, two hundred feet back, the man above the tunnel mouth sat calmly, his gun laid down and invisible. Bill put the bloody automatic back into its holster. Laurel was out of range. Old Thorsson struggled out of concealment, his face broken with horror. Bill turned Anne over so that she lay face up, blood trickling from her mouth.

A bullet cracked overhead. Far back above the tunnel mouth Laurel half rose, stumbled, and fell like a shot vulture to the rails below.

VK came down the train. When he climbed into the wagon his skin was green-white under the filth. He looked once at Anne, then knelt in the coal, his hands at his sides, shaking silently.

Bill leaned back against the woodwork, flattened. Between them they had killed her. VK, from his pride in refusing to recognize his own physical weakness; himself, for sparing Laurel when he had him helpless in Iceland; Mr. Thorsson, even, for the primal panic that had made him run so fast, so far, from the inescapable.

Yet they were not superhuman. This was how it was with people. People broke under strain. Cave fears stalked their twentieth-century lives. They misplaced their generosity. They acted without plan or logic.

"Laurel's dead. I think I shot him in the heart," VK said dully.

Bill said, "Tha-tha-tha-tha . . ."

He stared at VK. So it was all gone. He waited, shoulders hunched, for VK to say something more. VK said, "No one else knows we're on this train. The men who sent him will suspect the truth when they hear where and how he died, but by then it'll be too late. We can stay on the train."

Anne's open eyes reflected the deep blue and white cloud patterns of the high sky.

VK said, "I don't think any of the train crew heard the shots. If someone in the fields did, he'll keep quiet. . . . We must bury Anne's body, here in the damned coal." He frowned at Bill's involuntary cry. "We must, man! We must have time to get far away before she is discovered. What else can we do?"

Bill Hammond didn't speak. Somehow he doubted that he ever would.

Chapter 13

VK THOUGHT, afterwards, that in Bilbao their very weariness and numbed lack of caution saved them. The train ground into the outskirts of the city near half past seven. When a signal stopped it in a smoky warren of factories and slag heaps, soot-blackened rock on one side of the tracks and a coal-stained stream the other, the brakeman signaled to them to get off. With a whistle and a hiss the train clanked on, and they washed the worst of the coal dust off themselves in the filthy stream. Then they walked into the city, looking like Spanish working men—miners down from the hills perhaps, or dockers in from Portugalete.

In the city center the evening *paseo* was in full swing, the streets so jammed that the police would not have been able to chase them even if they had spotted them. Near the Gran Hotel Mr. Thorsson picked on an urchin who was working the gutter for cigarette butts, and beckoned him into an alley. There he gave him muttered instructions and fifty pesetas. When the boy had gone, Thorsson said, "I told him to find out whether Ingrid's there, and to tell her to come back with him if she thinks it's safe. . . . We should not all stay together. Bill and I will go into a tavern—that one, the third. You wait here for her, VK."

She came out in ten minutes, following the boy at a distance. VK walked away from the corner. The boy peered into the alley where Mr. Thorsson had spoken to him, looked up and down, and went away, puzzled. Ingrid examined a nearby shop window. VK could detect no one who seemed to be following or watching her. He went up to her, linked his arm into hers and started strolling down the side street, stopping to look into windows as they went.

Ingrid looked at him and said at once, "What has happened?"

He said, "Anne is dead."

Her arm squeezed his convulsively. "Oh, VK, no! How did—?"

VK cut in. "Any news?"

"Yes . . . I was able to telephone the American Embassy from a town on the road, the day we parted. We had no trouble—Miguel made us go very fast and we were almost in Bilbao before Trilby murdered the Civil Guard. Mother and I pretended to be Miguel's wife and daughter. Mother is hiding somewhere in the city now. . . . Mr. Monroe Barnett arrived here early today and we met secretly. He says you are to take my father to an American air base near Madrid, called Torrejón. Webber's there, and everything's ready. If that is impossible for you, tell me what you want, and I will get the message to Webber through Mr. Barnett."

The other side of the street two gray-coated men of the Armed Police passed, truncheons swinging. VK turned his head. Ingrid said, "Those louts are not dangerous. It is the plainclothesmen we must watch for. . . . You look very bad, VK . . . ill."

He turned into the third tavern. Bill and Mr. Thorsson were sitting at a table in the back of the crowded, noisy room, glasses in front of them. Bill jerked back a large shot of something that looked like cognac as he watched, and VK thought, Christ, that's just what we need now—Bill to start drinking the way he used to before Anne took his mind off it. He looked godawful in the wavering yellow light, too, pale, disheveled, unshaven, and above all, shocked. That must be how he himself looked, plus his black eye. The strange thing now was to understand that this big American, whom he had hated, was the only person in the world who really knew how he felt. And he was the only person who knew how Bill felt. Because they had both loved Anne. The thought of her gripped him like the pains of starvation, and he clung to the back of a chair for support, his eyes momentarily closing.

Ingrid clung briefly to her father, and sat down. Mr. T. murmured an order to a waiter. A radio behind the bar blared out a newscast at a deafening volume. Mr. Thorsson cocked an ear, listening, while Ingrid talked earnestly to Bill, her hand on his.

Mr. Thorsson said, "Nothing about us. That's one advantage of getting into trouble in a dictatorship. Franco doesn't want people to know that anyone could even think of killing a *Guardia Civil*. It was the same in Russia."

VK said, "We can't waste time. . . . Can we get the light plane out now? Did you check it, Ingrid?"

Ingrid said, "Mr. Barnett did. It's locked in a hangar. No one's there until eight o'clock in the morning. They haven't connected the plane with us at all, Miguel says—because we gave different names when we landed there. Miguel's in Bilbao, too. I can telephone him."

VK said, "What about the roads? Could Mr. Barnett get a car and drive Mr. T. to Madrid? With him in the trunk, perhaps."

Ingrid said, "Miguel says no, there are police blocks on all roads leading out of this area."

Bill scribbled on the notepad, which VK hadn't seen for days, *Must get airplane. Fly to Torrejón. Best way.*

Ingrid read it and nodded. "That's what Mr. Barnett thought. He thinks he could have the mechanics get the airplane out and ready tomorrow morning, if he has Bill's passport and papers. The ones he used when we landed here. Are they in your briefcase?"

Bill nodded. Ingrid said, "I have it, and all your suitcases, in the hotel."

Bill downed another brandy, beckoned the waiter, and made signs for the same again. While it was coming he wrote steadily. VK read the notes as Bill took the new drink: *Mr. B. should pay hangar dues, get plane serviced and gassed. Have mechanic rev up motor and taxi to airport building. Then B. should say he's going off to file flight plan and get clearance for nine A.M. takeoff. Actually he waits in building until plane taxis up, then comes out and gives us a sign. We wait in cafe opposite. At sign we walk straight through into plane and take off. Barnett stay behind to delay pursuit.*

Ingrid read the note carefully. She looked up. "I understand. We will try to have everything ready at nine o'clock. What sign shall we give?"

VK said, "Let Mr. Barnett come out of the airport building with his hat on. If he takes it off and puts it on again, everything's ready and we come at once. If he keeps it on his head, we wait. If he drops it we get away as quick as we can and try again through Miguel. Give me his number."

"474929 . . . Right. I will be with Mr. Barnett, or near, and when you go to the airplane I will go with you."

Bill shrugged. There was no animation in his face, only a slackening of the muscles holding it together as the brandies took effect. Ingrid said, "I will go back to the hotel now. Where will you sleep?"

VK said, "In a field somewhere near the airport. It's a warm night and we can't afford to risk being asked for identifications."

Ingrid said, "I've brought some passports for you—there, take them out of my bag—but they won't help much unless the policeman's never heard of you or what you're supposed to have done. . . . Good night."

Bill Hammond rapped the table sharply and called to the waiter, "Brandy. Double." Jesus, VK thought, you lucky bastard. You can drink yourself unconscious, and you've given her all of yourself, and she to you.

Over the rim of his coffee cup Bill watched the windsock swaying at the top of its staff. His head ached and his eyeballs throbbed. Here at ground level the wind seemed to be from the east, and weak; but the clouds racing out to sea showed a strong southerly wind at higher altitudes. The sun was up and there was no haze.

The Beechcraft came taxiing toward the airport building. Half a dozen red and gray policemen were lolling about in front of the building, but Mr. Thorsson had said there was no need to fear them. Their job was riot control in big cities, and their dull faces showed it. The lean men in the green uniforms and the black hats were out in the mountains, not here. The secret police they'd just have to risk.

Monroe Barnett walked out onto the steps of the airport building, looked around, and took off his hat. After a moment he put it on and went back inside the building.

Bill got up and the others followed. They crossed the road and went into the building. Through the far door Bill saw the Beechcraft on the tarmac, its engine running and the propeller turning. Monroe Barnett was talking to a respectful official, Ingrid at his side. As they passed Barnett handed them a big envelope and said, "I'll be with you in a minute . . . I have a message from Camp David—well done." Bill nodded and walked out onto the tarmac, followed by VK, Mr. Thorsson, and Ingrid. The airfield mechanic was in the pilot's seat. Bill gestured to him to leave the plane. A moment later he heard VK call, "Door shut!" As he gunned the throttle he thought his head would take off at the racket. Wincing with the pain, he slipped the brakes and turned the little plane onto the main runway. After a long lurching run it reached takeoff speed, and the tail rose. This was quite a load for a single-engined Beech, he thought. Finally the ground fell away, and they were airborne.

Bill turned east and held the altitude down to a hundred feet. In spite of all the brandy he hadn't slept much, through the long night under a stone wall. Anne came to him, not shattered and dead as he had last seen her, but alive, smiling, arms open for him. She was here now, between him and the dials in front of him.

He'd better try to concentrate on his job. A careless flyer was a dead flyer. Not that it mattered. VK wasn't going to care much, either. Mr. Thorsson was already under a death sentence, but there might still be time for him to unlock the remaining secrets of his remarkable mind. Ingrid . . . she had a life to lead. He especially owed it to her, maybe.

His head settled to a steady throbbing in tune with the beat of the engine. Now that they'd managed to get the Beechcraft airborne only fighter aircraft could stop them reaching Torrejón. Trilby's skill in involving the Spanish government was only matched by his ruthlessness in murdering innocent men to achieve it. That government already connected the Amieva murder of a Civil Guard with El Rubio, the unforgiven executioner of Prescendi. If someone now connected this stolen plane with El Rubio —and did it in time—they'd order the air force into the chase. So it would be best to fly low, inside what the pilots out at Edwards Air Force Base used to call "the nap of the earth." That would help to avoid radar detection, and make it dangerous for high-performance jet fighters to use their superiority, or their weapons, so close to the ground.

He glanced at the compass. Course 078—a little north of east. Below, a town suddenly appeared at the head of a long inlet of the sea. He looked at the spread map: Guernica. He waited till the town disappeared in the hills behind, then swung right until the compass needle settled on 180, due south. This course would take them west of Madrid. Torrejón was just east of Madrid, but it was important, as VK had stressed during the night, that they should not indicate their final destination too soon. Torrejón was a USAF base, but it was on sovereign Spanish soil, and the Spaniards were touchy about the uses it was put to, especially since the incident of the lost H-bomb back in '66. The government was quite capable of ordering all flights in and out of it suspended if it became known—again, in time—that El Rubio was heading for Torrejón.

Hills rose ahead. He pushed the throttle forward and put the plane into a steady climb, close to the rising earth. After fifteen minutes of steep ascent the land swooped suddenly down. A lurching updraught sent the Beechcraft soaring and his belly pressing into his feet. For a few seconds the plane swept and soared like a willful bird, almost out of control, then he got her nose down and leveled out again at a hundred feet above the brown earth and green vines. The airspeed indicator showed 120. He couldn't use the VOR to get the ground speed, so turned to VK in the copilot's seat, his hand on the map; but VK had understood already, for he said, "I've been working it out. We're here . . . doing about seventy-five across the ground."

Bill nodded. They were bucking a fifty-m.p.h. headwind. The dust trails across the plain showed it.

The plane droned on, very low. It passed over tangled rocks and gorges; tumbled precipices; a sudden view of a shepherd, with a dog like Baturro, alone on a brown waste . . . a curving river; red roofs and gray turrets; a medieval castle perched on an impossible crag . . . vultures swooping out of the way, wings spread in panic . . . Then the golden plain, wheat to the low horizon, and trails of dust drawn like pale plumes behind every cart on the side roads. On the black tarmac of the main road, trucks made black smoke like ships at sea . . . little cars, big cars, one or two cars actually passing the Beechcraft . . . women glimpsed, washing clothes, their faces suddenly up-turning—gone . . . ahead a thin glitter of white growing above the horizon . . .

Two hours on course now. His arms ached from holding the plane manually at its low altitude. The white glitter had become snow along the top of a steep mountain wall: the Guadarramas.

"Something high up," VK said. "Two planes. Fighters, I think."

Bill looked up through the perspex. Two jet vapor trails divided the sky out to the right. Now they were sweeping around in a great curve. Behind him he heard the click of safety belts.

Fighters. They might be just going from A to B. But they weren't. It would be nice to care. Or to feel good. He'd never had a hangover the whole time, since he'd fallen in love with Anne, though he'd drunk some. His head split and closed, split again.

The land rose. He gave the engine more throttle and inched up the trim tab. The Lear Jet would have gone up here at 450. There was a shallow draw a little to the right, hardly more than a fold in the skirts of the mountains. The Lear Jet couldn't have used it, nor could the fighters—but the Beechcraft could. He slipped over its rim and climbed up in it. Here he was not visible from either side, and it would require a very foolhardy jet pilot to dive on him from above, against the slope of the mountain.

Snow powdered the peaks on either side of the pass dead ahead. The city down in the plain to the right must be Segovia. Black shadows swept past on the ground and a fraction later the thunder of the jets' exhausts filled the cabin. The tail pipes passed overhead, the jets swept up into the sky, their wings wagging. They turned and started down again. The slope of the hill increased. Now he was barely fifty feet above the ground . . . thirty . . . the Beechcraft was ready to stall. He saw a hotel in the notch, empty ski lifts, plaques of snow, parked buses, sightseers, trucks grinding over the crest, a thousand startled faces, and the jets again, one high, one close—this one wagging its wings, going as slow as it could, just ahead and to the left, the pilot pointing down.

They were through the pass. He thrust the wheel forward and the Beechcraft dived down the southern slope. He sideslipped left, under the nearer fighter. For a moment, as he ripped down the south face of the mountain at zero altitude, the jet pilot couldn't have known where he'd gone; then he must have guessed, for the jet vanished behind a loud explosion and an orange burst from its afterburner.

The other jet came down like a rocket out of the sky. Bill tried to watch it as he held the Beechcraft on its steep downhill course. When puffs of smoke broke out along the jet's wing he forced his wheel to the right. The Beechcraft banked, hung in air, seemed to go backwards. Twenty smoke trails streaked by overhead. Red and orange flashes exploded among the rocks below. The jet went up in a climbing turn.

A lake with a big castle at its edge filled the valley floor ahead. VK, trying to hold the maps steady against the plane's violent twists and turns, shouted, "Manzanares." There were many cars parked on flat ground beside the lake, behind the castle. The first jet came at them again, from straight in front. Bill pulled the throttles back, lowered the flaps full out, and pointed the Beechcraft's nose at the flat space. The ground rushed up, a stream of smoking rockets passed overhead, followed by the bellow of the jet. In the cabin a horn blared in automatic warning, for at this speed he should have his undercarriage down. At five feet above the ground he lifted the nose, cut the throttles and put the Beechcraft down on its belly. It skidded across the flat space, rammed into the side of a small car, and burst into flames.

Bill shook his head. He was unhurt. VK looked groggy, and blood sprang from his forehead. The flames licked higher from the engine. Ingrid had the door open. She was getting Mr. T. out. He unbuckled his own belt, then VK's. Why was he trying to save himself? He didn't want to. There just wasn't time, or feeling, to work out an alternative. He dragged VK clear of the wreck.

They were all out, jet engines a hollow thunder somewhere above, but the fighters themselves not in sight. People were everywhere, running, shouting, lying down, crouching behind cars, looking up. Their own crash, and the burning Beechcraft, had hardly been noticed in the tremendous sound of the jets and the crash of cannon and rocket fire around the castle. Bill thought grimly, the people probably think a new Civil War has started, or an air force revolt against Franco.

VK could stand unassisted now, though groggily. Oily black smoke from the burning plane drifted over the parked cars and the lake. Bill ran to the cars . . . several SEATS, here and there a British Mini, some Citröen *3-chevaux*, Renaults, several Fords and Chevvies. A Mercedes 250 SE with German plates, and the key in the lock.

That would do. He scrambled into the driver's seat and switched on. Mr. Thorsson joined him, VK and Ingrid fell into the back seat and he started to back her out.

Ingrid panted, "Where are the fighters?"

VK mumbled, "Gone . . . must have radioed that we crashed here . . . look out for Civil Guard roadblocks . . . though they may think we're dead."

Bill headed the Mercedes down the castle drive. He pointed to a map in the side pocket. Mr. Thorsson took it out. VK said, "Give it to me, sir. . . . I'll guide you to Torrejón. Not on main roads if I can avoid them. Slow a second . . . Left here."

Bill turned onto a tarmac road along the edge of the big reservoir. The dam and hydroelectric plant were clearly visible on the far side. "Take it easy," VK said. "We don't want a road patrol to pick us up for speeding. . . . What weapons have we got?"

Bill thought. The rifle they had to throw away before the train reached Bilbao; he had taken off his shoulder holster—too awkward to fly a plane in it—so that was lost in the burning Beechcraft. VK said, "Only my pistol, right? I've got no ammunition except what's in it. Five rounds."

Ingrid said, "Give me the map. . . . Where are we? Where is Torrejón? I will tell you where to go. VK should be ready to shoot. We are not safe yet."

Bill drove fast with an eye on the speedometer. The gas gauge showed half: that was plenty. She didn't have a tach, but would probably redline at 6,200. She felt a little rough, but wouldn't fold on him inside the distance to Torrejón, which must be about forty, fifty miles.

"Chozas de la Sierra," Ingrid read aloud from a sign at the road side. "Straight on."

In the mirror he saw Anne's surprised, wide eyes, looking into his. Had he really seen them soften in love? He thought of her under the coal, and groaned aloud.

"Guadalix de la Sierra. Straight over . . . no, right! Head for El Vellón."

The road ran among barren rocks. A hawk swooped from the sky in twisting circles to snatch a mouse from the road almost under the Mercedes' wheels.

"The main road from Burgos to Madrid is coming. We have to turn left on to it, go two kilometers, then turn right for El Vellón."

Bill swung left onto the main road. The pavement was wide but the surface wavy, ridged, and uneven in the midday heat. The sun burned down from an empty sky, and tar glittered in melting lakes along the road surface. An endless column of big Barreiros and Pegaso diesel trucks ground up the hill toward Madrid with an ear-stopping, blatting roar. The dense smoke from their exhausts blurred visibility down the slope.

Bill drew out to pass a SEAT and quickly swung back as a big, cream-colored car passed at high speed in the center lane, going in the opposite direction.

VK said, "De Guise is in that car. And another of the men who was at Amieva. They saw us."

Bill accelerated, pulled out and went down the hill. The needle flicked past 80, 90, 100, 120 kilometers an hour.

Ingrid cried, "Slow! Next right."

Bill saw the turning, trod on the brakes and swung hard over. It would take de Guise several seconds to stop, get into the stream of traffic and come back down the hill. And then, although it was open country, he might not notice that they had turned off to El Vellón. He pushed his foot hard down.

VK said, "Stop at the first bad place you come to—bridge, curve —anywhere they'll have to slow. Leave me there. I can get them."

Bill ignored him. They wouldn't fool de Guise that way. In the mirror he saw the cream car making the turn off the main road. It was a Facel Vega Excellence sedan, five-passenger—the car Trilby and de Guise had come up to Amieva in.

VK said, "There are three men, plus de Guise, in it. Not Trilby. I'd be happier if he was. . . . Can we beat it?"

Bill shook his head. The Facel Vega was a French-made car with a big Chrysler engine. They'd stopped manufacture in '65, but that year he'd pushed one to 143 m.p.h. in a test at Riverside. This Mercedes would barely do 110 in the state its engine was in.

Ingrid said, "El Vellón. Through the village, over a canal, then a river, then right. The road will be marked for Alcalá de Henares. You won't have to leave it for twenty kilometers after that. It looks straight, on the map."

The Facel Vega crept closer. Was it worthwhile getting off this road onto one less straight, in the hope of shaking off the faster, heavier car? But that would turn them away from Torrejón, and allow the Spanish police time to block roads and start tracking them down. Besides—he took a quick look at the figure slumped in the seat beside him—Mr. Thorsson was not taking the ride well. The mountains had given him back a momentary health, but now he again looked like what he was—a dying man.

The kilometer gauge showed 180 and that was it, this car's limit. From the sound of the valve train he wondered how long she would take this without holing a piston.

VK said, "He's coming up quite fast."

The road was blacktopped, recently done. The Mercedes' rocketing passage raised some swirls of dust in the verges but not enough to cause any loss of visibility to the car behind. A car loomed ahead, going the same way. Bill slammed past with a blare of the horn. That gave him an idea . . . to pass close enough to a car, without warning, to frighten the driver out of his wits. Drivers surprised in that way often swung back into the middle of the road . . . which would be into the path of the Facel Vega. There'd be a crash. Involving the innocent car. He remembered it was Sunday and thought, That explains why there were so many picnic parties on the pass of the Guadarramas, and around the castle. No, he wasn't going to involve someone else if he could help it. VK and Webber could accuse him of lack of moral fiber—lack of a proper sense of values—and now he wasn't even sure that they were wrong and he was right; it came now simply to the fact, without making judgment or assessing values, that he couldn't do it.

The current of air changed and the noise level rose sharply. VK said, "I've opened a window. I'm going to have a shot. When I say 'Now,' brake hard and suddenly, so that they come close. I'll take a couple of shots—then you accelerate away again."

Bill watched the Facel Vega in the rear-view mirror. A nice-looking car, for its age. Heavy on corners. De Guise was a gutsy driver but maybe he hadn't raced. It might be possible to lead him into a corner faster than his car would take. Especially if the road was slick. But it was dry and good. Could he spill oil out somehow? There might be a can in the trunk . . . couldn't get at it . . . it wouldn't pour fast enough. . . .

"Now!"

He stamped on the brake and watched the Facel Vega close like a rocket to forty feet . . . thirty . . . VK's shots boomed like artillery behind his ear. He rammed the accelerator into the floor.

"I aimed at the tires," VK said. "Missed."

Ingrid said, "Try again? At the driver?"

"Better not. Only three shots left and at this speed I can't really aim. And they have a rifle. I saw. Next time they'll get us. They just weren't expecting us to turn on them, that time."

Ingrid said, "Eight kilometers to Cobena. Go through it, then bear right. The road should be signposted to Ajalvir and Torrejón de Ardoz."

At 170 k.p.h. it would take about three minutes to reach that village. The Facel Vega was closing again. A bullet hole appeared in the windshield, under the center mirror.

VK said, "He's aiming at you, not our tires."

Bill weaved the car from one side of the road to the other, still at full speed. That would make the target move laterally. Cobena church pointed skyward in an empty, ocher plain. The village lay slightly to the right of the road. . . . Houses, a barn, an old truck passed in a flashing blur. There was the road fork ahead about a kilometer, Torrejón straight ahead, the main road swinging left, a fast curve . . . but not this fast . . . a long stone farm building on the outside of the curve. This was the place.

He shouted suddenly, "Heads down." He held the accelerator to the floor . . . 170 . . . Now he was at the fork, bearing left into the curve. Ingrid screamed, "Wrong way!" The long stone wall flicked by on the right. Bill took a last lightning glance in the rear-view mirror and saw the Facel Vega keeping speed. He trod on the clutch, rammed the gear lever into third while the engine screamed in wild acceleration, let out the clutch and wrenched the wheel toward the inside of the curve, the left. The tail of the Mercedes took off like a rocket, swinging around, dragging the car with it. Bill held desperately to the wheel, his teeth rattling and head banging. The car spun like a crazy top, twice, three, four times, but losing momentum rapidly with each turn. On the third turn the Facel Vega passed, already off the road on the outside, still under full throttle. He caught a blurred sight of de Guise's face, then the big car hit the stone wall with a long, grinding roar. A flash of flame hurt his eyes with its intensity. Two bodies flew high, whirling and turning among pieces of the Facel Vega, splatted against the farm building, then fell down its stone side leaving huge blood splashes where they had hit. Flames erupted all over the twisted wreck below. At the wheel sat de Guise, up-right. The man beside him had his shoulders through the side window, and no head.

Bill jerked his door open and ran. The driver's door of the Facel Vega flew off its broken hinges at a touch and he dragged de Guise halfway out. VK was there, shielding his face from the heat of the fire, undoing de Guise's safety-belt buckle, dragging him out onto the road. De Guise was breathing.

People were running toward them from the village. Bill carried de Guise to the Mercedes and pushed him into the back with VK and Ingrid. Then he got behind the wheel. The motor kicked at once, though now it made a very sick clatter.

Ingrid said, "Reverse, and take the other road. . . . Are you all right, Father?"

Mr. Thorsson said, "I think so. Shaken up. Is de Guise alive?"

VK said, "Yes. He must be in shock. He may be mashed up inside. Can't tell. No blood."

Bill drove on, flames like a wavering curtain before his eyes. Surely those flames, the three twisted corpses, the blobs of blood on the wall, the smell of roasting flesh, would burn through the layer of deadness in which he existed? But no, he still felt nothing.

Except when he thought about de Guise. Then his chest tightened and his breathing hurt. Without de Guise Mr. Thorsson would be safe in Shiprock by now. And Anne safe in his own arms.

De Guise said, "VK . . . Whose car is this? My back hurts. My head. Trilby . . ."

"Yes? What about him?"

"Trilby said, 'It is I who will get them.' And he was right."

"What do you mean?"

"I forget."

"Try to remember."

"Yes. Of course . . . Whose car is this?"

Ingrid said, "Right," and "Left," and "Left," and—"Stop here."

Bill stopped. There was a wide gateway. Spanish and American airmen, in uniform, stood sentry at either side. Ingrid handed a card to the American and said, "Call the general personally with that message. It's very urgent."

"Yes, ma'am. Wait here, please."

He was back in half a minute, saluting. "Straight ahead, ma'am. To that building there, with the flag. The general's coming out right away."

Bill drove on. He braked the car outside the big office. A brigadier general, USAF, ran down the steps followed by two other officers and two armed air police. The general squeezed into the front seat with them, and now it was he giving instructions—left, right, straight ahead . . .

VK said, "General, do you know anything about a man called Trilby? Rouged-face, pearl-gray hat?"

The general said, "Never heard of him."

VK said, "He was in Spain, after us, but he wasn't in a car chasing us just now. This man, de Guise, said Trilby was going to get us, after all."

The general said, "No one's going to get you now. There's your aircraft."

De Guise gave a sudden violent laugh. VK said, "What are you laughing at? What did you mean about Trilby, just now?" Bill thought dully, Yes, what did he mean? It didn't matter.

De Guise said, "Trilby? Surely you mean Svengali?"

VK said, "He's over his concussion. He won't talk now."

They were getting out, the air policemen running from their

own car to assist Mr. Thorsson. A huge silver airplane squatted at the end of a wide black runway. The fourth of its engines whistled to purring life.

De Guise said, "I do not think I want to visit the United States again at this season." He turned to the general. "I am a French citizen, *mon général*. You do not wish to create more trouble than necessary with our President, I am sure." De Guise was dead white, one eyelid fluttering, one shoulder shaking. Bill stared at him in silent hate.

The general looked worried. He beckoned VK and Bill aside, and said, "Is that true?"

VK said, "Yes."

"The French are liable to kick up a goddam fuss, even if this man is a Red agent, if we snatch him onto a plane of ours."

VK turned to Bill. "I don't see any reason why we should take him with us, do you? The Spanish police will deal with him well enough—better than we would—once they learn that it was he who murdered the Civil Guard in Asturias."

Bill said, *"Non!"*

Ingrid came to them. "Father is in the plane. They have doctors there. And Webber. We are ready."

VK said, "What's the reason for taking de Guise, Bill?" They were all shouting now to be heard over the thunder of the idling jets.

Ingrid said, "So that we can make him talk, eh?"

Bill said nothing. Partly he had meant that, for de Guise obviously knew something; and his knowledge was making him shake with fear. But partly Bill didn't want the Spanish police to deal with him. Of their own volition his hands worked slowly, opening and closing.

VK said to the general, "We'll take him with us then."

The general hesitated, then said, "OK. You're the boss, according to these orders."

VK said, "Could anyone shoot down our plane as we take off? From a house in that village, for instance? Have you had it searched?"

The general said, "No one could harm you without an antiaircraft missile. Someone might try to shoot the pilot with a rifle or machine gun, I suppose. Hell, it's out of the question. Forget it. You're safe now."

They were moving toward the plane. The legend UNITED STATES AIR FORCE was spelled out large along the body. Uniformed officers waited beside an open door. Webber was there, grinning. The jet scream increased and Ingrid put her hands over her ears.

De Guise dragged back, yelling, "No, no! This is an outrage! This is Spanish territory! Where is a Spanish officer?" The air policemen snapped a pair of handcuffs on him and hustled him up the ramp and into the plane.

VK turned to the general. "Please have that village searched, General, at once."

"Right after you've gone."

Bill cried, "*Anne!*"

VK said, "I've told the general. He will see that she's properly buried. By that hut above the San Glorio. We'll come back when we can. . . ."

The general was saying, "You know Mr. Webber? This is your pilot, Lieutenant Colonel Jeffery . . . Major Phelan of the Medical Corps . . . OK, Bill, you're cleared for takeoff. Hike!"

Doors slammed, the whine dropped to a universal thunder. . . .

Chapter 14

VK WATCHED the long cabin tilt up, the yellow runway markers pass more slowly below, the view widen. There was the end of the runway . . . the boundary fence of the base . . . the village he had seen. Already it looked impossibly far for a rifleman to have a hope of hitting the pilot. But dumb unease filled the corners of his misery, and would not be quieted. He looked at Bill, across the center aisle from him. His eyes looked better than they had in the morning, but his hands had the shakes. His face was pale and taut, the corners of the mouth pulled down. He seemed to be staring fixedly at the back of de Guise's head in front of him.

The towers of Madrid spread across the plain as the Boeing aimed for the sky. Looking straight down, VK saw a lake, a castle, crowded cars, and what appeared to be one wing torn off a white moth. He looked at his watch. That was Manzanares, and the wing was the remains of the Beechcraft. Just fifty-seven minutes had passed since they scrambled out of it. . . . Higher reached the great jet, the thin snowfields of the Guadarramas drifted back, and the course lay northwest. The seat-belt sign had long been switched off, and he fumbled in his pocket for a cigarette. There were none, but one of the air policemen on guard over de Guise was ready with a pack of Camels.

VK lit one. He did not really feel alive. Otherwise, he thought, Anne's death would be hurting more. But nothing hurt—nothing gave either pain or pleasure. He breathed, but did not fully feel the breath passing in and out of his lungs. He saw, and the imprint rested on his retina; but that was all. There used to be further communication, a linking of the image with emotion, so that what he saw made him feel good or bad, made him groan or cry hooray. Now, nothing. Only unease.

The cabin was vast and silent as an empty tunnel. A tunnel . . . he shivered involuntarily. But the light poured in, and the sun flashed back from the rims of the jet intakes. Forward there was only a narrow passage to the flight deck; two private compartments on the right side took up the rest of the space. They'd put Mr. Thorsson in one; the other was empty.

Bill Hammond stared stonily at de Guise. De Guise, unmanacled, lit cigarettes, took a couple of puffs, stubbed them out, lit another. His face was greeny white and the tic in his shoulder worse than ever. A doctor ought to look at him. He had had amazing luck to come out of that crash at all. Perhaps he had suffered internal injuries. They might be fatal. It was hard to care. The air policeman, a Negro corporal, was watching him with lazy intentness from the aisle, his billy rocking in the crook of his arm.

Trilby. Where was Trilby? What had he meant by saying that *he* would get them? If that was so, de Guise ought to look a lot happier than he did.

VK leaned forward. "De Guise, how did you come to be on that road? You couldn't have been trying to intercept us because we didn't know ourselves that we were going to be on it."

De Guise stubbed out a cigarette. He said, "I need a drink. Bourbon."

VK said, "But you don't drink—I daresay we can find some." He glanced up at the corporal, who called softly to a companion. VK said, "Well?"

De Guise said, "That we met on the road was only luck. Bad

luck for me . . . and you, too. *We* would only have killed Mr. Thorsson. Not even that if we could have taken him away with us alive. . . . Where we met is the main road from Burgos to Madrid. I went to Burgos to be more central, when you disappeared into the mountains. Many of our people were out looking for you." He lit another cigarette and puffed jerkily. A cloud of blue smoke hung around his head. The second air policeman appeared with a juice glass half full of whiskey. De Guise downed it in a single motion. "Ah. Oh. Ow!" He gasped and choked. "Terrible! How can you drink stuff like that? Typical American taste . . ."

"Where were you going?"

"Barajas, the Madrid civil airport," de Guise said promptly. "I thought you would be flying to France, but my superior—"

"Trilby."

"—said that you would not risk crossing an international boundary without the proper papers and clearances, as you would certainly be held in prison when you landed. Our party is strong in France. We could have telephoned. You would not have left the prison alive. Rather, *he* would not. Now, none of you will live."

VK considered carefully. De Guise was saying that the HPS had expected them to head for Madrid and there try to get Mr. Thorsson onto a civil airliner bound for the U.S.A. But in fact they'd never thought of doing that: It was too difficult, and it was unnecessary, when the U.S. had an air force base nearby.

"Did no one think of Torrejón?" he asked suddenly.

De Guise said promptly, "No . . . I would like another drink."

Bill Hammond sat like a statue, his eyes glowing. VK chewed his knuckles. His mind scratched like a rat, a rat slowly going frantic at the walls of a cage that was not a cage. The sky was high and blue and absolutely clear.

The HPS *must* have thought of Torrejón. De Guise wasn't going to talk, but one must assume that something had been done about Torrejón. What?

Looking out of the window past Bill's silhouetted head, he saw far snow below high clouds. Those were the mountains where Marcos the shepherd boy walked with the great dog Baturro. That river, flashing beyond, might be Mr. Thorsson's Sella.

The door to the flight deck opened momentarily and he saw

Ingrid's rounded stern. She was leaning over the pilot as he explained something to her, her breast pressing into his shoulder.

De Guise burst out suddenly, "Why did you let the Americans buy you, VK? You are a man of taste. What do you have in common with this civilization of jukeboxes and Coca-Cola? Why offer them your friendship? You have risked your life for them several times in this affair, and you know what will happen? One day, you will apply for a tourist's visa, but the FBI will report that you once slept with a girl you were not married to. No visa. Only clean-living Boy Scouts for the U.S.A. Boy Scouts and Lee Harvey Oswald, and Lucky Luciano, and . . ." He took the air policeman's proffered drink and downed it. The corporal looked at VK and raised one quizzical eyebrow. De Guise went on, "It's too late now, but you're the sort of man who belongs on the other side, our side. . . ."

VK said, "What do you mean, it's too late now?"

De Guise said, "Because it is . . . rotgut bourbon whiskey instead of wine, fat Cadillacs instead of lean Maseratis, Mom instead of Bardot and Moreau . . . Those little towns I had to drive through—not one gram of culture, of breeding, of taste—nothing, nothing, except the money to do what they want, live their own stupid lives and pay their soldiers to interfere with everyone else's."

"And you think Communism—the Russians—are going to produce a better world?"

De Guise snapped, "Of course not. But they are the only people strong enough to destroy this . . . this blight of America."

VK said, "You aren't really a Communist. You just hate America."

"I will destroy America, if it is the last thing I do. And it will be. I only regret that they will never know in Washington who was responsible for their defeat."

VK leaned back. De Guise had made his testament. He looked like death. Below, a line of crawling foam marked the last fangs of the rocky land. Forty-five minutes from takeoff.

A young captain came back from the flight deck, a message form in his hand. "General Baisley at Torrejón sent this."

VK read, *Village near base searched as result your request. Two men escaped by car one possibly Trilby. In house left behind burned documents and electronic instrument of unknown purpose but apparently a type of radar. Instrument is large but would be portable by car. It was fitted with charge for self-destruction but charge failed to explode.* On the bottom Webber had written: *Seen, J.W.*

VK held the message across the aisle to Bill. But Bill did not see it. VK gave it back to the captain.

So de Guise has made his testament. Or, as Bill would have to say it, *de Guise a fait son testament.* Which also means, *de Guise has made his will.* De Guise expects death. Radarlike. Look at his face. Electronic instrument. He's been acting like a dying man. Because he thinks he is one. He knows.

VK jumped to his feet. He shook Bill's shoulder and said, "We've got to talk to de Guise. Alone. Come with me." To the corporal he said, "I'll take over. Put the handcuffs back on him. Now, stay outside the door. Ignore anything you hear."

He steered de Guise and Bill into the empty compartment and closed the door.

A big divan faced forward. A table and two chairs occupied the outer wall. A row of windows gave onto the broad wing and the starboard inboard engine thrusting serenely forward on its pod. There were two other chairs.

Bill felt the hairs on the back of his neck stirring like a dog's. De Guise suddenly seemed to notice him for the first time. "Hullo, Bill," he said. "You can't help being American, can you?" His mouth twisted into a sort of smile, and he held out his hand. Bill ignored it and de Guise's face altered. "Where's Anne?" he asked quickly.

VK said, "Dead." Bill felt his hands go rigid. VK pushed de Guise into a chair, and said, "Now, what do you know?" He felt in his pocket and brought out a penknife. "Something's going to happen to us. To this aircraft. What? Is it a bomb? Here?" He opened the knife and turned the blade under de Guise's eye. He said, "On that train your friends were willing to destroy a stranger's hearing just to learn what Mrs. Rapkin had told Bill. Believe me, I'll enjoy putting your eye out. . . ."

Bill heard a strangled gasp, and realized it was his own voice. His hand stretched out, palm up. VK looked at him in surprise, then dropped the knife into his palm. De Guise's face was the color of putty.

VK said. "Speak. This is your last chance."

De Guise said, "Ah, you will not learn, will you? You think I can be broken by pain?"

VK said to Bill, "Go on."

The knife lay rigid in his rigid hand. De Guise's eye looked just like the Pullman porter's. This was animal, what he was doing. He couldn't . . .

But not again. Not fail again. And de Guise said, "About Anne —it was—"

Bill's left hand shot out, seizing him by the back of the neck. The right hand pushed the knifeblade into his eyeball. De Guise shrieked and blood spurted from his eye. His legs jerked and kicked, but the rigid bar of Bill's arm held his head and neck still. The shriek died to a bubbling and stopped. The blood ran down his cheek into his mouth. Bill held the stained knife ready to plunge again. His strained breathing steadied.

VK said, "Now, we'll start on the other eye. But more slowly this time. Until you talk."

The door opened and Webber came in. "Say . . . Great Jesus Christ, what in hell are you doing?"

Bill smelled blood, and looked at the knife in wonder. He was on a plane, a bloody knife in his hand, and he had just pierced Robert de Guise's left eye with it. Webber was there, looking as if he'd seen the mouth of Hell.

VK spoke impatiently. "Sit down. De Guise knows something that's going to happen to this plane—or in America—I don't know. We've got to make him talk." De Guise rocked and moaned in his chair, held from falling by Bill's left hand.

Webber said, "Hold it! No, I haven't gone soft, VK. When you've supervised as much persuasion as I have, kid, you don't sweat over it. Also, you don't believe you can make anyone talk if you hurt 'em enough. People break not just under a different force, but a different *type* of strain. . . . First, wait'll I get the doctor."

He darted out, returning in ten seconds with the medical major.

The major whistled under his breath when he saw de Guise's face, then said, "Hold him firm. Got him?" Bill nodded. The major dabbed disinfectant on de Guise's eye, then quickly slipped a hypodermic into the gash made by the knife. "Local anaesthetic," he muttered. De Guise cried out again, and stiffened in Bill's grip.

Webber said, "That'll be all, Major. . . . As I was saying, VK, the first thing is to control the pain you're administering, very carefully. You don't get results if your man is hurting so much he can't think of anything else. Second, you got to find the right weapon for the particular individual. . . . How do you feel, de Guise? It doesn't hurt now, does it?"

De Guise said, "Yes. No. It is numb. I can't move the other eye."

"But you can see out of it? Good . . . This is the first chance I've had to speak to you for quite a while. I have an interesting paper here that was flown in this morning from Washington. It concerns you." He fished in his briefcase. "This. Can you see that, with your good eye?"

He pushed forward a sheet of paper, his hand covering the top half. De Guise turned his head and a drop of blood fell on the paper. His manacled hand shot out but Webber jerked the paper back.

"It's a forgery," de Guise said. "That's not my handwriting. Why would I try to get into your cheap horrible country?"

Webber said, "How do you know what the paper is? I've had my hand over the headings and all the details. . . . Come on. How do you know what it is if it's a forgery?"

De Guise's head rolled forward. VK pulled him up, slapped him viciously across the cheek and shouted, "Damn you! Come back. You're not going to escape that way."

Ingrid and the skipper of the aircraft, Colonel Jeffery, stood in the doorway. The colonel gasped with horror.

Webber said, "Come in. Close the door. Keep quiet. . . . See this paper? It's an application for U.S. citizenship, made by Robert de Guise on December 12, 1963."

VK said, "*De Guise?* Applying for American citizenship? But he hates America. That's the only reason he's a Communist. . . . This can't be true."

Bill thought, of course it is. Here was the missing clue to de Guise's behavior all along.

VK said, "Oh, I see. He meant to become an American so he could spy for the Reds from the inside? Get a defense job, or with the State Department perhaps?"

Webber said, "We don't think so."

Ingrid said, "This is amazing! See where he applied from."

Bill took the sheet and looked at the address: *The Continental Hotel, Dallas, Texas.*

De Guise moaned and stirred. Webber said, "Give him some water. There . . . The computers have only just turned up this application, and almost by chance. The file of rejected applications for citizenship isn't just the first place you'd think of to get information on de Guise's background. We don't know what was in his mind when he applied, and we haven't had time to find out, but the Director is sure it was the act of an idealistic young man—he was only just twenty—completely American in his outlook, his ways, his thoughts . . . who was so stirred by President Kennedy's assassination that he felt he had to come over and help carry on Mr. Kennedy's ideas."

De Guise groaned and Bill bent forward quickly to hear. "An examiner asked me if I had ever done anything that came under the heading of moral turpitude. I told him I had just been named in a divorce case. . . . He was one of those Americans who want to keep the dirty world, the dirty foreigners, out. My application was refused."

VK said, "What's this got to do with us? I tell you, we're in danger. It must be a bomb."

"The ship's been searched, before and after takeoff," the colonel said. "There's no bomb on board."

"Start on his other eye," VK snapped. Bill shook his head. One was enough, and he did not know, now, how he had done it.

"Give me the knife," VK said.

Webber said, "Wait . . . I think we will send this application to your bosses, de Guise. It should interest them."

De Guise giggled wildly.

Webber said, "Ah, you think we'll never send anything again? But this is a photostat, you know. . . . Look, you tell us what you know and you can have the original. We'll keep our mouths shut. You can go back to your place with the HPS."

De Guise swayed, and Ingrid saved him from falling. "He's fainted," she said.

"The eye must hurt in spite of the anaesthetic," Webber said.

Ingrid said, "I don't think it is that. . . . You know, when we came in here, VK was shouting, 'You're not going to escape that way.' But I think that is just what he *is* doing . . . because we are not offering him any other way of escape. I think he will talk if we give him the chance of escaping . . . now, here."

VK stared at her. "Suppose you're right—what escape can we give him?"

The colonel looked pale and queasy. The compartment reeked of pain and blood. He said, "We're flying along a heavily traveled ship lane. Suppose I took her down low and we gave him a parachute, and . . ."

De Guise suddenly cried, "Yes! Get down! Fast! Down!"

The colonel slipped out. A moment later the huge plane's nose tilted down and the whirring of the air grew louder on the metal skin. De Guise began to speak in rapid bursts, and now he was shaking all over. "The Soviets have a device—radar scanner and spectroscope combined—you aim it at a place, or thing—and it takes a picture—of exactly the kind of light which that place or thing—is emitting or reflecting. That joint picture, radar and spectroscopic, is frozen on tape—scanned into black and white dots—and converted into rows of figures—that tape is an exact fingerprint of that object—no two objects have the same signature . . ."

"Go on," Webber snapped.

"You can feed that tape—into a missile's guidance system and the missile—will home onto that particular place, or thing . . . once its radar can pick up the thing on its screen. . . . The final guidance has to be line-of-sight—Trilby flew to Moscow and back to Madrid, with a spectroradar while you were in the mountains— waited Torrejón for you. . . . Can't you tell the pilot—go down faster?"

Colonel Jeffery was in the door. "We're going down as fast as we can now," he said. "We're up to Mach point nine six . . ."

The long wings shook and the body shuddered. The dark slate of the sea grew momentarily more wrinkled. A big sergeant appeared with a parachute and a life jacket. The colonel said, "Put them on this man."

De Guise stood up and the sergeant began to get him into the life jacket. Webber said, "And a Communist on the post signaled when our plane was taking off? So Trilby got this radarspectroscopic picture of it . . . and presumably taped it. Then what?"

"Sent it by shortwave radio to a Red air force listening post . . ."

The sergeant stood up. "Excuse me, sir . . . You go out holding to this ring, see? Roll forward as you leave the door, count five, then give this a good jerk."

A grinding roar broke out and the plane gave a mighty heave. The colonel said, "He's lowered the main landing gear as an airbrake. He'll use the spoilers next." The slotted flaps rose on the wings and the shuddering increased, the engines bounced and swung on their pods. "We'd better get back to the rear door now. Do you want the doc to put a bandage on that eye before you go?"

De Guise was pushing toward the door. "N-n-n-no!" he stammered. "It d-d-doesn't matter. Let me out!"

Webber said, "Here, unlock the handcuffs."

They went out of the compartment and down the long aisle. The young captain and the big sergeant stood ready by the lever of the rear door. A voice on the intercom said, "Colonel, there's a freighter, eastbound, ahead. We'll be over it in about two and a half minutes. Altitude two thousand feet. Two hundred knots. Go on my signal."

"Open the door," the colonel said.

The sergeant leaned his weight on the big lever, the door jerked open. A tremendous roaring filled the plane, and a loose newspaper flew out and vanished.

"What then?" Webber shouted. "Hold him, Hammond." Bill grabbed de Guise with both hands. "What then, de Guise, after he'd radioed to the Red air force?"

De Guise stood in the open doorway, his hands stark-white, gripping the sides, trying to pull himself out. It was suddenly bitter cold.

"They were to send two Tigers to intercept," de Guise shouted. He tugged again.

"Hold him," Webber said.

"You promised," de Guise cried. "An American's promise!"

The voice on the intercom said, "Stand by to go on zero. Ten—nine—"

"Why Tigers?" Webber yelled. "They're the newest heavy bombers."

"Six—five—"

De Guise struggled with maniacal force to throw himself out of the open door. Bill held him from the side, staring coldly into the straining undamaged eye.

"Why?" Webber shouted.

"*Go!*"

De Guise screamed at the top of his voice "They're equipped with EAD! One thorup capacity! Compatible with spectroradar guidance!"

"Let him go," Webber said.

Bill released his grip and stepped back. De Guise stood silhouetted in the doorway. Second by second his rigid, straining attitude crumbled. Soon he was not straining to get out . . . he was not straining . . . he was not standing . . . A freighter appeared below, eastbound, and passed rapidly on. De Guise turned slowly away, sank into a seat and put his head in his hands.

"Get the doctor to him," the colonel said.

The voice on the intercom spoke. "Has he gone out? Shall I take her up again?"

The colonel seized a wall mike. "Hold her down, Jim. I'm coming forward. You fellows better come with me."

Webber said, "Why don't you ditch her right away, Colonel?"

The colonel said, "I could, but the sea's a little rough. Besides, I'm not going to give up that easily."

Webber said, "Miss Thorsson, let's talk to your father. See if he knows anything that can help us."

On the flight deck Colonel Jeffery said to Bill, "Put on that head set. Mr. Hawker, you take this one. Sit there. Chuck, get General Baisley at Torrejón on Band Two. Scrambler Mode." A moment later he said, "General, Kansas Six—we have reason to believe that the Soviets have sent out two Tigers to get us. They are EAD-equipped, one thorup, and can home on us as soon as they are in line-of-sight position."

The general's voice was sharp. "Roger. I'll get you a fighter escort and airborne radar to track the intruders. Will ask Nordefcom whether any military planes have taken off from Russian bases in the last two hours. Alter course for Station X-ray 467. Keep open on Band Eight for escort. You will command whole group."

"Roger."

The wings gradually tilted and the aircraft swung left, steadied, and leveled again. The colonel said, "X-ray 467 is a point over the Atlantic, seven hundred miles due west of Shannon Airport, Ireland. Our escort will probably come from Rhine-Main. . . ."

The general's voice cut in. "You're getting six F12's. They'll be airborne in one minute. Escort plus radar-equipped B58 from Brize Norton join you at X-ray 467. Altitude 39."

"Request negative," the colonel said. "The lower we fly the longer it will be before the Tigers reach line-of-sight position."

"Roger. Affirmative. Altitude zero."

The copilot pushed the half wheel forward. The big jet slid toward the sea. The colonel said, "Chuck, what's the horizon from a Tiger's maximum altitude?"

The radio operator handed him a message: NORDEFCOM REPORTS TWO TIGERS OVERFLEW TROMSO NORWAY 1343 Z, 70, COURSE 270.

The colonel clipped the message to the board on his knee. "Z means Greenwich Mean Time," he said. "This watch is set on it. 1343 was one hour forty minutes ago. Six minutes after we took off. 70 means 70,000 feet. Tigers cruise at about 1,200 knots, so they'll be between Scotland and Iceland by now, if they're heading for us."

The navigator said, "The Tiger's ceiling is one hundred thousand feet. From that height, an object at zero altitude comes over the horizon at 416 miles."

The colonel muttered, "My God, if we'd stayed at 39 we'd almost be in line of sight already. No wonder that Frenchman wanted down in such a hurry."

The surface of the sea, close below, showed long even crests and troughs, not steep but here and there flecked with whitecaps. The co-pilot eased back on the half wheel and the wings leveled out thirty feet above the ocean.

The radio operator handed the colonel a map and another message: NORDEFCOM REPORTS TWO TIGERS AT 00° 12′ E 64° 27′ N 1523 Z, 97, COURSE 223, TGS 1180.

The colonel looked at the spread map. "Four minutes ago they were here." He pointed at a spot in the sea southeast of the Faroe Islands. "They're headed southwest and . . . 1,200 miles from us, closing at twenty miles a minute if we both stay on present courses. TGS is true ground speed—they're making 1180. They'll be within line-of-sight range in, say . . . twenty minutes."

VK asked, "How soon do we reach X-ray 467?"

"Ten minutes."

VK said, "I think you'd better make preparations to ditch her, Colonel. They can't do anything to us if we get out into the rafts. It's only this plane they can aim the EAD at, because that's all they have the spectroradar picture of. And they can't come over-head to fire or bomb by sight, because we have a fighter escort."

The colonel said, "Those are big rollers. It's two to one on a crackup if I ditch in that. We'll stand a better chance if we jump individually. Chuck, tell all crew and passengers to dress for abandon ship. Crew take up readiness positions accordingly."

Webber stuck his head between them. "Negative on that, Colonel. The doctor's put Mr. Thorsson to sleep, so he can't jump individually. We'll have to take our chances together . . . and get away from the plane as soon as we're down."

"Roger," the colonel said. "Negative last order. Prepare for ditching."

A hand came over Bill's shoulder, giving him a life jacket. He got into it quickly, then strapped on the parachute and finally helped VK to get into his.

The colonel said, "I didn't know the Russians had made EAD portable yet. It's not much, only one thorup, but one thorup at, say, 1,000 miles is . . . where's my slide rule?"

"One equivalent ton of TNT," the navigator said.

"That's enough," the colonel said grimly.

"Kansas Six," a Southern voice drawled. "Gideon Two is thirty miles east of you at 103."

The colonel said, "There's our escort. . . . Gideon Two, detach two planes as close escort. Remainder vector course 287 degrees—target is two Tigers, 97, 223, 1180. I am turning to course 223 . . .

I'm turning away on the same course as the Tigers, going directly away from them. That'll cut the rate of closing to about twelve miles a minute." He turned a switch in front of him. "Kansas Six, Gideon One—report relative distance Tigers to us. Gideon Two, imperative to force Tigers to turn away before they close to 500 miles."

VK said, "If they won't, shoot them down."

The colonel said, "I'm just about to get clearance on that. Jimmy, did you hear?"

"Yes, sir."

"Cipher GKG request to Yoke 991." The colonel began scribbling orders on a pad.

"Yes, sir."

"Sir, Gideon One reports Tigers are now 826 miles from us."

The colonel said, "Gideon Two, we are seeking a GKG. Place Band Three on Auto for instructions. Jimmy, feed this into the Auto."

"Colonel, we have a GKG, Modification Baker, from Yoke 991."

"GKG Modification Baker confirmed. Lock signal confirmed. Identification confirmed . . . Transmitted on Auto to Gideon Two. Receipt confirmed. Lock signal confirmed. Identification confirmed."

"My God, Jimmy, no shooting? How in hell . . ."

VK said, "What's happening?"

The colonel said, "Four of the escort F12s went to intercept the Tigers. They're closing them at about fifty miles a minute. We asked authority to shoot the Tigers down. The President ordered us to use any means to turn them away, *except* shooting."

"Sir, report we are under URS . . . Decoding . . . Friendly."

The colonel said, "Probably the B58 R . . . URS means unidentified radar scan. We have means of knowing when we are being used as a target for radar devices. All radars send out their impulses in special patterns, which they can change every day according to a code book. By decoding we can tell whether the radar that's picked us up is friendly or unfriendly . . . well, we never know that. Just 'unidentified.'"

"Gideon One reports distance between us and Tigers is now 653."

The colonel said, "My God, they're closing fast! Intelligence has got their maximum speed way wrong. . . . I'll take her, Jim. I've got her."

"Gideon One reports Tigers have climbed to Angels 144."

"Report we are under URS. Decoding . . . Unidentified. Am naming UD 1."

The colonel swung the plane fiercely to the left. The wing dipped almost into the water. The figures on the compass dial scurried lower and lower. Bill saw that they were heading back toward the distant, unseen Tigers. "Flaps down," the colonel said. "Open all escape hatches." He pulled back on the half wheel. The plane's nose lifted.

"Report URS broken, sir." A roaring of air filled the cabin.

"Gideon Two, I am visual with Tigers. I am signaling them to turn away. Hold."

The colonel muttered, "With luck it'll take those Tiger radar men a moment or two to guess that we might be heading straight for them, and reset. Then they'll have to run our picture through their recognition gadget, whatever it is."

VK felt his lips tight and dry. He wouldn't be anywhere else for the world. He remembered a day near Nyeri when he'd gone out to stalk butterflies. A bad-tempered lion had decided to stalk him. He was sixteen years old, but he grew up that day. From that day on he had known in his bones that the hunter was always, somehow, within or without, also the hunted. To you, the game might be butterflies; to a lion, or God, the game might be you. On that day he had started on the road to becoming a great hunter. From that day he always knew what the quarry was thinking and feeling, because a part of him *was* the quarry. That day he had escaped the lion, and caught a rare butterfly. As the triumphant hunter, and as the wily quarry, he had known an exaltation that he could never again shake off. He was an addict, it was in his blood, he could not live without it. He was a hunter.

The voices in his headset became more sharply antiphonal. "Sir, report under URS. Decoding . . . UD 1."

"Gideon Two—Tigers will not turn away . . . Regret my craft is out of control."

"Sir, URS holds. UD 1."

"He's locked onto us now."

"Ready to ditch, sir."

"Gideon Two—it sure enough looks like I can't miss hitting the lead bogey. You-all please give my regards to Piney Notch, Georgia."

"Gideon Two—leader accidentally collided Russian Tiger Number M 928, both aircraft going down out of control. Leader bailed out. Two, three . . . seven chutes from the Tiger."

"They normally carry a crew of eight, sir."

"Gideon Two—my wing man is also out of control, just missed second Tiger. . . . He's coming around. . . . He's going to get him this time. . . . The Commie's turning away . . . he's still turning . . . he's heading back. Missed him by a goddam hair! Man, we nearly had another nasty accident there."

Colonel Jeffery said, "Congratulations. Keep on his tail. Report downing position to Coast Guard on Search and Rescue Band."

"Gideon Three—this is a Search and Rescue 52 with Gideon One . . . I have a bearing on that and should be overhead downing in seven minutes."

Ten minutes passed.

"Gideon Two—my wing man is also out of control, just missed 1220."

"Gideon One—Kansas Six, you are now 1010 from Tiger, increasing at thirty miles a minute."

"Gideon Three—overhead survivors. Rescue operations commencing."

The colonel's voice came up. "Negative abandon ship. Close doors and hatches. Return standard alert positions . . . Take her up to 39. Give us a course and ETA Andrews." He leaned back and lit a long, dark cigar.

VK said, "Thanks, Colonel. For my life, apart from anything else."

The colonel nodded. VK followed Bill into the main cabin, where the big sergeant took them out of their parachutes and life jackets. The wings shone more brilliant silver as the Boeing climbed back toward the sun.

VK said, "We won. We did it!"

Bill nodded soberly. Yes, they'd won. Some emotion was hovering close below the surface of his consciousness, but he could not yet make out what it was. He walked back into the main cabin, VK at his heels. Through the open door of the first compartment he saw Mr. Thorsson lying in bed, his eyes closed, his face calm. Ingrid arranged the pillow under his head, then came out, shutting the door carefully. "He was so tired," she said. "But otherwise, better. . . . Are we safe now?" Bill nodded. Ingrid touched his cheek suddenly, and he saw tears in her eyes; but she said nothing, and, turning, hurried toward the flight deck.

In the second compartment they saw de Guise lying on the divan, wrapped in a blanket. A big bandage hid most of his face and head. The doctor bending over him straightened up, unscrewed a syringe head and dropped it into the wastebasket. He glanced up and saw them. "Just given him morphia. There's no need for him to keep awake now, and the anaesthetic's wearing off."

De Guise uttered a sound halfway between a laugh and a moan. "Bill? VK?" he mumbled. "Are you there? Will we reach America now?"

"Yes," VK said.

"Thanks to me. That's what Webber said. Thanks to *me* . . . The stone which the builders rejected . . ." His voice trailed away.

The doctor beckoned them out of the compartment, leaving the door open. "He won't talk sense till he's had a long rest in the hospital. And he'll be in the hospital a long time. Whoever put that knife in his eye only just missed the brain."

"And then you know where we'd all be now!" That was Webber, cutting in from behind them as they stood crowded in the aisle.

"You heard him laugh just now? You know why? Because he's going to get his citizenship. . . . 'That's the way to do it,' he was screaming, rolling on the divan in there while we were dodging those Tigers. 'Try to become a citizen of this country and they throw you out,' he said. 'Come back when you've murdered a dozen people, they tell you'—he said—'join the Reds, spend a few years doing your damnedest to bury us, *then* we'll let you in.' Guys like de Guise don't understand about regulations. The immigration clerk back there in Dallas *had* to turn him down, or else what are regulations for? And now I have to let him in. . . . You saw him in the door, just after he'd told us everything? I knew he wouldn't jump then, because he realized he'd just made it impossible for himself to go back. The HPS know he's the only guy on board, anywhere, who could give the plan away. On our side, knowing what he knows, what can we do except let him live in the U.S.A.? Hell, we'll never use him. He's lost his nerve, his cool—everything. I know a few guys like him, ours and theirs, same sort of thing happened to them. They live like little old men—even if they're young—very quiet, mousy, read the paper, one beer at the tavern, and all the women saying Dear Mr. Witherspoon, such a defenseless little fellow, he needs someone to look after him. De Guise is going to be a lot better off than most because he has a special interest. He'll head for the Southwest, mark my words, and write the biggest goddam book you ever saw on Navajo junk jewelry. And if that fails, he can always be the Hathaway man, can't he?" He clapped Bill on the shoulder. Bill looked at him with cold distaste. Webber was too happy to notice, but continued euphorically, "I guess I ought to thank you two for all you did in this business. And I'm very sorry about Miss Hawker. I'll see that you get a good pension, VK, for—"

"*No!*" Bill said.

Webber's head snapped at the vehemence behind the word. Then he recovered his uncrushable confidence. "You know what?" he said. "And a few months back I couldn't have imagined myself saying this . . . I think there are jobs that fellows like you can tackle in our line of business that we can't. It's a matter of where you start from. We're big, national, powerful—and that's where we have to start from, that's our attitude, our approach. But you're small, personal. You can start from people, and look at the big, national things from down below. See what I mean? Maybe you should form a partnership. And if you decide to, I have a job coming up that I'll ask the Director to put you onto. Interested?"

Bill looked at VK. The creeping emotion in him was beginning to resolve itself. He was no longer uneasy. What he felt was certainty, the end of doubt. This was the work he had been searching for since his father died. This was the personal involvement that demanded all his determination, judgment, wealth, and influence: the involvement that could not be delegated or sloughed off, where the responsibility exactly matched the power.

Looking at VK, he nodded. VK said slowly, "All right. We're on. Where is it?"

Webber said, "Tierra del Fuego. And brush up on your sailing and navigation."

He nodded and left them. VK took Bill's arm in a rough grip— "She's dead, Bill. I'm not. You're not. She's the glass through which we understand each other. We will remember her."

Always, Bill thought.